Tessa Harris, born in Lincolnshire, holds a history degree from Oxford University. After four years of working with local newspapers, she set her sights on women's magazines. She is regularly heard on local BBC radio and over the years has interviewed such people as Margaret Thatcher, Jeffrey Archer, Anthony Hopkins, Susan Hampshire, Alan Titchmarsh, Jackie Stewart, Boris Johnson, and Uri Geller. She lives in Berkshire with her husband and their two children.

## Also by Tessa Harris

# SECRETS
## IN THE
# STONES

### A DR. THOMAS SILKSTONE MYSTERY

# TESSA HARRIS

Constable • London

CONSTABLE

First published by Kensington Books, a division
of Kensington Publishing Corp., New York, 2016

First published in Great Britain in 2016 by Constable

1 3 5 7 9 10 8 6 4 2

A CIP catalogue record for this book
is available from the British Library.

ISBN: 978-1-4721-1826-4

Printed and bound in Great Britain by CPI Group (UK) Ltd, Croydon CR0 4YY

Papers used by Constable are from well-managed forests and
other responsible sources.

MIX
Paper from
responsible sources
FSC
www.fsc.org    FSC® C104740

Constable
An imprint of
Little, Brown Book Group
Carmelite House
50 Victoria Embankment
London EC4Y 0DZ

An Hachette UK Company
www.hachette.co.uk

www.littlebrown.co.uk

*For Harry and Tom, because I made a promise*

# Author's Notes and Acknowledgments

A s a child I loved the stories of the *Arabian Nights*—or, *One Thousand and One Nights,* to give the collection its proper title. The first English language translation of these exotic fables was in 1706—a time when the West was really just waking up to the vast cultural and religious treasures of the East. Tales of far-flung kingdoms, fabulous jewels, fanciful creatures, and daring heroes fueled my imagination. Many of them had their roots in ancient Sanskrit legends as well as Buddhist stories.

One of my favorites featured the exploits of Sinbad the Sailor. The eponymous hero was transported by a giant bird, called a roc, to a land where the floor of the valley was "carpeted with diamonds." Between the fourteenth and eighteenth centuries many young explorers and adventurers were drawn to India and the Far East by such tales of riches beyond anyone's wildest dreams.

Little did I ever imagine, however, that in my adult life I would stumble across a true account of an expedition in India by an English traveler that could rival those stories. The *Narrative of a Journey to the Diamond Mines at Sumbhulpoor in the Province of Orissa* is a most extraordinary document. Published almost thirty years after the original journey was undertaken in 1766, it details the exploits of Thomas Motte. Motte was commissioned by Lord Clive, or Clive of India, to open up trade and purchase diamonds from the rulers of that region. The mission was a highly dangerous one. Indeed, Motte's English traveling companions and servants all died of fever during the trip. His account of the journey, however, is a fascinating travelogue, in which he explores not only the natural history but also the beliefs and customs of the tribes of that region. Among the many observations about the day-to-day life of these people we find extraordinary firsthand accounts of supernatural happenings, huge scorpions and spiders and—most amazingly of all—a monstrous snake with sacred powers. The name of the snake was Naik Buns, and it was worshiped by the mountain rajas in this area. If it died, so ran the belief, the world would end. To stave off the possibility, the sacred serpent was appeased with chickens and goats every week, which were deposited at the mouth of the cave where it lived. Motte actually witnessed the snake devour this prey and estimated that in diameter it was *"upwards of two feet."*

During the mid eighteenth century, Britain was one of several European powers vying for dominance in India. There was much to play for—spices, silks, and, of course, gems. Before the early 1700s, India was the world's only source of diamonds. The mines of Golconda were famous for yielding the most magnificent diamonds, including the famous Koh-i-Noor and Hope diamonds.

A succession of wars and various subsequent treaties led Britain to establish Fort William, which later became Bengal. Its first governor was Warren Hastings, who went on to be the first governor-general of India from 1773 to 1785. His story also makes for fascinating reading, as do the many love letters he wrote to his second wife, Marian, on which I have drawn for this novel.

So, it is against an exotic backdrop of oriental intrigue in the 1780s that I decided to set this, the sixth novel in the Dr. Thomas Silkstone mystery series. As ever, my research has taken me on my own fascinating journey, from the extraordinary ruins of the Golconda Fort in India to the British Library.

In my writing I have been helped and encouraged by the following people: historian and London guide Peter Berthoud,

David Baldwin, and Georgina Peek. As ever my thanks also go to my editor, John Scognamiglio, and my agent, Melissa Jeglinski. I am also grateful to Carolyn Cowing for her interest in the project. Finally, I wish to acknowledge the love and support of my husband, Simon, and my children, Charlie and Sophie, and my parents, Patsy and Geoffrey.

AUTHOR'S NOTE AND ACKNOWLEDGMENTS

*Good friend, for Jesu's sake forbear*
*To dig the dust enclosed here.*
*Blest be the man that spares these stones*
*And curst be he that moves my bones.*

—William Shakespeare (1564–1616)
THIS EPITAPH ON THE POET'S TOMB IN STRATFORD-UPON-AVON
WAS PURPORTEDLY CHOSEN BY THE BARD HIMSELF.

# Chapter 1

From high up on a loop of the great wall, the bania watched the pinpricks of flame blister the blackened city. Swords in hand, blazing torches aloft, the nizam's men gathered near one of the thirteen great gates. The citadel was sealed. No one could enter and no one could leave. But most of the ordinary inhabitants were cowering inside their dwellings, fearful for their lives.

Bava Lakhani was the bania's name. He was a Gujarati merchant who'd always lived by his wits. He'd known he was taking a gamble, but in a land where fanciful stories grew like pomegranates, he was certain this legend was seeded in truth. For years he'd acted as a middleman between the jagirdars who owned the diamond mines and the Europeans. He would be the first to admit that he did not always play by the rules, the few that there were. Yet the gods had smiled on him so far. The French, the Dutch, the Portuguese, and, of course, the English all knew him to supply a good bulse. They trusted him to select a few fine stones among those of poorer quality and to ask a fair price. When they opened the small purses, they were seldom disappointed: bloodred rubies, cobalt blue sapphires, and, of course, diamonds. Always diamonds. But what he had now was far too valuable to be included in an ordinary packet. What he had now might, just might, be a legend about to be uncovered, waiting to dazzle, delight, and amaze with its fantastical brilliance once it had been cut. What he had now might be worthy to grace the collections of the crowned heads of Europe, who would, no doubt, be willing to pay a most generous price for the privilege.

Yes, there was a risk. There always was, but this risk was bigger than all the swollen bulbs of the old rulers' tombs put together. And now it was looming over him like a monstrous cobra, readying itself to strike. There'd been an edict. Somehow, word had got out. Somehow the nizam's vakil had discovered that a miner had not declared his find and had escaped with a huge gemstone from the nearby diamond fields. The miner, a Dalit of the lowest caste, had come to him, and he, Bava Lakhani, had agreed to act for him. But the law was plain. Anyone who found a diamond of more than ten carats was required to hand it over to the governor of the mine. And that law had been violated. The Dalit risked death, and so, of course, did he. He knew that, should they be caught, their executions, the more torturous and gruesome the better, would serve as an example to others who might think of following in their wake. He tugged at his enormous moustache. The thought of his own death sent a runnel of cold sweat coursing down his back and set his heart beating as fast as a tabla drum. Now he must do, or die.

So secret was the mission and so precious the cargo that the transaction had to take place after dark. And how dark it was. Night coated the city's minarets and spandrels like melted tar. The air was close and the sky pregnant with monsoon rain. Everyone knew the Lord Indra would make the clouds burst any day now. Even though he was a good distance away, the bania could see the guards swarming like locusts on the poor quarter that oozed like a festering sore inside the walls. This was where the mosquitoes and rats were the fattest and the residents the thinnest. The stench was always bad, but at the end of the dry season, it was almost unbearable. Dust choked the narrow streets. And now it was mixed with something else. Fear. He could hear the shouts and screams, too. He knew the guards were approaching fast.

Scrambling down from the wall, the merchant nodded to his

naukar. The servant, spindly as a spider, waited below, standing by a handcart that held a large hessian sack. The trader's gaze settled on the bundle. He gave it an odd look, taking a deep breath as he did so. The deal he was about to broker could mean life or death. The exchange he was about to undertake would seal not just his own fate but that of his only son and his sons, too.

"Come, Manjeet," he whispered. "We must hurry."

*Nine years later, Brandwick Common,*
*the county of Oxfordshire, England*

The moment after the shot tore through the air there was silence. Silence and smoke. It was as if time itself stood still, caught up in the haze of gunpowder, watching to see what would happen. No one had to wait long. The man's mouth fell agape, and he gasped for the air that was already escaping from his punctured breast. He reeled backward, clutching his chest, then dropped, like a stone, to the ground.

"No. Please, God. No!" cried Lady Lydia Farrell. She rushed forward, careening down the hollow, followed by her maid, Eliza. When she reached the limp body, she slumped to her knees on the dew-sodden grass. A red stain was blooming on the man's chest. To her horror, she had seen the well-aimed shot hit Dr. Thomas Silkstone.

The apothecary, Mr. Peabody, was the doctor's second at the duel and the first to reach him. Lydia found him pressing hard on Thomas's breastbone, trying to stop the dark patch from growing. Jacob Lovelock, the groom, had been waiting with the carriage. As soon as he'd seen the doctor fall, he'd jumped down and begun to run over, too.

"Tell me he is not dead," Lydia whispered in disbelief. "He cannot be dead." She reached over and clutched Thomas's cold hand. Then her own heart missed a beat as she watched the apothecary rip open the bloodstained shirt to reveal the wound.

Mr. Peabody looked up. Even though it was a chilly morning, the little man's face was glistening with sweat. Lowering his head, he put his ear to Thomas's mouth, then felt for a pulse in his neck. "He lives," he told her after a moment. "But only just."

Lydia felt panic strangle her voice. "He can't die. He can't," she croaked. Eliza, fighting back her own tears, put an arm around her mistress, but Lydia would have none of it. She shrugged her off. "What must we do?" she asked Mr. Peabody.

"We must get him to the carriage, my lady," he replied.

The morning light was pearly, but a blanket of mist still hugged the ground and Lydia suddenly became aware of men's voices and the sound of horses. She struggled to her feet and could just make out a carriage on the opposite side of the hollow. A whip cracked and the carriage sped off, heading away from the common.

Jacob Lovelock saw it, too. "Coward!" he cried. "You bastard!" He coughed up a gob of spittle and sent it arcing in the carriage's direction.

The Right Honorable Nicholas Lupton was leaving the scene in all haste. It was he who had challenged the doctor to the duel. It was he who had fired the shot. And it was he who would face a murder charge if his opponent died.

"He'll not get away with it, m'lady," yelled the pock-marked groom, approaching fast.

Seeing her former steward make good his getaway, Lydia also felt the anger rise in her. Like the rat she knew him to be, he was deserting the scene, leaving his rival to die. She also knew her ire needed to be channeled. Now she must devote all her energies to saving Thomas and there was no time to waste.

"Jacob!" she cried to Lovelock. "Help here!" She pointed to Thomas lying motionless in Mr. Peabody's arms. "We need to get Dr. Silkstone to the Three Tuns."

A breathless Lovelock nodded and slid his arms under Thomas's legs.

"Be careful," Mr. Peabody instructed as he hooked his own hands under his patient's arms. Together the two men lifted him up.

"But he will live?" Lydia asked the apothecary as he staggered under Thomas's weight. Eliza steadied her mistress as they headed for the carriage.

Mr. Peabody, his face still grave, grunted, struggling with his burden. "We can but hope, your ladyship, but he needs great care," he told her.

Reeling across the wet grass, the two men arrived at the carriage and heaved their patient inside, laying him lengthways on a seat. The women followed and Eliza found a blanket to lay over him. Suddenly Thomas started to shake violently, and Lydia shot a horrified look at the apothecary.

"We must get him to the inn," said Mr. Peabody, feeling the pulse once more. "The professor should be there soon."

"The professor?" asked Lydia, frowning.

"Professor Hascher, from Oxford," replied the apothecary. "He will be on his way."

Puzzled, Lydia shook her head. News of the imminent arrival of Thomas's anatomist friend from Oxford, although most welcome, confused her. "But how did he . . . ?"

Mr. Peabody's eyes slid away from hers. "Dr. Silkstone made plans, m'lady," he said, returning to his charge and pressing on the wound.

"Plans?" repeated Lydia. "What sort of plans?"

Still not lifting his gaze, the apothecary bit his lip, as if trying to stop himself from divulging a secret.

"What sort of plans, Mr. Peabody?" she insisted.

The apothecary shook his head, and then regarded her for a moment.

"The doctor did not accept Mr. Lupton's challenge lightly," he began cryptically.

"What do you mean?" Lydia was growing increasingly irritated.

"I mean he conceived a way to thwart any possible injury, m'lady."

Lydia shook her head. "You are talking in riddles," she told him. "Please be plain."

The apothecary sighed, as if acknowledging defeat. "The doctor asked the blacksmith to forge him a light cuirass to repel the lead shot, m'lady."

"A cuirass!" exclaimed Lydia. "You mean armor?"

Peabody nodded. "I do, m'lady." He pointed to the bloody wound, and Lydia forced herself to look closer. She could see what he meant. There seemed to be some sort of metal sheeting under Thomas's shirt. "He also wore a layer of thick horsehair wadding beneath." The apothecary directed his gaze to a ball of coarse threads, now soaked in blood. "He hoped the lead shot would fail to penetrate the breastplate."

Lydia's red-rimmed eyes opened wide. "I see," she muttered.

Mr. Peabody shook his head. "Sadly, m'lady, the shot has clearly pierced the armor."

"But you say Professor Hascher is on his way!" There was a note of hope in Lydia's voice. She should have known that Thomas would not leave it to chance to dodge Lupton's shot. He was organized, meticulous, reasoned. He would not allow fortune to dictate his fate. There had been method in his apparent madness in accepting the challenge. But that method had most certainly failed him. She gazed at Thomas's deathly pale face and took his hand in hers once more. "Let us pray he can be saved," she whispered.

Back at Boughton Hall, Sir Montagu Malthus, the custodian of Lady Lydia's estate and official guardian to her young son and heir, Richard, was breakfasting in the morning room. A great raven of a man, and one of the finest lawyers in the land, he also carried a very personal grudge. He had made it his mission to prevent Lydia from marrying the American parvenu Dr. Thomas Silkstone, so destroying the English bloodline. So far, he had done rather well. The upstart doctor from the Colonies would surely admit defeat very soon, and as for poor dear Lydia, well, she was so highly suggestible that he could, and had, told her a pack of lies and she would believe anything he said.

Satisfied in such knowledge, he was now able to concentrate fully on his plans to enclose the whole of the Boughton Estate, fencing it off from the commoners and woodsmen. Over a bowl of hot chocolate, he was considering his day's tasks when Howard entered. From the anxious look on the butler's normally sanguine features, Sir Montagu could tell he had some urgent news to impart. Howard cleared his throat.

"Begging pardon, sir, but Peter Geech would speak with you."

Sir Montagu looked up from his bowl, then set it down.

"Geech?" he repeated. He wondered what the landlord of the Three Tuns had to relate that couldn't wait until later in the day. "Tell him to go away and return at a more civilized hour."

Howard looked uncomfortable. "He says it is most urgent, sir." Then, as if to press Geech's case further, the butler added: "It concerns Dr. Silkstone, sir."

"Ah!" Sir Montagu paused at the mention of Thomas's name and suddenly changed his high-handed tune. He dabbed the corners of his mouth with his napkin. "Then you better allow him in," he instructed.

Peter Geech, always with at least one of his beady eyes on the main chance, was shown into the morning room, clutching the brim of his tricorn. Sir Montagu eyed him like a hawk would a mouse or a vole before it struck, then signaled for Howard to leave.

"Well?" he said, as soon as they were alone. He did not invite the landlord to sit. "You have news concerning Silkstone?"

Geech thrust out his chin, as if he was proud to be the one to break the news. "I thought you'd like to know there's been a duel on the common, sir," he began. He paused for dramatic effect.

Sir Montagu paused, too, and arched one of his thick brows. "Tell me more," he said, leaning back in his chair.

"'Twixt Mr. Lupton and Dr. Silkstone, sir."

Now both of Sir Montagu's brows were raised in unison. He leaned forward, his interest piqued. "Has there indeed? And what, pray tell, was the outcome?"

Geech paused again, licking his thin lips, as if relishing what he was about to impart, but his silence spoke to Sir Montagu. He would say no more without a reward. The men's eyes met.

"A crown," said the lawyer.

Geech remained steadfast. "I was hoping . . ."

Sir Montagu frowned and leered toward the innkeeper. "I

could go to the village and ask any peasant on the street to tell me," he said coldly. "Then I could have your squalid tavern closed down!" He reached over the table and lifted the china lid of a jam pot, then shut it again to illustrate his point.

The landlord reddened and squeezed the brim of his tricorn. "Of course, sir," he said, suddenly losing his nerve.

"So?"

"Dr. Silkstone was wounded."

"Was he indeed?" There was a flicker of a smile on the lawyer's lips.

"Yes, sir. They brought him to the inn."

"They?"

"Her ladyship and her maid and the—"

"What? Lady Lydia?" At the mention of Lydia's name, the scowl returned to Sir Montagu's face. To the best of his knowledge, she was still sleeping soundly upstairs. He pushed himself away from the table and stood up. "Her ladyship is with him now?" The news clearly angered him. He strode over to the window.

"Yes, sir," continued Geech. "And now an arrest warrant for Mr. Lupton has been issued by Sir Arthur Warbeck."

Sir Montagu wheeled 'round, his hands behind his back. "Has it indeed? So the American might die?" He knew that if that were the case, a charge of manslaughter would be brought against the steward. "You have seen him?"

Geech nodded. "Hit in the chest, he was, sir. He's stone-cold out of it, sir, but Mr. Peabody is seeing to him."

Sir Montagu allowed himself a chuckle. "Peabody? That clown can kill a man as easily as any lead shot!"

Emboldened by the lawyer's response, Geech went on: "But I've been told to expect Sir Theodisius Pettigrew and another surgeon from Oxford presently, sir."

The news of the men's arrival wiped the smirk from Sir Montagu's face. "The coroner?" He walked forward and grasped the back of his chair. "And Professor Hascher, no doubt," he mumbled.

"Sir?" Geech did not catch the lawyer's words.

Sir Montagu reached into his pocket and produced two silver coins. He tossed them on the floor at the landlord's feet, one after the other. They rolled along the wooden floorboards and came to rest at the edge of a rug. "A crown for the information," he said, "and another to keep me abreast of the doctor's condition." As he watched Geech grovel to pick up the coins, Sir Montagu very much hoped that before the day's end the innkeeper would be the bearer of news of Thomas Silkstone's death.

# Chapter 2

In an upper room at the Three Tuns, three anxious onlookers—
Lydia; her maid, Eliza; and Mr. Peabody—were keeping vigil
at Thomas's bedside. There had been a glimmer of hope. The
doctor had opened his eyes, smiled at the sight of Lydia, and
then been lost to her again. At around midday Boughton's stable
lad, Will Lovelock, had come, bearing a message from Sir Montagu. The lawyer had, said his missive, heard the terrible news
and wished Lydia to know that if he could be of any assistance,
she had only to say. The carriage was at her disposal, and he had
instructed the Reverend Unsworth to say prayers for Dr. Silkstone. His words had offered her a little comfort, although she
could not be sure that he meant them. She continued to watch
and wait, and as she waited, she, too, prayed, prayed as never
before. And she made a vow: *Please God, if you let him live,
then nothing will stop us being together, I swear.*

By the time the clock in the room struck three, there was still
no sign of Sir Theodisius and Professor Hascher. Lydia felt her
anxiety mount. "Where are they?" she asked aloud, not expecting a reply.

No sooner had she posed the question, however, than Eliza
blustered in from a foray to buy fresh herbs to scent the room.
She was able to furnish her mistress with an answer.

"They've been spotted, m'lady," she told her breathlessly. "A
wheel came off their carriage just north of Woodstock, but 'tis
mended now."

Almost two more anxious hours followed until, just before the church bell struck the hour, a carriage drew into the inn's courtyard. Inside were Sir Theodisius Pettigrew and Professor Hascher, and their presence had never been more welcome.

"Thank God you are here!" cried Lydia, rushing forward to greet Sir Theodisius as he lumbered into the room. A corpulent gentleman, he enveloped the young woman in a warm embrace. Without children of his own, he had always regarded her as he would his own daughter.

"Dear child," he told her, "do not fear. Professor Hascher is here." He glanced at the elderly, snowy-haired man who was advancing straight to Thomas's side. "He will do everything he can."

Before the duel, Thomas had sent word of his intentions to the Oxford coroner. Sir Theodisius was fully cognizant of the doctor's plans, but it had come as a shock to him to learn from Peter Geech on arrival at the Three Tuns what had actually come to pass.

Professor Hascher, a Saxon by birth, set to work immediately while the others retired to a respectful distance. Mumbling to himself in his native tongue, he opened up his medical case and started to examine his patient. While Mr. Peabody was asked to remain to assist, Sir Theodisius thought it best if he took Lydia and her maid outside. He wasted little time in escorting them from the room, leaving the elderly anatomist to probe and suture away from their fretting gaze.

"I think some fresh air may be in order," the coroner suggested.

Lydia nodded, and together they stepped out into the courtyard of the Three Tuns. Eliza remained in the hall. By now it was early evening and the hostler was watering the carriage horses that had come from Oxford, bringing the coroner and the professor. Sir Theodisius and Lydia slipped unnoticed through a small gate into a shaded garden at the back of the inn. In the last few days, spring had made its presence felt. The grass was ankle-high and studded with drifts of bluebells. An unkempt flower bed teemed with periwinkles and yellow tansies. Lydia knew tansies were often wrapped in funeral winding sheets to ward off insects. She shivered at the thought.

"Here," said Sir Theodisius. His plump finger pointed to a stone seat that overlooked a stream, and there they sat.

"You mustn't fret, my dear," said the coroner, staring at the gurgling water. "The professor will see Thomas right."

Lydia sighed deeply, her breath trembling in her chest. "Please God let it be so, sir," she replied. She wanted to cry, but did not. Instead she made a confession.

"I've been a fool," she said suddenly.

Sir Theodisius's head jolted, sending his jowls wobbling. "What's this, my dear?"

She pulled the head of an oxeye daisy from its stem and began plucking the petals. "He's been the only one who's been true to me."

The coroner inclined his head. "Ah," he said, as if suddenly understanding. "Thomas."

"The thought of losing him . . ." She tossed the daisy head into the stream.

Sir Theodisius nodded and patted her hand. "I know, my dear. I know. Sometimes it takes the prospect of losing someone to make us realize how much they mean to us."

Lydia looked the coroner in the eye. "He means the world to me."

The coroner nodded. "Then you must tell him so."

"I intend to," she said with a nod, then looked away and muttered quietly, "If I have the chance."

Just then the latch on the gate clicked, and both of them switched back to see Eliza's head peering 'round. "Professor Hascher says you may return, m'lady," she said.

Sir Theodisius smiled at Lydia and squeezed her hand. "Yes, you must tell him so yourself," he said.

All of them made their way back inside and up the stairs to where Thomas lay. Lydia hurried in first, but stopped short of the bed when Mr. Peabody signaled to her to come no farther. She suddenly saw why. Professor Hascher, his hands still bloodied, was standing back to inspect his handicraft. Appearing to examine the closed wound with an artist's eye, he nodded to himself. Seemingly satisfied that the stitches were as neat as he could make them, and spaced at equal distances, he took a pair of scissors and snipped the catgut. His shoulders heaved as he allowed himself a deep breath, as if he had not breathed since he began the delicate procedure of tending to his patient's injury.

Still standing at the foot of the bed, Lydia glanced at the bowl on the bedside table. She was grateful to have been spared the sight of the removal of fragments of shattered metal from the wound, although there was still spilled blood on the white sheets. She was not alone in holding back. Sir Theodisius and Eliza did, too, nervous about what they might see. They were waiting on Professor Hascher's word, and it came very soon.

"*Das ist gut,*" he pronounced finally with a nod of his snowy-white head.

With the professor's announcement, all those in the room seemed to relax a little, as if their nerves had all been held taut by some invisible thread. They had been tense ever since they had known the seriousness of the injury. Now, at last, they could all breathe a little easier.

After another moment's deliberation, the professor, to everyone's surprise, addressed his patient. "Zat breastplate may have saved your life, but it still made ze nasty hole in your chest," he admonished.

Thomas, it seemed, was conscious, and Lydia rushed forward. From the bed, his hand rose, and he placed his fingers lightly along the row of stitches on his chest, as if playing the keys of a fortepiano.

"They feel even enough. You have done a good job, Professor," came the croaked reply. Although Mr. Peabody had dosed him liberally with laudanum, Thomas had remained conscious throughout the procedure. Through the fog of shock and pain, he had managed to follow the Saxon surgeon's work cleaning up a chest wound that would, most certainly, have been fatal had he not been wearing protective armor.

"Thank God you are back with us," exclaimed Lydia as soon as she saw Thomas's face. He managed to smile at her through his evident discomfort. As the professor reached for bandages from his case, however, Thomas switched his attention.

"A good dollop of aloe balm on the wound would surely not go amiss, sir?" he suggested.

Hascher paused at his words, glanced at Sir Theodisius, then rolled his eyes. The two older men exchanged weary smiles.

"The next time you're challenged to a duel, Silkstone, I beg you, do not accept, for all our sakes," exhorted the coroner as he lumbered up to draw alongside the injured young doctor.

Lydia clasped Thomas's hand in hers. "For mine, especially," she said.

Thomas, his eyes now fully open but his breath rasping, whispered his reply. "Fear not, sweet lady. 'Tis not grave," he told her. It was all she had needed to hear. His wound was ugly—she had seen it with her own eyes—but, barring infection, it no longer threatened his life.

"You must rest, now," Professor Hascher told his patient.

"I think we must all rest," agreed Sir Theodisius.

As the elderly anatomist set to work binding Thomas's torso, Sir Theodisius and Lydia, followed by Eliza, beat a retreat from the room.

Peter Geech jumped back as the bedroom door opened and looked sheepishly at Sir Theodisius, who returned a scowl. The landlord had clearly been listening on the landing outside.

"Dr. Silkstone . . . He is . . . ?"

"Alive, Mr. Geech," came the coroner's barked reply. The wiry innkeeper nodded his head. "Alive, but with a shattered breastbone and in need of rest," added Sir Theodisius. "And so am I. I shall have your finest room. And dinner." He rubbed his large belly, which suddenly felt very empty. "A chop or two will do nicely."

Geech nodded once more. "I have a room prepared for you, sir, and one for the foreign gentleman," he replied, casting a look through the door toward Professor Hascher.

"And her ladyship?" Sir Theodisius turned to Lydia.

"Her ladyship's carriage awaits," Geech informed him.

Lydia, drawing close, looked relieved. "Then we shall go back to Boughton, sir," she told the coroner.

Sir Theodisius smiled. "Yes, my dear," he said, taking her hand to kiss it. "I trust you will sleep better in your own bed."

She returned his smile and nodded. "I shall sleep better knowing that Dr. Silkstone is out of danger," she acknowledged.

Lifting up the hem of her skirt slightly, she made her way down the rickety stairs to the hall, where Lovelock was waiting. By now it was growing dark. The taproom was full of men carousing and laughing. The smell of pig fat from cheap candles tainted the air, and it was hard to see through the thick fug of pipe smoke. Nevertheless, the mood appeared much livelier than usual. The ale was flowing, someone had struck up on the pennywhistle, and it seemed to Lydia, as she glanced through the doorway, that the locals had not a care in the world. At the center of the merry throng she caught a glimpse of Joseph Makepeace, the bury man. Normally such a staid and dour fellow, as befitted his calling, he was quaffing his tipple and puffing his pipe as if he were lord of the manor. She wondered perhaps if she should instruct Geech to ask the grave digger and his friends to tone down their revelries so that the doctor would not be disturbed. But as soon as she drew level with Lovelock, shifting agitatedly at the foot of the stairs, the thought flew from her mind.

"My lady, is the . . . ?" the groom began anxiously.

Lydia quickly put him at ease. "Dr. Silkstone is recovering," she managed to relate, but it was clear she was exhausted and in no mood to tarry. She swept past him. Lovelock's pock-marked face relaxed, and he caught Eliza's eye. The maid smiled at him, and together they followed Lydia out into the warm night to the waiting carriage that would take them back to Boughton Hall.

## Chapter 3

Sir Montagu Malthus would never have called himself a man of faith, but he had been inclined toward prayer throughout the day. As yet, however, his request had met with no divine response. He had received no word from Geech. To his knowledge, Silkstone was still alive. Now his only supplication was that he would not survive the night.

The lawyer sat in the study at Boughton Hall. The evening was warm, and the French windows at the far end of the room were open. The noise of the guard dogs barking in the far distance made him look up and flatten his back against his chair. He was wading through unopened correspondence that had been left to mount over the past few tumultuous weeks. For most of the day his enormous shoulders had been hunched over the desk, and his neck ached. The occasional gulp of claret from a glass at his side had been all there was to break the tedium of the mound of documentation. Now, however, he allowed himself the indulgence of breaking off from reading his papers. It was not the sudden barking that roused him, but the appearance of a moth. Flying dangerously close to the naked flame of his candle, it was quite large and brindle brown. It skimmed and pranced in the enticing circle of light cast on the wall above his desk. Its quivering silhouette made it appear even bigger than it actually was. Fluttering in on the sultry night air through the open windows, the creature provided a welcome diversion. So now he set down his silver paper knife, eased back in his chair, and studied the insect with a macabre fascination.

The moth next settled on a volume of accounts on the desk, but Sir Montagu resisted the urge to swat it. It would be all the more pleasurable to watch it hover around the flame a little longer, thereby prolonging its dance toward inevitable death. He was therefore irritated when a sudden zephyr from the open doors rustled his papers and disturbed its rest. It flew toward the lighted candle, lingered for no more than a second, then succumbed to its fiery embrace. There was a slight hissing sound as a tongue of flame licked its wings before it fell like a singed fragment of parchment onto the desk. Sir Montagu's lips twinged with satisfaction. Could this be a sign that his prayers had been finally answered?

With a sweep of his hand he scooped the charred remnants of the moth to the floor and resumed his work. Another missive required his urgent attention, no doubt another plea requesting a larger allotment. There were times when he regretted abiding by the law of the land. It would have been so much simpler to fence off the commons and the woods and be done with it, rather than to subject himself to all these irritating legal procedures. Every Tom, Dick, and Harry, it seemed, felt entitled to protest against the plans to enclose the Boughton Estate. He had been forced to post his intentions and invite comments, and it irked him beyond measure that he was legally obliged to deal with all these petitions. Holding yet another missive toward the candlelight, the lawyer took the paper knife and began to slice through the seal. He acted with such gusto, however, that the blade slipped and nicked his finger. Sir Montagu grimaced, and the knife clattered onto the desk. The cut, although small, began to bleed, and two or three drops fell onto the bundle of papers, the color of the blood matching that of the seal. In fact he was sucking at the wound, a metallic taste on his tongue, when he heard a noise outside. Footsteps? He held his breath for a moment. Could it be Geech come with news of Silkstone's death? There it was again: the sound of feet crunching on the gravel below the terrace.

The lawyer rose and walked over to the open doors. He took a deep breath and advanced over the threshold, out onto the parterre. He was surprised to find it was slightly warmer outside than in. Palming his hands onto the stone balustrade, he cast his gaze over the gardens. The night was clear and the moon was almost full, so he could just about discern the outline of the rose garden with its clipped hedges. Somewhere in the woodland beyond an owl hooted. As far as he could see, however, nothing was untoward.

"Geech!" he called out in a hoarse whisper. He craned his neck into the darkness. "Who goes there?"

There was no reply. He allowed for a moment of quiet, just to satisfy himself that there was no one else in the grounds, before he wheeled 'round to return to the study. The doors remained ajar, although a little more open than he remembered. He supposed a breeze had blown them apart. Once inside, however, he decided to close them, just to err on the side of caution. It had suddenly occurred to him that Nicholas Lupton, now a wanted man, might pay him an unwelcome visit. They had parted on less than friendly terms, and the steward was a man with a hot temper. He could well do without his presence. He turned the key in the lock. It made a satisfying clunk as the latch dropped. He felt safe.

Convinced he must have heard a fox or a badger outside, he returned to his desk and sat down to resume his examination of the petitions. He started to unfold a paper. By this time, however, his candle had begun to gutter. Although there was another lamp in the room, the flickering annoyed him. It caused the circle of light on the wall to dim slightly. He reached for the wick trimmer, but just as he did so, he heard another noise—only now, it seemed inside the room.

"Geech, is that you?" he asked, glancing back over his shoulder before dropping his gaze to the candle once more. "Please tell me that Dr. Silkstone is dead," he quipped.

In the semidarkness, he waited for the message for which he so longed, trimming the wick as he did so. None came.

"Geech?" he called out, looking behind once more. When he saw no one, he shrugged, but still he fumbled for the tinderbox. He struck the flint. The flame burst into life and took hold of the candle. He was right. Someone else was in the room. From nowhere a silhouette suddenly loomed large against the wall. He started to twist 'round.

"What the . . . ?"

It was too late. A hand clamped across his mouth, and his hooded lids all but disappeared as his eyes opened wide with fright. From his mouth a strangled cry tried to emerge, but it was no use. The lawyer found himself fighting for breath, and his hands flew up as he gasped, flapping like a frightened bird. In the commotion the claret glass was knocked over, and its contents spilled across the desk. Sir Montagu felt his head yanked back, and he let go of his grip on his assailant. A gag was suddenly stuffed between his lips. In the next moment his arms were wrenched behind him. Through the mayhem, he could see something glint in the candlelight. The paper knife? Seconds later, he realized only too well that the sensation he could feel against the skin of his neck was the cold, hard steel of a blade.

*Chapter 4*

The journey to Boughton Hall, although short, allowed Lydia a few minutes' peace after the day's momentous events. She could take stock and reflect. It had been a day like no other: a day of high drama and deep emotion, of machinations and deceptions gone awry, and of anxious watching and endless waiting. And as the gates of the hall loomed up ahead of her carriage, she was suddenly filled with a terrible sense of foreboding. Previously they had signified home and security, but latterly they reminded her that she was a virtual prisoner and that Sir Montagu controlled her every move. Suddenly she knew what she had to do.

Those torturous hours spent at Thomas's bedside, not knowing whether he would live or die, had made her realize what was important to her in life. Tomorrow morning, at first light, she would leave. Taking Richard with her, she would escape from Boughton. When she feared Thomas had been shot dead, she had seen in the flash of a moment what life would be like without him. In those few short seconds, she knew she never wanted to be apart from him again. He was the only man who had ever truly loved her. Now she had made up her mind. As soon as he was fit, they would run away, all three of them—Thomas, Richard, and her—to America. Yes, America. To Philadelphia, perhaps. Thomas's home city. They could make a new life there, together, away from Boughton and the estate and away from England. No one would know her. And no one would care who she was. She would renounce her title, and once relieved of its burden, she could become Mrs. Thomas Silkstone. She mouthed her new name silently. *Mrs. Thomas Silkstone.* Her heart beat faster at the thought of it.

The chimneys and cornices of Boughton Hall suddenly came into view, silhouetted against the dark blue sky. The sight made Lydia tense. It seemed as if years had passed since she and Eliza had left that morning. After everything that had happened, the sight of its imposing walls now made it even more like a prison. She needed to escape. She must make plans immediately, but away from Sir Montagu's glare. Her own experience had shown her he would stop at nothing to prevent her and Thomas from being together. Ever since he had revealed to her that he was her real father, then immediately regretted it, Sir Montagu had shown her not a shred of humanity. He had tossed her feelings aside like a spent pipe. She thought of his threats to take Richard from her, his success in turning her against Thomas. She thought of Bedlam and how, even after her release, he had managed to control her.

"Not anymore," she muttered between clenched teeth.

"Are you all right, m'lady?" Eliza, sitting opposite her, broke into her thoughts. She had seen her mistress's eyes open wide as if she had suddenly had a revelation, then heard her mumble to herself and had become concerned.

Lydia turned away from the window and fixed her maid with the enigmatic look of a lost woman who had suddenly found her way. "Yes, thank you, Eliza," she replied with a smile. "I have never felt better."

As her carriage drew up outside, Lydia saw that only in the ground-floor study did a light burn dimly. She assumed Sir Montagu had stayed up late attending to his business affairs. A small part of her also thought that he might wish to learn whether Thomas was alive or dead. The doctor's death would, of course, suit his purpose. She suddenly imagined his expression had she been the bearer of such news. He would have dipped his brows, feigned shock and concern, and reached out to put a comforting arm around her. Yet underneath, his dark heart would be leaping for joy.

Lovelock helped his mistress down from the vehicle, and Howard was there on the steps to greet her and Eliza. He had obviously seen the carriage lamps on the drive, although it was clear he had not expected them back.

"Your ladyship," said the butler with a worried frown. "Dr. Silkstone . . ." The whole household had been on tenterhooks for the entire day, waiting to hear news from the village about the doctor's state of health. The gossip among visiting trades-men had forewarned of serious injury and possible death.

"The wound is bad enough, Howard. But God willing, Dr. Silkstone will make a full recovery," she told him as he helped her off with her cape.

The butler relaxed his stiff stance a little. "That is most grat-ifying to know, your ladyship." Then after a moment he added, "Will you require refreshment, m'lady?"

Lydia shook her head. "No, Howard. I will call in on Sir Montagu, then Eliza will see me to bed."

"As you wish, m'lady," he replied with a bow, and he padded off back to his quarters.

Eliza looked at her mistress. "Shall I go up, your ladyship?"

Lydia nodded. She would inform her of her plans to leave Boughton in a moment. She would need the maid's help in order to make ready Richard's escape, too, but she knew she could trust Eliza. She might even ask her to accompany them. After all, she was the one who showed her that Thomas had been fighting for her freedom from Bedlam. Before she could make the maid privy to her plans, however, Lydia first had to inform Sir Mon-tagu of the doctor's condition. It was a task she would relish, a victory for her after such a long series of defeats at her father's callous hands. A shaft of light lanced into the hallway from un-derneath the study door, telling her that he was still working. She crossed over and took a deep, steadying breath before she tapped lightly on the door. She waited a moment. There was no reply.

With her mouth to the door she called softly: "Sir, 'tis Lydia." Still no reply. Not wishing to disturb the peace of the household, she turned the handle quietly and walked inside. A single candle burned.

Glancing to her right, she saw that her father seemed to have dozed off at the far end of the room. His head was resting on the desk, but curiously, his goat-hair wig appeared to have slipped from his scalp and now lay at the foot of his chair. Suddenly she shivered. The temperature in the study was much cooler than in the hall, and turning, she saw the French windows were wide open.

"You'll catch your death of cold," she muttered, even though she knew her father would be oblivious to her warning.

She made her way across the room toward the windows when suddenly she felt something below her shoe. Looking down, she saw she had stepped on some stray papers that had fallen on the floor. She frowned and raised her eyes to the desk. Her father had not stirred. It was then that she also noticed all the drawers in the cabinet ahead of her had been pulled out. Quickly she turned 'round and squinted into the gloom. The shelves on the facing wall were half empty. The ledgers normally kept there had been thrown to the ground. Panic suddenly flared in her chest.

"Sir," she called. He did not move. "Father!" She hurried over to him. As she did so, she noticed the odd position of his body. His arms appeared to be behind his back. It was only when she drew level with him and the pool of light from the candle illuminated the surface of the desk that she saw the upturned claret glass. For a moment she thought the liquid that was spreading across the desk was red wine. Without thinking she dipped her finger into the crimson fluid, and felt it warm and syrupy against her skin. The piercing scream that emanated from her lips a split second later came from the realization that what she was touching was not spilled claret but fresh blood.

# Chapter 5

The shock of Sir Theodisius's words caused Thomas to jolt. He raised his head from the pillows. Heaving himself up on his elbows, he contorted his face in a grimace.

"Sir Montagu dead? But how?"

The coroner, his shoulders sloped and his eyes to the floor, floundered to find his words. "I had not wanted to tell you, Thomas, but I knew there was no way to avoid it. The shocking manner of it . . ."

"What?" wheezed Thomas, the pain in his chest making it hard for him to breathe.

Sir Theodisius shook his head, as if he, too, found it difficult to digest the news. "He was murdered."

"Murdered?" echoed Thomas incredulously. He slumped back down on his pillows, unable to bear the pain any longer. "Murdered," he whispered again, as if to convince himself that he had heard the coroner correctly the first time. His initial thought had been that the aneurysm on which he had operated last year had burst, or that the lawyer had suffered heart failure or apoplexy. But murder? "Who . . . ? Where . . . ?"

"In the study at Boughton," the coroner replied, reluctantly adding: "Her ladyship found him."

Thomas's eyes widened. "Lydia found him?" Suddenly, summoning what little strength he had, he flung back the bedclothes and shot up as if he'd been fired out of a cannon. "I must go to her."

Mr. Peabody rushed forward. The apothecary had been left in charge of the doctor's ministrations while Professor Hascher took a well-earned rest.

"No, sir. I must urge you not to move." The little man grabbed hold of the sheets and gave Thomas a disapproving look. He need not have worried. The exertion was too much for the young anatomist, and he fell back onto the mattress like a limp doll.

"But Lydia . . . I must . . ." cried Thomas as Mr. Peabody reordered the bedcovers.

"Dr. Fairweather has given her a draft," Sir Theodisius reassured him. "The last I heard was that she was sleeping."

It was some comfort to Thomas to know that she had been sedated, but it did not compensate for his frustration at his own injury and his inability to be at her side.

After a moment he asked: "Do you know who did it?"

The coroner's jowls wobbled as he shook his head. "I wish I did," he replied. "You know I loathed the man, but I would never have wished the manner of his death on anyone."

Thomas's gaze shot up. "How, sir? Tell me how?"

Sir Theodisius swallowed hard. "He was all but beheaded."

"Holy Christ!" muttered Thomas. "And Lydia found him?" Once more he flung back the covers and tried to leave his sickbed, and once more Mr. Peabody tried to prevent him.

"You must allow your wound to heal, sir," advised the little apothecary.

"But I must go to Boughton," replied Thomas, wincing as he planted his stockinged feet on the floor. He shot a glance at Sir Theodisius. "Is that not right, sir?"

The coroner eyed the anatomist sheepishly, then addressed Mr. Peabody. "I fear the good doctor is right," he assured the apothecary. "Dr. Silkstone is needed urgently at the hall."

In less than an hour, Thomas, accompanied by Sir Theodisius, arrived at Boughton Hall. Leaning on Lovelock, the doctor had to be helped from the carriage and up the front steps into the hallway, where a flustered Howard greeted him.

"Dr. Silkstone, sir!" There was a note of relief in the butler's voice at seeing the anatomist both alive and about to take charge of a most unsettling situation.

"Howard," Thomas acknowledged. The effort of walking up the steps had left him short of breath. "Her ladyship?"

"She was in a most distressed state, sir."

"I am sure."

"But she is resting now, sir."

"Then I shall not disturb her," said Thomas. Instead he turned to Sir Theodisius, who had waddled in behind him. "Shall we get to work?"

Being privy to the anatomist's methods, the coroner had instructed that no one should enter the study. Nothing had been touched, and the chaotic scene that greeted the two men was just how Lydia had chanced upon it late the previous night.

Daylight now flooded into the room, revealing the full extent of the horror. Drawers had been tipped out, curtains slashed and, amid it all, blood spilled. A great deal of blood. There was something else, too. Thomas sniffed at the air around the desk. A strange perfume lingered, sweet and exotic. He looked for cut flowers but could see none. It troubled him, but then this was clearly a most troubling case.

The French doors were wide open, and Thomas walked over to them. Glancing down, he spotted a large bloody footprint on the threshold. Tracing the path back to the desk, he found more.

"The murderer entered from the garden?" ventured Sir Theodisius.

"He certainly escaped that way," replied Thomas, circling the desk where Sir Montagu's body sat in its chair. "Footprints." He pointed to the floor.

Already the flies were buzzing around the source of the blood. Moving closer, Thomas blanched at the sight, and a cold feeling ran down his spine. Before him lay the man who had stood in the way of his happiness, his nemesis, his archenemy, and now he had been defeated. But not in the way he would have wished. Patience, logic, and reason were his own weapons of choice. That was how he had always planned to triumph over Sir Montagu, but now someone else had beaten him to it. And in one of the most savage ways imaginable.

Thomas paused to inspect Sir Montagu's head. Like a surveyor, he skirted it and eyed it intently, sizing up angles and taking measurements. Presently, he lifted the cranium gently in his two hands and turned it to its side. Sir Theodisius shuddered, wide-eyed, as he saw the lawyer had been gagged. A piece of fabric had been thrust into his mouth to stifle his screams. It was sodden with blood. Unconsciously, the coroner balled his own kerchief in his hand and held it to his mouth. "A most brutal murder," he mumbled.

"Indeed," agreed Thomas, still clutching the dead man's cranium. He peered at the back of his neck, but there was so much blood it was difficult to determine the nature of the wound, so he rooted the head on the deck once more. Taking a step away, he reached for his own kerchief to wipe his bloodied hands.

"The list of people who would have liked to see the scoundrel dead is as long as my arm," continued the coroner, backing away from the corpse. "Any one of the villagers, for a start."

Thomas cast about the room, this time settling his eyes on the scattered documents and ledgers that covered the floor amid the general disarray. "Whoever murdered Sir Montagu was searching for something," he ventured.

The coroner looked up. "What?"

"This chaos was not caused for amusement," replied Thomas slowly. His eyes suddenly settled on a skewed portrait of an elderly Crick ancestor.

Sir Theodisius followed his gaze. "Money?" he suggested.

"There is a safe." Thomas's look locked onto the wall.

The coroner headed toward the lopsided picture. The doctor followed as the painting was pushed to one side. Behind the portrait the safe door was unlocked.

"Empty," pronounced Sir Theodisius, sticking his hand into the space.

Thomas eyed the pile of papers that lay on the floor immediately below. "Our murderer was looking for something specific," he said. Clearly visible among the documents was a banknote. He bent down slowly and picked it up. It was worth fifty guineas. "And it was most definitely not money."

As the anatomist began leafing through the other discarded bills and documents on the floor, Sir Theodisius craned his neck and cupped his hand 'round his ear.

"Hear that?" he asked, moving as fast as his bulk would allow him toward the threshold.

There appeared to be some sort of altercation in the hallway. Voices were raised. Feet were marching across the marble floor. Thomas looked up to see the coroner fling open the door, and there, in the hallway, stood Sir Arthur Warbeck, the magistrate. Wearing a bouffant wig and carrying a cane, which was clearly for effect rather than any physical need, he was accompanied by the stalwart constable, old Walter Harker, and another sideman. From the way he was addressing Howard, he was obviously annoyed about something. On hearing the door groan on its hinges, the magistrate turned to see Sir Theodisius glowering at him from the study. From his reaction, it was clear he had not expected to see his colleague.

"Pettigrew!" he exclaimed, somewhat taken aback. He pursed his lips and, after a short pause, added: "The murder brings you here, no doubt."

The coroner tugged indignantly at his waistcoat, which had ridden up over his large belly. It was clear he felt he had every right to be at the hall, and needed no permission from Warbeck to attend. "Indeed it does. A most troubling and gruesome affair," he replied. And as if to demonstrate his point, he took a couple of paces back and opened the door wide, silently inviting the magistrate to view the scene of the hideous crime for himself.

Warbeck swaggered in, brandishing his cane, clearly wishing to take charge of the situation. He cast his eyes about the room, yet as soon as he was confronted by the sight of the bloody footprints and the scarlet splashes on the walls, his swagger seemed to desert him. Startled by what he saw, even before he caught sight of the cadaver, he began to heave as if to retch. He would probably have swooned had he not clapped eyes on Thomas as he turned away.

"Silkstone!" he cried. "But I thought . . ." The magistrate's normally florid complexion, reflecting his penchant for port, turned decidedly pale, as if he had seen a ghost.

Thomas had remained in the study to inspect the safe, but by this time his throbbing wound had left him feeling a little lightheaded. He was steadying himself on a nearby chair. "I was injured, sir, but I am pleased to report I am very much alive." He arched his head in the direction of the desk, where the body remained. "Unlike Sir Montagu." A quick glance at the lawyer's corpse, its head at an odd angle, was sufficient for the magistrate. The pooled blood was clearly visible from a few paces away, and the ferrous smell of the corpse was making its presence felt as the sunlight warmed the room.

Sir Arthur, catching a glimpse of his old ally's face, shot away quickly.

"Dear God!" he muttered, jerking his head as fast as if his cheek had been slapped. Blinking away the shocking image of his murdered friend, he forced himself to focus on the desk. His eyes soon settled on the smeared paper knife in among the crimson-soaked papers. There was blood on the blade. His eyes snapped back to Sir Theodisius.

"The weapon, I presume."

Thomas intervened. The scene of the crime was his domain. He did not want quick assumptions made. "We cannot be certain, sir."

The magistrate turned to face the doctor. "We? *We* cannot be certain? And what do you think you are doing here, Silkstone?" he sneered, his voice like acid.

Sir Theodisius stepped in with a reply. "As coroner for this county, I asked Dr. Silkstone to investigate the death."

Warbeck, whose wig added at least three inches to his height, looked at his colleague narrowly. "And as magistrate for this part of the county, I am also here to investigate with a view to making an arrest."

Thomas, his eyes wide, balked at the very suggestion. It was far too soon to accuse anyone. "An arrest?" he repeated. "Who?"

The magistrate's expression became even sterner. "It is no concern of yours, Silkstone," he snapped, stalking toward the door.

Thomas would not be deterred. He followed him. "You have evidence on which to base your arrest, sir?"

Sir Arthur turned. "I have sufficient reason," he said, and he carried on walking through to the hall, where his men were waiting alongside an anxious Howard.

The magistrate addressed the butler directly. Drawing himself up to his full, yet not considerable, height, he said: "I would see Lady Lydia."

Howard shot a look of dismay toward Thomas, who stood on the threshold of the study, then back at Sir Arthur. "But, sir, her ladyship is resting," he protested.

"Fetch her immediately," ordered the magistrate, tapping his cane on the marble floor. "I will wait in here," he told the distraught butler, and he brushed past him on his way to the drawing room.

"Warbeck!" barked Sir Theodisius. "What do you think you are about?" The coroner began to trail Sir Arthur.

The magistrate wheeled 'round, a smirk on his face. "I am about to question Lady Lydia," he replied.

"But you heard. She is resting," Sir Theodisius repeated forcefully.

Sir Arthur merely smiled. "It is a luxury I do not usually allow those under suspicion," he countered.

By this time, Thomas had also progressed painfully into the hallway. The shock of Sir Arthur's intervention had unsettled him and left him gasping for breath. He clung onto the hall table to steady himself. "What are you saying, sir?"

Sir Theodisius looked askance as he shambled toward the magistrate. "Surely you do not suspect her ladyship?"

Warbeck gave a slight nod of his bewigged head. "I have been reliably informed that Lady Lydia was found with blood on her hands and robe."

Shocked by such a revelation, Thomas wondered who could have betrayed Lydia; then he recalled that Dr. Fairweather, the duplicitous physician, had been called to attend her. He suddenly found his strength. "That proves nothing," he interjected, lurching forward. "She was simply unfortunate enough to be the first to find Sir Montagu."

The magistrate remained unmoved. "May be," he began. "But couple this with the fact that her ladyship has just been released from a mental institution and that the knife was already to hand—we may well be looking at the deranged and impetuous actions of a madwoman."

The glib assessment bewildered and angered Thomas in equal measure. Momentarily stunned, he watched Sir Arthur proceed toward the drawing room door, which was held ajar by a footman. He refused to allow him to have the last word.

"But that is all circumstantial," he called out. He clenched his fists. Then he had an idea. "Better to question Nicholas Lupton."

The magistrate turned once more, slowly this time, as if the very action of the turn allowed him to think. He inclined his head and arched a brow. "Your rival, I believe, Dr. Silkstone?"

Thomas felt the blood return to his cheeks. "My personal circumstances have nothing to do with it, sir," he replied firmly.

"Is that so?" There was contempt in the magistrate's voice.

Unsure as to whether his words might hold some sway, Thomas launched into his justification. "He has the motive."

"Oh?" Sir Arthur's interest was clearly piqued.

Thomas continued. "I know he and Sir Montagu quarreled the day before the duel and he left his employ." He recalled Lupton's visit to his room at the Three Tuns.

The magistrate nodded in agreement. "I had heard rumors, too."

Perhaps, thought Thomas, he was making progress. "And then there are the footprints," he blurted.

"Footprints?" repeated Sir Arthur, intrigued.

Thomas nodded. "Bloody ones that lead from the body back to the doors and out into the garden," he replied. "If you but let me, we can compare those footprints with Lupton's."

The magistrate paused in thought for a moment, stroking his long chin. "Lupton, eh? There is already a warrant out for his arrest."

Thomas coughed back a laugh. "For my murder?" he asked with a wry smile.

Sir Arthur flashed the anatomist a haughty look. "Happily it is no longer valid."

Sir Theodisius stepped in. "Happily indeed, but you could let the warrant stand to give Silkstone more time to carry out his investigation," he suggested.

The magistrate paused to gather his thoughts. After a moment he nodded. "Very well," he said, adding: "And I shall engage a thieftaker, too."

"Most judicious," agreed Sir Theodisius.

"A thieftaker?" Thomas's eyes darted from one man to the other.

"To track down Lupton," explained the coroner.

Sir Arthur arched his head in the direction of the study. "I owe it to an old friend."

"Of course," acknowledged Sir Theodisius with a nod.

The magistrate turned again, this time changing course and heading toward the front doors. "But I shall still need to question her ladyship," he shot back, waving his cane in the air.

Sir Theodisius frowned. "But perhaps tomorrow, when she will be better able to cope?" he ventured.

Sir Arthur stopped dead and pivoted 'round on his cane. First he glanced at Thomas, then back at the coroner. "Very well," he conceded, adding to Sir Theodisius: "But in the meantime Silkstone will accord Sir Montagu's body the dignity it deserves."

The coroner was about to offer his assurances when Thomas butted in. "Of course, you have my word, sir," he said. He gave a shallow bow, but his seeming courtesy masked what he muttered under his breath. "Just as soon as I have gathered more evidence," he whispered to himself.

The magistrate deferred to the two gentlemen and made his way toward Howard, who waited with his tricorn and cape. The footman had hurried to open the front door. "I shall return tomorrow," warned Warbeck, plumping his hat onto his large wig. "And I shall expect some answers."

Thomas and Sir Theodisius waited until the top of Sir Arthur's tricorn had disappeared from view down the front steps of the hall before they exchanged anxious looks.

"You have much work to do," said Sir Theodisius, shaking his head.

But Thomas did not seem to hear. Instead he slumped into the nearby chair, clutching his chest. The coroner clamped a hand on the doctor's shoulder and clicked his tongue. He was suddenly angry with himself for forgetting Thomas's injury. "Forgive me. You should be resting."

If Thomas had not been in so much pain, he would have sighed. As it was, all he could do was give a shallow nod. "It is a luxury I must do without," he replied, heaving himself up from the chair. He lifted his hand and signaled to Howard. "My case, if you please. It is in the study." The butler bowed and went to retrieve the bag. "I need to conduct a thorough search of the room before the light is lost," he continued.

"And the postmortem?" asked Sir Theodisius.

Howard returned a moment later with the case and set it on the nearby console table.

"I fear Sir Montagu will have to wait a while in the game larder until I can perform one," replied Thomas, unlocking his bag.

Sir Theodisius frowned as he watched his ailing friend retrieve a phial of brownish liquid and uncork it. "I am sorry to put this upon you, Silkstone," he said, mindful of the doctor's own condition.

Thomas shook his head before swigging back the contents of the phial. His face registered a look of disgust as he swallowed the fluid. "My discomfort is irrelevant. Whoever committed this terrible murder is still abroad," he said, plugging the phial once more. "He needs to be caught as soon as possible."

## *Chapter 6*

Sir Montagu's corpse was beginning to turn. Thomas knew at least sixteen hours had passed since the murder and probably more. Rigor mortis had spread to all the muscles and could remain for several hours until they relaxed again. It was a warm spring day and already the flies were infesting the body. Thomas had promised Sir Arthur he would accord the eminent lawyer his dignity, and while his professional priorities certainly took precedence, he nevertheless had no wish for the cadaver to remain in the study a moment longer than necessary. Standing by the mantelpiece, he pulled the bell. Howard appeared a moment later.

"Dr. Silkstone?"

"Tell Lovelock that Sir Montagu's body needs to be taken to the game larder, will you?"

The butler nodded grimly.

"We'll need sheets and some sort of stretcher to transport him."

"Yes, Doctor."

In preparation for the removal, Thomas inspected the body once more. Lifting the head, which was bereft of its wig, he could see a short gray bristle hazed the scalp. It was the first time he had seen the lawyer thus, and such nakedness made him look oddly vulnerable.

Still pained by his chest, Thomas knelt down to retrieve the wig. The lawyer's hands were bound behind his back with rope.

The binding had been tied so tightly that it had cut into the flesh at the wrists. He would examine the resulting wounds during the postmortem. For now, however, it was the cord itself that caught Thomas's attention. He ran a finger along the surface of the rope. It was harsh and almost prickly. Taking a pair of tweezers from his case, he plucked at one of the fibers that protruded from the length. He peered at it through his magnifying glass. It seemed to him as if it might be from a plant of some sort, but not standard linen. Nor was it wool. He dropped the fiber into an empty phial. He would examine it under the lens of a microscope later. For the moment, he knew he would have to cut the rope to free up Sir Montagu's arms so that he could be transported more easily.

Using a scalpel, he severed the cord cleanly, but the dead man's hands were so stiff, they did not move. Thomas rescued the rope and saved it for a later inspection. Just as he had finished the grisly task, there came a knock at the door and the head groom's pock-marked face peered 'round it.

"Ah, Lovelock," Thomas greeted him somberly. "I fear I have an unpleasant undertaking for you. You are not alone?"

The groom moved gingerly into the room. "No, sir. I have Will with me," he said, clutching a large white sheet to his chest.

"Good," said Thomas. "And I'll take that," he added, pointing to the sheet. He moved forward and relieved the groom of the drapery, which the latter held at arm's length, his eyes darting everywhere but on the ghastly spectacle. Seeing Lovelock's discomfort, the doctor was quick to cover the gaping wound at the back of the neck with the murdered man's own wig. "To the game larder, if you please," he instructed. "Oh, and avoid the footprints," he warned, pointing to the floor.

Lovelock was all too familiar with the routine. The larder had become a mortuary on more occasions than he cared to remember over the past three years. With its marble slab and drainage sluice so the blood could be washed easily away, it made the most suitable setting for a makeshift dissecting room. The groom signaled to his reluctant son, who had remained, shivering, at the door. Together they heaved their unwieldy cargo onto a wide plank that had been purloined from the woodshed and marched as quickly as they could out of the room.

"I will be along presently," Thomas assured them, although he could not say when. He still had much to do in the study. He wanted to take advantage of the bright spring sunlight that flooded the room, illuminating dust motes that danced in the air and specks and flecks that had landed on the surfaces. Any miniscule one of them might prove vital in identifying the killer.

As he took a deep breath, as if to gird himself for the task ahead, he was, however, immediately reminded of his wound. He also registered the smell again, the one he had first noticed as soon as he walked into the room. It was sweet and rich, but he could not quite place it. He did not recall that Sir Montagu wore such pungent cologne, but he might have been mistaken. He would ask Lydia if it was his habit.

Peering through his magnifying glass, he next turned his attention to the bloody footprints that led from the desk to the French window. There was only one that was almost complete. The other two were really only red-rimmed contours. He eased himself gently to his knees to study them and was immediately puzzled by what he saw. The outline of the footwear was lighter and less defined than would normally be expected. Nor was there any sign of a heel mark. It was as if the imprints were made by slippers. And yet the prints were quite large, too large for a woman.

Thomas scanned the desk and quickly found a clean sheet of paper. Bending down, he pressed it hard on the bloody footprint, then removed it. Only a bare outline was left on the paper, but such evidence could prove vital in the hunt for Sir Montagu's killer.

Next he examined the desk. Some of the papers that were strewn across it were spattered with blood. Various bills and documents had been showered with splats, presumably when the blade had severed the carotid artery, sending a crimson jet spewing across the surface. At the edge of the congealed pool of blood, Thomas spied the paper knife that Sir Arthur assumed to be the murder weapon. Wrapping his own kerchief around his hand, he picked it up by the hilt to inspect the blade. He walked to the window for a better look. There was a light smear of blood toward the tip, yet the pattern was very different from the spots and splashes left behind by the gushing of the slit artery. He placed it carefully into his handkerchief and laid it in his case. He was almost certain that Sir Arthur had been incorrect in his assumption.

A moment later, he heard footsteps approach. Looking up from inspecting a pile of documents on the floor, he saw Howard at the doorway. The butler cleared his throat.

"Sir, her ladyship is awake and asking for you."

Thomas smiled. "Then I shall come right away," he replied, wincing as he straightened himself.

Following Howard slowly and painfully up the stairs, he was directed into the boudoir. He found Lydia dressed and seated on the chaise longue by the window. Richard was by her side, his curly head resting contentedly just below his mother's breast. Lydia was clutching him to her, stroking his hair and gazing out across the lawns. She looked pale and drawn, but as soon as she saw Thomas, she seemed relieved. Richard immediately sat up as he strode toward them, then rushed forward to greet him.

"Dr. Silkstone," cried the young earl, tugging at the doctor's coat. "Mamma says we are to be friends again," he said, fixing Thomas with large brown eyes.

Thomas smiled at the boy, then shot a glance at Lydia, who remained seated but calm. He bent low to level himself with Richard. "I am most glad of it," he replied. He proffered his hand, and after a quick glance back at his mother, who gave him a reassuring nod, the boy took it and shook it.

As if she had been hovering outside on the landing, watching events, Nurse Pring appeared at the threshold. "Shall I take the young master now, m'lady?" she asked. Lydia nodded, but assured her son she would see him again later in the day. Both she and Thomas watched him go; then, as soon as they found themselves alone, Lydia rose and Thomas moved forward.

"My love!" she muttered, pressing her head to his chest.

Thomas let out a muffled cry of pain, and she withdrew quickly.

"I am so sorry," she apologized, pulling away from him. "Your wound . . ."

He smiled at her and shook his head. "There is no need," he replied, taking her hands in his. "I can endure anything as long as I know that you trust me again."

She threw back her head and looked up at him. "I should never have doubted you in the first place. I am so sorry, I . . ."

"Shush," soothed Thomas, placing his forefinger across her lips. "No apologies. No recriminations. We are together."

She led him to the window seat and bade him sit beside her. For a moment their reunion meant they both set aside the horror that had unfolded downstairs only a few hours before.

"I thought I'd lost you," Lydia told him, harking back to seeing him lying wounded on the common.

"You should've known I would outsmart Lupton," he told her, brushing off the duel as a trifling incident.

Seeing he was jesting, Lydia smiled, too, but the respite was short-lived. She gasped and pulled away suddenly. It was soon apparent that her nightmarish discovery in the study was still very real.

"What's wrong? What is it?" Thomas followed her gaze to see that her eyes were fixed on a dark red stain on his coat cuff. It was smeared with blood. Seeing her revulsion, he took the coat off immediately, flinging it on the floor and out of sight, as if it were plague-ridden.

"Forgive me," he said. He had washed his hands of Sir Montagu's blood, but the stain on the sleeve had gone unremarked. He put a comforting arm around her once more.

Lydia was holding her handkerchief up to her mouth. "His head! It was . . ."

Thomas pulled her to him again. "You have had a terrible shock," he told her, "but we will find whoever did this."

She regarded him with doleful eyes that reminded him of the first time she had come to his laboratory, pleading for him to probe her brother's death. Her look still sent an electric charge through his body, yet there was something more assured in her expression. Time and successive bereavements had taken their toll on her face and hardened her features. Her vulnerability remained, but it was tempered by a new steeliness. From the look on her face Thomas knew there was something more.

"You have a suspicion?" he asked.

"I do," she said, nodding.

"Lupton?" Thomas preempted her reply.

Lydia frowned. "Sir Montagu told me there had been a disagreement between them, and then I remembered a carriage flash past me as I returned to Boughton. I later realized Lupton was inside." She shook her head in disbelief. "Could he really have done such a thing?"

The anatomist took a painful breath. "Until I have examined all the evidence and conducted a postmortem, I cannot say," he replied. He folded his hand over hers. "All I know is there is a warrant out for Lupton's arrest and when he is found he has some serious questions to answer."

# Chapter 7

The thieftaker—one John Thrupp—and his three men were on the road heading north shortly after noon. Thrupp, a hatchet-faced veteran well versed in the ways of villains, had been briefed by Sir Arthur. The magistrate had told him that the murder suspect, a gentleman by the name of Nicholas Lupton, came from a family who owned land in Yorkshire and might try to make his way homeward. There was a possibility he was planning to join the Great North Road at Biggleswade in order to catch the coach from London to York. He would also, most probably, be armed with a dueling pistol and was almost certainly accompanied by a thuggish sideman called Seth Talland. It went without saying both men were extremely dangerous. Any approach, instructed Sir Arthur, must be made with extreme caution. If they had executed Sir Montagu in such a savage and unholy way, the fiends were obviously crazed and might well lash out again.

Armed with a description of the wanted men—unfortunately no small likenesses were available—the four thieftakers set off at the gallop. The fugitive pair had more than a day's head start on them. The posse planned to stop off at the many inns and hostelries they passed on their way. This would obviously slow their progress, but the two guineas that Sir Arthur Warbeck had personally pledged for the scoundrels' apprehension was as good an incentive as they could wish for. There was a reward for information, too. A guinea to the man, or woman, who could lead them to the fugitives.

Everywhere they went, they asked questions and spread the word. A murderer, or murderers, was abroad. More rumors had surfaced among other travelers come from Brandwick. News of Sir Montagu's murder was circulating on the morning of market day, and already those who had visited the village were leaving with more than just cloth or food or other wares. They were weighed down with gossip and accusations, too.

"You 'eard about the murder up at Boughton?" asked a woman buying ribbons from a haberdasher.

"Terrible business."

A cross-eyed passerby butted in, drawing his finger across his throat. "Fair near cut off 'is 'ead," he interjected gleefully.

The trader, a plump woman with a whiskery chin, ignored the man. "They say 'tis the steward."

"The one that shot that American knife man?" asked her customer.

"One and the same."

"'E must have gone mad."

"Aye, the devil's got into 'im right enough."

By midday the murder was already the talk of inns and shops within a ten-mile radius of Boughton, but the news needed to spread farther and quicker. So, as soon as the thieftakers were engaged, they decided that one of them should ride ahead in haste to scour the coaching inns at Biggleswade so as to prevent Lupton from boarding the York coach at first light. At the same time, the other men would stop and make inquiries at the inns in the more immediate vicinity.

Meanwhile, much farther south, another young chancer had recently arrived in London. One took one's life in one's hands around the foul stream of the Fleet after dark. Any London gentleman would tell you that. In the tumbledown courts and alleyways that surrounded it dwelt the desperate and the damned. That would have been reason enough to make anyone nervous, but Captain Patrick Flynn, formerly of the Irish Dragoon Guards and lately of the East India Company, had cause to be doubly so. He had shouldered his way through the slums of Calcutta and traded with the hardest merchants in Golconda, but this area of London, the haunt of many a robber and murderer, beat them both. Normally his dress marked him out as a man of substance, but on this occasion he had resorted to an old fustian coat and a shabby tricorn over his ginger-colored hair so as to blend in with the surroundings. Circumstances had forced him to call upon the services of such lowlifes in order to achieve his plan. But he did not feel comfortable in such company.

A little welcome moonlight squeezed through the gaps in gable ends and down narrow alleyways as his carriage journeyed deep into the black heart of the city. It was an area where the roofs of dwellings slumped like exhausted dockers after a hard day's work. Painted women stood on every street corner, feral dogs roamed freely, and brawling men could spill out of a tavern at any turn. Up ahead he caught sight of an upstairs window suddenly flung open to disgorge a pail of slops. The reeking contents narrowly missed an old man shuffling below, who cursed loudly as piss splashed his breeches.

Flynn's carriage came to a halt behind the unfortunate pedestrian. The way ahead was too narrow. The captain put his head out of the window to find out what was happening.

"You're on your own from now on," the driver shouted down from his seat.

It was what Flynn feared. He knew he and his naukar, Manjeet, would have to make some of their way on foot. This was the part of London where the Fleet River met the Thames just by Blackfriars. It was here that the lascars would often gather. These were the Indian sailors who were conveyed to the shores of England by the powerful and prolific traders of the East India Company. It was here that they were often abandoned to their own fates once they had outlived their usefulness. Droves of the hapless men would huddle around braziers on the dockside to keep warm, their thin cotton shifts and pantaloons affording little protection against the cold English climate. For victuals they were forced to beg or to rely on the uneven bounty of the captains of their erstwhile ships. In short, they were a wretched band. Finding themselves ignored and discarded, they had no way of returning to India unless they accepted that cruel treatment and rampant disease were inevitable elements of their hazardous voyages. Left to fend for themselves in a foreign land, they were desperate men. And desperate men did desperate things, in Patrick Flynn's experience.

After a few tentative steps through the thread-thin streets, Flynn and his naukar arrived at the Cockpit Tavern. Manjeet had been with him these past nine years, ever since an unfortunate debacle in Hyderabad when his previous Indian master fell afoul of the law. The former had transferred his loyalties quite easily and remained a good and reliable servant ever since. The only problem arose with his disfigurement. He was without a nose. It had been sliced off as a punishment for his thievery when he was but a youngster. In his homeland he was accepted—there were so many like him. In London, however, he was an object of curiosity and revulsion. The captain insisted he cover the bottom half of his face in public with a silk scarf.

Flynn looked about him warily, then up at the inn sign that dangled drunkenly off a single rusting hinge. He'd been warned about coming here. He'd heard the stories about unsuspecting patrons dispatched through trapdoors that opened out onto the river, never to be seen again. But he was a man of the world. He'd learned well in India. He was aware he was playing a dangerous game, but he'd shown a penchant for deception at the card table and wagered he was a good match for any of the scoundrels who frequented these parts.

They were not far from the quayside. At this part of the Fleet, ships could moor three abreast, and the tavern was frequented by merchants and adventurers, too. Here deals were done and fortunes made and lost. Flynn and his man took a table in the corner, away from prying eyes. There master and servant waited, an uneasy silence between them, even though all around there was the constant noise of talk and raucous laughter.

"A brandy," Flynn told the serving girl who came to the table after a minute or two. He noted the hair that hung in straggles below her cap was the color of a tallow candle.

"And for him?" She eyed Manjeet, who sat, head bowed, next to his master. The naukar lifted his face to her unthinkingly, and his scarf fell down. The girl gasped in horror and backed away. Heads turned, and curious eyes fixed on the strange pair.

"Have you never seen a man without a nose before?" barked Flynn. There was a tinge of an Irish accent in his voice. It always resurfaced when he was angry or nervous or both, as on this occasion.

The girl's lip began to tremble, and she scurried off to fetch the captain's order, leaving him hunched over the table waiting.

"You are certain they will be here?" he asked Manjeet after a short silence.

"Yes, sahib," came the reply. Even after nine years of service Manjeet's English remained rudimentary.

Sure enough, the captain did not have to wait long. At the appointed time the two lascars approached, seating themselves opposite him. Flynn could tell they were men of the sea. Their dark faces were weathered, and they stank of stale sweat mixed with a pungent smell he could not quite place. They were strong and intimidating, one a whole head taller than the other. Their hair, black as tar pitch, was tied at the napes of their necks, and they wore the flimsy cotton pajamas of their class. He eyed both Indians with a look of eager anticipation and bade them sit. Manjeet was to be his interpreter in the negotiations.

"Well?" he began, leaning forward across the table that separated them and then returning his gaze to Manjeet.

One of the lascars, the one who appeared older and wilier, spoke.

"You have money?" translated Manjeet.

Flynn signified he was irritated by such an opening question. He let a sigh of frustration escape to make his point, then delved into his pocket to bring out a small purse. "Five shillings," he said grudgingly, flinging it on the table.

The lascar slid his eyes toward Manjeet. "He said ten," he protested in his native tongue.

Flynn did not need his naukar to translate. "The rest when you have told me what I want to know," he replied. His many years at the card table had taught him never to gamble everything at once.

Manjeet conveyed the deal, and the lascars swapped looks before nodding in agreement.

The older spoke a few words and Manjeet listened intently. "The *Atlas* reached St. Helena six weeks ago with the *Besborough*," he told Flynn.

"And Mrs. Hastings?"

The taller man nodded and seemed positive in his account.

"She good, sir, so they heard," Manjeet relayed.

Flynn was relieved. At the back of his mind lurked the fear that Marian Hastings, formerly known as Baroness von Imhoff and now married to Warren Hastings, the governor-general of India, might have declined during the long and hazardous voyage from Calcutta. Her poor health was the reason her doting husband had insisted on her trip to England's fresher climes.

Flynn allowed himself a tight smile. "And when is the ship due to reach these shores?"

Manjeet put the question to the men, waited for the answer, then replied. "It is due in Portsmouth late next week, sahib."

Another smile, only this time broader, graced the captain's lips. He showed a row of small front teeth. "Good," he said with a nod. From what he knew of the celebrated Mrs. Hastings, once she had seen the diamond, she would surely fall under its spell. Reaching into his pocket, he brought out another purse. "The rest of the money," he told the men. This time Manjeet did not have to translate.

*Chapter 8*

Sir Montagu's corpse remained overnight in the game larder. It lay beneath a sheet on a long marble slab. Its stockinged feet, spattered dark red, stuck out at the end, and a hand, now flaccid, had emerged from under the sheet to point to the floor below. Day had just broken, although the light remained poor as Thomas entered the outbuilding to begin the postmortem. Once again, he had enlisted the help of Professor Hascher. The elderly Saxon had been due back in Oxford, but had postponed his journey to assist. The latter busied himself stripping the body in a workmanlike fashion as Thomas went through his well-rehearsed ritual of laying out his medical instruments.

When all the clothes were removed, Thomas asked Professor Hascher to arrange for a pail of water and some cloths, allowing him a moment alone to compose himself. This would be an examination like no other. He once had heard Sir Montagu, in one of his tirades, protest to Lydia that he, Thomas, was nothing but an artisan, and now, as Thomas struggled to adjust the lawyer's limp body on the slab, he had to acknowledge there was some truth in the words—the way he was so often obliged to shoulder a corpse, wash a body, sew up dead flesh. There were indeed times when he felt more artisan than artist. But on this occasion, he voided himself of all emotion. He had a job to do and do it he must, to the best of his ability, without stopping to think whose flesh his knife was cutting.

The Saxon professor returned after a few minutes with the requested items, and together the two men swabbed down the body in silence, performing the routine with a priestly reverence.

Thomas appreciated the quiet. He wanted to be alone with his own thoughts, and Professor Hascher, he knew, could respect that. Before them, on the dissecting table, lay the body of a man who had wished him all the ill in the world. Sir Montagu had wanted him dead, no doubt. He would have been delighted had Lupton's shot penetrated his heart and put paid to what the lawyer regarded as his incessant meddling. How ironic, then, mused Thomas, that their fortunes had been so reversed. He checked himself. He had no intention of gloating. It was a base emotion, certainly not worthy of his profession.

Because of the paucity of light, the two men agreed to a division of labor. Thomas would take the top half of the body, and the professor would concentrate on the bottom, where Thomas had already carried out a cursory examination.

As Sir Montagu's head had been partly severed, it rested at an odd angle on the slab. The force from behind had severed the spinal cord, but the anterior of the neck had been left intact. Thomas squeezed out a cloth and began to wipe away the congealed blood from the chin and the front of the throat. It was then that he noticed it: a laceration around the front of the neck, a thin line like a red necklace that stretched two or three inches on either side of the epiglottis. He reached for his magnifying glass to take a closer look. On the left side the skin had been incised, as if a blade had been hooked into the flesh, then drawn across it. On the right, however, the mark was little more than a scratch. The wound had not been intended to kill, of that Thomas was sure—more to frighten or, the thought occurred to him, to torture, to extract information by inducing fear and pain. He put down the glass and paused for a moment, causing Professor Hascher to look up.

"Something wrong?" he asked.

"Something puzzling," replied Thomas, inspecting the strange yet superficial wound. He went over to his case and retrieved the paper knife he had found in the study. Returning to the corpse, he laid the blade of the knife across Sir Montagu's throat. At that point he was most thankful he had already closed the hooded lids. Holding the knife slightly above the skin, he drew it across quickly to reenact the murderer's probable motion. Yet try as he might, he could not see how the paper knife, with its straight, double-edged blade, might make such a mark. No ordinary knife had made it, he was forced to conclude, but rather a curved blade.

"A sickle?" he asked out loud.

Professor Hascher peered across. "Or some such ozer farm implement, perhaps?"

Thomas's mind switched quickly to the Brandwick commoners who had stood to lose their land at a stroke of Sir Montagu's pen, not to mention the coppicers and sawyers. The planned enclosure of the whole of the Boughton Estate would have put an end to their livelihoods and threatened their very existence. He pictured their woodland billhooks and spoon knives with their sharp curved blades, used to slice the larch and hazel. In the wrong hands they could kill a man with one fell blow. So many of the villagers had the wherewithal, and all had the motive to commit such a heinous act. As he examined the wound, it seemed that one of them had done just that.

"You could be right, Professor," he replied.

Next Thomas moved down to the dead man's wrists. There were yet more puzzling fibers. He was plucking them out with tweezers when a knock at the door broke into his routine.

"Silkstone, 'tis I," came a booming voice.

Thomas nodded to the professor and wiped his hands on a clean cloth nearby.

"Sir Theodisius," he greeted the coroner, opening the door.

"Good God, man. You look like death yourself."

Thomas nodded. "I have felt better," he said, allowing Sir Theodisius to pass.

The coroner nodded to Professor Hascher, who took his cue. "Please to excuse me, gentlemen," he said, bobbing his snowy-white head and leaving the room. He knew that the coming conversation was not going to be easy for Thomas.

Once the two men were alone, Thomas walked over to the

corpse. "I fear what I am about to show you will disturb you, sir," he said, beckoning toward the slab.

The coroner's brow furrowed, and he swallowed hard. He did not need to be warned. He could already tell from Thomas's expression that what he was about to witness would unsettle him. Even though he had seen almost as many corpses during his tenure in office as he'd had hot dinners, he still balked at the sight of a dead man. The fact that this particular cadaver belonged to someone he knew in life made it all the harder for him. Nevertheless, he tugged at his waistcoat, as if to prepare himself for what was to come. He took a sturdy breath. "I am ready," he said.

Thomas stepped aside to reveal the body, and Sir Theodisius shuddered.

"Poor devil," muttered the coroner, shaking his head as he looked with pity on his old adversary.

"'Tis not a pretty sight, sir," said Thomas softly. "And there is much that puzzles me." He pointed to the red necklace around the corpse's neck.

"What's this?" The coroner frowned, then looked up with eyes that were questioning and troubled at the same time.

"I fear Sir Montagu was tortured, sir." There was no easy way to say it.

"Tortured?" The word hung between the two men as both of them contemplated the barbarity of the act. The coroner could not disguise his repulsion at the thought. He began to shake.

"Who? Why?" he asked, seeking the support of a seat. Thomas fetched a nearby crate to take the coroner's weight.

"This wound is cursory, designed to shock but not seriously injure," the doctor explained, walking back to the slab. "Whoever inflicted it either wanted to put the fear of God into Sir Montagu or make him divulge information."

Bringing a lamp closer to the dead man's head, Thomas next turned the corpse onto its front to show the coroner the fatal wound. But Sir Theodisius was most reluctant to take advantage of the view.

"I shall accept your word," he told Thomas, holding his kerchief to his mouth.

Undeterred, the anatomist peered into the crimson cavern of the gaping neck with his magnifying glass. The cut was clean. The blade was very clearly honed to be as sharp as a scalpel.

"There is no evidence of chattering," he mused.

"Chattering?" repeated Sir Theodisius, clearly unfamiliar with the term.

Not bothering to look up from the corpse, Thomas explained: "Yes, I've sometimes noted a distinctive cutting pattern when a thin blade jumps slightly from side to side during use."

"But not in this case?"

"No. The implement, whatever it was, has sliced easily through the cartilage and muscle. A straight blade cuts well enough, but if it encounters a bone, it will tend to shear it, or break it, while the curved blade usually slashes through it more cleanly."

"So what sort of weapon might it have been?"

Continuing to examine the wound, Thomas told him: "There is no doubt in my mind that the blade was sizable and belonged to a formidable weapon that could, if desired, cut through bone."

The coroner arched a brow. "So 'twas not the paper knife?"

Thomas straightened his back and reached once more for the suspect knife. For a second he studied its smeared blade. A tallow stump lay cold in a nearby holder, and he ran it along the length of the knife. It scoured the wax, but nothing more.

"Not the paper knife," repeated Thomas. Then, as if to reinforce his point, he traced the path of the blade along the wound and could tell immediately.

"But the blood on the blade!" protested Sir Theodisius.

Thomas shook his head. "It must have come from another source other than the mortal blow," he concluded. He began to turn the corpse onto its back once more. The effort, however, was too much for him. He winced in pain. Reluctantly, the coroner stepped forward and, without a word, used his considerable weight to lever the body over.

"Thank you, sir," said Thomas, gasping for breath.

Now standing by the corpse, Sir Theodisius seemed impervious to the anatomist's gratitude. He was eyeing his former colleague's ashen face and, in particular, the bloody gag that was still stuffed between his blue lips. Its presence, thought Thomas, explained why no one in the household was roused during the attack. He could just make out the initials *M. M.* embroidered at the corner. The kerchief was Sir Montagu's own.

"Curious," remarked Sir Theodisius.

Thomas followed the coroner's gaze. "Sir?"

"If the murderer went to the trouble of gagging him, he did not intend to dispatch him with haste."

Thomas knew the gag backed up his theory that Sir Montagu was subjected to an interrogation prior to his gruesome end. "If, as I believe, the killer was looking for something specific, a movement of the eyes or a nod of the head would have been a sufficient means of communication."

Sir Theodisius took up the thread of his argument. "But what if the information the murderer sought was not forthcoming, either because Sir Montagu was not privy to it or because he refused to be intimidated?"

"Either way," said Thomas, taking his forceps and carefully removing the bloody rag, "he paid the price with his life for refusing to cooperate." And what, he asked himself privately, could be worth killing for in such a callous and fiendish manner?

*Chapter 9*

The thieftakers had cause to be very pleased with themselves. Later that night they apprehended not one but two wanted men in one fell swoop. Nicholas Lupton and Talland, the bald and burly ruffian, had been found at an inn in the village of Aston Abbotts. A wily hostler at the Royal Oak had suspected the men were fugitives from the way their horses had been ridden so hard. Foaming at their mouths, their fetlocks swollen, the poor creatures were clearly in need of a proper rest and watering. The hostler alerted the landlord, whose wife had heard the warnings of undesirables on the loose earlier in the day. The thieftakers were duly summoned to the suspects' chamber as they bedded down for the night.

As was to be expected, the ruffian put up a fight, landing blows and breaking chairs in an effort to avoid capture. The other man, a more refined sort, had attempted negotiation rather than brute force. He challenged the thieftakers to call upon his good acquaintance, the Earl of Rainton, who owned a few thousand acres around the town. The earl would, he said, vouch for his good character. His claims, however, carried no weight, and he was bundled, along with his unsavory cohort, into a carriage bound for Oxford Castle, a day's journey away, to await trial.

His own pain was proving Thomas's most pressing enemy as he sat to write his postmortem report. Pain followed swiftly by uncertainty. Sir Arthur had requested that the work be completed with all haste. The doctor worked as best he could, trying to ignore his throbbing chest and a nagging headache that refused to shift. After finishing the document, Thomas was required to deliver it to the justice's residence on the other side of Brandwick. Because of his injury, he prevailed upon Jacob Lovelock to harness the gig and drive him to Sir Arthur's home, an elegant Palladian mansion framed by oaks and beeches.

Thankfully Thomas was not kept waiting long, but neither was he accorded much courtesy. The magistrate did not even bother to invite his guest to sit—an invitation that would have been most welcome. Instead he started to thumb through the report.

"I am sure you would like to read it at your leisure, sir," ventured Thomas, watching the scowl spread across Sir Arthur's features.

"What?" barked the magistrate. He threw the report down on the desk, sending it sliding across the polished surface. Thomas shifted uneasily as, brows dipped, Sir Arthur looked up. "I'll see them hang for this," he growled as he tented his fingers.

Thomas was confused. He had not laid the blame at anyone's door in his report. "Who, sir? Who'll hang?"

"Why, the villagers of course, Silkstone."

Thomas, feeling the room pitch about him, steadied himself on a nearby chair. "The villagers?" he repeated.

Whether he was unaware of Thomas's discomfort or simply chose to ignore it, Sir Arthur carried on, opening the small silver box on his desk. "'Tis clear they did this to exact revenge," he muttered, taking out a pinch of snuff and laying it on his hand. "Sir Montagu was the man who wanted to deprive them of their livings by closing the common lands to them."

The explanation was a wasted one. Of course Thomas was fully aware of the tension between the villagers and the Boughton Estate. He shook his head in despair as he watched the magistrate inhale the snuff, first through his right nostril, then the left.

"This does not prove who was responsible for Sir Montagu's death, sir, only the manner of it." He waved his hand at the document.

Sir Arthur sniffed loudly, mucus dislodging itself in the back of his throat. "And the manner of it!" He glanced away in disgust. "You say his head was almost sheared off by a curved blade, possibly a coppicer's tool."

Thomas had wavered before committing that possibility to paper. He feared the magistrate would seize upon it as proof of the woodlanders' complicity. In Sir Arthur's attitude toward the villagers, and indeed toward him, Thomas found him to be very like Sir Montagu. It was as if both men had been educated in the same school of superciliousness toward those they considered of inferior birth. "There are certain pieces of evidence that remain inconclusive," he protested weakly. He felt too ill to put up a real fight.

Sir Arthur arched a brow. "Such as?"

Thomas leaned forward toward the document. "The rope fibers and the footprints, sir . . . I . . ."

Yet clearly the magistrate remained unmoved by the doctor's protestations and cut him short. "'Tis well-known that your sympathies lie with the commoners, Silkstone," he sneered. "But please, do not make excuses for them." He handed back the report to Thomas with a glare. "Believe me, whoever murdered Sir Montagu Malthus will be given no quarter."

As soon as he returned to Boughton Hall, Thomas took to his bed.

"You have a fever, my love," said Lydia, seated at his bedside. Thomas knew what she said to be true. He feared his exertions had brought on an ague, and he had seen many a man die of a similar affliction after an infection of a wound. His forehead was wet with sweat, and even though his skin was searing hot, his teeth chattered with cold. He knew he would have to take charge of his own care.

"Over there," he said, pointing to his medical case. Lydia followed his hand and fetched it. Returning to the bedside, she opened the latch as he directed her to reveal several small bottles and phials all secured in rows. "Laudanum," he croaked. She poured him out a dose from the labeled phial and watched anxiously as he downed it. After a few minutes, his breathing steadied and his pain seemed to trouble him less until he lapsed into sleep just as night fell.

For the next few hours, he slept fitfully, sometimes calling out, sometimes mumbling. Lydia remained at his side until his fever broke shortly before dawn. He managed to settle into a better sleep, but less than three hours later, he awoke. At the sight of a maidservant opening the shutters, Thomas heaved his head up from the pillow.

"What goes on?" he asked, shielding his eyes from the bright morning light.

"Forgive me, my love," said Lydia, suddenly appearing at his bedside and taking his hand. She laid her other palm on his forehead and gave a satisfied nod to reassure herself. "Your fever has gone," she told him with certainty, adding, "And there is more good news." Thomas focused on her. "I have just had word that Mr. Lupton has been apprehended."

Thomas rubbed his eyes. "Has he indeed?"

"They have transported him, and that brigand Talland, to Oxford Castle." She smiled as she spoke, but her pleasure quickly turned to apprehension once more as Thomas began easing himself gently into an upright position. "What are you doing?" she asked.

"I am about to get dressed," he said, throwing her a guileless look.

"Dressed? But you need rest."

Any thoughts of spending the day in his sickbed were suddenly banished from Thomas's mind. He reached for her hands and smiled. "You know there is no rest for the wicked, my love," he told her with a wry smile. "And I have much work to do." Oxford Castle and its forbidding prison would be his next port of call.

## Chapter 10

The coach carrying Thomas thundered through the huge portico of Oxford Castle and deposited him once more into the familiar domain of the fearful and the condemned. Waiting for the footman to bring the steps, he spied the ever-eager gibbet that stood waiting to receive its steady stream of victims. He wondered if Nicholas Lupton would soon be one of them.

Presenting himself at the head keeper's lodge, Thomas was escorted to a cell on an upper floor of the debtors' tower.

"Why is the prisoner assigned here?" the doctor asked the craggy-faced jailer as he was led through a corridor with cells on either side.

"'Cos he greased the old palm," came the turnkey's reply. He held up a grubby hand, then rubbed his thumb against his fingers to signify that money had been exchanged.

Thomas had to admit to himself that he could not blame Lupton for investing in his own welfare. His mind switched to the vermin-infested dungeons that he'd been unfortunate enough to visit before. If the wretched inmates didn't end up on the scaffold, they were just as likely to suffer from jail fever. These upper cells were cramped. He could tell that by the number of arms that wormed through the door bars as he passed and the volume of the voices raised in pathetic pleas. At least, however, they were favored with a little natural light, and the stench, although gut-wrenching, was diluted by the odd draft of fresh air. Seth Talland, Thomas assumed, would be wallowing with the majority of the accused below. His would be an even worse fate, awaiting trial in the most squalid of conditions that harbored even more diseases than rats in the many nooks and crannies of the dungeon. He would be in good company. Together Talland and Lupton had formed a tight unit: Lupton the master, the brains behind the smuggling ring that had terrorized the village of Brandwick for months, and Talland the brutal enforcer. Those who had crossed them had paid with their lives. Thomas's thoughts turned to Aaron Coutt, the peg-legged stable lad whose charred body had refused to submit fully to the charcoal burner's flames. Lupton had not killed the boy himself but had surely instructed Talland to put a bullet through his brain. The bald-headed brute was a murderer, no doubt, but had he murdered Sir Montagu? Had Lupton ordered Talland to hack his erstwhile master's neck with a sickle or a machete to make it appear as though a coppicer or some other commoner were to blame? Thomas was about to put his theory to the test.

Through the rusty bars Thomas could see Nicholas Lupton sitting on a low bed. His large head had sunk right down into his shoulders, and the air of arrogance that had previously exuded from him seemed to have dissipated. Stripped of his fine frock coat and all the trimmings of the English aristocracy, his pomposity and contempt appeared to have deserted him. It was a phenomenon Thomas had witnessed before. He recalled Captain Michael Farrell had undergone a similar transformation when he languished in a cell in the selfsame prison, accused of murdering Lydia's brother. It seemed that the prospect of dangling from the end of a rope concentrated the mind seriously. And, in Thomas's own experience at least, from the tight bud of contemplation and introspection, a little humility usually emerged to see the light of day.

The door creaked open onto the small cell, with a window high up in its wall. Only a little sunlight penetrated the room, but the wing was south-facing and inside the heat was stifling. A bluebottle buzzed frenetically around an untouched platter of bread and cheese on the floor. The supply of such victuals served as a minor consolation for those prisoners rich enough to pay for it.

Lupton jerked his head toward the door at the sound of the key. When he set eyes on Thomas, however, his only reaction was swift and loud. Leaping up from the bed, he cried out with all the terror of a man convinced he had just seen a ghost.

"Good God! Silkstone!" His normally ruddy face whitened. "They told me you were dead, that I was charged with murder."

Thomas held back an ironic laugh. "And you still may be," he replied calmly, "but not mine."

"What!" Lupton's arrogance suddenly resurfaced for a moment. "What goes on?"

Thomas signaled his desire to be left alone with the prisoner, and the jailer acceded. The doctor walked over to the chair under the window. "Please," he said, pointing to Lupton's low pallet. It was a gentlemanly gesture so out of place in such surroundings.

The prisoner obeyed, even though he remained agitated. Thomas, still suffering from his wound, eased himself onto the seat, but just as he did so, his adversary rose once more in anger.

"You have come to gloat," he snapped, a fleck of spittle arcing across the floor. He turned his back on Thomas to face the door. The thin cotton shirt he was wearing was plastered to his sweat-soaked back. The fly started to circle his head, and he batted it away with his hand.

Of course Thomas had no such intention. Pity was rather the emotion elicited by the former steward of Boughton. Admittedly, there was a certain justice in seeing a man of such powerful and evil intent, a man who thought little of swindling and cheating and even killing anyone who was fool enough to stand in his way, in such dire straits. And yet, in Lupton's dealings with the young earl at least, Thomas knew the man to possess some humanity. The boy seemed to adore him, and to Thomas's mind, if a child could see good in someone, then it had to be there, albeit in small measure.

"You should know me better than that," replied the doctor.

The sentiment seemed to calm Lupton a little. He studied Thomas for a second, then returned to his bed. Seating himself, he slouched forward and started scratching and rubbing the palms of his hands, as if they had been tainted by something.

Both men sat in silence for a moment, but rather than divide them even further, the peace seemed to soften the steward.

"I am relieved you are not dead," he said finally, still playing with his hands. Thomas registered the surprise on his face. He raised a brow and nodded. But there was more. "I did not intend to kill you, you know," mumbled Lupton. Slowly he lifted his gaze to address the anatomist directly. "I had no intention of challenging you to a duel, but I'd been drinking and by the time I'd sobered up it was too late."

Thomas nodded once more, like an earnest confessor. "Your honor was at stake."

"Precisely. I had to go through with it."

"But you thought you'd killed me."

"I knew you were still alive, but I feared for how long. They told me you were gravely wounded."

"So you fled."

Lupton let out a long sigh and let his eyes drop to his hands once more. "I knew I no longer enjoyed Sir Montagu's protection. I had no other choice."

Thomas tensed. Lupton had traveled to the nub of the matter without being steered in that direction. His captors had been under strict instructions not to mention Malthus's murder in the hope that the steward could be led into a trap. Despite the obvious conclusion drawn by Sir Theodisius and Sir Arthur Warbeck, and indeed by Thomas himself, it was becoming apparent to him that Lupton knew nothing of the brutal murder.

The irritating fly settled in a corner, only to find itself entangled in a cobweb. Both men watched, fascinated, as a large spider suddenly stirred.

Thomas decided to play the devil's advocate. He took a gamble. "Is that why you killed him?"

Lupton's head jerked up. "What?"

Thomas tried to remain composed even though he felt his heart barreling in his chest. "Sir Montagu Malthus is dead."

"No." The reaction was tinged with incredulity, and the noise roused the struggling fly, which immediately buzzed off again, avoiding the spider's clutches. "How?" asked Lupton.

"I think you know how."

"What are you saying?"

"He was murdered in a most brutal and barbarous way." Thomas did not prevaricate.

Lupton leapt up. "And you think I . . . ?" He raked his fingers through his hair and paced to the cell door and back, to stand over Thomas. "No. No." He shook his head vigorously, then slumped back down on the bed.

"So that is why they refused to release me?" He gasped, as if thinking out loud. "But I did not . . . I . . ."

"Where did you spend the night after the duel?"

Lupton regarded Thomas with a frown. He was being asked for an alibi and frantically searched his memory. "In an inn. Yes. The Unicorn at Deddington. The landlord will verify it."

Thomas nodded. "Rest assured he will be asked." He cast a look into the corner and saw that the spider had retreated once more. "You were making your way back to your estate in Yorkshire, I assume."

The nobleman nodded. "I had nowhere else to go. Being a fugitive limits a man's choices, Silkstone."

"So does being a murderer," Thomas countered. His eyes hooked onto Lupton's as he thought of the stable lad at the Three Tuns who had been dispatched by Talland, his body partly burned in a charcoal kiln.

As if reading Thomas's thoughts, Lupton snapped: "I did not order Coutt's death."

Thomas was not inclined to show mercy. "Please, do not try and distance yourself from that brute. He was acting on your orders."

Lupton shook his head. "I did not order him to kill the lad."

"And you expect me to believe that?"

Lupton nodded. "I do because 'tis true." His eyes met Thomas's. "I know you are a man of integrity and I confess I am not. But when I say I had nothing to do with Sir Montagu's murder, I swear, I am telling the truth."

Thomas said nothing for a moment, allowing the tension between them to hang in the air.

"I believe you," he finally conceded, "although I cannot be certain that Talland would not kill."

Lupton nodded. "I am sure the brute is capable of it," he said, wringing his hands once more. "But I swear, he could not have murdered Sir Montagu. He was with me from the moment we left Brandwick."

Thomas resolved to question the henchman later, but for now, he felt he should draw the interview with Lupton to a close. Pushing against the arms of the chair, he rose slowly, and the pain of the movement manifested itself in his face.

"Your wound troubles you?" asked Lupton.

"Not as much as you would have liked," retorted Thomas with a wry smile. He walked toward the door to summon the jailer.

As he did so, Lupton said suddenly: "And her ladyship . . ."

Thomas switched 'round. "How is she taking all this?"

The doctor noticed his old adversary's features seemed to have softened a little at the thought of Lydia, but he spared no punches. He spoke angrily as he recalled her horror.

"It was she who discovered Sir Montagu's body. She saw the blood, the wound . . ."

Lupton tensed at the thought of it. "God, no. A terrible shock," he mumbled.

"A terrible shock indeed," conceded Thomas. He wanted Lupton to dwell on the thought for as long as possible. He wanted him to share in the nightmarish vision that had confronted Lydia and feel remorse for all the ill he had caused her. But it was not to be. The jailer's key suddenly turned in the lock.

As Thomas made his way to the door Lupton rose to his feet. "I am innocent," he protested. "You have to believe me," he implored.

"It is not up to me to decide, Lupton," the doctor replied just before the door slammed shut.

The steward's hands grasped the metal bars of the small grille in the door as he cried out once more: "I didn't kill him, I tell you. I swear I didn't."

Thomas did not respond, even though, on this rare occasion, he believed the steward to be telling the truth. Instead, the interview over, the doctor allowed himself to be escorted by the turnkey back to the main entrance, where his carriage remained. He stepped out into the relative fresh air of the courtyard just in time to see a prison conveyance trundle through the gateway. Watching the carriage disgorge its wretched cargo to four waiting jailers on the other side of the yard, Thomas counted a dozen men. Shackled together, they were being jostled through the open doors. It suddenly struck him that there was an odd familiarity about them, something in their dress and their demeanor. But it was not until the final man jumped down from the carriage that he recognized the large frame of someone he knew. It was none other than Adam Diggott, the coppicer who had spent the last few months challenging Sir Montagu's plans.

"Adam!" Thomas called involuntarily. Of course the coppicer did not hear him. He was too far away. But the head jailer nearby did. He cocked his head at the doctor and frowned.

"Those men," said Thomas. "Why are they under arrest?"

"Them lot?" The turnkey shrugged. "They're in for murder. They killed that lawyer at Brandwick."

Thomas suddenly felt the weight of responsibility press down even further on his shoulders. As he had feared, Magistrate Warbeck had clearly ignored everything he had said and used the findings of his report to justify the arrest of the villagers. Now they were shackled and doomed to hang on the gibbet within his sight. The onus was on him to prove their innocence. It was even more imperative that he examine the evidence he had gathered from the scene of the crime. But he could not do it alone. He needed to pay Professor Hascher a visit as quickly as possible.

*Chapter 11*

"Thomas, my dear fellow! Vat on earth!?" Professor Hascher's effusive greeting was tempered with such shock that it made his white hair seem to stand on end even further. The young anatomist was the last person he had expected to find on the threshold of his Oxford rooms. "You should be resting, *Willkommen*. Come in."

Thomas secretly concurred with the Saxon professor. He should indeed be resting. His light-headedness and breathlessness persisted, but he managed a smile as he flopped into a chair.

Hascher had left Boughton two days ago, fully conversant with the appalling affairs at the hall. "You are here about Sir Montagu?" he asked, pouring Thomas a schnapps into a small glass.

The young anatomist nodded. "I am here to prevail upon your kindness yet again, sir," he replied, taking the glass in a trembling hand. "I have certain items retrieved from the scene of the murder."

The professor nodded his white head while pouring himself a drink.

"But of course. Vat do you have?"

Opening his case, Thomas produced a phial containing the strange fiber from the rope that he had retrieved from Sir Montagu's wrists.

"I would examine this specimen under your microscope, if I

may, sir," he said. He put down his schnapps, untouched, and heaved himself up from the chair.

Together the two men walked over to the professor's workbench, where he kept his scientific apparatus. Hascher took a glass slide and placed the fiber upon it. Fixing his eye to the microscope, he adjusted the lens and invited Thomas to look through it.

"Zis is no ordinary hemp or vool," he ventured, as the young anatomist bent low to view the specimen.

Through the magnifying lens Thomas could see the professor was right. The cord appeared foreign to English shores. He had come across it for the first time only recently when he was tasked by Sir Joseph Banks to examine the specimens brought back from the Jamaican expedition. The fiber was extremely narrow and hollow, and the lignin on its walls yellow. It was coir.

"It is fiber from a coconut," Thomas pronounced, straightening his aching back. "Such rope is not made in England. It comes from a tropical clime."

The professor raised a brow. "And you think zat might be relevant?"

Thomas shrugged his shoulders, momentarily forgetting his injury. He winced and shook his head. "We must neither rule any possibility in nor out at this stage, Professor," he replied earnestly. "There is another piece of evidence that puzzles me, too."

"Oh?" queried Hascher. He narrowed his eyes as he watched Thomas produce a sheet of paper from his case.

"Does anything odd strike you about this footprint?" he asked, handing it to him.

The Saxon squinted at the clear dark outline of the bloody print. Raising his finger, he traced the shape of the print in the air. After a moment he declared: "A shoe wizout a heel."

Thomas nodded. "Quite so. More like a slipper," he said, returning them to his case.

The professor gasped. "You are not saying a voman . . ."

Thomas stopped him short. "No." He shook his head. "It is too big."

"Pattens, zen. I know ze English peasant to vear zem."

Thomas had already thought of the overshoes favored by many of the villagers, but had discounted them on the grounds that they were made of heavy wood that was less porous and would not have left such a clear imprint. "For the moment, I am at a loss to—" Thomas began before he was interrupted by a loud knock at the professor's door. Hascher caught his breath and cast a worried look at his young friend.

Answering the urgent summons, the professor hurried over to the door to find Jacob Lovelock standing, panting, on the threshold. His pitted face was flushed and spattered with mud. Thomas joined Hascher at the door as soon as he saw the Boughton groom.

"What is it, Jacob?" he asked.

"Oh, Dr. Silkstone, sir, my lady asks you return to the hall as soon as you can." Lovelock gulped down his breath and added: "Something terrible has happened."

*Chapter 12*

It was hard to say what compelled Lydia to pay a visit to her late husband's grave. She had told herself, and her servants, that she wished to be alone a little while. The events of the last few days had been so shocking that she needed time to herself away from the hustle and bustle of the hall. She asked Lovelock to ready the dogcart so that she might drive up to the pavilion. This was her favorite spot on the whole of the estate. The small wooden structure had been designed by the fifth earl, who was inspired by the architecture of India. Painted white and bordered on three sides by a veranda that offered superlative views, it was her refuge. In difficult times, it was where she always sought solace. She wanted to blot out the horrific events of the last three days: the duel, Thomas's injury, and, of course, Sir Montagu's murder. The sight of the blood, the smell of it, the stickiness of it on her fingers still lingered. She needed to be rid of it, to slough it off, and simply by being in this beautiful place she hoped she would feel cleansed.

The sky was streaked with white mares' tails, a sign that the weather was set fair as she started off up the stiff hill. On either side of the track, the blades of grass that had been so browned and broken by the Great Fogg last year had grown back even stronger and were now verdant and flourishing. The leaves on the trees, too, had been coaxed out by the sunshine of the past few days, clothing the wood in a green haze. Up ahead the red kites wheeled and dived on the warm thermal currents that formed below the ridge, and a skylark in full song hovered over a nearby cornfield.

The track was dry and dusty, although the rainstorm earlier in the month had scoured deep ruts that she was careful to avoid. Two of the house dogs, the spaniels Jipp and Juno, set off with her, bounding up ahead of the cart, then stopping suddenly when they caught a scent and running off at a tangent. The pony was a hardy little beast and responded well to her commands, and soon they reached the top of the ridge. Tugging at the reins, Lydia paused for a moment to take in the view. There had been times during her incarceration in Bedlam when she thought she would never see such a sight again. At one point, shackled to her narrow bed, she had been forced to content herself with the memory of the hall. Thoughts of its honey-colored stone, its fine pediments and its barley-twist chimneys, had kept her sane in her darkest hours. And Richard, too. Her dearest Richard. How his short life had been blighted by the wiles of men. Sir Montagu's aim might have been to control Boughton through her son, but surely he had cared for him, his own flesh and blood, in his own strange way.

Down below she saw the men and women planting in the fields, scattering corn from their panniers onto the furrows of the rich brown soil. She saw, too, the sheep grazing on the higher pasture, their wool providing a staple of the estate. It was a scene that gladdened her heart, a scene she had no wish to change. Any plans to enclose Boughton had died with Sir Montagu, and the commoners and coppicers, the pit sawyers and the charcoal burners, could rejoice in the knowledge that she would not deprive them of their ancient rights. The villagers of Brandwick would remain free to glean for corn at harvest time and to put out pigs to pannage in the forest in autumn. The coppicers could carry on working their coupes, and the power of water, not steam, would turn the fulling stocks that pounded the wool cloth.

The sight of the estate from her perch comforted her, but her memory was also tinged with sadness. Up ahead on the ridge, just beyond the pavilion, she could make out the simple wooden cross that marked her late husband's grave. The dogs had run on ahead in that direction, no doubt chasing after a rabbit or hare, so she decided to follow. She could pay her respects, perhaps even pick a few spring flowers and lay them at the foot of the cross. The Church's strict laws regarding those who took their own lives meant that Michael had been denied his rightful place in the family vault. She had chosen his resting place herself, near the pavilion where they both used to ride in the early days of their short marriage when they were briefly happy together.

After his death she had intended to erect a more permanent memorial to the captain on the site. At the time she had taken care to bury him in his best clothes and to see that his precious diamond ring, the one that he had brought back from India, was placed on the fourth finger of his right hand. He had worn it thus in life, before she had told him it was vulgar and that he should remove it, and he had in her presence. Yet there was another reason she did not approve of the magnificent gemstone. It had, it seemed, a checkered history. She had heard rumors, although she had never shared them with her husband, that he had stolen it from a dead merchant in Hyderabad. Such accusations would only have widened the rift that grew daily between them. At the memory of it, however, she felt a tinge of regret. Perhaps she had been too harsh on Michael. At any rate, events had conspired against her so that she had never even managed to commission a fitting headstone. Now, however, there was nothing to stop her. She could design an elaborate mausoleum or even a mortsafe to protect him from sack-'em-up men, if she chose to. Not that there had ever been any likelihood of anyone trying to steal the captain's corpse in such a remote spot. But it was up to her to erect a fitting memorial.

As the pony walked steadily along the ridge, past the pavilion, she noted how dilapidated the building looked. The roof was covered in moss, and ivy was creeping up the columns of the veranda. She made a mental note to ask her new steward, whoever he might be, to make its renovation a priority. She could not allow it to fall further into disrepair.

She was contemplating the expense of such an endeavor

when the pony came to a sudden and unbidden halt. It shuffled backward and snorted through its flared nostrils. Lydia frowned and gave it a tap with the whip, but to no avail. She tried a different tack and pulled gently on the reins to soothe the creature, but again it was no use.

"Steady, girl!" she called. "Steady!" Hearing its mistress's voice, the pony seemed to calm down, yet despite Lydia's best efforts, it could not be coaxed on. "What is it?"

The dogs, a few yards away by the grave, also began to bark. Knowing it was useless to urge on the pony, Lydia lifted her skirts and, still clutching her whip, clambered down from her perch. Frowning, she hurried toward the wooden cross.

"What the . . . !"

Instead of the smooth green burial mound where she had stood in silent prayer on her last visit, there was a mound of earth, freshly dug. She surveyed the scene incredulously. An animal must have been pawing at the grave, she told herself. A badger or a fox. But surely there was too much dark mulch to have been shifted by a single wild creature. She drew closer, the nausea suddenly rising in her throat.

The dogs were no longer barking. Instead they were growling at each other. They were fighting over something, baring their teeth, snatching at whatever it was: a bone perhaps.

"Jipp! Juno!" she called, but they ignored her voice. She walked toward them, her heart beating faster with each step. "Jipp! Juno! Away!" she repeated, only louder, but the dogs continued to tug at something, slavering and baying in turn. She felt her body start to tremble as she drew level with them. She cracked the whip. The dogs parted. And then she saw it. Beyond the pile of earth, a few fragments of material lay ragged on the grass, and beside them was a small carcass of some sort: a bird or a rabbit.

Still wary, she moved forward until she could see more clearly. A bird or a rabbit, she kept telling herself. Then her stomach lurched and her eyes widened in sheer terror.

"No!" she said. Her voice was soft at first. Her eyes had to be playing tricks on her. She looked closer. "No!" she repeated, this time in a scream. She tried to blink away the sight, but the horror of it only drew her even further toward it, as if she had fallen under some ghoulish spell. Her mouth opened, allowing another faint cry to escape her lips, but she remained transfixed by what she saw. It was part of an arm. A human arm. Surely not Michael's? Her eyes shot to the material, the ragged silk that lay nearby. She recognized it. It was a fragment of the shirt in which she had laid him to rest. She looked back to the arm. The skin on it was the color of lead, prinked with purple, and great hunks of it clung to the white of the bone like filthy rags. It suddenly dawned on her that the grave must have been opened. No animal could have done this, she told herself. Her breathing came in short, sharp pants as she realized this had to be the work of some depraved resurrectionist. The fiend must have been looking for a corpse to sell to an anatomist, but his despicable errand had been interrupted. Her own hand suddenly flew up to her forehead, and she felt it dotted with sweat. She gazed upon the sight in a morbid daze, bewildered and outraged at the same time. It was then, through her shock and revulsion, that it struck her that an even greater sacrilege had been committed. She forced herself to look again at Michael's arm—his right arm—and, more specifically, at his hand. His once-elegant fingers stuck up in the air like rotten twigs. But there were only three. One was missing; the one that had borne the captain's ring. The diamond was gone.

*Chapter 13*

It was early evening by the time Thomas reached Boughton Hall. He found Lydia pacing the drawing room in a most distressed state. Eliza was with her, but seemed unable to calm her mistress. Before the return journey Lovelock had primed the doctor about the horrific findings at Michael Farrell's grave.

"One of the shepherds 'eard 'er scream," the groom had said. "In a terrible state, she were."

As soon as he entered the room, Thomas saw that Lydia's face remained ashen gray. She hurried to him, still trembling. "Who would do such a thing? Who would do such a thing?" she kept asking, over and over again.

"Calm yourself," soothed Thomas, taking her by the hand. Dismissing Eliza with a nod of the head, he led Lydia to the sofa and together they sat. "I know what happened," he said. He put his arm around her shoulders. "And I must go and see the grave for myself before I can try and answer your question."

She acknowledged the sense of this, but he could tell she was still in a state of shock. He reached for his medical case and took from it a glass phial.

"Drink this," he told her, handing her a draft.

Closing her eyes, she downed the dark syrup and shuddered a little at its bitter taste.

" 'Twill calm your nerves until I return," he told her, but she immediately opened her eyes and tugged at his coat.

"No. No, you can't go. Please don't leave me."

"I will not be long," he promised, "but I need to see the site for myself." He touched her shoulder gently. "Lovelock is waiting to take me to the grave." He paused. "You will not be alone," he added. "Eliza will stay with you."

Lydia gulped a lungful of air and nodded her acquiescence. "Of course," she agreed, placing her hand on his.

Lovelock was indeed waiting at the reins of the dogcart, with Will, his son, in tow. The sun was low over the Chiltern Hills, leaving a pinkish glow in the sky as they headed up toward the desecrated grave. The crows, gathering like black rags blown by the breeze, were already roosting high up in the trees of the nearby woods, and although no one said anything, they all knew that any remaining carrion might be picked clean by now.

Without delay Thomas dismounted from the cart. He did not relish the thought of what he was about to see. He had been informed of the grisly remains and the disturbed grave. Whoever had opened it to steal the diamond might well have left behind some vital evidence. Moreover, whoever was responsible might also have murdered Sir Montagu. A careful examination of the area could well throw up meaningful clues.

"Stay back," Thomas ordered Lovelock and his son, even though the pair seemed in no hurry to move nearer the grave. It did not take long to find the severed arm. As he feared, much of the flesh had been picked off the bone and only a few flies buzzed around it, but Lydia had been correct. Just three fingers and a thumb were left. Moving up the heft, only the ulna remained. But it was the cut that interested Thomas most. He examined it carefully. The bone had been hacked through cleanly, possibly with an ax.

Next he turned to the grave itself. The earth was patted into a mound. Bending down, Thomas felt the top. It was dry to the touch. He lifted a handful of dirt, and it crumbled through his fingers like stale cake. It was obvious to him that this topsoil had been baking in the sun for a while. He cast his mind back to the terrible storm two weeks before that had drenched the earth. There had been no rain since, although he noted there were ruts and gullies in the soil where it had been exposed to the torrential downpour. He hazarded a guess that the mound had been dug before the storm. Taking out his magnifying glass from his coat pocket, he scrutinized the brown loam more closely. He could see shoots of grass already. The ones that had been in full sun during the day had already germinated. From their growth he estimated they had burst forth from their seeds at least a week ago, but probably much earlier. He paused. This meant that the act of desecration was certainly not committed on the same night as Sir Montagu's murder but well before it. Possibly several days prior.

It was three years since Thomas's last visit to the grave, three years since he had opened Michael Farrell's coffin. The captain had been newly dead, the flesh putrefying and wet, the stench gut-wrenching, but at least Thomas had been able to confirm his suspicions. Lydia's husband did not take his own life and, from the nature of the wound on his neck, he had been able to identify his killer. He did not relish the thought of reacquainting himself with the corpse. Nor, judging by their reluctance to stay near him, did Jacob Lovelock and his son. The head groom's memories were still raw, too, but at Thomas's request, father and son shuffled forward. The doctor had no intention of putting them through an unnecessary exhumation. He would not make them witness the work of the worms in the last three years. They would have feasted on the skin and soft tissue, leaving only the white pearl of bone in their wake, he told himself. He was as reluctant as they were, but he knew what needed to be done.

Armed with shovels, Jacob and Will started to dig away at the loose mound. After a few minutes their spades hit what sounded like wood. Renewing their efforts, they uncovered the whole of the lid. Mercifully it was still in place, although no longer secured, making the men's task much easier.

Squatting low on their haunches, with Jacob at the top and Will at the bottom, they grabbed the lid and, instinctively holding their breaths, pulled it upward and toward them. They both fell backward, away from the grave, Thomas suspected by design, so that they did not have to confront the body in the coffin. He, however, had no choice. He peered down into the grave.

And there lay what remained of Captain Michael Farrell. For yet a second time his interment had been disturbed.

Thomas and Lovelock exchanged anxious looks, but it was the former who took off his hat and coat and made to descend.

"You can't go down there in your state, Doctor," protested the groom.

"I can and I must," replied Thomas. "Here." He handed his belongings to Lovelock and, kneeling down, lowered himself into the grave. His chest wound still caused him pain, but without too much grief he arrived at a point where there was just enough room for him to stand. There was Farrell's familiar white brocade jacket—the one he had asked to wear for his sentencing in court. The robber had slipped it off the corpse's shoulder to get a better purchase at the arm. Reaching into his pocket for his magnifying glass once more, Thomas inspected what remained of the mutilated limb. The thief had been in such a hurry that he had simply hacked it off above the elbow with a sharp blade. Thomas's previous thoughts were confirmed. The motion had been downward. The pattern on the bone indicated a chop, not a slice. A sickle rather than a knife. Could this mean that the weapon used to mutilate Farrell's corpse had been employed to murder Malthus, too? He could not be sure. What was undeniable, however, was that whoever did this unspeakable deed knew exactly what he wanted. This was no opportunistic theft but a carefully planned and executed crime. It would have been no mean feat. It was robbery to order, undertaken by someone skilled who knew precisely what he was about. Someone who knew that Michael Farrell was buried wearing a diamond ring.

Thomas was just about to call for Jacob to help him scale the steep wall of the grave when he stopped. His memory flashed to an image of Farrell's hand and the diamond ring that Lydia had placed on it in death. He recalled her telling him that the gem had been acquired during her husband's time in India.

India. He whispered the word.

"Sir?"

Thomas wheeled 'round, aware that Lovelock and his son

had been watching him in the grave trench from a distance. The groom's voice jolted the doctor back into the moment.

"What? Nothing, Lovelock." Thomas stretched out both arms, and gently the groom and his son helped ease him out.

"You think they knew the diamond was there, sir?" asked Jacob Lovelock as the doctor sat on the soil on the other side of the grave.

"I have no doubt," he replied, sifting the loose earth between his fingers. He stopped suddenly.

"What is it, Doctor?" asked Will, watching Thomas's eyes casting around him.

"Footprints," he replied. His gaze settled on a single indentation left at the edge of the mound.

"What have we here?" he asked suddenly. Thomas moved closer on all fours. "Did either of you make this?"

Father and son both shook their heads in unison, so Thomas took the tape from his pocket to measure it. Would it match the print in the study? To his surprise he found it was much longer than the other, bloody print. It was a different shape, too. Made by a sturdy boot, he'd wager. The grave robber and Sir Montagu's murderer might not, after all, be one and the same person. Rocking back on his haunches, Thomas looked toward the grave.

"You can secure the lid," he told Lovelock, clapping his hands to rid them of extraneous soil.

"Aye, sir," replied the groom.

Man and boy set to work while Thomas investigated a little farther afield. It occurred to him that whoever had prized open the coffin would have used heavy tools that might well have impeded a getaway. He decided to venture into the nearby woods, hunting for a discarded pickax or shovel, perhaps. Keeping his eyes on the beech mast of the woodland floor, he had gone only a few yards when his acuity was rewarded. He had homed in on what he thought, at first, was a piece of broken-off bark. But no. He bent down to pick up something brown the size of a man's hand. It was a fragment of leather, the tongue of a boot perhaps. His mind flashed to the poachers who plied their trade at night in Raven's Wood. Mayhap they hunted here, too, on occasion. He picked up the fragment, turned it in his palm, then sniffed it. It was leather all right and as stiff as if it had been starched. It had been left out in the rain, but there had been no rain for several days, not since the terrible storm. The leather tongue might have nothing to do with Sir Montagu's murderer. It could have lain there for many days, if not weeks. He thought better than to discard it. He could not rule out the possibility that whoever robbed the grave had some connection to the dead lawyer. Perhaps it was something. Perhaps not. He slipped it into his pocket. Nothing could be discounted, nothing ruled out, but at the moment, in his hunt for the killer, Thomas was forced to admit to himself that he was grasping at straws in the wind. And now a most burning question had surfaced: Who knew that Michael Farrell was buried wearing the precious stone?

Thomas's thoughts were suddenly interrupted by a shout that went up from the direction of the grave. He looked up from the shadows of the wood to see young Will running toward him and waving frantically.

"Dr. Silkstone, sir! Come quick."

Breaking into a run, Thomas arrived at the open grave in seconds to see Jacob Lovelock clambering out, holding an object.

"Whoever robbed the grave left this behind," said the groom. He handed Thomas a flat wooden shovel, the sort used by grave diggers—and grave robbers, too. It was encrusted with dirt, but as he rubbed off the soil that clung to the shaft, the anatomist's eyes snagged on its handle. Taking out his magnifying glass once more, Thomas made out two roughly carved nicks on the wood. He looked up to see a stunned expression cleave to Jacob Lovelock's face.

"*It can't be,*" muttered the groom.

"Them's Jo Makepeace's marks!" cried Will instantly.

"No," said his father in disbelief. "Old Jo could never—" He broke off suddenly, recalling how he and his son had helped the bury man dig many a grave last year in St. Swithin's churchyard during the Great Fogg.

"Joseph Makepeace?" asked Thomas. "You think . . . ?"

" 'Tis nothing," snapped the groom.

Thomas persisted. "You must tell me what you know, Jacob."

The groom chewed his lip. "The last time I see'd 'im was at the Three Tuns, the night you was shot."

"The night of Sir Montagu's murder?"

"Yes. I was waiting in the hall for her ladyship to come down, and the men was making a real racket, drinking and laughing, they was."

Thomas thought of the smoky taproom. It was often quite a lively place, so for Jacob to remark upon it, the atmosphere must have been raucous indeed. "Was there a particular reason?"

The groom nodded. "The drinks were on Joseph Makepeace," he said.

"Were they indeed?" Thomas mused. He thought of the down-at-heel bury man.

"He said he'd been paid handsome for a job."

Thomas could not hide his surprise. "What sort of job?"

"He didn't say. Only that he'd been told to lie low for a few days. With Lupton gone, he must've thought it safe."

"And he were showing off a new pair of boots," chimed in Will.

"New boots," repeated Thomas. He looked down at the fragment of stiff leather he still held in his hand. Joseph Makepeace was one of the villagers locked up in Oxford Jail. Perhaps Sir Arthur had arrested the right man after all.

*Chapter 14*

As his carriage jounced along the streets of Mayfair, Captain Patrick Flynn reflected on what he saw. It was the color he missed most. He had returned to England only the previous month and was still acclimatizing himself after his many years in India. He found the cooler weather suited him better, although the gray skies, even on relatively temperate days, did nothing to lift his mood. The people, the common-or-garden Englishmen and -women, seemed to him less deferential than when he departed, too. Not only were they insolent now, they were drab, too. Brindle browns, dull taupe, and funereal blacks were the staple shades of their garb. How different from the rainbow hues of Madras and Calcutta, he mused—the peacock blues, the emerald greens, the fuchsia pinks, the saffron yellow and brilliant crimson. He missed the smells, too, the pungent wafts of coriander, turmeric, and silky cinnamon that hid a multitude of malodorous sins. Rather than the fabled gold of Dick Whittington's day, the streets of London now seemed to be paved with rotting cabbage and horse dung. They no longer held any allure for him.

Presently the carriage delivered the captain and Manjeet to a jeweler's shop in fashionable New Bond Street. There were more dandies here, and perhaps a little more color to break up the drabness, but Flynn still found it a relatively dull affair. A liveried footman helped him down and ushered him inside the shop. *I can still carry it off,* he thought to himself. The captain retained the bearing of an officer and a gentleman even though he wore no wig. Instead his flame-red hair was tied back with a black ribbon, and he sported an expression of superiority so often espoused by those with the least claim to it. He had abandoned his fustian coat in favor of a deep blue frock coat trimmed with gold braid. Manjeet, too, was decked out in his finest silk sherwani and white turban with a plume at the front.

"Doth thir have an appointment?" asked the young man behind the counter. He spoke with a pronounced lisp. His head was tilted in a slightly patronizing manner that put Flynn on his mettle straightaway.

"No. I am here for a valuation."

"May I ask thir the nature of the item?"

"A most precious diamond," replied Flynn, producing the gem from the bag.

The young man's eyes lit up at the sight of it. "Thir hath indeed come to the right plathe."

The captain did not need to be told that he was in the right "plathe." He had done his homework. He knew that the owner of this shop, one William Gray, was jeweler to Prince George. There were rumors that this was a less than satisfactory arrangement on the craftsman's part because the prince never paid his bills on time. Yet as Flynn glanced around him, he could see the royal patronage obviously brought in custom. The shop was an elegant space, lined with display cabinets that held not only trays of rings and bracelets, necklaces and tiaras, but elaborate swords, too.

"I will thee if Mr. Gray ith free," said the young man, taking the diamond with him. He disappeared through a door that lay behind a red curtain. He reappeared a moment later. "Thith way pleathe, thir," he said to Flynn. Manjeet was signaled to wait for his master.

William Gray sat hunched over the diamond like a hungry hyena over its prey. With his mouth open wide to accommodate a thick loupe that was jammed into his eye socket, the jeweler, Flynn thought, looked almost comical. The stone itself was held in the grasp of a pair of pincers. It sparkled under the glare of a lamp, a thousand stars twinkling on its brilliant surface. He did not acknowledge his visitor at first.

As he watched the jeweler at work, Flynn held his breath. He held his breath, and he listened to his own heart beating, beating faster than he had ever heard it in his life, even though he was standing quite still. That was because his future depended on what this old man had to say any moment now. This was his first foray into the hub of the capital. A month had passed since his return to England. It was a month in which he had learned what it felt like to be betrayed. First Farrell, then Lavington had thought he could do as he wished with the gem behind Flynn's back. They had humiliated him. They had made a mockery of him. It reminded him of a punishment he had seen inflicted on an Indian father who failed to pay his daughter's dowry. He was stripped and publicly flogged. Although he had suffered no physical wounds, the mental ones were just as real. But now Flynn had won the day. He was having the last laugh. He had the diamond. He'd heard nothing, so he assumed his crime had not been uncovered. Not yet. His secret was still safe. So he had seen fit to act.

"Well?" he asked. He could wait no longer. The old jeweler finally eased himself back into his chair.

"It is indeed a fine stone, sir," he mumbled, still not lifting his gaze.

"Fine?" asked Flynn indignantly. "It is surely the finest you have ever set eyes on!"

The loupe popped from the jeweler's eye socket. He turned to face the captain, but from the old man's glum expression, Flynn gleaned he was not about to hear good news.

"Not the finest, I fear," Gray replied. He wiped his forehead with the back of his hand.

Flynn stiffened, then let out a little laugh. "There must be some mistake." His nostrils flared resentfully. "That ring was cut from one of the largest stones ever found in Golconda."

The jeweler nodded his head. "I am sure it was, sir," he replied. "But it was cut in India, yes?"

Flynn's face fell. Yes, it had been cut in India. The smaller stones had been sold off and the proceeds shared among the three of them, Farrell, Lavington, and himself, but the brilliant remained. It had been mounted on a gold ring to be kept in Farrell's possession.

"What of it? Surely it makes no difference where the stone is cut."

The jeweler screwed up his eyes. "I fear so, sir. The method of cutting is very different there. The Indians are unable to give the stones such a lively polish as we give them in Europe."

"What?" The captain's color was rising.

The jeweler pointed to the large steel wheel on his workbench. "Their wheels do not run as smoothly as ours." He pulled his lamp toward him and shone it on the stone, then unlocked a small drawer nearby and brought out another, smaller diamond, which flickered and dazzled under the light. "You see there," he said, a diamond in each hand. "Yours is dull compared with this one."

"What!" The molten anger that had been simmering inside Flynn suddenly exploded. "This is preposterous. You will never find a finer diamond. Never!" He slammed his fist on the workbench, then took two paces to the door and banged on that, too.

"Sir, calm yourself, please!" urged the old man. "I would tell the king of England the same if he came to me with such a stone."

The workshop door suddenly opened and the younger man reappeared. He saw the captain, then switched his gaze to the jeweler. "Ith everything in order, Father?" he asked.

The old man slid a look at Flynn, then back to his son. "Quite," he said.

The young man nodded. "If you're thure, thir," he replied with an uneasy bow. He cast a wary look at the captain, then closed the door behind him.

The interruption seemed to have soothed Flynn's ire a little. He tugged quite deliberately at the cuffs of both his coat sleeves, as if to signify he wanted a fresh start. He kept his voice flat. "How much will you give me for it?" he asked.

The jeweler turned the stone in his palm. "A thousand guineas."

A look of disdain settled on Flynn's features. "A thousand guineas," he repeated.

The old man's tone was apologetic. "It needs much work and even then . . ."

"You insult me, sir. I shall take the gem elsewhere."

Flynn snatched the stone away and, flinging the workroom door open wide, strode into the front of the shop. Manjeet was waiting for him, his hands clasped behind his back.

"Come!" barked the captain. "We have no further business here."

Outside the shop, the footman hailed the captain and his servant a carriage. Inside, Flynn's simmering rage erupted once more at this second betrayal. Questions collided into one another as they roiled around his brain, then spilled out as expletives aimed at a silent Manjeet.

"Curse the bastards! If they were here, I'd . . . Damn them. I hope they are both rotting in hell!"

Had Farrell and Lavington known that the diamond was not the priceless stone they'd led him to believe? he wondered. If so, why had he not been told? His plans now lay in ruins. Somehow he had to work out how to pay off his mounting debts and salvage a reputation that was even more tarnished than his lackluster diamond.

# Chapter 15

"James Lavington." The name that cleaved to the roof of Lydia's mouth suddenly broke loose. She had been gazing into the empty fireplace in the drawing room at Boughton, but now her eyes latched back onto Thomas's as she managed to say it. "Somehow he knew."

"Lavington?" repeated the doctor. His mouth suddenly turned dry.

James Lavington was a name he had never wanted to hear again, let alone say. It resurrected memories of a dark episode in the past. The lawyer had served with Farrell in the East India Company and purported to have been his best friend. He had been hideously disfigured in an explosion near Golconda and lived in a house on the Boughton Estate. Bearing a simmering resentment, it seemed, he always blamed Farrell for his injuries and had murdered him in jail. His plan was to slip into the dead man's bed with a hasty marriage proposal to Lydia. Forced by monetary circumstances to acquiesce, Lydia had married the monster, only for him to be murdered on the very same day. His remains had been buried away from the estate and with them, Thomas had hoped, his memory.

Lydia looked down, as if suddenly ashamed. "After you returned to London, he told me Michael had died owing him vast amounts of money"—she switched back—"and that if I did not consent to marrying him, he would sell the house."

Thomas tried to console her. She had told him before of her trials at Lavington's hands. "You were under a terrible strain," he assured her, holding her close.

"Yes." She nodded. "I had no choice but to agree. He would have thrown Mamma and me out." Thomas thought of the swarthy lawyer with his prosthetic nose that had been made for him in India from ivory. He now understood him to be ruthless enough to make Lydia and her aged mother destitute.

"I know," he told her gently, but he guessed there was more to come.

Suddenly she pulled away and sat upright. "But I remember one day he made a curious remark," said Lydia.

Thomas sensed she had been holding something back. "What did he say?"

She looked wistful, as if in thought. "He said how foolish I had been to bury the diamond with Michael."

Thomas frowned. "But if you did not tell him about the diamond, then how . . . ?"

Lydia broke in. Her gaze hovered over the hearth and settled on a portrait of her late mother that hung on the wall near the fireplace. "That was the strange thing. I only told Mamma, and I know she would never have—"

"Of course not," snapped Thomas. He was keen to steer clear of any mention of Lydia's mother for fear she might uncover the secret that he had guarded so closely for the past four years. Yet he could tell by her look she was still holding back. "And?" he pressed.

"Lavington said, 'If the sack-'em-up men get wind it's there, they'll be buzzing 'round the grave like flies.' " Lydia's eyes widened, as if the recollection, retrieved from so far back in her memory, had surprised even herself.

Thomas took a deep breath before voicing a thought he had been formulating ever since the discovery of the theft. "I am thinking Sir Montagu's murder has nothing to do with his plans to enclose Boughton, nor indeed with Nicholas Lupton."

"You think this has something to do with Michael?"

"I do," he replied with a nod. "With his time in India."

She narrowed her eyes. "Because of the diamond?"

He did not tell her about the odd fibers or the strange foot-prints he had found at the scene of the crime. Or the fact that Sir Montagu's head had been all but severed with a curved blade that he was beginning to think might not have been a sickle after all. There was also the matter of what the murderer was searching for in the study.

"Yes," he replied, fixing her with a frown.

Lydia reached for his hand and regarded him with a look of resignation. "Then I am to lose you again?"

Thomas returned her sad gaze. "Whoever stole the diamond will be looking for a buyer," he told her, covering her hand fondly with his. "I shall leave for London tomorrow."

"Tomorrow," she echoed.

"I fear so," he replied, and he drew her toward him and kissed her on the forehead.

"There is always something that keeps us apart," she whispered forlornly, lifting her face to his.

"Not for much longer," he told her. He found her lips and kissed them; then, pulling back, he wiped away a lone tear from her cheek with his thumb. "I swear that as soon as I have found Sir Montagu's killer, nothing will keep us apart again," he said. "Nothing."

Jacob Lovelock and his son, Will, readied Thomas's horse at first light, as planned. For the past two weeks the weather had been fair, and the roads, so rutted and muddy from the terrible storm earlier in the month, had recovered well.

"You should have a good journey, sir," ventured Will. He cupped his hands to help Thomas mount.

The doctor's chest wound, although healing well, still troubled him, so it was with the greatest care that he heaved himself up and flung his leg over the saddle. Despite the early hour, the sky had lightened to a pale blue and the June sun was already warming the land. As the groom adjusted his stirrups, Thomas squinted toward the drive that led down to the village. He had to agree.

"Let us hope so, Will," he replied with a smile, but the second he said it, his expression changed. "Although I fear my journey may be delayed."

Lovelock rubbed his forehead and straightened to see the doctor was no longer smiling. "Delayed, sir?" He saw a frown had settled on Thomas's brow, and he followed his gaze. A horseman was approaching fast and a moment later was clattering into the stableyard. "Who goes there?" shouted Lovelock.

A squat young man in a battered hat pulled up his horse. "A message for a Dr. Silkstone!" he called down, breathless from riding hard.

Thomas urged his mount toward the disheveled courier. "I am Dr. Silkstone."

Remaining in the saddle, the messenger took off his hat with a sweeping gesture; then, reaching into his leather satchel, he handed Thomas a letter. The doctor recognized the script immediately. It was Sir Theodisius's hand. The previous afternoon Thomas had sent word about the terrible violation of Captain Farrell's grave and the theft of the diamond. This, he anticipated, would be the coroner's response. With his pocketknife he broke the seal and read the message. Yet it was not the communication he had anticipated. After a moment Thomas looked up.

"It seems Lupton and his man have been released from prison. They both have solid alibis," he told Lovelock.

The groom nodded, and then frowned. "But what of the commoners, Doctor? Of Adam Diggott and Abel Smith?" he asked.

Thomas gave a resigned shrug. "They remain in jail, I fear." Lovelock's shoulders slumped at the news.

It did not come as a surprise to Thomas to learn that the former steward had been telling the truth. What was more, the barbarity of Sir Montagu's murder was surely beyond even Talland's capacity and Lupton had vouched for his innocence. Yet the intelligence gave the doctor no further assistance in tracking down Sir Montagu's murderer. Until he did so, the commoners, of whose innocence he was convinced, still faced the prospect of rotting in Oxford Jail, or worse.

The messenger's horse began stomping on the cobbles and snorting through its nostrils. "A reply, sir?" asked the young man.

Thomas looked across at him, his own horse champing at the bit.

"There will be a reply," he told him. "But in person. I shall go directly to Oxford to see the coroner myself."

*Chapter 16*

Great Tom, the Christ Church bell, was tolling ten as Thomas rode into Oxford. Originally he had planned to call on Sir Theodisius, but as the sturdy keep of the castle loomed over him, he thought of the Brandwick men entombed in its prison dungeons below. He needed to offer them a crumb of comfort and, quite possibly, dress any wounds they might have sustained during or since their arrest. Po-faced Joseph Makepeace and Abe Diggott were not young men and were the most vulnerable. And even though Adam Diggott and Will Ketch were strong enough, youth was no guarantee of survival in a place where death stalked every nook and cranny.

On presentation of a letter of authority from Sir Theodisius—the coroner had helpfully enclosed it with his original message—the guard allowed Thomas to ride through the gates and into the great festering wound that was the prison. The stink was all too familiar: the dirt, the tang of urine that stung the eyes, the coppery smell of blood.

The doctor had followed a cart inside, and he watched as it disgorged its delivery of new prisoners, two men and two women. From a row of grilles at ground level, hands were suddenly thrust out, some holding bowls, begging for food or money or both. At the pathetic sight one of the women took fright. As she was shoved toward the entrance, she let out a shout. "I didn't do it, I tell ye!" But her protestation was quickly silenced by a turnkey who coshed her about the head. She dropped to the flagstones and had to be dragged inside.

In the courtyard several debtors, allowed to roam during the day, took advantage of the sun. They leaned against the walls or squatted on the cobbles that they shared with the rats. A ragged boy scampered along the line of men, seemingly running errands for them. There were three or four women, too, carrying panniers of bread or laundry on their hips.

Thomas dismounted and handed his horse to a hostler. As he did so, some activity in the far corner of the courtyard vied for his attention. A huddle of men was being shepherded out from the lodge into the sunlight by two jailers. They reminded him of dazed fledglings that had fallen from their nest. It seemed they had just been discharged. One man in particular caught Thomas's eye. He was especially tall and rubbed his eyes as he blinked away the darkness of the jail. He recognized him almost immediately as Adam Diggott.

Thomas covered the few yards between them quickly and drew closer to see the familiar faces of the villagers who had been so maligned. They had only been detained for three days and yet they already appeared to be changed men; their faces were drawn and their skin was like ash. He had expected them to be chained, but looking at their wrists and ankles, he saw no restraints.

"Are these men free?" he asked one of the jailers.

Before the man could scowl back his reply, however, Adam Diggott piped up: "Dr. Silkstone!" In his excitement he rushed up and grabbed hold of the doctor's jacket. "We knew it had to be you!"

Thomas backed away a little, gagging on the coppicer's stink. Bewildered, he shook his head. "They are setting you free?"

"Aye, Doctor. Free to get out of this hellhole," replied Diggott, baring his few remaining teeth at his erstwhile jailers. One of them raised his cosh, but the other stayed his hand, knowing that very soon they would no longer have any authority over the men. Sneering at their impotence, Diggott turned to Thomas once more. "And 'tis surely thanks to you." He held out a grateful hand.

Thomas shook it, but remained perplexed. "Me? But I do not understand. I fear I've had nothing to do with your release."

Diggott let his hand drop and cast around at the other men who were gathered about him, searching their eager faces for answers. When none were forthcoming he turned back to Thomas. "But we was told that Captain Farrell's grave had been robbed on the night of Sir Montagu's murder." His tone was most insistent.

Again Thomas shook his head. "There is no proof of that," he protested, thinking of the sprouting grass on the soil heap. Even if the murder and the robbery had a direct connection, he was still at a loss to understand its bearing on the men's freedom.

Adam Diggott moved closer, his eyes growing wilder by the second.

"But that's when old Joseph came clean!"

"Joseph Makepeace?" Thomas thought of the grave digger, whose shovel they had found to incriminate him in the robbery. He had not noticed his absence before. He was not among the motley gaggle of commoners. "What has become of him?"

Diggott coughed out a sarcastic laugh. "He only owned up to robbing the captain's grave."

"Did he indeed?" Thomas feigned surprise, even though he was still at a loss as to why the bury man would do such a thing. Diggott soon provided his motive.

"Put up to it by an old friend of Farrell's, he was. Claimed the diamond was rightfully his."

Thomas saw that his theory might be confirmed. "Who?" he pressed. "Who claimed the diamond?"

"Said he had an agreement with the cap'n." Diggott turned back toward the others, seeking support. Several ayes rose into the tainted air.

Thomas rolled his eyes in despair. "No, no," he muttered to himself and took a few paces away from the man, as if the distance might help him think. He snatched off his hat and raked his fingers through his hair. He was angry that his words had been misinterpreted. Somehow his message to Sir Theodisius about the robbing of the grave had leaked out. Someone had put two and two together and made five, deducing that whoever stole the diamond murdered Sir Montagu. Yet Thomas could show that these acts were executed at different times and might not be connected at all.

Plumping his tricorn back down on his head, he marched back to the huddle of men. "I can prove that the diamond was stolen days before the murder," he told Diggott.

The coppicer shrugged. "That don't matter to us no more, Doctor," he said with a half smile.

Thomas frowned. "Why not?"

"Because old Jo says a gent paid 'im to steal the stone!"

Thomas's eyes widened. A man could swing for robbing a grave, and Old Jo certainly risked the noose, unless, perhaps, he could name the commissioner of this foul crime.

"And where is Makepeace now? I must speak with him." There was an urgency in the doctor's voice that wiped Diggott's smile from his face.

The coppicer shoved his thumb behind him toward the grilles of the stinking dungeon he had just escaped. "He's still to go to court, Doctor. We've left him in there."

"Then I must go," said Thomas, fixing his gaze on the door of the keeper's office next to the lodge. He switched back to Diggott. "I am glad you are free," he said; then, lifting his face to the other men, he added: "I never doubted your innocence." They acknowledged his words with low mumbles. But as they started their walk to freedom, Thomas headed deeper inside the jail.

The keeper's rooms were on the second floor of the wing that offered the governor a commanding view of the courtyard. From his vantage point the man responsible for the prison could oversee the enduring misery that was suffered by his inmates firsthand. The keeper's ill-advised name was Solomon Wisdom, and from their previous encounters, Thomas knew him to be a hard overseer with scant regard for those in his charge, be they convicted felons, debtors, or, for a short while before their dispatch, murderers.

As he made his way toward the office, Thomas mulled over

the shocking news he had just learned. Joseph Makepeace. Yes, it made sense—the way the grave had been so skillfully entered, the special trowel, the boot leather in the woods. He already had enough evidence to convict him even without his confession. Money was his motive. But he needed to speak with him face-to-face, to find out who paid him to steal the diamond from the grave—and quickly.

Thomas stopped at a desk at the bottom of the stairs.

"Yes?" said the guard, eyeing him suspiciously. His nose, the doctor could tell, had been broken and set, badly, at least once.

Thomas took a deep breath. "I wish to see Mr. Wisdom, if you please. My name is Dr. Silkstone, and I am come on an urgent matter."

The guard let out a mock laugh. "It's always urgent," he mumbled; then, fixing Thomas with his bloodshot eyes, he smirked. "There's a gentleman with the gaffer at the moment, you'll have to wait your turn." He pointed to a solitary chair near the stairwell.

Thomas removed his tricorn and made his way to the seat. Above him, on the next floor, he could hear voices. A handle turned, and he looked up to see the office door open. A gentleman sporting a high peruke stood in its frame.

"Warbeck," muttered Thomas to himself.

At that moment, the magistrate peered down from the landing and caught sight of him.

"Silkstone! Is that you?" he called.

Thomas swallowed hard. He had not anticipated seeing the Brandwick magistrate, but was eager enough to take advantage of the chance encounter. He strode toward the bottom of the stairs.

"Aye, Sir Arthur," he replied.

By this time, Wisdom had joined the magistrate at the threshold. He was broad in stature, and his face was streaked with a meanness that so often engrained itself on the expression of such officials. The two men swapped looks from their vantage point.

"How fortuitous," said Sir Arthur before turning to the keeper. "I am sure we would both like to speak with the good doctor."

Thomas noted the touch of relish in the magistrate's tone and suspected that this meeting might not be weighted in his favor.

"Come up, Doctor," barked Wisdom.

"But slowly, now," added the magistrate, his lips curling in a knowing smile. "You must take care after your ordeal."

Thomas duly obeyed and managed to negotiate the stairs, even though the effort robbed him of his breath. Once on the landing he was shown into an airy office with a large window at one end. Unlike every other window in the castle, it was not barred. The room was simply furnished, but his eyes latched onto a glass cabinet that was given pride of place behind the large desk. Inside was displayed a single leather whip, hanging as if it were a prize exhibit in a museum. Thomas had heard it was the keeper's personal lash, reserved for those prisoners unfortunate enough to be singled out for his "special" treatment.

"Take a seat," said Wisdom. It was an order rather than an invitation.

Thomas did as he was bid, while Sir Arthur sat at his side and the head keeper resumed his seat.

"So, Dr. Silkstone." Wisdom planted his elbows on his desk in a no-nonsense fashion. "What brings a *colonist* here?" He placed a deliberate emphasis on the word "colonist."

Thomas hoped his nervousness did not show. The two men were clearly setting out to intimidate him, but he would not let them know that they were succeeding. He lifted his chin.

"I understand there has been a development in the case of Sir Montagu Malthus," he began.

The keeper's shoulders heaved in a laugh. "My, my. News travels fast," he sniggered, directing his comment at Sir Arthur.

The magistrate nodded in agreement. "I got word of the un-savory robbery at Boughton and I naturally told Mr. Wisdom straightaway."

The keeper butted in. "And I had a word with the men in my custody."

*A word,* thought Thomas to himself. No doubt it was the usual euphemism for torture. Even though it had been officially abolished under English law more than a century ago, he was under no illusion that such inhumane methods had actually ceased in institutions such as this. "And the bury man Makepeace confessed to robbing the grave?"

Sir Arthur nodded. "Indeed he did." He shot a look at the keeper. "Most accommodating he was." The magistrate tugged at his lace cuff. "He told us he was paid two crowns for his travails."

Thomas could not dispute his words. There was no denying that Makepeace had, in all likelihood, taken the diamond from Farrell's grave. But on whose orders?

Sir Arthur, in full flow, continued. "It follows that whoever commissioned such an act had Sir Montagu murdered, too."

Thomas could feel his anger roiling inside him. He shook his head. "There is no evidence to link the two crimes, sir."

"Evidence!" snorted Wisdom.

"Ah!" Sir Arthur held up his hand, as if to stop the keeper from any further outburst, and gave a tight smile. "Your famous science, Silkstone, eh?"

"My science is based on facts, sir, and facts trump allegations, if I am not mistaken."

Unable to contain his temper, Wisdom now butted in. "So Sir Montagu is murdered at Boughton, and three days later Captain Farrell's grave is found robbed, and you think it a coincidence?" He slapped his palm on the desk as if to swat the notion like a troublesome fly.

When it was put so plainly, Thomas admitted to himself that his theory did sound a little far-fetched, but he knew that all the evidence he had collected pointed to two separate incidents. He refused to be moved. Switching his regard from one man to the other, he reiterated: "All I can do is convey to you what I have found."

The keeper narrowed his eyes in anger. "So whoever ordered the grave to be robbed is a thief but not a murderer?" He slapped the desk again in exasperation.

Thomas decided it was time to reveal his hand. "The grass on the disturbed earth on Farrell's grave was already growing back when I saw it. It had been disturbed several days before the murder. Surely the grave digger will testify to the date?"

The magistrate and the keeper exchanged wary glances once more.

Sir Arthur raised his brows. "It seems you may have a point. But that still does not clear the diamond thief of Sir Montagu's murder."

Thomas felt he was finally making progress. "No, it does not," he conceded. "But from what I understand, 'tis likely that the man who paid Makepeace, whoever he is, will have taken the diamond to London to be valued and to find a buyer. Did Makepeace give a name?"

Wisdom's eyes widened. "Who do you think you are?" he barked.

Thomas refused to be bowed. He continued: "Whoever he is, I would track him down and—"

Sir Arthur's hand flew up immediately. "You will do no such thing, Dr. Silkstone," he snapped. "May I remind you, you are an anatomist. It is not your place to hunt down criminals."

Yet again Thomas had let his desire to pursue the truth lead him over the boundary of his profession. He had strayed into foreign territory and was duly chastised.

"If this thief is in London, then 'tis up to the justices' men to track him down," chimed in Wisdom.

Thomas pictured the worthy band of men known as the Bow Street Runners, who could arrest offenders on the authority of the magistrates, traveling nationwide to apprehend criminals. He had no confidence in them at all.

"Mr. Wisdom is right, Dr. Silkstone." Sir Arthur twirled his cane in his hand. "It is not your business to pry into these affairs, even though you seem to have made it a habit of yours. I suggest you get back to your dissecting room and leave the pursuit of justice to those of us Englishmen who are more qualified to execute it."

The slight wounded Thomas, even though he was used to such barbed comments about his motherland. Still he endeavored to remain measured. "If that is your wish, gentlemen," he conceded.

The magistrate shook his head. "It is not a wish. It is an order, Silkstone," said Sir Arthur, tapping his cane sharply on the floor.

Thomas rose slowly. The throbbing in his wound was growing more fearsome with each passing minute. Remarking his pained expression, the magistrate threw a parting insult.

"You should consult a physician, Silkstone. I am sure he would advise you to rest."

Thomas did not rise to the bait. Instead he smiled. "As I always say, there is no rest for the wicked, gentlemen," he shot back, then mumbled under his breath: "So I am sure you have much work to do, too." He threw them a parting nod. "Good day to you both." And with that he left the keeper and the magistrate and made his way back down to the prison courtyard. In his quest to track down the diamond thief and solve Sir Montagu's murder, he knew that, yet again, he was on his own.

*Chapter 17*

"Oh, my dear boy, I cannot tell you how relieved I am to have you back safely!" Dr. William Carruthers struggled to heave his arthritic frame from his chair to welcome Thomas home to Hollen Street.

"I am relieved to be back, sir," replied the young anatomist, laying his hands gently on his mentor's shoulders. "Please, do not trouble yourself," he said cheerfully, trying to hide his own pain. The coach journey from Oxford was challenging at the best of times, but with several stitches in his chest, Thomas had found it even more so. He had been bounced around so much, he thought it a wonder that his wound had not burst open. Thanks to Professor Hascher's excellent needlework, however, the sutures had held. Nevertheless his discomfort remained.

Settling himself back into his chair once more, Dr. Carruthers shook his head. "Sir Theodisius sent word of your injuries after the duel." He suddenly let out a chuckle. "And that old bugger Hascher patched you up, I hear. I trust he did a good job!"

Thomas eased himself down in his usual chair facing Carruthers. Each time he returned after a period of absence, the old anatomist appeared to him even frailer. On this occasion, for the first time, he noticed that his cheeks were beginning to hollow.

"Do not worry about me," replied Thomas, reaching over to pat the old man's gnarled hands. He suspected he did not know about Sir Montagu's death. Without access to the newspapers, which Thomas usually read to him in the evenings, there was every chance he did not. He would inform him later. It would come as a huge shock.

"And what of you, sir?" he asked. "What news do you have?"

Carruthers huffed and craned his neck toward the door where Mistress Finesilver, the pinch-faced housekeeper, was crossing the threshold.

"We have plenty of news, do we not, Mistress Finesilver?" he called out. There was a mocking note in his voice.

The woman, who had entered the room with a tray of glasses, threw her master a peevish look. "That we do, sir," she replied grudgingly. "Rushed off my feet, I am," she mumbled, setting down the clean glasses on the side table nearby. She poured a tumbler of brandy.

"How so?" inquired Thomas.

"My brother is staying with us," came the old anatomist's excited reply. "He arrived at the end of last month." He clapped his hands and rubbed them together like a small child at Christmastide.

"The professor?" Thomas took a glass of brandy from the housekeeper.

"Yes, indeed," replied Carruthers, grinning broadly. "'Tis many years since I last saw dear Oliver." Despite being completely blind, the old anatomist insisted he still "saw" people in his mind's eye. "About a year before I lost my sight, in fact," he added.

"He is an Oriental scholar, is he not?"

"Indeed. Most learned in Sanskrit."

"The ancient Hindu language," ventured Thomas.

"Quite so. He is staying for a few weeks, I am pleased to say, although the Lord knows he has been out all hours visiting old friends. He is away tonight in Oxford, although I expect him back tomorrow."

Thomas nodded thoughtfully. "I've heard the Indian climate is very unforgiving."

Carruthers agreed. "Yes, Oliver suffers constantly in the heat, and of course he is not getting any younger."

"None of us is," mumbled Mistress Finesilver, handing the anatomist a brandy.

The old anatomist tilted his head and smiled in her direction. "But like mutton, dear lady, the longer you stew, the more tender you become. Yes?"

Thomas could not help but smile, much to the housekeeper's obvious annoyance.

"Flattery will not air the beds or do the laundry, sir," came the barbed reply, and with a derisory flick of her duster, Mistress Finesilver left the room. She did not slam the door behind her, but she did not close it quietly, either.

"She is not a happy woman," Dr. Carruthers told Thomas once he knew the housekeeper was out of earshot. Mistress Finesilver believed her lot to be difficult at the best of times. Circumstances so very often conspired against her. It might rain on wash day, or the milk might curdle, or she might find ants on the sugar cone—they seemed to be everywhere this summer—but still she was expected to soldier on. Now, however, she was almost at the end of her tether, according to the old anatomist.

"Oh?" Thomas had always believed that she considered her glass in life not just half empty, but completely dry. "What ails her now?"

"Sajiv, my brother's naukar."

"His servant?"

"She is most put out by him," the old anatomist confided. "They do things very differently in India, you see."

"I am sure," replied Thomas sharply.

Carruthers sensed that Thomas was troubled. He shifted in his chair, easing himself back. "But you have intelligence of a confidential nature to impart," he said.

Thomas took a deep breath. He had always wondered at the old man's perception, as if his wits were sharpened by his lack of physical vision. He swallowed down a gulp of brandy to give him courage to deliver his news as much as to relieve the constant, nagging pain in his chest.

"I fear, sir, that I do have intelligence, but it is not confidential. It is already the talk of taverns and coffeehouses in both Oxfordshire and London."

Dr. Carruthers's expression suddenly changed. "And it concerns you, dear boy?"

"It concerns Sir Montagu."

The old anatomist grasped the white stick at his side and thumped the floor with it, as if the very mention of the lawyer's name riled hm. "What's that scoundrel done now?" he growled.

Thomas leaned forward. There was no easy way to say it. "He has done nothing, sir."

"Oh?"

"He is dead."

The old anatomist jerked his head back in his seat. "Good God!" he exclaimed. For a moment he appeared stunned until finally he asked: "How? The aneurysm?" Carruthers knew that Thomas had operated to unblock an artery in Sir Montagu's leg a few months back.

Thomas shook his head. "No, sir."

"Then what?"

Thomas's reply was measured. "I fear he was murdered."

There was a sharp intake of breath, and the sudden motion caused the old anatomist to spill his brandy in his lap. Thomas quickly relieved him of his glass and produced a handkerchief.

"By whom, dear boy? By whom? Surely not the Brandwick commoners?"

Thomas, mopping his mentor's breeches, sighed. "I am convinced the people of the village have nothing to do with it, although the local magistrate thought differently. He rounded up those who protested over the enclosure of the Boughton Estate and threw them into Oxford Jail again."

Carruthers flapped away Thomas's hands. "Don't bother about that. Just pour me another drink," he told him.

Thomas obeyed and refilled his own glass from the decanter, too.

"But now the men are released?"

Thomas decided to tell his mentor the whole story from the beginning: how Lupton and Talland had first been suspected but now were cleared, and how Captain Farrell's grave had been robbed of the diamond ring by Joseph Makepeace, acting for some villain whose identity was not yet known.

Dr. Carruthers paused, his razor-sharp mind whirring away. "So tell me what you have found," said Thomas's mentor after a moment. "You have conducted a postmortem on Malthus?"

The questions came thick and fast. Thomas handed Carruthers his brandy and took another gulp from his own glass. As the evening drew on, he started to relate the chronology of the terrible misfortune that had befallen his old adversary and the effect it was having on Lydia.

"It was she who found Sir Montagu in his study, blood everywhere," he said.

"The poor child!" interjected Carruthers. "She must have been distraught."

"I fear so, sir. The whole household is shocked beyond measure."

"Quite so. Quite so." The old anatomist tapped the floor with his stick. "And cause of death?"

Thomas's breath juddered in his chest, causing him to tense in pain. "His head was half severed from his neck, sir."

"By Christ!" At the news the old anatomist almost leapt from his chair, slopping more brandy onto his lap.

"A single blow with a sharp blade cut the spinal column in half."

"Good God!" cried Carruthers.

Watching the fire burn low, Thomas related the findings of the postmortem on Sir Montagu: how he believed the blade to be curved, and the odd fibers he had found embedded in the superficial wounds around the wrists.

"There was something else, sir," continued Thomas.

"Oh?"

"A shallow cut around the front of the neck. As if the blade had first been held to his throat."

Carruthers gasped. "So you think he may have been threatened initially?"

Thomas nodded. "His murderer, it appears, tried to obtain information from him before he hacked off his head."

The old anatomist nodded, then sipped his brandy in thought. "And now you will tell me whom you suspect of committing such a terrible act."

Thomas always felt flattered by his mentor's unwavering faith in his abilities. On this occasion, however, he had to disappoint. "I wish it were so," he replied.

"Come, come, dear fellow," pressed Carruthers. "If I know you, you are at least formulating a theory."

Thomas let out a sharp laugh. "One is taking shape," he replied, "but it is only embryonic at this stage, sir."

The old anatomist drained his glass and held it out to Thomas with the ardent look of a man who had no intention of going anywhere until the whole story had been told. "Then I will let it gestate. In the meantime you can pour me another and tell me all about the postmortem," he said.

## Chapter 18

As the shadows on the wall lengthened, Thomas relayed to Dr. Carruthers not only the graphic details of the postmortem on Sir Montagu's corpse, but also the shocking desecration of Michael Farrell's grave. The old anatomist listened intently, interjecting and querying now and again. Soon, however, it was clear that the brandy and his advanced age were taking their toll. Thomas ached to settle in his own bed, too. He was relieved when the mantel clock struck ten.

"So there you have the case so far, sir," he concluded. He hoped his mentor would take the hint and allow them both to retire. The brandy had eased the nagging pain a little, but he knew he would be unable to sleep unless he took something stronger.

"A most interesting and perplexing one," came Carruthers's considered reply. Holding out his hand, he counted off the evidence that Thomas had imparted on his fingers. "First the coir fibers, the footprints, and a curved blade, then the depraved theft of the diamond from Farrell's grave. Surely there must be some connection between the two crimes?"

"If there is, I have yet to find it, sir," replied Thomas. "As I said, the grave was robbed several days before the murder, and until we find the man who commissioned Makepeace . . ." He broke off as the old anatomist tried, unsuccessfully, to stifle a yawn.

"A task for tomorrow, I feel," Dr. Carruthers suggested, trying to heave himself out of his armchair. His old joints cracked like unseasoned wood on a bonfire.

Thomas was glad when he finally pulled the cord to summon the housekeeper. Escorting his mentor to the door and into Mistress Finesilver's care, the young doctor bade him good night. From the study doorway, Thomas watched him shuffle across the hall, but before he began to climb the stairs, his mentor paused.

"It is good to have you back, dear fellow," he said with a smile.

"It is good to be back, sir," he replied.

Thomas's gaze followed the old man as he struggled up the stairs to his bedroom; then, helping himself to a lighted candle from the console table, he lifted the key to the laboratory from a hook in the hallway. He needed to go in search of more laudanum.

The night was still and balmy. As he crossed the courtyard, Thomas could hear the usual sounds of the city: the watchman calling the half hour and the trundle of the soil truck as it made its way along the cobbles. Reaching the laboratory, he turned the key in the lock. It groaned open. The light from the street lamp above shone through the high windows and went some way to illuminating his path. In the gloom a lantern flared into life from his candle flame. The lofty room was lined with shelves crammed with jars and goglets full of all manner of apothecarial ingredients. Pungent and exotic smells exuded from their lids and lingered on the stale air.

Thomas headed straight for a small cage in the corner where he kept his pet rat. The creature went by the name of Franklin, in honor of his father's polymath friend. He had been rescued from the dissecting table four years back, much to the housekeeper's dismay. Yet Mistress Finesilver, no doubt cajoled by Dr. Carruthers, had been true to her word and always fed and watered the white rodent in his absence. His candle aloft, Thomas peered into the cage and smiled to see the rat alive, seemingly well and keen to embrace freedom.

Franklin darted out as soon as his master opened the little door, before scuttling along the workbench. Thomas reached into his coat pocket for his napkin. He had saved some scraps for his own light supper, and the rat ate them eagerly. The sight brought a smile to his lips, but it was not long before another twinge of pain reminded Thomas of his mission. A red-hot poker plunged into his chest, doubling him up for a moment. Once recovered, he scanned the shelves, narrowing his eyes to read the labels on the bottles. It did not take him long to find what he was looking for. Carefully he reached up toward a bottle and winced as the pain returned with the stretch.

"Laudanum," he said out loud. But something was wrong. He weighed the bottle in his hand. It felt light. Too light. He uncorked it and would have poured its contents into a nearby glass had he not found the receptacle empty.

"Mistress Finesilver," he muttered. The housekeeper was rather too partial to her tipple. He had always doled out a good dose of tincture whenever she asked for it, but now, it seemed, she was taking liberties, obviously thinking it her place to help herself when she felt like it. She had been at the bottle. By the looks of it, in his absence, she had consumed it liberally, so now there was none left for him. He would have to make up another batch for his own ministrations, even though the mixture would take several hours to steep before it was ready.

Slightly peeved at the discovery, Thomas fumbled for the key to the store cupboard. He went inside. Thankfully the staple ingredients were easily to hand: a flagon of white wine spirit, a pot of saffron, and two phials of essential oils, one of cinnamon, the other of cloves. There was just one more thing required for the manufacture of laudanum. He reached for a canister. Again he was careful in his movements, and he managed to retrieve the jar without any further distress and left the cupboard with his arms full of vessels and phials. Setting them down on the workbench, he gently prized off the lid of the canister. It was then that it hit him. A vapor wafted up so sweet and enticing that he recognized it immediately. A memory was triggered. Suddenly he saw Sir Montagu's bloody corpse at the desk once more. It was the smell that had pervaded the study where the body was found. It was the smell of opium. "Of course," he said to himself at the realization.

Holding the recollection in his mind, he had just reached for his weighing scales when he heard the door creak on its hinges at the far end of the laboratory. He turned.

"Who's there?" he called, squinting toward where a silhouette had suddenly appeared on the wall behind him. He listened for the tapping of Dr. Carruthers's stick. There was none. "Sir? Is that you?" he called out. No reply, but footsteps approaching through the gloom. As his heart raced, he reached for a coal shovel by the grate.

"Who goes there?" he called out again. He lifted the shovel aloft as the cloaked figure of a man moved toward the pool of lamplight on the flagstones.

"Lupton!" The steward's familiar features emerged from the shadows.

"I am glad to find you, Silkstone," came the reply.

Thomas laid down the shovel and walked toward him. "What in God's name are you doing here?" he asked. Lupton was a free man. Why, Thomas wondered, would he pay him a visit?

Lupton removed his hat and ruffled his sweat-dampened hair. "I cannot return to Boughton," he said. "And I needed to see you." There was a note of humility in his voice that surprised Thomas.

"You have information?"

Lupton nodded. "Perhaps."

Thomas guided him over to the stools by the workbench and lit another lamp so that he could see his old adversary's face clearly. He had the flushed complexion of a man who had ridden hard. Across his body was slung a leather pouch, the sort used by messengers. He settled himself down, still a little out of breath from his exertions.

"Well?" Thomas was in no mood for courtesies.

Lupton sighed. "I spent many a long hour in prison racking my brains about Sir Montagu's murder," he began. "I was so caught up in trying to push through the plans for enclosure that I became blind to everything else. But there was something I did recall. Something unusual." He seemed, to Thomas, to have the air of a penitent about him.

"Yes?" he pressed.

"A few days before the attack a stranger called at Boughton."

"A stranger?" repeated Thomas.

Lupton lifted his hand, as if to stem the tide of questioning. "The butler dealt with him and 'tis a pity I did not."

Thomas looked puzzled. "Howard did not mention anything to me."

"And why should he have? There was no reason to link the two events."

Thomas nodded. Such testimony stacked up with his findings. "The evidence showed that the grave was disturbed several days before the murder," he confirmed.

Lupton continued. "Howard told me a gentleman called and asked to see Mr. Lavington."

"Lavington!" echoed Thomas, his face suddenly blanching.

Lupton nodded. "When Howard told him Lavington was, in his words, 'deceased,' the stranger apparently became vexed. He asked when and where, but did not wait for a reply."

Thomas stroked his chin in thought. "And Howard did not think to call you?"

Lupton shook his head. "It was just after the riots in the village and I'd told him I was not to be disturbed."

Thomas pictured the steward surrounded by petitions, the blood of innocent villagers on his hands after the recemt mayhem.

"And Lydia was not informed?"

Lupton's neck, slung so low into his shoulders, suddenly straightened. "I would not trouble her ladyship," he replied indignantly. "You forget I was, in effect, the master of the estate."

Thomas drew his lips into a thin line. He was also all too aware that, despite his denial, Nicholas Lupton still harbored feelings for Lydia. For a moment the unspoken truth hung in the air between them. "Of course," he said finally. "So, do we know the name of this stranger?"

A look of self-satisfaction scudded across Lupton's face as he reached into his frock coat pocket. "I made inquiries. He stayed the night at the Three Tuns and signed the register."

Lupton was holding up a scrap of paper to the candlelight.

Thomas narrowed his eyes to focus on the lettering and read out loud: "*Captain Patrick Ignatius Flynn, East India Company.*"

Thomas retrieved the note and brandished it. "If this Flynn is in the employ of the East India Company, it should be possible to trace his whereabouts," he said.

"Yes. It may be possible," agreed Lupton.

"And when I find him, he will certainly have some questions to answer," said Thomas.

Lupton nodded and began fumbling with the strap on his satchel. "But some of those answers may lie in here," he replied enigmatically.

"What have you there?" asked Thomas, peering at the leather pouch. He watched as Lupton produced a small parcel wrapped in brown-tinged paper and secured with string. The steward placed it in front of the anatomist.

"Something that might help in the search for Sir Montagu's killer," he said.

Thomas gave him a quizzical look. He wondered why his old enemy was suddenly being so helpful. "Tell me, why should this interest you any longer? You have been cleared of any involvement."

The corner of Lupton's mouth lifted slightly. "Sir Montagu and I may have had a major disagreement, but I did not wish to see him dead any more than I wished to see you die. His killer must be brought to justice."

Thomas nodded and returned a flat smile. The shoots of decency and honesty that Lydia had reportedly seen in Lupton when she engaged him as her steward might still resurface, he told himself. "Amen to that," he replied.

Taking a nearby scalpel to the string that secured the parcel, Thomas cut it and opened the paper binding.

"Letters?" He shot Lupton a questioning look. With his forefinger and thumb, he picked up the topmost and held it up to the lamplight. It seemed aged and tattered, but it was what was written on the front that caused him to shudder. He recoiled at the name. In bold letters on the front of the packet was written:

*Mr. James Lavington, Esquire, Boughton Hall, Brandwick, Oxfordshire, England.*

"James Lavington," he said out loud, his eyes latching onto Lupton's. "What the . . . ?" For a second time the name sent chills down his spine. "Where in God's name did you find these?"

Lupton cleared his throat. "I came across the first one in Lady Lydia's unopened correspondence shortly after she engaged me. The other four arrived over the course of last year. Their nature made me conceal them from her among my own papers."

Thomas frowned as he started to unfold the first letter. "You know . . . ?"

Lupton nodded. "Sir Montagu told me all about the scoundrel," he replied. "I know that he was an ex-army friend of Farrell's and that an explosion in India left him severely injured."

Thomas shrugged. "Both in body and in mind," he said, opening out the brittle paper. "While to all the world he was a friend to Farrell, he was, in reality, plotting to kill him."

"He represented the captain at his murder trial, did he not?" Lupton butted in.

"He did," acknowledged Thomas, "but when Farrell was found hanging in his cell and it seemed he had killed himself, I had my doubts."

"Well-founded ones, I believe."

Thomas sighed. "He tried to force her ladyship to marry him in haste, to pay off Farrell's gambling debts and gain control of the Boughton Estate." He paused for a moment. That was four years ago, yet it suddenly seemed as if it were yesterday. An image of Lavington's battered skull flashed into his brain.

"But he got his just deserts," remarked Lupton.

Thomas returned his gaze to him. "Yes, he came to a terrible end, bludgeoned to death in Raven's Wood."

Lupton nodded. "Thus ended the life of a career liar, cheater, schemer, and ultimately killer," he summarized.

"Or so I had thought," said Thomas, peering down. "But he seems to have come back to haunt us." He scanned the first letter as he spoke and noted the date: October 28, 1781. He frowned and looked up at Lupton. "How so?" he asked. "Lavington was already dead when this was sent."

The sender's address was written at the top right-hand corner of the dog-eared paper: Hyderabad, India. It read:

> *My Dear Lavington,*
> *I have heard of your good fortune and trust*
> *that you are enjoying marital bliss with your new*
> *bride. I am sure that now that you are in such a*
> *felicitous position, you would wish to share some*
> *of your newfound wealth with your old friend. I*
> *would therefore remind you of our agreement*
> *and, as a true gentleman, you will, of course, be*
> *bound by it.*
> *I await to hear how you propose to implement*
> *the transaction.*
> *Yours sincerely,*
> *Patrick Flynn*

"Flynn?" muttered Thomas, looking up from the letter.

Lupton nodded. "The very same stranger who called at Boughton."

Thomas nodded. "The very same stranger who needs to be tracked down as soon as possible," he said.

*Chapter 19*

In the dead of night, Thomas retreated to his room. He sat at his desk with the neatly written missives from Captain Flynn to James Lavington in front of him. The summer heat allowed the stench from the London gutters to rise to the second floor of the town house, from where it refused to budge. It was too hot to close the sash window, so the sounds of the street below joined the stink and together they made their unwelcome presence felt.

In the absence of laudanum Thomas had resorted to brandy as he pored over the letters. Seated at his desk, a bolster cushioning his aching back, he squinted over the second. There were only five letters in total, their dates spanning the period between October 1781 and just eight weeks ago. Dated seven months after the first, this second communication took a more severe tone.

> *Dear Lavington,*
>
> *I am most disappointed that it seems you have chosen to ignore my last letter. If this is not the case and the fault lies with unreliable messengers, then forgive me. If not, then I would choose to remind you of our agreement. On Farrell's death the proceeds of the diamond were to be divided equally between us. Yet to date I have received no payment. I understand the stone went to the*

> *grave with Farrell on his widow's insistence, but*
> *you assured me it would be retrieved in good*
> *time. That time has now elapsed.*
> *I await with the utmost impatience to hear*
> *your explanation for the unpaid monies.*

The voyage to India, Thomas knew, usually spanned six months, although messages conveyed overland sometimes took only four. He noted the next letter was dated five months after the first one. The tenor was even more urgent. A particular sentence leapt out at him: *If my demand is not met, then I fear I shall have to return to England and claim what is rightfully mine in person.* The tone of the letters was becoming more threatening. The following one even more so, with Flynn declaring he would "take by force" what was his, if necessary. But what was "rightfully" his? The diamond, Thomas presumed. It seemed in the correspondence that Flynn had no idea that Lavington was dead. How could he have before he visited Boughton in person and was told by Howard?

Thomas was about to reread them all yet again when he noted something that had escaped his notice before. Attached by a pin to the fourth letter was a torn fragment from a newspaper. Across the cutting, Flynn had scrawled: *I kept this archived report as proof that there is no danger that the merchant will speak.*

Thomas reached for his magnifying glass. The report was dated May 1, 1775. The print was small, but there was no mistaking what it said. The headline ran: *Merchant executed for theft of diamond.* It appeared the report's author had witnessed firsthand the public execution of the man, one Bava Lakhani, who allegedly acted on behalf of a miner who'd escaped with a huge diamond from the Golconda mines. It read:

> *In the presence of the nizam and in front of a huge*
> *crowd, the wretch's legs were secured by ropes to*
> *the ground. These ropes were then fastened to a*
> *ring on the right hind leg of the elephant. At every*

*step the animal took, it jerked him forward, dislo-*
*cating his limbs. After an hour of such torture, the*
*unfortunate man, still alive, was put out of his*
*misery when the beast, given an order, stamped on*
*his head.*

Thomas pushed the paper away from himself as a wave of repulsion washed over him. He felt the nausea rise in his stomach.
He could not comprehend such cruelty. He knew, however, that
he had to force himself to read the rest of Flynn's letters. He was
glad he did. It was the fifth letter that provided the most information. He looked at the address. London. This final missive,
dated June 16, 1784—just over two weeks ago—gave East India
House as the address. So Flynn was true to his word, thought
Thomas. He had traveled to England to claim what was "rightfully" his. The words suddenly took on a chilling significance in
light of what had happened: *I shall be arriving at Boughton
Hall on Thursday next.* Thomas reached for his almanac on the
bookstand by his bed and thumbed through it. June 16. Twelve
days before Sir Montagu's murder. He looked up from his book
and stared out of the window. The date might well tally with the
theft of the diamond, the day that Joseph Makepeace was paid
to rob Michael Farrell's grave. But why would Flynn return the
following week to murder Sir Montagu if the diamond was already in his possession?

"It doesn't make sense," Thomas muttered to himself. He
flung down the almanac in frustration and, rising slowly from
the table, he walked over to the mantelshelf, lost in his own
thoughts. Whatever the truth, now that he had a recent address
for this elusive Captain Flynn, he could pick up his scent and
track him down before the bumbling Runners got to him first.

*Chapter 20*

M anjeet looked on as his master fitted and shivered like a naked madman in the mountain snows. Captain Flynn had taken to his bed as soon as they had returned from the jeweler's shop two days before. At first the naukar put his master's fever down to his anger. He knew that discovering the diamond was worth much less than his friends had led him to believe had stirred his blood. The captain had a hot temper and would strike him for the slightest mistake, so he'd hoped that the chills would serve to quell his black humor. Unfortunately, he had been much mistaken. Some things he wished he could have brought with him from India, but others, he knew, were best left there. This ague was one of them. The fever had struck his master every now and again for years and laid him low while it ravaged his body. To Manjeet's dismay, it had followed his sahib back across the ocean to his motherland. And now his teeth chattered like so many women at a water pump and his sheets were damp with sweat as his whole body burned.

Although he did not let on, Manjeet understood a great deal more than his master ever credited him with. The naukar knew, for example, that it did not help that their lodgings, in Clerkenwell, were not what the captain was accustomed to. The open sewer they called the Fleet was not half a mile away, and the stink crept in through broken panes and chinks in the plaster where the rain could penetrate. Until his master sold the diamond, however, Manjeet suspected his means were somewhat limited. The offer of one thousand guineas he had received from the jeweler, his master had revealed in an unguarded moment, would just about pay off his current debts, but no more.

Manjeet was, of course, used to Flynn's episodes; sometimes they lasted a few days, sometimes only hours. Thankfully this one seemed to know it was not welcome and was subsiding after less than forty-eight. But not before the captain had suffered his customary delirious rantings. Although Manjeet's grasp of the English language was fairly rudimentary, he could always make out the names of the captain's friends. "Farrell! Lavington!" he often called out. "Quick!"

Manjeet had a good idea what caused his master such distress. He, too, still lived with the nightmares. He also recalled the night it happened as if it were yesterday. He drifted back, back to the fateful night in Hyderabad.

"They're coming!" he had warned his old master

Even though he had no nose, he could smell fear on the air, like a dog that knows another of its kind has passed that way. The pair of them quickened their pace, heading away from the nizam's guards. He, Manjeet, was pushing the cart over the cobbled lanes, sending clouds of dust into the sultry air. Snaking through the back streets that ran like veins inside the city, they finally saw a cluster of buildings through the pitch black. One of them was his master's office. Perhaps "office" was too grand a name for it. It was a small ramshackle lean-to next to a warehouse that he rented from a Portuguese merchant at the back of the souk. It was where the trader kept his scales and his safe and where he carried out his business transactions. The ceiling always leaked in the rainy season, and now and again a snake managed to slither through a crack in the wall. He knew his master wanted no such intrusions that evening. Everything must go according to plan.

They stopped outside and he put down the cart. A muffled protest filtered through the hessian, but he hit the sack and the noise stopped. His master shot him a disapproving look, then reached for his belt. He could see his nerves were jangling like the keys he held in his shaking hands. A chorus of crickets sere-

naded them from the surrounding mango trees, and it had occurred to Manjeet that if someone approached them now, they
would not hear them over this symphony of insects. His master
was putting the key in the lock when, from out of the deep shadows of a nearby pakar tree, Manjeet saw someone moving toward them. The trader saw him, too, and punched his own chest
with his fist as he recognized the man.

"Sir Surgeon! You gave me a fright," he mumbled in a hoarse
whisper.

"I kept my word," replied the man. "And here are my associates."

Out of the darkness stepped three smartly dressed white men.
The trader bowed his head and pressed his palms together in the
traditional greeting. As they came closer, Manjeet could tell these
men were officers—they wore East India Company uniforms.
One of them was Captain Patrick Flynn. Within the hour he was
his new master.

*Chapter 21*

On the third day of his ague Patrick Flynn awoke from his very long sleep. It was past noon. He emerged from his soggy bed linen weakened but fully in charge of his faculties. He heaved himself up on his elbows, his nightshirt still clinging to his skin, and lifted up the bolster. Peering under it, he saw the bag was still there. He picked it up, and after a quick glance at the door to make sure it was shut and Manjeet was not watching, he peered inside the neck. The ring, the magnificent diamond, was still there. Yet knowing now that it was not worth the fortune he had envisaged tarnished its shine. It no longer dazzled like before, in his eyes at least. But his judgment was informed by the stone's value, and he remained convinced that Marian Hastings, when she set eyes on the brilliant, would feel compelled to buy it, no matter how much he asked for it. He'd heard that her passion for her fortunate husband paled by comparison to her love of diamonds and precious jewels. Her appetite for such gems verged on avarice, and this stone, he told himself, would be the one to satiate her cravings. Drawing the string once more, he patted the bag. All was not lost.

Hearing his master move, Manjeet arrived a few minutes later bearing water to wash and a towel. Quite soon the captain was changed into a clean nightshirt and a banyan and was seated in a chair, eating a hearty breakfast of eggs and bacon. As he ate, Flynn's mind returned to the diamond. Breaking the yellow yolk of his egg with his fork, he was reminded of what the Indian trader told them when he first set eyes on the gem all those years ago.

The three of them, Farrell, Lavington, and he, had found their way through the warren of muddy streets in Hyderabad to the shabby shack where the Gujarati merchant conducted his business.

There they made a rendezvous with the surgeon, an Englishman. Farrell had enlisted him for the procedure. A miner had escaped from the mines with a huge gem. He'd accomplished this in a most unusual way, secreting the stone within his own body. He had made a large incision in his calf muscle and hidden the diamond inside the wound before making his getaway. It would be the surgeon's task to remove it.

Remaining in the deep shadows of a nearby pakar tree, they watched in silence. A few minutes later, the merchant arrived with his naukar. That was the first time he saw Manjeet. He was pushing a handcart, and as he waited nervously in a pool of light, it became clear the servant had no nose. He recalled how Farrell had remarked on the fact and smiled cruelly at James Lavington, who had also lost his nose and part of his face in an explosion the previous year. There was always a vicious streak in Farrell that should have told him he should not be trusted.

They continued to watch as the cart came to a halt, when suddenly they heard a muffled protest filter through the hessian. Manjeet hit the sack, and the men smiled at one another knowingly.

They could tell the trader was nervous. His keys jangled in his shaking hands. They slipped through his clammy palms twice before he found the lock. The surgeon signaled that he would make his move and walked toward the merchant, who twisted 'round at the sound and punched his own chest with his fist.

This had been their cue to step out of the darkness. Bava Lakhani greeted them, and they had replied with shallow nods. They, too, were on edge, although obviously they tried to hide their concern. They were mavericks. They were a band of brothers. Or so he had thought.

"Come," the trader whispered, opening the door to his office.

He showed them into a long room with a low ceiling. Flynn recalled there were cushions on the floor, a chest, and very little else apart from a machete in the corner, he assumed for the trader's own protection. Manjeet followed swiftly behind with the cart. Lamps were lit quickly, and the shutters remained closed. No one wanted to be seen.

"He is in there?" Farrell asked, craning his neck toward the cart. He'd stepped forward, bullish and assertive as ever. From his expression it was clear he had no time for pleasantries, but the trader was not fazed. He tacked sideways, shielding the cart from view. He tensed as if summoning his courage and lifted his chin.

"You first," he said, then added, almost apologetically: "Sir."

The three of them had swapped wary looks, but Farrell had nodded to Lavington. It was the signal for him to produce the map. He opened the satchel that was slung across his shoulder and brought out the scroll. Lifting it up by its wooden shaft, he let it unfurl itself to reveal a length of parchment so long that it almost reached the ground.

He recalled the look on the bania's face. His eyes opened wide at what he saw. Then he blinked, as if to reassure himself he was not dreaming. It was clear that this map exceeded his expectations. Against a yellowing background, he could see the inked outline of mountains and valleys and rivers. There were place names, too; names written in his own language, names he could understand. These were places he had heard of: Aurangabad, Seringapatam, and Sira. His eyes played on the minute depictions of palaces and camels before settling on the northwestern corner of the map. And there it was. His eyes bulged from their sockets.

"The Great Snake!" he cried. He lunged forward for a closer look, but Lavington took a step back.

"Not too close," he had warned. "Not yet."

So the trader stood in awe for a second or two longer, regarding this purportedly ancient map of the region that detailed the exact location of the diamond mines that everyone thought had been lost forever. And there, at the center, was the Great Snake, the guardian of the greatest treasure trove of all.

"It is good?" asked Farrell.

The Gujarati could barely speak. "Good, yes," he'd muttered.

He, Flynn, had watched the transaction from the doorway. He was supposed to be the lookout, so when shouts suddenly cut through the thick air, he switched his attention.

"The nizam's men. They are closer!" he had called.

"The miner," Farrell hissed. "Quick!"

The command jolted the trader back into the present, and from then on everything happened quickly. Manjeet untied the neck of the sack in the cart to allow a small emaciated body, wearing nothing but a loincloth, to emerge. But it was the dirty rag, dusted with red earth, that was wrapped around the man's left leg that everyone wanted to see.

"Here he is," announced the trader excitedly.

The man, a dazed look in his eyes, lurched forward as he left the cart. He was clearly unable to stand unaided, and quick-thinking Manjeet grabbed a large cushion and he slumped onto it.

The surgeon, who had been silent during the proceedings, studied the man for a moment. "An untouchable?" he asked.

Lakhani nodded. "Yes, a Dalit, Sir Surgeon, but I believe him to be honest. You see his leg." He pointed to the bloody rag and added: "He must not die, sir. You know that."

The surgeon, a man in his late fifties with an air of calm efficiency, arched a brow. "I shall take the greatest of care," he assured the merchant. He knew the murder of one of the local jagirdar's miners would be punishable by death. "Then let's get to it, shall we?" he'd said. "He needs to lie down."

The shouts of the guards could be heard in the near distance now.

"Hurry it up, can't you?" Flynn had urged from the doorway.

The trader nodded to Manjeet, who rushed the Dalit over to the small alcove and pushed him down roughly on a filthy straw mattress. The lamp, encircled by all manner of small flying insects, was duly fetched and placed on the ground nearby.

"You have examined the wound?" asked the surgeon, unwrapping the dressing.

The trader nodded. "I have seen the bulge. Big as an ibis egg, it is."

"Big as an ibis egg," Flynn now said out loud. It was not an exaggeration. He regarded the drawstring bag that lay on the worm-eaten table beside his plate. Despite the jeweler's low valuation, he would not give up hope of a lucrative sale.

"Sahib feel better now?" inquired Manjeet, hearing his master's voice.

"I do," replied his master.

The naukar poured coffee. "Sahib would also like his newspaper?"

The captain nodded, and Manjeet handed him a copy of the *London Gazette*. Flynn scanned it for news of Marian Hastings's arrival. He could see none and was about to rise and call Manjeet to help him dress. As he folded the newspaper and placed it on the table, however, he stopped suddenly. His attention snagged on a lurid headline on the front page. He craned his neck to read: *Barbarous murder at Boughton Hall.* For a moment he froze as the words swam in front of him. This time he felt his hands tremble not because of the ague but from trepidation. As he delved deeper, his fears mounted. He forced himself to concentrate. The victim of this vicious crime was called Sir Montagu Malthus. He searched his memory. The name was unknown to him. He read further: *The murder is being linked to the theft of a diamond from the grave of the late Captain Michael Farrell.* Again he felt that same terrible jabbing sensation, the bolt of electricity that charges through a man's body when something awful and calamitous descends upon him like a catastrophic storm. Flynn thought of the bury man and his promises to make good the grave—"So as no one'll ever know," the dour peasant had assured him. He had rewarded him handsomely for his work, too. The old fool had even joked that he would buy new boots with the money and lifted a foot to show him the tongue of his boot hanging loose. Everything, he assumed, had gone smoothly. How wrong he was.

In a fit of unbridled rage, Flynn swept his coffee cup from the table. It smashed to pieces on the floor, splattering its contents as it went.

"Sir! Sir!" Manjeet hurried in from the other room.

He found his master pacing up and down, shaking his red head.

"What is it, sahib?" he cried. "You ill again?"

Flynn eyed his servant. "'Tis worse than the ague, Manjeet. Much worse," he said. "I fear I am wanted for murder."

*Chapter 22*

The morning dawned clear and bright over the south coast of England as the sailing ship *Atlas* weighed anchor off shore. Another vessel, the *Besborough*, accompanied it. But if there was much excitement, and indeed relief, on board the vessel that the long and arduous passage from India had ended safely, there was also much anticipation on shore. The ship's most precious cargo was neither spice nor silk, but none other than the wife of the governor-general of India, Mrs. Marian Hastings. Her husband had sent her, most reluctantly, back to England on the grounds of her poor health. The subcontinent's climate had not agreed with her, but it had been reported that, even before her arrival in St. Helena en route, she had recovered her spirits. Now, some six weeks later, the ship was mooring in the Channel and its very important passenger appeared fully restored.

As soon as the Indiaman ship was spotted, the commissioner of the dockyard at Portsmouth ordered the king's yacht be dispatched to fetch the esteemed visitor. To the peal of church bells, many of the town's inhabitants turned out with the intention of greeting the celebrated lady. For many weeks now, the talk had been of the manner in which the governor-general had spared no expense in fitting up the roundhouse of the ship for his lady's luxurious accommodation. Much had been made of the profusion of sandalwood and carved ivory that adorned her cabin, not to mention the dazzling array of jewels that were said to accompany her. Hence handkerchiefs were laundered, wigs powdered, and carriages readied to greet such an important visitor.

Unbeknown to those aboard the king's yacht, however, Mrs. Hastings and her companion Mrs. Bibby Motte, escorted by a friend, William Markham of Benares, had left the ship off Dunnose Point, on the Isle of Wight. Consequently they missed the yacht. Nevertheless, as soon as the mistake was realized, all those in authority rallied 'round and the party was still accorded every civility on landing.

Among the first to greet Mrs. Hastings was the eminent surgeon and physician Sir Percivall Pott. A few months previously he had received a personal letter from the governor-general, asking him to examine his wife when she arrived in England. The meat of the letter ran thus:

> *My dear wife is most out of sorts. Her mood is lively and depressed by turn and her appetite waxes and wanes like the moon. She blames the Indian climate and we can all attest to its severity and extremities, however, sir, I fear that there is something much more serious that causes her general malaise. I would therefore be most beholden to you if you, as a most esteemed physician of the highest character, could examine her and give me your honest opinion of her health.*

And so it was that the most respected Sir Percivall, an avuncular gentleman who walked with a pronounced limp, was engaged. He visited Mrs. Hastings at the inn where she had taken rooms for her first night on terra firma in weeks. Her salon was modest, even by English standards, but by all accounts the landlord was aware of his guest's importance and had spared no expense to make her stay a comfortable, if not luxurious, one.

Sir Percivall found his new patient seated in a chair, looking out of a window with a view onto the sea. At her side was another woman, whom he took to be Mrs. Motte, her companion on the voyage. Both looked up and smiled when he was announced.

"Sir Percivall," Mrs. Hastings greeted him warmly, holding out her fingers bedizened with several colored gemstones. She remained seated.

The surgeon duly took her hand and kissed it. Lifting his gaze, he saw that he was addressing a most handsome woman. For weeks the gossip columns in the newssheets had trumpeted her voyage from India, and now that she had arrived he could easily see why. Her high cheekbones gave her a most noble countenance, and her aquiline nose added strength to her face. Despite the fact that she had landed earlier in the day and had only a few personal effects with her—the rest being still on board the *Atlas,* which was sailing on to London—her attire was extremely decorous. Her elaborately embroidered dress of blue taffeta was complemented by a row of sapphires around her neck, while matching earrings hung from her lobes.

Before Sir Percivall could say another word, however, Marian Hastings preempted him. "I know my husband has sent you," she told him with a coy smile. He detected the sharp clip of a Germanic accent in her voice.

The surgeon returned her smile. "You also know that the governor-general ranks your welfare as high as that of India itself, madam," came his swift and accurate reply.

Marian Hastings nodded and fingered the gemstones at her throat. She twitched her lips to show that she knew what her visitor said was true.

"And so you vish to examine me."

Sir Percivall tilted his head. He could tell from her manner that she had a strong will and would do nothing that she did not feel inclined to do. He replied: "If that is amenable to you, madam."

She sighed in a rather dramatic fashion and glanced at Mrs. Motte, who watched attentively. "I suppose ze sooner you report back to my husband, ze sooner he vill stop fretting," she ventured. "Come, let us get on with it."

*Chapter 23*

A stranger sat next to Dr. Carruthers at the breakfast table in Hollen Street. At least he was a stranger to Thomas. Yet even though he had never clapped eyes on him before, the young anatomist knew his identity straightaway.

"Professor Carruthers," he greeted the visitor cordially.

"Dr. Silkstone," came the reply as the gentleman rose to shake hands. Although ten years younger, Oliver Carruthers bore a striking resemblance to his brother: He had a small, flattish nose and prominent cheekbones, but appeared much taller and carried less weight. It was as if he had been lifted up at both ends and stretched to make him longer and thinner, thought Thomas. Then, of course, there were the eyes. Dr. Carruthers's were most often shut. When open, they were dull and swiveled in their sockets. But his brother's, by contrast, were sharp as scalpels.

"I'm delighted to meet you," said the professor, fixing Thomas with an intense gaze. "William has told me so much about you and your work." His delivery was extremely quick and precise as he offered his hand to the young doctor.

Thomas had also gleaned much about Professor Carruthers from his letters to his brother. For the past six years, he had read them out loud to Dr. Carruthers because of the latter's failed sight and had gained the impression that here was a man in love with India and entranced by its ancient customs and culture.

"It is a pleasure to meet you finally, sir," Thomas replied, taking him firmly by the hand. "You are restored after the voyage?" he asked as he took his seat.

Professor Carruthers smiled at Thomas's remark. "I've been two weeks ashore but have only just recovered my balance," he told him, adding, "which is more than can be said about English politicians."

Dr. Carruthers paused as he munched his toast. "We were just discussing Mr. Pitt's India bill, dear boy," he explained. "My brother is most concerned by it."

Thomas knew there was talk of a bill going through Parliament that would give the British Crown control over the territory of India. He also knew that Warren Hastings was under fire. Blamed, some said unfairly, for the recent and ruinous wars in the subcontinent, he was losing hold of his position.

"What will happen to the governor-general if the bill is passed?" he asked, helping himself to coffee from the pot.

The professor turned in his seat toward Thomas, as if the very thought had fired him up. "Such is the strength of feeling against him that I fear he will be forced to resign and return home," he replied, without pausing for breath.

The old anatomist nodded his head in agreement. "Hastings has many enemies." He chuckled and looked pointedly at Thomas. "He even fought a duel with that cad Philip Francis, dear boy!" The enmity between the two men was well-known in certain English circles, but the professor was clearly puzzled by the teasing tone of his brother's remark. He turned his questioning gaze toward Thomas again. The latter, sipping his coffee, put down his cup to explain.

"I have also just fought a duel, sir," he said, a little awkwardly.

"And he has the wound to prove it, don't you, dear boy!" chimed in Dr. Carruthers, rather too cheerfully than was seemly.

The professor raised a brow. "I trust you are well used to my brother's rather odd sense of humor by now, Dr. Silkstone." He shook his head and shot a disapproving look at the old anatomist. "I hope your injury is not serious."

"Thank you. I'll survive," replied Thomas, gently laying a hand on his chest. His wound still irked him.

"Which is more than can be said for Hastings's political career," gibed Dr. Carruthers with a chuckle.

Steering the conversation into what he thought might be less choppy waters, Thomas jumped in. "We hear that Mrs. Hastings is due to arrive any day now," he said.

The professor, who had taken up his spoon and was about to resume eating his porridge, nodded but did not smile. "Ah, the dazzling Mrs. Hastings." His left eye twitched slightly as he spoke.

"You know her personally?" inquired Thomas, draining his cup.

"Only by reputation," said the professor, framing his reply carefully. He downed a spoonful of his porridge before adding: "Yes, I am sure London society will be clamoring to see her."

"Ah, this is the lady famed for her love of precious stones," said the old anatomist, dabbing a dollop of butter from his chin.

"You are well informed, brother," said the professor, continuing to eat.

Dr. Carruthers chuckled again. "Dr. Silkstone keeps me abreast of all I need to know," he said. "Don't you, Thomas?"

His protégé smiled. "I try my best, sir," he replied, rising and scraping his chair away from the table.

"But you are leaving us so soon, dear boy?" responded the old anatomist.

Thomas dipped a shallow bow to the professor. "I fear I have a great deal to do, sir."

Dr. Carruthers nodded. "Ah, the ghastly murder," he said knowingly.

The professor's expression registered both surprise and alarm.

"I shall tell you all about it," the old anatomist assured his brother as Thomas strode toward the door. Just as he did so, however, there came a loud knock from outside. So clearly could it be heard, and so confident was it in its execution, that it sounded official.

"What the deuce?" cursed Dr. Carruthers as Thomas opened the dining room door just in time to see Mistress Finesilver answer the caller. A moment later, Thomas could hardly believe his eyes. None other than Sir Percivall Pott was standing on the threshold, leaning on a walking stick. He was small and round in stature, and his face was kindly yet learned. An old leg fracture left him with a limp. It was clear, however, that Mistress Finesilver, who had planted herself firmly across the entrance in a belligerent manner, had no inkling of the importance of the visitor. Thomas would never forget when, newly arrived in London, he attended one of Sir Percivall's lectures on scrotal cancer in chimney sweeps at St. Bartholomew's Hospital. It had been an enlightening experience—the first time he had ever heard of anyone linking a malignancy to a patient's environment. Ever since that day, he had held Sir Percivall in the highest regard, and had had the privilege of meeting him, too. Now, fearing the great man was about to be barred from entry by an overprotective housekeeper, he stepped up quickly before any more damage could be done.

"Sir Percivall," Thomas greeted him with an outstretched hand. It was a calculated maneuver that forced Mistress Finesilver to step aside.

Seeing the anatomist approach, the surgeon, who had appeared a little disconcerted by the housekeeper's manner, broke into a smile.

"Dr. Silkstone," he said, shaking Thomas's hand.

"We are honored by your visit, sir. Come in, please," replied the young doctor, gesturing toward the study. Sir Percivall gave an open-mouthed Mistress Finesilver his hat and limped across the hall and through the open study door.

"Forgive my unannounced call," said the surgeon as he was shown to a chair, "but I am come on an urgent matter."

"Oh, and what might that be, sir?" asked Thomas, perching himself on an opposite seat.

The surgeon leaned forward. "I shall get straight to the point, Silkstone," he said earnestly. "You may have heard that the governor-general of India's wife has lately arrived to these shores."

Thomas's eyes widened in surprise. "Indeed I have, sir. The lady is the subject of great admiration in polite society, I understand."

Sir Percivall slapped the arm of the chair as if in agreement. "Yes. Yes. But do you know the reason for her sojourn in England?"

Thomas nodded. "I believe the harsh climate was taking its toll on her constitution."

The surgeon responded, "Correct. His Excellency commissioned me to examine the lady when she arrived and to report back to him on her physical and mental state."

"And I trust she is in good spirits, sir."

The surgeon's lips drooped slightly at the corners and he shrugged. "Her spirits are good enough, but there are certain symptoms that cause me concern."

"Concern, sir?" repeated Thomas.

The surgeon nodded. "And that is why I am come to you, Silkstone."

Thomas was taken aback. That England's foremost surgeon, a pioneer in many chirurgical practices, should consult him was indeed flattering, to say the least.

"Me, sir?" he asked with a frown.

"I believe you were recently involved in the study of tropical plants for the curation of certain diseases and conditions."

"Yes, sir," replied Thomas. "I was given the honor by Sir Joseph Banks. He entrusted me to catalog various specimens returned from an expedition to Jamaica."

The surgeon smiled. "And you treated a plantation owner for a parasite, too, I believe."

"You are well informed, sir."

"I make it my business to be, Silkstone," he replied. "That is why I am asking you to examine Mrs. Hastings, too."

"You wish me to give a second opinion?" Thomas felt flattered.

"Indeed I do, just to check that I have not overlooked anything of a serious nature."

"Then of course, sir. It would be a privilege," he replied, adding, "although totally unnecessary, I am sure."

Sir Percivall proceeded to furnish the details. "The lady arrived in London last night. She had rooms prepared for her by an advance party, I believe. Everything has been executed with military precision. The house is in South Street, close to Hyde Park."

Thomas pictured the area. "I am told there are fine views of the park and the Surrey Hills from there," he ventured.

"Yes, yes," snapped Sir Percivall, clearly in no mood for light conversation. "I understand some of her retinue is already in residence. I will call for you at two of the clock tomorrow, and we can consult better to see what treatment, if any, she will require." With these words he heaved himself out of the chair, his leg clearly still troubling him, and rose.

Thomas followed suit and bowed. "Let me assure you of my utmost attention, sir."

Sir Percivall smiled as one smiles at an equal. "I would expect nothing less of you, Dr. Silkstone. Tomorrow afternoon it is," he reiterated.

Thomas watched him go. He was grateful for the opportunity to attend such a lady of rank, yet at the same time, he did not wish to neglect his own investigation into Sir Montagu's murder. Today he would have just enough time to visit East India House to see if he could trace the whereabouts of Captain Flynn. The arrival of Marian Hastings and her entourage was just another unwanted complication.

*Chapter 24*

The headquarters of the East India Company were housed in a grand, imposing building in Leadenhall Street. The intention, Thomas supposed, was to reflect the power and global reach of an organization that stretched from London to the smallest islands in the Pacific Ocean, many thousands of miles distant. Yet there was also a solidity to it, designed, no doubt, to inspire confidence while impressing investors.

His coach drew up a few yards away from the main entrance. It was the last in a line of perhaps four or five conveyances that were either parked or about to pull away.

Thomas ducked down his head to peer out of the carriage window at the mighty edifice. The curtilage outside was crowded with merchants and company men. They milled about and talked earnestly, assuredly hatching their grand moneymaking schemes, no matter the human cost. Fortunes would be made and lost in this building, Thomas told himself, and lives, too. Trade might have been the engine that powered the world, but people were the cogs in its wheels.

A liveried footman opened the carriage door, and Thomas stepped down. He gave the driver his fare, and then made his way under a great Doric pilaster into the cavernous entrance hall. The building was much deeper than he had imagined and stretched far back from the road. Its wide corridors seemed to run for many yards into the distance. Around him clusters of men stood deep in conversation or, with heads down, hurried past him. Somewhere in this vast labyrinth of rooms and passages and warehouses, there had to be information about Patrick Flynn. It was Thomas's supposition that the captain's entry on a passenger manifest from his voyage from India might also give a forwarding address. Although he thought it unlikely and believed it to be a vain hope, he had to try. In the absence of any prominent signage in the great entrance hall, he suddenly felt very lost.

Up ahead of him loomed a large, wide marble staircase, and at its foot a stone tablet was set into the wall. He noticed two or three men seemed to be consulting it. He wondered if it was some sort of directory and he headed toward it. Just as he was within a few feet of it, however, he suddenly became aware of something or someone hurrying toward him, quick footsteps pattering along the marble floor. He jerked 'round just in time to see a young woman rushing out of a nearby corridor with her forlorn maid in tow. Seemingly in an agitated state, she was waving her fan vigorously, as if she were at the center of a swarm of bees. Such was her anxiety that she clearly did not see Thomas in front of her. Quickly he tried to sidestep out of her way, but she clipped his shoulder with such force that he staggered back and feared, for a moment, that he might fall. He gave out a muffled cry as a stab of pain lanced his chest again. His tricorn went flying, and the maid gasped. The lady, however, although momentarily stunned, shot Thomas a look of disdain and carried on her way toward the main exit. The maid slid the doctor an apologetic glance as he retrieved his hat with great difficulty from the floor, then hurried after her mistress.

The strange encounter was watched by several onlookers, who, for a second or two, broke off their conversations and interrupted their errands to gawp. As soon as the petulant woman was out of the door, however, some shrugged, a few chuntered, but they all resumed their own affairs, leaving Thomas to pursue his. For a moment he stood rubbing his chest and was left wondering what could have irked the lady so. That she was a lady, Thomas was sure. He could tell from her dress, if not from her manner. His eyes followed her through the main portico and outside, where he saw her being helped into a waiting coach. It was one of the vehicles he had noticed when he had first alighted: a private coach and particularly handsome. On both doors were painted a coat of arms in red and yellow, although the heraldic symbols meant nothing to Thomas.

"Can I help you, sir?" A voice behind him made him turn away from the door. A livered clerk regarded him warily, as if he knew that Thomas was not in his usual environment and was floundering to find his way.

The relief on the doctor's face gave way to a smile. "Thank you," he said. After he explained the purpose of his visit, the footman pointed him in the direction from where the mysterious woman had appeared.

"The office is the third door on the right, sir," he told him helpfully. So Thomas set off down the corridor and duly reached a door marked *Records Office*. The room was large and lofty, and ledgers were arranged around the walls on huge shelves. Three clerks sat, quills in hand, at three desks. Thomas approached the nearest one.

"I am seeking an employee recently returned from India," he said.

The clerk looked over the rim of his spectacles. "India is over there," he replied, pointing with his quill.

Thomas walked to the farthest desk and repeated the purpose of his visit.

"Yes, sir," replied the clerk straightaway. He even gave a reassuring smile. "The name of the vessel?" A large ledger lay open before him, and his hand was already hovering over the pages. He looked up when his question was greeted with silence.

"I fear I have no idea," said Thomas, embarrassed. "All I do know is that the vessel arrived from India in the last few weeks and that the passenger's name is Captain Patrick Flynn, formerly of the Irish Dragoon Guards but lately of the East India Company."

On hearing Thomas's words, the clerk suddenly clasped his hands together and placed them firmly on the ledger. "Captain Flynn, eh?" he repeated.

"Yes." For a moment Thomas allowed himself to feel more confident, only to have his hopes dashed seconds later.

"He is a popular man," said the clerk.

Thomas smiled nervously. "How is that?"

The clerk nodded. "You're the second person to ask for the captain this morning."

A cold feeling slid down Thomas's spine. "And the first was a lady?"

The clerk's brows lifted in unison. "How . . . ?"

"She was in a great hurry to leave the building and did not look where she was going," the doctor replied. "I assume you were unable to furnish her with the information she sought?"

Unclasping his hands, the clerk began to turn the pages of the ledger. "I'm glad to say I could be of some help, sir." His finger prodded a tightly written entry before him. "Captain Flynn arrived from Madras on the *Aurora* on the thirtieth day of May." He looked up with a self-satisfied smile, as if anticipating Thomas's gratitude.

The doctor was indeed grateful for the information. It was proof that Flynn was in England at the time of the theft and, moreover, at the time of Sir Montagu's murder. But he needed more.

"There is a forwarding address?" Thomas could feel his heart barreling in his chest as the clerk gave the page a perfunctory glance.

"No, sir," he said almost immediately. "The lady asked the same. All I can tell you is Captain Flynn resigned from the company almost as soon as he came ashore. We have no record of his whereabouts."

Thomas felt his heart sink. He took a deep, steadying breath as he eyed the clerk. "Thank you," he told him. "You have been most helpful," he added, even though he found himself no nearer to tracking down the errant captain. The one man who could hold the key not only to the theft of the diamond but to Sir Montagu's murder, too, was proving as elusive as ever. And not just to him. He pictured the angry lady with her fan. Someone else wanted to find Flynn as much as he did.

\* \* \*

Thomas returned to Hollen Street in the late afternoon to find Dr. Carruthers in the small courtyard outside the laboratory. He was sitting on a bench, his face lifted toward the waning sun. The fragrant herbs that were planted to dilute the overwhelming stench that often emerged from the dissecting room were in full bloom. Their powerful fragrance perfumed the warm air. Wafts of sweet thyme and rosemary came and went on an intermittent breeze, and on the nearby lavender bush, the bees were hard at work. Thomas could see there was a smile on the old anatomist's lips. He felt uncomfortable disturbing him, but he knew Dr. Carruthers would want to be updated on his progress or, rather, the lack of it. He had already informed his mentor of Flynn's letters and their revealing contents.

On hearing footsteps, Dr. Carruthers turned his head toward the sound. He recognized Thomas's step immediately.

"No joy, young fellow?" he asked. It seemed that simply by listening to the speed and resonance of his tread the old man could gauge his protégé's mood.

"I fear not," replied Thomas. "The East India Company has no forwarding address," he told him, settling himself beside his mentor. "What's more, Flynn resigned from his post shortly after he came ashore."

Carruthers nodded. "No doubt to free himself for the task ahead. He clearly planned to visit Boughton and confront Lavington all along."

Thomas closed his eyes and also lifted his face toward the sun. He pictured an angry Flynn calling at the hall, only to be told that his erstwhile colleague was dead. He imagined his frustration at having been ignorant of his death all those years, believing that his one-time friend had betrayed him. He had decided to take matters into his own hands and retrieve what he described in his own words as something that was "rightfully" his. He was a gambling man, that much Thomas knew, and he had either bet on the assumption that the diamond had remained buried with Farrell, or had somehow found out. That was why he engaged Joseph Makepeace. He trusted the grave digger to do a good job. He was to plunder the corpse, then reinter it as best he could so that his crime would go undetected for a long time, if not forever.

"There was something else," said Thomas, remembering the clerk's words.

"Something else?"

"I was not the only person looking for Captain Flynn this morning."

"What?" The old anatomist tapped his stick on the paving stones, disturbing a resting butterfly.

"The clerk told me someone else had inquired about him a few minutes previously."

"Who?"

Thomas thought of the young woman who had been in such a hurry to leave the building that she careered into him. "I cannot be sure," he replied. "A lady. I saw her, although I do not know her name, but . . ." Thomas trailed off, suddenly remembering the crest on her carriage.

"What is it, dear boy?"

"There was a heraldic device on the side panel of the coach. It was red and yellow and bore an image of a knight's helmet with great flowing plumes."

The old anatomist twiddled his thumbs. "Well, well," he mused. "If that isn't the coat of arms of Warren Hastings."

"Ah," replied Thomas. He had wondered as much.

"Your visit to Mrs. Hastings tomorrow will be interesting," observed Carruthers playfully.

"Indeed it will," replied Thomas.

"You think she has something to do with the diamond?"

This latest revelation certainly put a spoke in the wheel of Thomas's line of investigation.

Dr. Carruthers's thoughts, however, followed his protégé's thinking.

"So if Flynn has the diamond, you think he may approach her?"

"Not until he has a verified valuation," replied Thomas. "He has no position and, I suspect, little income. He will want to sell it, but he will need it authenticated."

The old anatomist pursed his lips and tapped his stick on the ground. "Surely if you have a large diamond that you believe is worth risking jail, if not your life for, then you will want the best possible price for it? You would take it to a place where the jeweler is highly skilled yet discreet."

Thomas's eyes suddenly opened. "Of course," he replied, blinking away the sunlight. "A jeweler used to dealing with clients of the highest caliber." He twisted in his seat. "A jeweler who deals with royalty."

The old anatomist chuckled and slapped his thigh. "By Jove! Yes, indeed, dear boy. And I know just where that would be!"

*Chapter 25*

"Is the professor not joining us this evening, sir?" asked Thomas of Dr. Carruthers as he sat at the dinner table later. Mistress Finesilver was already ladling out thin brown soup into their bowls.

"He will be here shortly," replied the old anatomist, tucking his napkin into his stock. "He must be mediating, or meditating, or whatever he calls it."

"Forgive me, brother," came a voice from the doorway. Professor Carruthers strode toward the table. "I lost track of the time." He sat down opposite Thomas, and Mistress Finesilver set a bowl in front of him and slopped the unappetizing liquid into it.

Dr. Carruthers bent low and sniffed. "Venison broth, if I'm not mistaken," he said cheerfully as soon as Mistress Finesilver had left them. "I should've known. We had venison stew yesterday and roast venison the day before."

Thomas smiled at the gibe and picked up his spoon. The professor, neither understanding nor caring to understand the quip, did not smile. Yet his cheek did twitch quickly three or four times. It was an affliction the young doctor had noted before in patients who suffered with their nerves.

Ignoring the strange mannerism, however, Thomas made polite conversation. "So, sir. I am interested to hear about the Indian way of meditation. Might you be able to describe it to me?"

The professor stared intently ahead as he considered the question for a moment. "It is the quest for enlightenment," he said thoughtfully.

Thomas raised a brow. "Many of us are seeking that at the moment," he commented dryly.

"Yes, Doctor, but this is an ancient means of transforming the mind. It encourages concentration, clarity, and emotional and spiritual well-being by seeing the true nature of everything."

"I'll drink to that!" chimed in Dr. Carruthers with a hearty laugh.

The conversation continued as the soup plates were cleared away and Mistress Finesilver deposited a roast capon on the table. As Thomas carved, the professor continued expounding Indian philosophies. "You see, some of the ancient texts teach us that much of man's ability to heal lies within himself."

"And this meditation helps one achieve that?" Thomas latched onto the thought that one's physical state might be controlled by the mental. He assumed it was an exercise that might help ease the professor's nervous twitch.

"I believe it does," said Professor Carruthers, helping himself to potatoes from a dish. "The governor-general has even expressed an interest. Yes, indeed."

Thomas had heard that Warren Hastings was championing a new movement that no longer regarded India as merely a source of profit. He also knew that his views made him unpopular with several other politicians. "Mr. Hastings has a great affection for India, does he not, sir?"

The professor began to blink very quickly as his gaze latched, limpet-like onto Thomas. "His Excellency knows India has more to give the world than lakhs of rupees and bales of silk. It has vast stores of wisdom, too."

"And you believe we can learn from the ways of the native Indians?" Thomas asked. He knew from his own dealings with the Delaware and Mohican tribes in his homeland that some of their medicines were far superior to anything even the best European physicians could offer.

The professor let out a strange laugh. "We English are like

jackdaws," he said, relinquishing his soupspoon so that he could gesture with his hands. "We pick and pluck at other countries' dazzling riches at whim, but we glean nothing from their cultures." His fervor, it seemed, caused him to blink rapidly once again. "We can learn so very much from India—its many religions, its cultures, its social organization—if we but open our minds, Dr. Silkstone. Yes, indeed."

Dr. Carruthers pushed away his plate. "I fear I am far too tired to open anything other than the door to my bedchamber," he chimed in, cheerfully. He declared himself utterly defeated by the food and wine, and Mistress Finesilver was summoned.

The professor also pronounced himself ready to retire. "We must continue our conversation another time, Dr. Silkstone. Yes, indeed," he told Thomas, rising.

Thomas also rose and bade him good night, but then sat down again, choosing to remain at the table. Mistress Finesilver had just poured him a brandy. He sipped it slowly, contemplating his visit to Marian Hastings the next day. It would be difficult to frame his questions about Flynn and the diamond in such a way as to not arouse suspicion.

By the time he'd downed his nightcap he was still no nearer to a solution. He snuffed out the candles and walked into the hallway. From under the study door he could see a light still burned. Thinking Mistress Finesilver had neglected her duties, he went to remedy the situation when, as he reached for the handle, the door suddenly opened and out came Professor Carruthers, burdened down by a pile of books and bundles of papers. Unable to see Thomas, he bumped straight into him, sending his load flying.

"Forgive me, sir!" cried Thomas, even though the fault was not his. "Let me help you," he volunteered, bending low to start retrieving the fallen papers.

The professor seemed most agitated and dropped to his knees. "No!" he barked. "I can manage. Yes, indeed. I can manage," he told Thomas; then, to himself, he started muttering "Quickly! Quickly!" as he scrambled to gather his books, which were strewn across the hallway.

Thomas noted the professor's face was now twitching violently. "I can manage," the professor repeated in a more measured way. But it was too late. Thomas's eyes had already strayed. In his hand he held something extraordinary, something he was clearly not supposed to see. He had caught sight of an open notebook. The left-hand page was covered in a strange hieroglyphic writing made up of lines and symbols, while the right-hand was filled with images: pen-and-ink drawings depicting men engaged in vile practices. Thomas's eyes widened at a drawing that showed an executioner dropping hot balls into the cavity of his victim's head so that his boiling brains bubbled and spilled over. On the same page men were surrounded by their own amputated noses and ears, blood spurting from the relevant orifices.

Thomas shot a troubled look at the professor, who was frantically scooping up his papers. *He does not realize what I saw,* Thomas told himself. He continued gathering the books, feigning ignorance.

"Here, sir," he said, managing a beguiling smile. He handed the professor a bundle, among which was the notebook.

"I am most obliged, Dr. Silkstone," the professor said, holding out his hand to take the papers. For a moment he regarded Thomas intently, as if gauging whether or not he had seen the contents of his notebook. His violently twitching left eye betrayed his anxiety. After an awkward pause he said finally: "I bid you good night, Doctor."

"Good night, sir," replied Thomas, and he watched the professor slope off upstairs, still trying to make sense of what he had just seen.

*Chapter 26*

Thomas glanced up at the sign hanging above a bowfront window on New Bond Street. On it were painted two crossed swords overlaid with a circlet of precious stones, and in gold lettering below it proclaimed: *William Gray and Co.* Yes, this was the shop, he told himself. Mr. Gray senior was apparently a master cutler, turning out the finest of swords for the nobility, but he also prided himself on his knowledge of gems, and diamonds in particular. Agents for none other than Prince George were known to consult him when wishing to acquire various pieces of jewelry for His Royal Highness's lady friends.

Judging by the fashionable gentry he saw promenading around him, this was the place to frequent—during daylight hours at least. The street was lined with various shops catering to those with wealth, though not necessarily good taste, Thomas thought, noticing a woman with garish plumes in her hair. Several of the younger ladies had abandoned their powdered wigs and covered their hair with shepherdess hats in the style of the French queen, while a few men adopted what Thomas considered a most foppish look, all lace and ribbons. He even spied a dandy walking along in a very odd manner. At first he assumed he was suffering from some sort of embarrassing ailment until he realized it must be the famous Bond Street roll. Most of the promenaders seemed more eager to be seen by their peers rather than to shop, although some of the women would pause now and again outside a milliner's window or venture into a mantua maker's establishment.

Thomas, however, was not tempted to browse. He was on a mission. He moved forward toward the door, and a footman, dressed in a fine crimson livery, opened it for him with a bow.

Inside the shop felt quite small and was made even smaller by the fact that it was crammed with glass cabinets. Some displayed swords of various styles and sizes. Most of the cases were, however, taken up with fine jewelry. An exquisite diamond tiara sat on a blue velvet cushion. Below it was a gold bracelet encrusted with rubies and emeralds, and in another case there were several rings made of a myriad of stones.

"May I help you, thir?" lisped a voice behind.

Thomas looked 'round to see he was being studied by an elegant young man, his bewigged head tilted in the polite manner of one who wishes to be of service.

"I do hope so," Thomas began. He had concocted a story. "I intend to ask for a young lady's hand in marriage and I am looking for a suitable ring. A diamond ring."

The young man's tilted head suddenly righted itself. "A diamond ring, thir. Of course." He gave an imperious smile.

Thomas remembered what Lydia had told him about the stone. "But my intended is very particular. It must be a brilliant."

This time the young man nodded, although his obliging smile suddenly waned a little.

"And it must be the size of a shilling coin." The assistant's eyes slid toward the red velvet curtain. "And it must be from Golconda," Thomas added.

The young man's tone hardened. "Thir is motht thpethific in hith requirementh."

"I am," agreed Thomas, "because I was told that you may have recently acquired such a stone."

Another glance at the curtain, and the young man shifted uneasily. "I cannot imagine who told you that, thir," he said, clasping his hands together. Despite his undoubted discretion, Thomas could easily read the telltale signs. He was lying.

"My fault. I must have been mistaken, then," said Thomas. "Do forgive me." He turned and was about to head for the door when he saw the red curtain swish aside. An elderly man in an apron stood in the doorway. He had obviously been listening to the conversation.

"You seek a particular diamond, sir?"

Thomas eyed the man and smiled. "That is correct. I hope to be engaged to be married, and I understood that you may have recently acquired a particularly fine brilliant."

The older man, in possession of the same nose as the younger one, shook his head, and Thomas prepared himself for another denial.

His son jumped in. "You are mithtaken, thir. We have not rethently acquired a diamond." Thomas could see that the young man had been groomed in discretion by his father. That was why he was even more surprised by the older man's intervention.

"Although we were offered one," he said.

Thomas held his breath. "Oh?"

The young man shot a reproving look at his father, but unperturbed, the older man continued. "But 'twas not fine. It was slightly flawed."

Thomas frowned. "Flawed?" he repeated.

The jeweler nodded. "Polished in India, it was. Not a good shine. I declined it, of course."

Thomas nodded. "Of course," he said, adding: "You have your reputation to maintain, after all." He was playing for time, wondering how he could gain more information without appearing to pry. "All the same, I would very much like to see this diamond. It sounds exactly like what my intended described. Do you have the gentleman's contact details?" Thomas asked, even though he knew he was clutching at straws.

"No, sir," the old jeweler said, his hands on his hips. "He left in quite a hurry. He seemed most disappointed in my valuation."

Thomas did not have to feign his own disappointment. "A pity. My beloved will be most disheartened," said Thomas. "But thank you, gentlemen, all the same."

The older man left, with a swish of the curtain, while his son followed the doctor to the door. With his hand poised over the handle, he suddenly turned to Thomas. In a low voice he said: "The gentleman with the diamond . . ."

"Yes?" said Thomas with a frown.

"I recall the footman hailed a carriage for him and hith thervant."

Thomas tried to sound nonchalant. "Do you recall where he wished to go?"

"Field . . . Field Lane, I think it wath. Yeth, that wath it, in Clerkenwell."

"I am most grateful to you," said the doctor, and as he, too, hailed a carriage to take him to the east of the city, Thomas felt he was finally making progress.

Within the hour Thomas exchanged the fashionable streets of Mayfair for the less salubrious environs of Clerkenwell. The area was one of faded gentility. Once favored with several well-tended gardens, these were now overgrown or built upon, and Thomas found himself standing outside an unprepossessing block of houses that was in stark contrast to Bond Street. Instead of satins and silks, those who trudged along this street wore coarse wool and worsted and seemed to carry the weight of the world on their shoulders. He lifted the knocker and rapped hard. He waited for a moment, then knocked again until he heard a voice: "All right. All right. I'm coming. Lord give me strength." The bolt was drawn, and Thomas was confronted by a fat squat woman fixing him with small beady eyes that sank back into the fleshy folds of her cheeks.

Standing on the front steps, she looked Thomas up and down. "Well, well. A real gent, I'll be bound," she said in a mocking singsong voice. Then suddenly her expression turned on a sixpence and she scowled. Leaning forward, she thrust her large bosom into Thomas's face. "If you're looking for Captain Flynn, he ain't here," she yelled, and she began to slam the door. Thomas, however, was too quick for her and jammed his foot over the threshold. "Owes me rent, he does."

"Captain Flynn has left?"

The woman's face reddened under her grubby cap. "What's it to you?"

The news of Flynn's arrears did not surprise Thomas. The captain had been relying on the sale of the diamond to provide him with a welcome windfall. Now that he knew the stone was tainted not only by its association with Sir Montagu's murder but also because by its disappointing quality, he would be forced to sell it to less than scrupulous traders.

Thomas thrust his hand into his pocket and brought out a shiny coin.

"Might this alleviate some of his debt to you?" He held out a crown.

The landlady's expression suddenly switched, and she snatched it and bit into it as if it were a biscuit.

"What d'you want?" she asked, dropping the coin down her cleavage. "I ain't no 'ussy, you know."

Thomas smiled politely, but ignored her innuendo. "In return, I would gain access to his lodgings and ask for your"—he broke off, searching for the right word—"discretion," he said, even though he doubted she had any.

The woman narrowed her eyes. "Very well," she agreed. "I don't expect he'll be back anytime soon."

"What makes you say that?" asked Thomas, watching the woman open one of the doors off the hallway. A ginger cat scampered out and hurtled down the passage.

"Went yesterday morning, 'e did. 'Im and 'is Indian without a nose." She cringed at the thought as she began to climb the stairs.

"Do you know where they were going?" asked Thomas, following her up the sagging treads.

She paused on the half landing. "All I sees is them coming and going," she replied, breathless from the ascent.

Thomas, also forced, by his wound, to gasp for breath, looked downstairs at the door from where the cat had emerged. The landlady was indeed well placed to see Flynn's movements.

"Did Captain Flynn have any visitors?" he wheezed as they resumed the climb. He had to wait until they reached the top landing for a reply. The woman puffed so vigorously that her upward breath ruffled the lace frill of her cap.

"Now you mention it, there was one yesterday," she replied, reaching for a key on her belt.

"A visitor?" asked Thomas.

She put the key in the lock. "The one they left with," she replied flatly.

The door creaked open on rickety hinges to reveal a small, shabby room. Paint was peeling from the walls, and in the far corner, bare timbers were exposed where a section of the ceiling had fallen in. It was not the sort of accommodation where Thomas had expected to find one of Michael Farrell's closest associates. He stepped over the threshold and sniffed. There was the familiar smell of damp melded with dirt in the air.

"I keeps the room clean enough," said the landlady. She folded her chubby arms across her body defensively.

Thomas ignored her and walked past a threadbare sofa, through into another room. In it was a large bed neatly made, a chair, and a cheval mirror. Under the window sat a traveling trunk. It was padlocked. He went over to the bed. A small chest of drawers stood at the bedside. Making sure the landlady was not looking, he opened the top drawer. A pistol lay inside. He lifted it out and inspected it. It did not surprise him to find it was primed. If word got out that Flynn was in possession of a diamond in these parts, no matter its poor quality, his own safety could not be guaranteed. Yet he wondered why the captain had ventured abroad without it.

"Find anything?" the landlady called through.

Thomas hastily placed the pistol back in the drawer. "No," he replied. He sneaked a look under the bolster. There was nothing. He glanced again at the trunk. If the diamond was not on Flynn's person, then he knew it might well be inside, but the lock was a sturdy one, beyond his own capabilities.

He put his head 'round the door into the third and final room. It was little more than the size of a large cupboard. There was a pallet on the floor. This would be where Flynn's Indian servant slept, he supposed.

"Owes you money, too, does 'e?" asked the landlady, suddenly appearing in the doorway.

Thomas let out a muted laugh. "Not exactly."

Brushing past her ample bosom, he returned to the first room. He stopped and inhaled the air once more. Walking to the mantelshelf, he picked up a clay pipe and sniffed the bowl. It smelled of nothing more than stale tobacco.

"What you after then?" queried the landlady.

Thomas frowned. "I will let you know when I have found it," he replied distractedly, casting an eye along the dusty mantelpiece.

"If that's all . . ." She was clearly eager to be shot of him and grabbed hold of the door handle. Just as she did so, she stopped suddenly and let her hand fall as she watched Thomas seize hold of a small card next to a candlestick. His eyes appeared glued to the script, and as he read, the landlady saw the color drain from his face. The card belonged to none other than Lydia.

"Bad news, sir?" she asked, her tone suddenly softening.

"You said the captain left with a visitor?" asked Thomas, the card in his hand.

The woman scowled disapprovingly. "Yes. It was 'im that gave 'im that card. Said 'e was some lady's agent."

"What?" asked Thomas. An uncomfortable feeling suddenly solidified inside him like ice. He strode toward her.

"What is it? What's wrong?"

"What did this visitor look like?"

The landlady suddenly went on the defensive. "'Ow should I know? 'E kept 'is 'at on. All bundled up, 'e was." Opening the door for Thomas, she followed him out into the hall.

He could tell that there was no use pressing the point. It was clear she could not identify this stranger who had, so evidently, lured Flynn into a trap.

"You have been most helpful, mistress," said Thomas, not being entirely truthful. He secreted the card in his breast pocket and slipped another crown into her hand. "For your pains," he told her. What he did not reveal was that now he feared not only for Captain Flynn's safety but also, with the discovery of the calling card, for Lydia's.

*Chapter 27*

"**W**ho gave this to Flynn?" Thomas, back in the study at Hollen Street, was barely able to control his anxiety. In his hand he brandished the card he had retrieved from the captain's lodgings.

"Might it have been stolen from Sir Montagu's study on the night of the murder?" the old anatomist ventured.

Thomas slapped his forehead in frustration and flung the card onto the mantelshelf. "Of course!" he said. "And now Flynn has walked right into a trap. The landlady heard the man say he was acting on Lydia's behalf."

Carruthers tented his arthritic fingers. "So, do you have any idea where he may have taken the captain and his man?"

"Not Boughton Hall, I'll wager." Thomas stomped across the room like a man trudging through deep snow. He looked out of the window.

"So Flynn is not Malthus's killer?"

Thomas whipped 'round. "It seems not. But whoever has lured him away from his lodgings could be."

The old anatomist shook his head. "Be careful, dear boy. Remember, you are first and foremost an anatomist," he warned. "It is not your place to chase after villains. You would do well to let those with authority take over."

His mentor's words of caution brought Thomas up sharp. His expression remained grave. "You know that if I do, Flynn will never be found," he replied.

Carruthers's devilish chuckle lifted the moment. "Of course I know," he said with a wink of his unseeing eye. "That is why I only warn. I would never prevent."

Once upstairs in his own room, Thomas palmed his chest. It still throbbed and his breath was tight. Easing off his coat, he flung it onto the bed and rolled up his shirtsleeves. Still uneasy, he sat down at his desk and, taking paper from his drawer, started to compose a letter. As he did so, something Dr. Carruthers once said to him reverberated inside his head. "You are an anatomist, and the dissecting room and the lecture theater are where you belong, not the courtroom," he had chided when Thomas had first become embroiled in the search to uncover how Lydia's brother had died.

Of course he knew the dear man to be right. The courtroom was a foreign territory to him, and yet, over the past four years, it was where he had fought so many of his battles. His old enemy was most often injustice, and it paraded in the garb of corrupt attorneys like Sir Montagu Malthus. Now that his biggest adversary was dead, however, perhaps it was time for him to change course. He had taken the Hippocratic Oath. He had sworn to do no harm. Perhaps now he should return to concentrating on healing the living rather than bringing the dead back to life by making their bodies talk.

He dipped the nib of his pen into the inkwell. He would write to his old ally Sir Stephen Gandy, the Westminster coroner, regarding his investigation into Sir Montagu's murder and the subsequent discovery of the theft of the diamond. He would tell him he had traced Captain Farrell's erstwhile associate in India, Captain Patrick Flynn, and that he believed him to be in possession of said stone. Sir Stephen could then bring his authority to bear and request that the Westminster magistrate issue a warrant to search Flynn's lodgings. There they would find the diamond and have grounds to arrest the captain and his servant. Under questioning, they would reveal their connection, if any, to Sir Montagu's murder. And that would be that. The perpetrator of the crime would hang and justice would be done. Or would it?

As Thomas wrote the words, they began to seem hollow. He suddenly felt what little confidence he had in the judicial system ebb away as fast as the Thames at low tide. Had he placed his faith in the courts before, at least three innocent men and two women would have finished their days dangling at the end of a rope. He laid down his pen, rubbed his tired eyes, and thought of Lydia. He recalled her warm smile and her tears and how she nestled her head gently on his shoulder. He could not wait until they were man and wife. But there was his mentor's nagging voice again. Perhaps it was time he distanced himself from murderers and their methods. Perhaps from now on his actions should begin and end at the autopsy. Perhaps he should no longer put himself in danger in the pursuit of justice, risk life and limb in his quest to protect the innocent and condemn the guilty. After his marriage, perhaps he should leave it to others to follow up on his findings and recommendations. From now on, should his first duty not be to Lydia and to young Richard? He blotted the letter and sealed it. He was washing his hands of the investigation.

*Chapter 28*

The fine carriage jounced and clattered its way through Mayfair toward the fresher air of Hyde Park and the temporary residence of Mrs. Marian Hastings in South Street. Inside, seated opposite Sir Percivall Pott, sat Thomas. The latter, now in his finest frock coat and wearing a hint of cologne, did his best to hide his apprehension over his decision to walk away from his inquiries into Sir Montagu's murder. The ailments, either real or imagined, of a wealthy and by all accounts unscrupulous woman were not uppermost in his mind. It seemed, however, that Sir Percivall mistook his anxiety for apprehension over the upcoming encounter.

"I am told that Mrs. Hastings enjoyed a good night's sleep. Hopefully she will be in a relaxed frame of mind when we examine her," Sir Percivall informed him, clearly trying to put him at ease.

Thomas nodded. He only wished his own frame of mind could be equally unperturbed. The disappearance of Captain Flynn and his servant had only complicated matters further. The trail that might have led him to Sir Montagu's murderer had gone cold. It was unfinished business, and it irked him. A visit to this famous Mrs. Hastings was not at all what he would have wished, even though Professor Carruthers had assured him that he would be the envy of every physician in London. Nevertheless he knew he owed it not only to his new patient but to Sir Percivall, too, to give the governor-general's wife his undivided attention during the course of the consultation.

"You are concerned about the lady's health, sir?" asked Thomas as the carriage trundled along Bond Street.

Sir Percivall nodded gravely. "I have heard there is a new and very virulent strain of phthisis in India. It causes great fatigue and a cough."

"And these are the symptoms displayed by Mrs. Hastings?"

The eminent surgeon sucked in his cheeks and answered Thomas with a question. "You have brought your listening device with you?"

Thomas patted his case. A few years ago he had discovered that a rolled-up tube when held to a patient's chest might magnify the sounds made by the heart and the lungs, making it possible to diagnose certain conditions. It had proved invaluable when dealing with the poisonous cloud of gas that had settled on Brandwick and the surrounding area several months back.

"Good," said Sir Percivall. "Let us hope we find nothing of a serious nature."

The door of the imposing town house in South Street was opened by a servant in eye-catching garb. Instead of a formal frock coat, he was wearing saffron-colored robes and a turban. More servants could be seen in the hallway carrying boxes and heaving trunks upstairs. Great vases of fresh blooms, some of which Thomas recognized from his cataloging of exotic plants, must have come from Kew, and were being transported into various rooms. A few feet away, near the staircase, stood a man who appeared to have a military bearing. Keeping his back ramrod straight, he boomed out directions as if they were commands to the regiment of servants.

"Take that into the dining room," he cried, pointing to a crate. "And in God's name be careful with it!" He was about to deal with another sepoy who was buckling under the weight of a large chest when, amid the mayhem, he spied Thomas and Sir Percivall.

"Gentlemen!" he called. He made toward them, and bowed low as he reached them. "Major Scott at your service, sirs." He switched his gaze to the older man. "And you must be Sir Percivall Pott," he said with a studied smile. Thomas noted his face bore scars sustained, he suspected, from a battle with the bottle rather than on the field.

A bemused Sir Percivall nodded. "I am, sir, and this is Dr. Thomas Silkstone. We are here at the request of His Excellency to examine Mrs. Hastings."

"Then you are most welcome," replied the major. "Please, come this way." He gestured toward double doors that lay ahead, and Thomas followed Sir Percivall into what he assumed was the drawing room.

There were several people in the salon, both men and women, all dressed in garments that were de rigueur. Scents of sandalwood and exotic spices fought with body odor. But Thomas had no difficulty in marking out the famous—or, in some circles, infamous—Marian Hastings. The huddle of people around her high-backed chair suddenly parted to reveal an appealing woman in her thirties. She was of slender build and pale-skinned, with auburn hair that she wore piled loosely on top of her head. Ordinarily she would have been regarded as a woman of modest attributes. Her eyes were large yet perhaps a little too far apart, her nose slightly hooked in the Germanic way, and her lips quite thin. Yet she was dressed in such a flamboyant fashion that one could not help but be dazzled by her. At her neck there was an amethyst necklace, in her hair there were feathers, and almost every finger of her hands displayed a ring. Yet these outward shows alone would not have impressed Thomas in the least. It was something in her speech and in her manner that made him think her quite captivating.

". . . and this is my colleague Dr. Silkstone," he suddenly heard Sir Percivall say.

For a moment Thomas had allowed himself to be pulled into this woman's sphere, as gravity attracts objects to earth. Suddenly he realized that all eyes in the room were on him. Quickly he drew himself upright, gave Mrs. Hastings a polite smile, then bowed low.

"Dr. Silkstone," she addressed him directly, "my husband has told me about you."

"He has, madam?" asked Thomas, unable to hide his surprise.

Mrs. Hastings nodded. "Sir Joseph Banks has praised you for ze vork you have done for him."

Thomas felt the color rise in his cheeks. There was something in this woman's attitude that made him feel like a child once more. "He flatters me, madam," came his hurried reply.

Noting that Thomas was quite taken by his newest patient, Sir Percivall stepped in. "We are here at your husband's request, madam," he told her.

Mrs. Hastings rolled her eyes. "My dear husband," she cooed. It appeared it was the signal for those who remained in the room to smile and nod politely. "He vorries too much. I can assure you zere is nothing wrong with me zat a little London society vill not cure." This time her words were met with a ripple of laughter, which she acknowledged with a nod of her head to the assembled coterie. "And once zose abominable customs officers allow me my creature comforts, I shall feel most at home here."

Sir Percivall had told Thomas on the journey there that officials had confiscated all of Mrs. Hastings's muslin gowns and silks when her ship had docked at Blackwall.

"Do you know, Sir Percivall, zey have even seized my red velvet riding habit because it vas vorked vith pearls?" she complained.

"For shame, dear lady!" Sir Percivall commiserated.

Buoyed by such a response, she continued to rant. "Zey virtually threatened me vith ze loss of my entire vardrobe but for zose items I had carried to shore."

Major Scott, hovering beside her, rallied to her cause. "There never were such a set of vermin as the customhouse officers," he told the assembly, whose collected heads nodded as one.

Thomas swapped a bemused look with his senior colleague. His newest patient seemed rather highly strung. Anxiety, he had read, might cause the force of blood, as measured by Mr. Hales some years earlier, to engender palpitations. This in turn might lead to hard-pulse disease. Conventional wisdom would dictate bloodletting to reduce the force. He suspected, however, that Sir Percivall and he were of the same mind: Venesection was not the way forward. Nevertheless, in his experience it was often those with the most severe issues of health who shrugged off their conditions, refusing to acknowledge them until it was too late to treat them. A good dose of cajoling and encouragement was the first treatment required, thought Thomas.

Sir Percivall knew it, too. "Then, madam, let us make sure that you are at the peak of your health to enjoy all the delights that this fine city can offer," he told her firmly, but with a smile. It was clear he would not take no for an answer.

Mrs. Hastings fluttered her fan with a studied coquettishness.

"Oh, Sir Percivall," she said with a coy shrug. "How can I refuse you?" Then, turning her fan from an instrument of flirtation into a vehement weapon, she flapped it vigorously at the others in the room as if to ward off a flock of marauding pigeons. "Off you go, now. Go, if you please," she called out. "Zese good gentlemen must attend to me."

The room was quickly vacated, the men skulking out and the ladies tittering, leaving Mrs. Hastings still seated. One other woman remained close by her side. Sir Percivall gave a questioning look.

"I shall require a chaperone, gentlemen," she told them. Thomas's unfortunate encounter with Lady Thorndike suddenly rose to haunt him. He would never allow himself to be exposed to such an attempt at seduction again and was only too happy to examine Mrs. Hastings in the presence of another lady. He had not, however, expected her to be someone who was strangely familiar to him.

"Gentlemen, zis is Mrs. Motte," said Mrs. Hastings, reaching out for her friend's hand.

Thomas was forced to stifle a sharp intake of breath with a cough as it struck him there was a remarkable similarity between this lady and the woman who had ploughed into him at East India House the day before. The likeness was too much of a coincidence.

"Of course," he replied, recovering his composure.

Mrs. Motte eyed Thomas, but whether she recognized him, the young doctor could not be sure. Her expression was inscrutable. All trace of the anger and frustration that she had expressed during their first encounter had melted away to be replaced by a placid mien. She was a little younger than her friend and, to Thomas's eye, much more feminine, with dark eyes fringed by long lashes and black hair swept back from an oval face.

"Zen pray sit," said Mrs. Hastings, pointing to a nearby chaise longue.

Thomas parted the tails of his frock coat and sat alongside Sir Percivall, who seemed content to make small talk. They spoke of London's unusually warm weather and of the voyage from Madras. Politics reared its controversial head, and Mr. Fox and his "ghastly" Whigs were soundly castigated by Mrs. Hastings. Thomas nodded in agreement now and again or smiled politely as he followed the conversation. It seemed to him that Mrs. Motte, seated by her friend's side, was often employed as a sounding board, called upon to endorse various statements. "Didn't ve, Mrs. Motte? Do you not agree, Mrs. Motte? Have ve not, Mrs. Motte?" She sat quite passively, but with an expression that denoted she was perfectly at ease with the situation. Thomas suspected that she was absorbing all that was said and storing it in a mental notebook to be retrieved as and when necessary.

At a point where there was a natural pause in the conversation, Sir Percivall clearly thought it was time to act. He began by taking Mrs. Hastings's pulse. Thomas was heartened when the surgeon declared it "satisfactory." Next, with a nod of approval from Sir Percivall, Thomas reached for his listening tube from his case. He rose and approached Mrs. Hastings.

"I shall rest this on your chest, madam, and listen to your breath and your heartbeat," he explained.

His patient appeared slightly alarmed and looked to Mrs. Motte for reassurance, then switched back to Thomas.

"I am to breaze normally, Doctor?" she asked.

"If you please," he told her. "And I will need silence."

She let out a nervous giggle and once more glanced at Mrs. Motte, who gave a measured smile.

Thomas moved toward her bodice and pressed the cold tube on her décolleté. She shivered a little as she felt the instrument on her naked skin.

"Have no fear, Mrs. Hastings," he assured her. "'Twill not hurt."

Leaning forward, Thomas put his ear to the tube. For a moment there was silence as he listened intently to the throb and thrust of the woman's heart as it pumped blood 'round her body. Her breathing seemed steady enough. He could hear no sign of congestion in the lungs. He righted himself, then passed his tube to Sir Percivall, who likewise listened intently for a few seconds.

"Vat can you hear? Oh, do tell!" said Mrs. Hastings, as if she could bear the suspense no longer. Thomas detected that underneath her bravado there was an underlying anxiety.

"I hear the machinations of a most wondrous organ, dear lady," Sir Percivall replied with a wicked smile, adding, "But first I must consult with my colleague."

The senior surgeon guided Thomas over to the fireplace, away from their patient. He spoke in a low voice.

"In my opinion there is nothing wrong with that lady that a stricter and less doting husband wouldn't cure," he whispered.

Thomas stifled a laugh. "I agree, sir," he concurred, even if he would not have worded his conclusions so honestly. "Her pulse and heartbeat are normal. Her eyes, her skin, and her tongue give no cause for alarm. She appears in generally rude health."

The two medical men returned to their waiting patient and her companion.

"We are pleased to relate that we find nothing amiss, dear lady," pronounced Sir Percivall.

Marian Hastings's fan instantly began to flutter. "I am most relieved, Sir Percivall." Her voice was tinged with laughter. "I trust you vill inform my husband of your findings." She swapped looks with Mrs. Motte. "I am sure he vould not believe me if I told him zere was absolutely nothing to vorry about."

"We will indeed tell him, madam," replied Thomas.

Mrs. Hastings eyed him for a moment. "Sir Percivall is dining vith us, Dr. Silkstone. I trust you vill stay, too."

Although flattered by the invitation, Thomas felt disinclined to accept. He could sense that he was expected to bring wit and joie de vivre to the company, and he felt himself lacking on both counts in his present mood.

"I fear I am already committed," he told her.

Mrs. Hastings fluttered her fan again. "Such a pity. Another time, zen."

Thomas gave a shallow bow. "I would like that very much, but for now I must be away." He took her hand and kissed it; then, bowing to Mrs. Motte and Sir Percivall, too, he took his leave. He really did have to make haste. In the mayhem he had all but forgotten that Sir Montagu's funeral was to be held the following day. He would need to hazard his chances on catching the mail coach that left for Banbury that evening. It was his duty to be at Lydia's side to give her the support she deserved on such a challenging occasion.

# Chapter 29

The clatter of cups and cutlery in the drawing room greeted Thomas when he returned to Hollen Street. The sound, coupled with the low hum of conversation, told him that Dr. Carruthers and his brother were taking tea. Thomas put his head 'round the door to see the professor's naukar, Sajiv, swathed in a cloud of steam, pouring boiling water into a teapot. It was not a ritual that was usually observed in the household, but Professor Carruthers had presented his brother with a canister of the most prized leaves from Darjeeling and suggested that Sajiv serve them. This the turbaned young man did with a calm and silent efficiency.

"Dear boy, do join us," called the old doctor, sensing his protégé's presence.

Thomas balked at the idea. He needed to pack, but felt he might appear rude if he refused.

"Thank you," he replied, smiling at Professor Carruthers, who had already noted his hesitation. He settled himself into his usual chair as the professor addressed his servant in his native tongue, directing him to serve Thomas.

"So how did you find the famous Mrs. Hastings?" asked the old anatomist between slurps of tea.

"Most charming," replied Thomas as the young naukar handed him a bowl. Patient confidentiality did not permit him to take the matter further, so he steered the conversation on a different course. He turned to the professor. "And I believe you continue to work on your translations, sir?" The thought of the gruesome images of torture in the folio had suddenly resurfaced to haunt him.

"That is so," replied the professor with a sheepish smile. He let his gaze drop for a moment, then seemed to rally. "I fear I have neglected William. But I resolve to make it up to him and shall stay put for at least the next week," he replied, reaching out and patting his brother's hand.

The next five minutes were spent in idle, but polite, chatter, although Thomas was so keen to get away that he scalded his mouth on the hot tea. He downed it far too quickly, but was relieved to be able to relinquish his bowl and make his excuses.

"Gentlemen, I must not intrude on your company a moment longer," he said, rising. He needed to pack quickly and head off as soon as possible if he was to make the overnight coach to Banbury. If all went to plan, he would arrive at Draycott House in time for the funeral. He had just made it into the hallway when there was a loud rap on the front door.

"Prick my liver!" he heard Dr. Carruthers curse.

Thomas turned. Mistress Finesilver was nowhere to be seen, so he strode to answer the call just as another thunderclap of knocking burst forth.

"Yes?" cried Thomas, flinging open the door.

A young messenger in the livery of the Westminster coroner's office stood breathless on the threshold. His horse snorted at the foot of the steps.

"Dr. Silkstone?" asked the hollow-cheeked youth.

"Yes."

"I am come from Sir Stephen Gandy, sir."

Thomas could not hide his shock. He had not expected such a swift response to his letter sent earlier that same day. He held out his hand as the youth planted a note into it.

"I am to await your reply, sir."

Thomas scanned the words quickly, then once more, only this time more slowly to make certain he had not misunderstood what he had just read. He lifted his gaze to the messenger, who suddenly straightened his back to receive his reply.

"Tell Sir Stephen I will be at the mortuary within the hour," Thomas said. There was nothing else for it. This news would force him to miss Sir Montagu's funeral. He would pen a letter of apology to Lydia and send it to Boughton Hall in the hope it would arrive before she set off for the service at Draycott House. All of a sudden there was another dead man who was vying for his attention.

Thomas fixed his gaze on the long, thin bundle that lay covered on the table. A pair of feet protruded from beneath the sackcloth. Even before the sheet was drawn back, he knew the dead man was not of European origin by the color of his skin. He could tell, too, by the soles of his feet, that he had spent many years without wearing shoes, so calloused and scarred were they.

Even though the mortuary was in the basement of the building, the sweltering heat seemed to have penetrated its walls. It was already working on the gruesome offering on the slab. The stench clung to the air, and although he was more used to it than most, even Thomas felt himself retch as the porter drew back the sackcloth and a waft of turning corpse assailed his nostrils. It hit him like a slap in the face. He turned away in an instant, composed himself, then turned back, and in that moment, he smelled something else, too: an underlying note, both sweet and exotic, of opium.

In his message, Sir Stephen Gandy had simply told him a man's mutilated body had been found near the docks. He had not said he was an Indian. Nor had he warned him about the nature of his injuries.

"I thought he would interest you, Silkstone," came a voice from behind. Sir Stephen, solemn and gray-wigged, stood in the doorway, a nosegay of fresh herbs in his hand. He inhaled a lungful of its scent before venturing farther into the airless room. "Found this morning. I was about to contact you in any case, then I received your timely letter." The whites of the coroner's eyes were as yellow as ever. Thomas had secretly diagnosed a problem with his liver months ago. Careful to keep a good distance from the corpse, Sir Stephen persisted, his gaze dancing around the room to avoid the gruesome sight. "You told me of your suspicions regarding a Captain Flynn in your letter," he said. "Is this his Indian?"

The young anatomist studied the dead man's face. At its center was a single black hole, obviously once graced by a nose. Remembering the words of Flynn's landlady about the servant, he nodded. "It may well be," he replied. He knew that she could be called upon to verify the man's identity.

"The nose . . ." began Sir Stephen, shaking his head.

Thomas nodded. "Such a disability is common in India, I believe," he replied. He opened his medical case to retrieve his magnifying glass.

"Oh?"

"Among thieves, or adulterers, or even those vanquished by marauders," explained Thomas. He knew, too, that the frequency of such injuries had given rise to a particular form of reconstructive surgery, performed by the Kooma, a small caste of Hindu bricklayers. Using a long, thin strip of skin from the forehead, they turned it and sutured it onto the stump of the nose, like the handle on a pitcher, until new blood vessels grew back and secured it to the face. This man, this servant, had, however, not been so fortunate. His was an old wound. The edges of the nose stump were ragged and vulnerable, allowing all manner of detritus to pass into the nasal passages without the benefit of filtering nostrils. The Indian's face was badly contorted into a grotesque mask, and his eyes protruded from their sockets. What Thomas found most strange, however, was the fact that much of the lower half of the face was covered in a sticky substance. There were odd dark specks dotted here and there that were stuck to the skin.

"Where was he found?" asked the anatomist, running his fingers around the man's jawline.

"Some porters spotted him in a warehouse near the Fleet at first light," replied Sir Stephen.

Thomas glanced at the man's wrists, lacerated by twine, then moved down to his ankles to find the feet fixed together with more rope. "So he was tied down."

"Apparently so," replied Sir Stephen.

It was then that Thomas pulled away the hessian that covered the man's chest and stiffened with shock.

"What is it?" asked the coroner, forcing himself to approach the slab.

Thomas looked up, his forehead puckered in a frown. "His chest," he began. It was peppered with small red welts, but as well as these marks, there were other, more curious ones.

"What of it?" Sir Stephen's eyes strayed reluctantly. "Good God!" he cried. It seemed that the man's killer had carved strange symbols into the flesh of his chest. "What is that?"

Thomas was peering at them through his glass. They reminded him of the symbols he had seen in Professor Carruthers's notebook the night before. "A word, perhaps?" he suggested. Taking a pencil, he copied the symbols into his notebook. He would quiz the professor on their meaning later.

Leaning over the victim's face, the anatomist remarked that a torn fragment of hessian had been stuffed into his mouth. And this sticky substance that coated his cheeks, chin, and neck seemed to have been applied deliberately.

"What are you doing?" asked Sir Stephen. He sounded almost cross.

Thomas drew back, then ran his fingers once more over the man's jawline and neck. Sir Stephen, still awaiting a reply, watched, puzzled, as Thomas rubbed his thumb and forefinger together, then sniffed those, too. Finally he shook his head and said: "Honey."

"Honey?" repeated the coroner. "What the deuce . . . ?"

Thomas stood back from the corpse a little. "The man's face and neck have been smeared with honey. And these dark specks," said Thomas, peering at the curious dots through a magnifying glass, "are ants."

"Ants!"

"I'll wager he was deliberately placed near a nest. Warehouses are full of them at the moment. And those red marks are bites. 'Twas no coincidence that the ants found him."

"What in God's name . . . ?"

Thomas sighed. "I shall need to pry more deeply," he said pointedly. Sir Stephen took his meaning.

"Then I shall wait outside," he said, slightly relieved that his own personal ordeal was coming to an end.

Thomas turned to stare at the dead man's agonized face. Dr. Carruthers had an expression for it. He called it the "grotesque pantomime of death," but it never became any easier to stomach. Over the years Thomas had forced himself to become inured to the hideous expressions that froze themselves upon corpses' faces in their last agonal throes. Eyes often bulging from their sockets, mouths twisted in a scream—the image was always unsettling, but he never failed to overcome his feelings of revulsion to conduct a postmortem. This corpse, however, was unlike anything he had ever seen before.

As soon as Sir Stephen was out of the room, Thomas began his preliminary examination, looking for a likely cause of death, a stab wound or a blow to the head. Yet apart from the lacerations where the rope had cut into the flesh, there seemed no obvious explanation on the torso. The cause, he reasoned, must lie in the region of the face and neck.

The room was designed to store the dead, not to conduct postmortems, and the light was exceedingly poor. What little daylight there was shone in through a window grille. Thomas laid out his instruments in order and took up his magnifying glass. Holding it over the large black cavity in the Indian's face, he noted it was bordered by a thick crust of scar tissue. Taking a pair of tweezers, he thrust them into the hole in the center of the corpse's face and peered into it with his glass. As his eyes focused into the darkness, he could just make out a foreign body that should not have been in the nasal cavity. He probed and picked it out, then held up the object to the light.

"*Myrmica rubra*," he muttered under his breath as he inspected the creature caught in the pincers of his tweezers.

"What's that you say, Silkstone?" Sir Stephen had been hovering in the anteroom outside, happy to leave Thomas to his grim task. Now he appeared on the threshold, keen for news. "You have found something?" The coroner shuffled reluctantly toward the mortuary slab.

Thomas felt his breath quiver. "I have, sir," he replied as the coroner drew level with him, although still keeping his eyes away from the cadaver. He held up the tweezers that had within their grasp a small dead ant.

By now Thomas had returned to the table. Prizing open the cadaver's mouth with a spatula, he peered inside and reached once more for his tweezers. He took out another ant, followed by another and another. "His mouth is full of them," he said, his voice tinged with amazement. "His ears, too," he added, retrieving another dead creature from the auditory canal.

"But surely a man cannot be killed by ants?" Sir Stephen's face crumpled into a horrified scowl.

"Not normally, sir. But this victim was tied down and his face smeared with honey to attract them." Thomas had heard tales—he did not know if they were true—of cases where Indians in his homeland had tortured white settlers in this manner. Particularly vicious fire ants were allowed to tear through the fabric of their victims' tissues, chomping away at lungs with their razor-like pincers, thereby causing suffocation in a most brutal and agonizing fashion. Sir Stephen bit his lip as if to stifle a yelp.

"The insects have entered the man's body through his orifices, as you see, and then gained access to his lungs."

"His lungs?" repeated Sir Stephen, clamping his kerchief over his mouth to suppress a sudden cough.

Thomas knew what he was saying seemed far-fetched in London, but the evidence lay plainly before him. "These are common red ants. Normally they present no danger, but the man's face was smeared with honey. They managed to enter his respiratory tract via his large nasal cavity."

A dark shadow crossed Sir Stephen's expression as he realized what he had just been told. "Sweet Jesu. You mean to say . . . ?"

Thomas nodded. "Of course I shall need to open up the chest to confirm my theory, but I believe he was asphyxiated." The coroner remained glued to the spot, but Thomas was eager to proceed. "You would like to watch, sir?"

The offer to allow him to observe the procedure seemed to stir the coroner to action. "No. No. Carry on without me, Silkstone," he told him, waving his kerchief and beating a hasty retreat toward the door.

Left alone once more, Thomas took his knife and opened up the chest cavity. The lungs lay resting like great bellows below the rungs of ribs, and several ants had managed to find their way into the bronchial tubes. It would have been a slow and excruciating death, thought Thomas. When it finally came, it would have been a great relief for its victim.

*Chapter 30*

Bibby Motte winced suddenly and made an odd hissing sound as she sucked in air through her clenched teeth. A ruby-red droplet of blood was blooming on her forefinger, and she thrust it into her mouth.

"My dear Bibby," exclaimed Marian Hastings, seated opposite her. "But you have pricked yourself." She laid down the embroidery she was working in a frame and patted her companion's skirt.

Bibby Motte, sucking at her finger, tried to make light of it. "'Twas my own fault, Marian."

Her companion looked sympathetic. "You are distracted," she told her. "I can tell you are not yourself zese days."

The two women sat by the window of the upper drawing room in the South Street residence to catch the late-afternoon light. The sun had, however, long dipped below the roofline of the elegant mansions, sending deep shadows onto the wooden floor. On the thoroughfare below, carriages and sedan chairs rushed hither and thither along the Mayfair street. Observing such activity through the large casements provided the occasional welcome distraction for the ladies.

"You have heard news of your husband?" asked Marian Hastings after both had resumed their embroidery.

Bibby Motte sighed deeply and rested her needle again. "It has been four months now. All I know is he must be growing weaker and more despondent every day in that terrible place."

Marian Hastings shook her immaculately coiffed head. Even during the day, her hair was studded with sapphires and diamonds. "But you must be strong for him, my dear. Our sex must bear the veight of a thousand hardships so often."

The younger woman's back stiffened as she shifted in her chair and her eyes fell to the floor. She suddenly looked even more vulnerable.

"Zere is something you vant to tell me, dear Bibby?" asked Marian, ducking her head slightly so that she could catch her companion's attention. She had not spent the last six months on board ship with her not to know when she was deeply troubled.

Bibby Motte nodded with the look of a penitent about to confess to a priest. "The other day I went to East India House," she blurted.

At this news the governor-general's wife set down her embroidery on a nearby chair as if such a revelation required her undivided attention. "To inquire after Captain Flynn?"

"Yes."

"And?"

"Apparently he resigned from the company soon after he came ashore. They have no record of him." She lifted her palms from her lap in a gesture of both acceptance and despair.

Marian Hastings's lips tightened into a flat smile. "It vould seem he is trying to avoid his creditors," she ventured. But the younger woman's expression suggested there was more and the older woman picked up on it, like a seamstress on a bad stitch. "You know something?" She leaned forward conspiratorially.

Bibby Motte glanced over to the door to make sure they were not overheard. "One of the sepoys brought me news. There is a tavern by the docks, frequented by the lascars. There is talk that Flynn is trying to sell the diamond."

Marian Hastings leaned back. "Vell, vell," she muttered to herself before addressing her friend once more. "Zat could prove most useful to you, could it not?"

"I am hoping so. The word is out that I wish to see the captain."

"To negotiate with him?"

The younger woman hesitated. "I am not sure 'negotiate' is the right word." A steely expression suddenly crossed her face. "'Tis because of him that my husband languishes in jail. He owes him not just money but his reputation, too."

"So vat do you propose?" asked the older woman, intrigued.

Bibby Motte took a deep breath, as if to gird herself for battle. "I have put a price on his head," she said emphatically. "Two guineas to the man who brings him to me."

Marian Hastings lifted both brows simultaneously, but before she could say a word, there came a knock at the door. She tutted, annoyed at the interruption, but called out: "Yes."

An anxious-looking Major Scott stood on the threshold. "I apologize for the interruption, ma'am"—he bowed, then turned to Bibby Motte and gave another bow—"but I have news from the customhouse which I thought you would be anxious to hear."

The two women swapped glances. "From ze expression on your face, it is not good, Major," said his mistress, shooting the officer a wary look as he approached.

"I regret to say the customs men have detained not only the ivory bedsteads and the chairs but the horses, too, ma'am."

Marian Hastings looked scandalized. Her large mouth dropped open in shock. "But zat is preposterous. First my silk gowns, zen my bed? Now ze horses. Am I to sleep naked on ze floor?"

An image of the lady in such a predicament clearly flashed through the major's mind as he reddened at the thought, but he soon composed himself. He went on to say: "They assure me that you are not being singled out and that everyone arriving from India is subject to the same rules."

"Do you think I care about everyone else, Major?" she snapped, walking to the window. "I should not be subject to ze same rules as everyone else because I am not *everyone*." She turned back to face him. "I am the vife of ze governor-general of India. Would Queen Charlotte's belongings be impounded? Tell me zat?"

The major's mouth opened, then shut again before he could

think of a reply. His mistress answered her own question. "I think not.

"No, you must continue to press for ze release of my belongings, including my silk robes. How can I be expected to attend all zese social engagements, let alone be presented to ze king and queen, vith only four gowns to my name?" She pointed to the mantelshelf that groaned under the weight of several gilt-edged invitation cards. "And vat am I to give Zeir Majesties?" she continued. "You know as vell as I zat zose Arab horses vere intended for zem."

"I shall tell them of your displeasure, madam." The officer's brow was crumpled in a frown.

"Yes, Major, please do," she said, dismissing him with a wave of her fan.

Bibby Motte watched him leave in silence, then asked her friend: "What will you do?"

"Vat can I do but vait, dear Bibby?" came the reply. Marian Hastings's eyes slid along the mantelpiece at the numerous invitations to balls, a concert, and a soiree. But there was one card, smaller than the others, that took her fancy. Major Scott had left it up there unthinkingly when the two medical men visited her the other day. She picked it up, studied it, and smiled. "And vile ve are vaiting, ve can organize an intimate dinner party," she said.

"A dinner party?" repeated Bibby Motte.

Marian Hastings nodded thoughtfully. "Yes, just five or six vell-chosen guests," she replied; then, taking her friend by the hand, she assured her: "It vill take your mind off your travails, my dear. And I know just the person to invite."

*Chapter 31*

It was later in the day, and Thomas had been toiling over the Indian's corpse in the mortuary for at least four hours. His grim work complete, and the Indian stitched up as neatly as possible, the doctor began clearing away his tools. As he stretched over the body to reach one of his knives, his arm caught a scalpel. It clattered to the stone floor below, and he bent down to pick it up. As he did so, he noticed what looked like a leather thong under the dissecting table. Curious, he picked it up. He frowned. It was a shoe, a strange shoe that must have belonged to the dead man. The leather on its upper had been pricked and worked into a simple pattern, while the sole was flat and without a heel or a back. It was like a lady's slipper. Its sole, he realized after a moment, was surely like that of the mysterious shoe that had left a bloody imprint in the study at Boughton Hall.

Sir Stephen Gandy's arrival interrupted his train of thought. He knew the coroner was expecting his preliminary findings in a written summary. He also believed that Sir Stephen would be eager to know what conclusions could be drawn from the examination. He was, only not in the way that the anatomist had envisaged.

Once again the coroner loitered near the doorway.

"You have finished the autopsy?" he asked, seeing Thomas dip his hands in a ewer.

"I have, sir," he replied, shaking the water away and reaching for a cloth.

"Good," snapped Sir Stephen.

Thomas walked toward him, picking up his notes as he did so. He drew level with him and handed them to him for perusal. But the coroner shook his head and pushed them away.

"There is no need for those, Silkstone," he blustered. "Just as long as we can say that Flynn is the murderer."

"I beg your pardon, sir?" blurted Thomas, taken unawares. His aching back stiffened. "I don't understand."

The coroner jutted out his chin, making it clear to Thomas that he felt he had overstepped the mark. "Surely 'tis obvious? The Indian stole the diamond. Flynn caught him, but the thief refused to divulge where he had hidden it, so was subjected to this." He waved his hand disdainfully at the corpse.

Thomas suppressed his rising frustration. "It is plausible, sir, but we cannot lay the blame on Captain Flynn without evidence."

Sir Stephen sniffed at his nosegay once more. "Of course not, and that is why I called you, Silkstone, to find evidence against this Flynn. I cannot have such a madman running around my streets. There will be mayhem. Riots. The lascars are already gathering in numbers to protest at the brutal slaying of one of their kind. We need to pin the blame on Flynn and quickly." The coroner paused and allowed his eyes to slide toward the dead man for a moment. "Have you ever seen anything like it before?" he muttered. He turned his head away again quickly, unable to stomach the sight of the corpse.

Thomas wished he could take a deep breath to ease the tension in his chest, but his own wound had begun to throb once more. Instead he shook his head. "Never, sir," he replied. And as the coroner beat a hasty retreat to the door, he muttered under his breath: "But Flynn isn't your man."

By the time Thomas arrived back in Hollen Street, Dr. Carruthers had taken to his bed. He found Mistress Finesilver in an even worse mood than usual. She barely greeted the young doctor in the hallway when she took his hat, and even then made a show of how bad it smelled. Only when she was recovered from the stench did she ask grudgingly if he wanted anything to eat. He did and said as much, although he was not sure his request for bread and milk registered with her. When, however, he asked her what troubled her, she was more than willing to vent her spleen.

" 'Tis that servant, Sajy or Sajiv, I neither know nor care which," she blurted, hanging Thomas's hat on the hall peg.

"What has happened?" asked Thomas.

The housekeeper huffed. "He insisted on washing the professor's clothes in the copper. I told him the washerwoman calls next week. Lord knows I don't have time to iron and starch them myself. But no. He seemed to think they needed boiling."

"Boiling?" Thomas picked up on the word.

"Yes," said the housekeeper. She produced a duster from her apron pocket and ran it over a picture frame as she talked. "Mark you, the shirt did look real filthy," she added.

"Did it?" asked Thomas. "And where had he been to make it so dirty, I wonder?" He did not receive an answer. The housekeeper was flouncing off downstairs in the direction of the scullery. So, abandoning all hope of any food, Thomas lit a candle and hauled himself up the stairs, his mind simmering away like a stew pot.

*Chapter 32*

The funeral of Sir Montagu Henry Ambrose Malthus, King's Counsel and Solicitor at Law, was to be held in the chapel at Draycott House, near Banbury. Lydia sat stony-faced in the carriage that was taking her and young Richard to the service. Nurse Pring and Eliza were in attendance and sat opposite as all four of them were jounced and buffeted through the Oxfordshire countryside and over the border into Northamptonshire.

Lydia had hoped Thomas would travel with her. Before he returned to London, he had assured her he would attend the funeral; then his letter arrived just as they were about to leave Boughton. In it he had spoken of a murder. The Westminster coroner needed him urgently. He begged her forgiveness for his unexpected absence, yet still she clung to the vague vision of him awaiting her arrival at Draycott, even though with each passing mile that vision faded slightly.

"Sir Theodisius and Lady Pettigrew will be there, m'lady," ventured Eliza cheerfully, trying to reassure her mistress.

"Yes, of course," replied Lydia with a tight smile. She would be strong. There were those who would be surprised to see her at all after what had passed between herself and Sir Montagu. All eyes would be upon her, but she would not break down. She would not show the emotion she felt. It was not grief alone but anger, too, that welled up inside her and needed to be suppressed. She now knew her incarceration in Bedlam had been on Sir Montagu's orders, and she could never forgive him for what he had put her through there.

As her carriage drove up the lane that led to the chapel, she could hear the slow toll of the bell. Its mournful sound made her recall how she had found Sir Montagu caked in blood in the study. She shivered at the recollection. Seeing her mistress shudder, Eliza handed over her silk embroidered shawl.

"Here, m'lady. You are cold."

Lydia looked at the wrap. It was one that Michael had brought back from India and given to her as a wedding gift. He would be smiling now from his place in heaven or hell, or wherever the Lord had seen fit to place him, she thought. He had loathed Sir Montagu almost as much as he loathed her late brother. Few had mourned Edward, and few would mourn Sir Montagu.

"Thank you, Eliza," she replied. "But I do not need it." She was not cold. She was full of fear. It was dread that made her shudder. The fact that whoever killed Sir Montagu and stole her husband's diamond was still on the loose filled her with trepidation. For all she knew, the malefactor might even attend the funeral. Her stomach lurched at the thought. Instead of wearing it herself, however, she took the shawl from the maid and covered her sleeping son.

As the carriage breasted the final hill before the ascent to the mansion, Richard awoke. Still nestled on Lydia's shoulder, he rubbed the sleep from his eyes, then propped himself upright to peer out of the window.

"We are here, Mamma?" he asked her, looking up.

Lydia gave him a warm smile. "Yes, my darling," she told him gently. Today would be hard for him. He understood that Sir Montagu was dead. Even though he was still only seven years of age, Richard was no stranger to death. He had seen it too often in his short life. In his nightmares, he so often relived the times when he was a pipe boy. Lydia knew that more than once he'd witnessed a fellow sweep being dragged dead from a flue, choked by soot in his lungs. His past still haunted him, as it did her. She held him close to her and kissed the top of his curly head. She had to be strong for him.

Hers was not the first carriage to arrive outside the chapel. There were at least half a dozen more lined up on the drive outside. Several men in black suits congregated like so many crows along the path. As Lovelock helped her from the carriage, Lydia saw their heads turn and felt their eyes boring into her. She dared not return their looks, keeping her own gaze to the ground, although she did recognize the occasional familiar face. There was Sir John Thorndike, for one. He was confined to a bath chair that was being pushed by a liveried servant. He wore the deathly pallor of one not long for this world and appeared painfully aware that his own funeral, in all probability, would be next. Then there was the Earl of Rainton, sly as a fox, and even in the subdued mood of the moment, she heard Lord Fitzwarren's irritatingly loud laughter, more apt at a bordello than a burial, ring out. There was Gilbert Fothergill, too, the fussy, jumpy little clerk, too officious for his own good. He bowed low when he caught sight of Lydia, and she nodded back but quickly switched her gaze to the ground once more. She did not dare search for Thomas amid the dozens of mourners. Of him there was no sign. She had hoped that he might have won against the odds and ridden hard overnight to be there with her. But he had not. Even though she was sure his absence was no fault of his own, she could not help but feel the slightest bit let down, the slightest bit tested by him. Like a small stone in one's shoe, his absence irked her. It was therefore with great relief that she heard a familiar voice.

"My dear." She looked up to see Sir Theodisius, a warm smile splitting his flaccid face. He folded his hand over hers. "How are you faring?"

Lady Pettigrew came to his side, her black-veiled head inclined. "Lydia." She held out her arms and kissed the woman she had come to regard as her own daughter on either cheek; then, bending down, she acknowledged Richard. "Dear boy," she said.

"Let us go in together," suggested Sir Theodisius, crooking his arm and offering it to Lydia. She smiled and took it. Lady Pettigrew gave her hand to Richard, and the four of them walked somberly into the chapel.

They sat in one of the box pews with a good view of the altar, but shielded from most of the other mourners. Lydia was relieved. The only other person privy to her secret, apart from Thomas and Dr. Carruthers, was with her, inside this wooden palisade. No one else knew that Sir Montagu was her real father. None of these black-clad vultures now gathered to pick over the remains of his life had an inkling. Or had they?

As the pipe organ struck up, the congregation rose in solemn unison. All eyes were upon the funeral procession as it progressed up the aisle. Six pallbearers, their faces hard as granite, shouldered the draped coffin to the altar. Memories of her brother Edward's burial came flooding back, and she was forced to dig her nails into her palm to keep herself in the moment. It was then that the thought suddenly occurred to her: What if Sir Montagu had confided in someone? What if he had revealed that he was her real father and that person had sought to use the secret against him in some way? Blackmail, perhaps? Could the same person who robbed Michael's grave have returned to kill Sir Montagu? And if so, why? While Jo Makepeace had been unable to furnish much useful information about his paymaster, her personal plea to Sir Arthur meant that at least he had been spared the gibbet, if not a jail sentence. At least his death was not on her conscience. But it was small consolation when her father's killer was still at large. She surveyed the flock of black crows that stood with their heads bowed, looking to pick over the carrion. They were scavengers, all right, but were they murderers? Right now there was no way of knowing.

"Your ladyship!" The shrill calling of Gilbert Fothergill followed Lydia as she left the chapel. "Your ladyship!"

The service over and the interment in the family vault complete, Lydia found herself more than a little relieved to be out in the fresh air once more. Sir Theodisius had remained at her side throughout. The two of them swapped bemused looks at the sound of the clerk's voice and stopped.

"Mr. Fothergill," said Lydia as the little man presented himself in front of her. He was slightly out of breath.

The clerk removed his large brimmed hat and gave a studied bow. "My condolences, your ladyship," he told her, fingering the brim of his hat. "A most distressing affair."

Lydia did not need to be reminded of the circumstances surrounding Sir Montagu's death. Her look betrayed her own distress, and Sir Theodisius stepped in.

"You have something to say, Fothergill?"

The clerk, seemingly embarrassed by his own awkwardness, apologized. "I wished to tell her ladyship, sir, that the reading of Sir Montagu's will is on Friday in London. I would advise her that she will be requested to attend." He delivered his speech without once looking at Lydia.

Sir Theodisius drew himself up to his full height and plumped out his chest before deferring to Lydia. "Her ladyship has heard the request and is obliged to you," relayed the coroner. Lydia nodded her assent. "And she will indeed make sure she is present."

Seemingly satisfied, the clerk bowed low once more and took his leave.

"So, you are remembered in Sir Montagu's will, my dear," said Sir Theodisius in a low voice, making sure he was not overheard.

Lydia was not so sure. She suspected she was being asked to attend the reading in her capacity as the young earl's mother. "I believe Richard will inherit the Draycott Estate," she said, in an equally low voice. It was a proposition to which she had given some thought, and her conclusion, she felt, was quite probable. Sir Montagu had been widowed many years, and he had no other natural heirs, to her knowledge.

Sir Theodisius's forehead creased in a frown, and he shifted on his large frame, yet he did not look at her. His eyes danced about the chapel grounds at all those still milling around, huddled in small groups, whispering and, perhaps, even plotting. Lawyers always plotted and schemed. It was their natural state, just as ravens roosted at dusk. "If that is the case, my dear," he began, finally switching his gaze to hers, "then you may both be in very grave danger."

Lydia frowned. "I don't understand."

"Whoever killed your father was looking for something. The murderer may return, and if you and Richard are the heirs . . ."

She digested the thought and felt it settle uncomfortably inside her. "I fear you may be right," she said. Her breath juddered as she inhaled deeply. Like the bell that tolled for Sir Montagu, the coroner's words clanged through her mind for a moment. She was in danger, he had counseled, grave danger. "There is something else you must know," she told him, recalling Thomas's letter.

"Oh?" Sir Theodisius was looking about him as if he had landed in a den of thieves.

"Captain Flynn is missing."

"What?"

"According to Thomas, he and his man left their lodgings three days ago and have not been seen since. Then Thomas was called to attend a postmortem by Sir Stephen Gandy."

Sir Theodisius straightened his back. "Flynn's servant?"

"He could not say."

The coroner stuck out his fleshy chin. "Then that settles it," he barked.

"Settles what, pray?"

"You and Richard shall stay with Lady Hattie and me at our London residence until this most terrible business is brought to a satisfactory conclusion."

Lydia felt her mouth open in a natural protest. But then she thought better of it. She did not refuse.

*Chapter 33*

The day after the postmortem, Thomas rose early and made his way to his laboratory to finish writing his report on the murdered Indian. Before he settled himself at his desk, he scanned the bookshelves for studies on insects until he came to his trusty copy of Carl Linnaeus's *Systema Naturae*. Propping the dusty volume on the nearby work surface, he thumbed through the leaves until he found the object of his search. "Formicidae," he muttered to himself; then, carrying the still open volume, he set it down on his desk, sending a cloud of dust billowing into the musty air.

A glass jar in front of him contained what might have been mistaken for small dried fruits, currants or raisins, at first glance. They were, in fact, the desiccated corpses of at least twenty red ants that Thomas had removed from the innards of the unfortunate Indian. There had been many more, but it would have taken too long to extricate them all from both lungs. A cold chill suddenly shot down his spine as he thought of the insects swarming in the dead man's lungs. The hot weather seemed to have triggered a plague of them in the city. They were to be found anywhere where there was anything sweet, and the Indian's killer had used this to his advantage.

Thomas opened the jar and delved inside with a pair of forceps to retrieve one of the creatures and set it on a glass slide next to an illustration in the well-thumbed reference book.

A knock at the door interrupted him. He groaned at the

thought of Mistress Finesilver airing yet another complaint about the Indian servant's manners or some such triviality.

"Yes," he called. He did not even bother to look toward the door when he heard it open, but simply waited to hear his housekeeper's waspish invective.

"Forgive the intrusion, Dr. Silkstone," came a voice. It belonged not to Mistress Finesilver but to Professor Carruthers.

Thomas leapt to his feet. "Good day to you, sir," he said, suddenly feeling on edge. There was something about his mentor's brother that made him uneasy. Catching sight of the professor's grotesque and disturbing images had not endeared him to Thomas. Nor had the fact that his clothes needed boiling so soon after the Indian's murder. There might be innocent explanations for both. And there might not.

The professor, however, seemed unabashed as he moved toward Thomas. "I am sorry to disturb you, Doctor. I know you are working, but I wondered if I might offer you some assistance." His gaze was as intense as ever, and his left eye flickered as he spoke.

"Oh?" Thomas registered surprise.

"I heard about the naukar's murder, you see."

Thomas tensed. "The murder?" he repeated, wishing to draw out the professor.

"Sajiv told me the lascars are up in arms over it."

Thomas was reminded of Sir Stephen's words. "I believe so," he said, offering the professor a seat.

"There is talk that the Indian was killed in—how shall I put it?—a most irregular fashion," he continued, seating himself by Thomas.

The young anatomist resumed his place at his desk. "That is one way of putting it, yes," he said, wondering just how much was common knowledge.

Carruthers drew close to Thomas, close enough that the anatomist could feel his breath on his skin. It smelled familiar, sweet and pungent. He did not relish the experience and drew back a little. Then the professor said something that unnerved him.

"I know you saw my notebook." His stare locked onto Thomas's face.

Thomas was uncertain whether he was being accused or upbraided or both. "I am not sure what you mean, sir," he said, hedging his bets.

The professor's left eye began to twitch again. "I think you do, Dr. Silkstone," he said. "You saw those heinous images."

Thomas decided to go on the offensive. "I saw them, yes, Professor, and I have to admit, I wondered why they were in your possession."

This time both the professor's eyes blinked rapidly. "And I have to admit I have not been entirely forthcoming about my work, Dr. Silkstone," he began.

Thomas was intrigued. "Pray, go on."

"There are few Europeans familiar with the ancient texts of India, let alone Englishmen," he began. "And knowing the governor-general to be a good but much misunderstood man, I offered my services as a translator."

Thomas nodded and watched the professor produce the notebook he had rescued from the floor the other night. He set it on the desk and opened it at one of the shocking images.

"As you are no doubt aware, Dr. Silkstone, this is a catalog of the most unspeakable practices known to man. A litany of the vilest tortures ever devised." His voice was flat as he began to turn the pages, each featuring cruel and twisted torments.

Thomas looked at them in horror. "You are translating these texts?"

"Quite so," Carruthers said with a nod. "There are some fearsome rulers in power in India at the moment who delight in such punishments. These forms of torture are widely employed to subjugate slaves and citizens alike. Even widows are often forced to climb on funeral pyres with their dead husbands to burn."

Such an explanation did nothing to enlighten Thomas. "And why should Mr. Hastings take such interest in this . . . this . . ." Thomas tried to find the words. "This barbarity?"

The professor's neck stiffened and he twitched again. "You misread my meaning, Dr. Silkstone," he replied indignantly. "Only when we understand the full extent of these practices can the governor-general outlaw them."

Thomas suddenly felt relief flood into his tense muscles. His shock at seeing the vile images had led him to jump far too quickly to the wrong conclusion. He had fallen into a trap of his own making and felt very foolish. "Of course, sir," he said.

The professor fixed his glare on Thomas once more. "I can assure you I do not condone them, but I do know something about them. That is why, when I heard of this Indian's fate, I wondered if I could be of assistance to you."

Thomas felt his color rise a little. Perhaps he had rushed to judgment after all. "I would welcome such help," he said with a smile, and he saw no reason to prevaricate. Reaching for the glass jar that contained several dead ants, he set it down before the professor. "In your research, have you come across a method of torture that employs ants or biting insects?" Thomas waited for the professor's reaction as he held the jar up to the light.

"I have heard of such a practice, yes." The professor grimaced at the sight of the shriveled insect corpses.

"Can you elucidate?" Thomas pressed.

Carruthers's gaze settled on the glass jar. "The victim is usually tied down, unable to escape, and a particularly vicious genus of ant, native to Africa and certain parts of Asia, is unleashed on his face and neck. He is forced to endure the slow gnawing of his soft tissue; his nasal passage, his aural cavities, even his eye sockets become fodder for these marauding savages." His mouth contorted as he spoke at the very thought of such barbarity.

"And he dies by the venom?" asked Thomas.

The professor shook his head. "No, Doctor. Small children and animals have been known to suffer death by their poison, but 'tis by entering the body through the airways and swarming through the mouth and down the bronchial tract and into the lungs that these creatures are able to kill a man."

"So he is asphyxiated?"

"Precisely. A most gruesome death." Carruthers set down the jar and pushed it away from him in disgust. "But surely the Indian . . . ?"

Thomas explained. "The ants were not of the same genus, but commonly found in England, and they were set on the victim's face."

"But English ants do not kill," exclaimed the professor.

Thomas remained silent but, opening his case, took out a phial. He had managed to scrape off some of the honey from the dead man's neck and face with a spatula. Uncorking it, he sniffed at it. It gave off quite a distinctive aroma.

"The victim's face was covered in this." He held the phial up to the professor's face, allowing him to sniff it, too. "And he did not have a nose."

The professor's eyebrows lifted. "Ah, there are many such unfortunates in certain parts of India. It is a common punishment."

Thomas nodded. "So I believe," he said. "The ants must have been poured onto his face and were free to invade his respiratory system through his widened nasal canal, causing death by suffocation." The mental image of such an invasion led both men to pause for a moment so that even before Thomas could replace the cork on the phial, the tap-tapping of Dr. Carruthers's stick was heard at the threshold. They turned to see the old anatomist shuffling into the room.

"Ah! There you both are!" he cried, waving his stick in the air. He stopped as he drew level with Thomas, then twitched his nostrils. "Honey," he said suddenly.

Thomas swapped looks with the professor. "Yes, sir," he replied. "Here." He wafted the glass tube under Carruthers's nose.

"Acacia honey," barked the old anatomist instantly. His olfactory perception and his ability to instantly name any scent were, Thomas knew, quite remarkable. "My favorite. What's it doing here, by Jove!?"

Thomas pulled out a stool for the old man, and he sat.

"It had been smeared over the face and neck of the Indian servant whose autopsy I conducted yesterday, sir."

"What?" Dr. Carruthers had barely settled on the stool before he jolted upright.

"It was used to attract ants, sir. They invaded his lungs and suffocated him," Thomas explained.

The old anatomist's forehead was ridged with deep furrows as he floundered to find words. "But who could . . . I cannot . . . Such devilry!"

"I fear it is a method of torture exercised in India, brother," explained the professor, this time quite calmly.

It had already occurred to Thomas that no one would go to such elaborate lengths to kill another man unless he wished to extract information from him before he died. Just as the turn of a handle can increase the exertion of a rack wheel, so an inquisitor could have added more and more ants onto his victim's upper torso in the hope that he would divulge any secrets he might have been keeping. In this case the Indian either could not or would not tell, or perhaps his fate was sealed from the outset and he was a dead man the moment he was pinioned by the ropes.

"The rope," Thomas muttered to himself, reaching once more into his case. He had salvaged a length of it from the dead man's feet.

"Rope?" repeated Dr. Carruthers.

Thomas pulled a few fibers from the length and placed them on a glass slide. Walking over to the window, where his microscope could best take advantage of the light, he peered down into the eyepiece. It was as he suspected.

"Coir rope," he announced, straightening his back.

"There is a connection?" The old anatomist was thinking out loud.

"Between this death and Sir Montagu's? 'Tis possible," Thomas replied.

"But I thought you had ruled out Flynn?" interjected the old anatomist.

Thomas raked his fingers through his hair in thought. "I could not see—I still cannot see—why, if he was in possession of the diamond, the captain would have returned to murder Sir Montagu. It makes no sense."

"But the captain is still missing?" asked the professor.

Thomas nodded. "Sir Stephen has informed the local magistrate, and the Runners are on the case, but I do not hold out much hope of them finding him."

The old anatomist tapped the floor with his stick. "Then what is our next move?" he asked just as there was a knock at the door.

"Come in," called Thomas.

Mistress Finesilver, her face as dreary as a wet Sunday, entered carrying a small tray. She gave a shallow curtsy. "Beg pardon, Doctors, Professor," she said, "but this just came for Dr. Silkstone." She shoved the tray in front of Thomas, and he reached for the letter on it. Breaking the seal with a scalpel that was to hand, he read the contents.

"What is it?" snapped the old anatomist tetchily. He was used to bad news being delivered in such a fashion.

On this occasion, however, Thomas regarded his old mentor with a smile. "An invitation, sir," he replied.

"Oh?"

"I have been invited to dine at Mrs. Hastings's residence."

Dr. Carruthers chuckled. "Have you, by Jove? The dear lady must have taken a shine to you."

"You are indeed honored," chimed in the professor.

Thomas felt his cheeks flush slightly. From her look, Mistress Finesilver noticed his color rise.

"That will be all now," Thomas told her. But as she turned to go, Dr. Carruthers raised his stick.

"No, wait," he trilled. "Acacia honey."

Mistress Finesilver stopped in her tracks. "Sir?" she replied with a bemused look on her face.

"We have some, do we not?" Before his housekeeper's answer

was forthcoming, the old anatomist turned to Thomas to explain. "An old patient of mine sent me a few jars, and I do so enjoy it."

Mistress Finesilver nodded. "I believe there's some in the pantry, sir," she replied.

Dr. Carruthers smiled. "Then I would have it for my breakfast, dear lady," he told her. "Spread thickly on my toast." He licked his lips as if imagining the taste of the honey.

"Very good, sir," she told him, and with that she aimed another curtsy at the gentlemen and was away.

Thomas wondered that the old anatomist could countenance eating acacia honey ever again after what he had just been told. For him the taste of it would always remind him of the ravaged corpse he had examined the night before.

Dr. Carruthers turned to the professor once more. "I came to see if you would accompany me to the park this morning, Oliver. The weather is set fair, I believe," he said. "But I vouch you are enjoying your time back in a laboratory after all those years of absence, eh?"

Thomas shot a puzzled look at the professor. "I didn't know you were interested in such matters, sir."

From the far end of the large room, the old anatomist chuckled. "You haven't told Thomas?" he asked.

"Told me what, pray?" pressed Thomas. He turned a quizzical look on the professor, who suddenly seemed most uncomfortable.

"Oliver was a surgeon before he dropped his scalpel and took up his pen," revealed the old anatomist cheerfully.

The professor shot Thomas an embarrassed look. "It was a very long time ago, William," he replied, his left eye starting to twitch.

*And one you clearly wish to forget,* thought Thomas, judging by the professor's pained expression. He let the matter drop.

"If I am not needed here . . ." said the professor, by way of an excuse to leave.

"You have already been most helpful," Thomas assured him. "Please do not remain on my account."

"That settles it," announced the old anatomist, tapping his stick on the floor. "Then let us ready ourselves."

The professor nodded and began walking to the door with his brother. As he did so, Thomas called out.

"There is just one more thing, Professor."

"Yes, Doctor?" Carruthers turned to see Thomas approaching as his brother continued to the door.

"Do you have any idea what these characters mean?" he asked, his own notebook in his hand. He was pointing to the strange marks he had seen on the dead Indian's chest and copied down.

The professor glanced at them for a moment, then frowned. "Why yes," he replied, his eyes blinking in rapid succession. "This says 'Gaddar.'"

"'Gaddar'?" repeated Thomas.

Carruthers twitched again. "It is a Hindu word. It means 'traitor.'"

Thomas took a moment to digest the translation. "Traitor?" He looked up at the professor.

"Oliver!" Dr. Carruthers called out as he reached the laboratory door.

"Coming, brother," the professor replied, switching back to Thomas to take his leave.

"Thank you, sir," Thomas said. "That is most helpful."

*Chapter 34*

The coffeehouse was as busy as a beehive, but then it always was. Tucked down an alley off one of the main wharves lined with warehouses, it made an excellent meeting place for those involved in commerce. It was also a favorite haunt for those in the East India Company. Merchants in drab, dusty coats hawked and haggled around the many wooden tables that cluttered the sprawling rooms. They had their cargoes to sell: sugar, ginger, and dyewoods from the West Indies and spice and silk from the East Indies, not to mention goodness knows what else from all points in between. While the merchants were hard men, enduring hell and high water to bring back their goods to England, the buyers were made of even sterner stuff and always drove a difficult bargain. There would be the odd challenge, the occasional fight, but by and large everyone knew his place and the order of things, and more often than not deals were done and hands shaken.

Nevertheless Nicholas Lupton did not feel at ease in this sort of place. He preferred White's on St. James's Street, where punters could place bets on how long customers had to live, then gamble away their entire estates. He'd heard of a fellow who'd done just that, only to be found drowned in the Thames the next day. He had bagged himself a seat in the far corner, away from the merchants and moneymen. He'd ordered a dish of thick, grimy coffee that tasted like brewed soot, but it kept him alert. In fact he was sipping it with particular relish because he was savoring his freedom after his wretched sojourn in Oxford Jail. Yes, he was savoring and he was waiting. For the past few days he'd stayed in London. He'd told Silkstone he would search for this reprobate Flynn. He had not meant it, of course. He no more intended to help the American upstart than return to that stinking prison. True, he had caught sight of the redheaded varlet mounting his horse and riding off from Boughton. He would be best placed to find him, but for what? If he had murdered Sir Montagu, then he had rid the world of an overbearing tyrant. If he had dug up Michael Farrell's grave and stolen a diamond, then good luck to the man for his enterprise. He only wished he had known that such a stone had been buried in Boughton's grounds. He'd have been onto it in a trice.

No, he had lied to Silkstone, but the situation had subsequently changed. Keeping his ear to the ground, he had heard that the anatomist was not the only one who wanted to talk with Captain Flynn. There was someone else. And what was more, that someone had put a price on the captain's head and a good one at that, although he knew he could raise the stakes. So that was what brought him here, to this shabby haunt of brokers and wheeler-dealers, at the behest of someone who wanted to find Flynn just as much as Dr. Thomas Silkstone but who was willing to pay for the service.

And there he was coming into view, scanning the tables, seeking Lupton out: a stocky man with a military bearing, his back as straight as if he were at court. An officer undoubtedly. He had told Lupton in his note that he would be carrying a copy of the *London Gazette,* but there was no need. He stuck out among the merchants like a vicar in a brothel. Well-groomed but with a drink-bloated face, he had an air of a man who would brook no nonsense. Lupton had heard of his needs through an old friend of his father's. It was all about who you knew, not what you knew, in this game. Any good businessman would tell you that. This gentleman chose to remain anonymous. Such a position always rendered a man vulnerable, in his experience.

"Nicholas Lupton at your service, sir." He rose to greet his new associate as he looked around him warily. They exchanged handshakes before sitting opposite each other.

"You would have coffee, sir?"

In reply, the gentleman pursed his lips as if the very thought of the taste repulsed him. "I'd rather drink water from the Thames," he snapped back, settling himself on his chair. "Let us get down to business, shall we?"

"By all means," retorted Lupton.

"You come on good account," began the gentleman. He eyed Lupton as if trying to convince himself that he could place his trust in the slightly rakish man across from him whose head was slung low into his shoulders.

Lupton did not reply. He did not feel he should be forced to justify himself. He simply twitched his lips into a smile. That the gentleman was reticent, nervous even, was obvious from the sheen of sweat around his upper lip and on his forehead. He continued, "My m—" but then stopped himself. It seemed he had no wish to incriminate his employer by disclosing his or her sex. He bit his lip and started once more. "I am bidden to find Captain Flynn. He owes a great deal of money to an associate of mine who now finds himself in jail because of his debts."

Lupton nodded. "And you believe Flynn has the diamond?"

The gentleman looked uncomfortable. He fingered his stock to try and loosen it. "You know about that?"

Lupton let out a little laugh. "It is the fodder of the newssheets. All of London knows that a diamond was stolen from a grave at Boughton Hall."

The gentleman took out his kerchief and dabbed his forehead. He might as well have been waving a white flag in surrender. Lupton knew he had wrong-footed him. "There are grounds to believe that it is in his possession, yes," he conceded.

"So you would have him sell it to pay off this unfortunate gentleman's debts?"

"In summary, yes."

"By all accounts it is a very large diamond. I read it is the size of a plover's egg. Surely such a stone will fetch many thousands of pounds?"

"Perhaps."

"And you are offering two guineas to find this scoundrel Flynn, asking me to risk my own life in the bargain, and bring him to you?"

The gentleman suddenly realized he was being played for a fool. He leaned forward in his seat.

"Now look here!" he snarled indignantly.

Lupton cast his gaze at the men around him as if he thought he might draw courage from their steely business acumen. "I will accept two," he said, taking another sip of his coffee.

The gentleman's back stiffened as if he had snatched a victory from the jaws of defeat. He nodded and his lips curled. "Good," he retorted. But his conquest was short-lived.

"Yes. Two and twenty percent of the value of the diamond," added Lupton.

The other man's face flushed crimson. "What!" he growled.

"You forget, sir. I have friends in high places. 'Twould not be hard to find out on whose behalf you are acting. And I suspect your employer would not appreciate your actions being broadcast among polite society."

"You would blackmail me, sir!"

A huddle of merchants at a nearby table switched 'round in unison, hoping to witness a fight. But Lupton pulled the conversation back from the brink. "Like all these good men around us," he said, gesturing toward the merchants, "I would merely strike a fair bargain. I have a service I can provide, and if I succeed, you will have the wherewithal to pay me for it. What could be fairer than that?"

The gentleman drummed the table. It was clear a strategy was playing through his mind. Finally he declared grudgingly, "Very well."

"Excellent," said Lupton, offering his hand to seal the deal. The gentleman took it reluctantly. "Give me a week and you shall have your man." He enjoyed the thrill of the chase, especially when there was such a sizable reward at the end of it.

Lupton watched the gentleman stride out of the coffeehouse. He, too, was eager to be gone from the place, and rose to leave immediately after. He now had a mission to undertake, inquiries to make. He would call in a few favors from his old company associates, prod a few vipers' nests. He would surely turn up some information that would lead him to his quarry.

So preoccupied was he in planning his modus operandi that he did not notice a shadowy fellow seated only a few feet away from him. Bundled by the nearby chimney breast, his hat planted so far down on his head that his face could not be seen, he had been listening to every word. In front of him was a dish of coffee, which he stirred slowly and deliberately. He watched Lupton for a few more moments, then began to drink. His was a hatred that bided its time.

## Chapter 35

Thomas's latest encounter with Sir Stephen Gandy had ended disastrously, as he had feared it would. He had held his breath as the coroner flicked through his report and settled straight on its conclusion. It was not, of course, the one that he wanted. Thomas had found no evidence to connect Captain Flynn with his servant's murder, and in a fit of pique, Sir Stephen had flung the document on the fire in his office.

"A waste of your time and mine, Silkstone!" the coroner had exclaimed as the flames licked the report he'd consigned to the grate.

So, newly returned from his bruising encounter and having fulfilled his duty to examine Mrs. Hastings, Thomas found himself free to travel to Boughton. He planned to spend two days there. He hoped it was not too much to dare that Lydia would have already forgiven him for not attending Sir Montagu's funeral. He knew she would have missed him sorely, but Thomas was sure he could still be of some comfort to her.

Upstairs in his room in Hollen Street, he began to pack a few clothes into his small trunk. Then he remembered. Walking over to the window, he opened the drawer of his writing desk and took out a round case in red leather. And there it was: a modest sapphire surrounded by small diamonds and set on a gold band. It had belonged to his late mother and Lydia was the only woman he had ever wished to wear it, but he had not given it to her—yet. They had never formally announced their betrothal. There had been a tacit understanding between them when he rode away from Boughton after her mother died. Six months later, however, she had shattered his dreams when she told him she was breaking off their unofficial engagement. After that, of course, she had tried to take her own life, and then they had searched for Richard. In among all the upheaval and the drama, their own future seemed to have been lost. Not that he had abandoned any hope that Lydia would one day consent to wed him again. A light had always burned inside him. Surely now was the right time to propose?

He closed the case and placed it in his coat pocket. He would pick his moment and then he would ask her, once more, to be his wife. With Sir Montagu gone, surely she had no reason to refuse. He smiled to himself as he patted his pocket, but then he looked out of the window once more when he thought he heard a carriage pull up outside. He was right, and the sight wiped the smile from his face. He thought it odd. To his knowledge no visitors were expected, and in his experience unexpected visitors usually brought bad news.

Deciding to ignore the carriage, he returned to his packing until, moments later, he heard voices in the hallway. He stopped, then looked out of the window once more. The carriage was still there, and now footsteps were coming up the stairs. He recognized the familiar tread.

"Yes, Mistress Finesilver?" he called through the closed door.

"Dr. Silkstone," she told him, out of breath and clearly out of sorts, "Sir Theodisius Pettigrew is downstairs to see you."

"Sir Theodisius?" repeated Thomas, opening wide the door. His first thought was for Lydia. Had something terrible happened? He brushed past his peevish housekeeper, forcing her to flatten herself against the wall as he rushed onto the landing.

"Sir Theodisius!" he called down, then began his descent, striding two stairs at a time.

The Oxford coroner's great bulk was standing in the center of the hallway. He lifted up his large head to greet Thomas. He was clearly feeling the heat and was mopping his brow.

"Silkstone! Pray do not alarm yourself, man!" he cried as Thomas made it to the half landing.

"No?" asked a breathless Thomas, carrying on down the stairs. He felt his chest muscles relax at such an assurance.

"No. I bring good news!" replied the coroner.

"Then you are even more welcome than usual, sir," replied Thomas, finally making it to the foot of the stairs.

"Yes, dear fellow. I bring you a visitor." Spreading his arms wide, like some theatrical impresario, Sir Theodisius shifted his rotund frame to reveal a petite figure behind him.

"Lydia!" exclaimed Thomas. He rushed forward and, forgetting all decorum, embraced her. She offered no resistance and allowed Thomas to take both her hands in his.

"What goes on here?" Dr. Carruthers's cheerful inquiry interrupted their reunion. The old anatomist appeared at the doorway of his study, waving his white stick.

"Lady Lydia is here, sir, with Sir Theodisius," Thomas explained.

Young Richard, Nurse Pring, and Eliza followed on over the threshold, and in an instant all was noise and bluster in the house.

Dr. Carruthers beamed. "What a wonderful surprise!" he chuckled.

"Indeed, sir. Most wonderful," replied Thomas, forgetting his wound and playfully scooping up Richard in his arms.

"Then let us adjourn to the drawing room," declared the old anatomist, tapping his stick excitedly on the floorboards. "And we shall have some tea."

"And perhaps some cake?" suggested Sir Theodisius.

"Cake, yes. And muffins. I shall call my brother, too." Dr. Carruthers turned toward the stairs—"Oliver! Oliver!"—then back again. "Oh, what a time we shall have!" he cried.

Hooking his arm into Sir Theodisius's, the old anatomist headed up the stairs to the drawing room on the second floor. The young earl took Nurse Pring's hand. Thomas held back with Lydia.

"I planned to catch the coach to Oxford later today," he told her, taking her hand in his.

"Then we are fortunate that our paths did not cross," she said earnestly.

He saw something troubling in her expression and lowered his voice. "What is it? Is it Flynn?"

She nodded. "Your letter said he was missing, and I have learned that Richard or I, or both of us, may be beneficiaries of Sir Montagu's will." She swallowed hard. "Sir Theodisius thought it best if we stay at his London house for a few days until the captain is apprehended."

Thomas nodded. "He is right. As long as no one finds out that you are here, then you are safer than at Boughton." He squeezed her hand tightly. "Flynn will soon be found, I am sure of it. Lupton is on the case."

"Mr. Lupton?" Lydia pulled away.

Thomas understood her reaction. Lupton was, after all, the man who had tried and almost succeeded in killing him. "We are reconciled," he explained. "I can assure you he wants to help us." He corrected himself. "Or rather to help *you*." Lupton's jealousy, he knew, could never be fully exorcised.

She nodded and smiled. "Very well," she whispered.

Thomas returned her smile. "Then come. Let us join the others," he said, holding out his arm for her. Lydia took it, and together they walked up to the drawing room.

By now Professor Carruthers had joined the party and introductions had been made.

"Come, come, you two," called Dr. Carruthers as he heard Thomas and Lydia enter. "Sajiv here is going to make us tea the Indian way," he announced gleefully.

Thomas shot a look at Mistress Finesilver, standing redundant in the corner. "And perhaps we might have some of Mistress Finesilver's excellent pastries, too," Thomas said, looking directly at the housekeeper. "I know jam tarts are Master Richard's particular favorite."

The kettle was already singing in the hearth, and Sajiv set to work making the tea.

"This is such a pleasant surprise," reiterated the old anatomist, shaking his head as if he could not believe his good fortune.

Sir Theodisius's face wobbled as he nodded. "We agreed it would be best for all concerned," he said, then added, "given the circumstances." He shot a glance at the young naukar, who was pouring out the tea. It was clear he did not want to say too much in front of a servant, and the professor picked up on his suspicion.

"You may talk freely in front of Sajiv, sir. His English is really quite limited," Professor Carruthers told him, watching the youth grasp a particularly large lump of sugar in the silver tongs.

Seeing this, Lydia politely raised her hand. "Not so much sugar, if you please," she said, switching her appeal to the professor for fear of not being understood.

The professor smiled. "Have no fear," he told her, swiftly producing an implement from his pocket. "Here," he said, leaning forward to the sugar bowl and unsheathing a knife from an elaborately decorated scabbard. In one fell chop, he had severed the large lump in two. Lydia caught sight of the curved blade at the same time as Thomas. They swapped an awkward glance.

Professor Carruthers saw the exchange. Latching onto Thomas's thoughts, he butted in with an explanation. "A khanjar, Dr. Silkstone," he ventured, slipping the dagger back into its scabbard. "It is most practical. I find it especially useful when peeling fruit, particularly mangoes."

The perfectly plausible explanation left Thomas feeling a little uncomfortable. It had become his habit to read meaning into the slightest detail, sometimes to his own embarrassment. "Yes, very practical, I am sure, sir," he agreed, picking up his bowl to sip the tea.

Sir Theodisius rescued the young doctor with a question for the professor. "How long have you lived in India, sir?" he asked.

"More years than I care to remember," came the reply. "But I still find its diversity and customs endlessly fascinating. And I hope to persuade my fellow Britons of their merit, too."

"A laudable aim indeed," said the coroner, his fork poised over a large slice of chocolate cake.

Much of the rest of the afternoon was spent in conversation

about life in Hyderabad. Thomas was glad that any mention of Captain Flynn had been brushed aside. He would need to talk in confidence with Sir Theodisius and with Lydia to inform them of developments, but he knew that such conversations would best be conducted in private. Any indiscretion might make the captain even harder to track down.

The chimes of the mantel clock brought proceedings to a close.

"Good lord, is that the time?" asked Sir Theodisius, licking sticky crumbs from his fingers. "We must away, my dear," he said to Lydia. "Lady Hattie will be expecting us."

Thomas and the professor rose to bid them farewell, but only the former accompanied his guests into the hallway. His intention was to catch a moment with Lydia.

"I am forgiven?" he whispered to her as Mistress Finesilver handed Sir Theodisius his hat.

"There is nothing to forgive," she replied with a smile as Eliza and Nurse Pring arrived from below stairs. Aware that they were being watched, Lydia offered Thomas her hand to kiss. "We shall meet again soon, Dr. Silkstone," she told him formally.

The coroner echoed the sentiment. "Indeed we shall, Silkstone." Both men knew there were pressing matters to discuss.

"Soon," Thomas repeated as he watched the party walk down the steps and, one by one, climb into the waiting carriage. He patted his frock coat pocket. The ring was still there, and very shortly he would, he hoped, be placing it on Lydia's finger.

# Chapter 36

There was a new spring in Nicholas Lupton's step. Like a man just cleared of the clap, he strode cheerfully down Fenchurch Street toward the Magpie Ale House. The air was as steamy as the hot springs at Bath after a heavy shower, and mist rose from gutters and ruts in the roads. He leapt over a filthy puddle with ease and even avoided the splashes from a chamber pot that was being discharged just ahead of him. His fortunes seemed to have changed. He'd quarreled with Sir Montagu and left Boughton in a rage. Then he'd allowed his jealousy over Lydia Farrell to get the better of him when he challenged Silkstone to a duel. But he'd seen the inside of a jail cell and lived to tell another tale, and now he was on what might, hopefully, prove a most lucrative mission.

This was not a salubrious area. Every few yards he had thrown a sly look over his shoulder to make sure he was not being followed. It was not yet dark, but everywhere there were shadows. The stern stock brick terraces faced one another across the narrow lanes, blocking out the fading sun. He'd thought about hiring a moon-curser to ease his path, but he knew that their sort could never be trusted, either. So he'd decided to chance his hand and venture out alone, although he did have an ace up his sleeve. Or rather a pistol in his pocket. He patted his coat lightly, as if to reassure himself. He hoped he would not have to use it, but he would not hesitate to do so.

The inn was tall and thin, and from the open windows, clouds of pipe smoke billowed and mingled with bawdy laughter. Taking a deep breath, he went inside. There was an odd smell in here, too. It was not just the reek of the sweat or the dirt, but a sweet, pungent, spicy smell that was unfamiliar to him. He had felt ill at ease in the coffeehouse, but scanning the motley collection of patrons, he could tell this place was a hundred times worse. As he looked down at the sawdust that covered the floor, he couldn't help but notice the splats of newly spilled blood, either. It was a sailors' tavern, one where jack-tars rubbed shoulders with seamen from the four corners of the globe. Women with bulging bosoms that spilled out from their bodices like foaming beer from tankards sat on men's knees. There was spitting and there was cussing. There were lascars, too. This was the place the Indian seamen favored. And this was the place he would begin his hunt for Patrick Flynn.

Heads turned as he walked to the bar. A one-eyed sailor barked something at him as he elbowed his way toward the landlord. He could not make out what he said, although he gathered, from the scowl, it was not complimentary.

"Rum," he cried above the din. In his hand he brandished a half crown. It was the only language they understood in taverns like this. He looked nervously about him. He would start with the huddle of lascars who sat on a settle at the far end. It was unlikely that they spoke English, but his money would do the talking. He had just begun to make his way over to them when he felt a tap on his shoulder. He turned and dropped his gaze to see a short young Indian at his side.

"Yes?"

The youth was not dressed in the white uniform of the lascars, but wore a silk turban and a heavier embroidered robe that reached below his knees.

"You seek information, sahib?" the Indian asked with a knowing look in his dark eyes.

"How do . . . ?"

The youth made an odd movement of his head, as if it were held onto his neck by a thin thread. "Men like you, sahib, only come to place like this if they look for someone or something," he said. "You have money, yes?"

Lupton frowned. He had not expected to find such a helpful accomplice so soon after setting foot in the tavern, but then they both spoke the same language. The Indian was already holding out his palm.

"First we talk," Lupton told him firmly.

They walked over to a table in the corner, curious eyes following them until they sat down.

"What you want to know, sahib?" The Indian cut to the chase.

Lupton leaned forward. "I am looking for a captain, from the East India Company."

The youth stuck out his bottom lip and nodded. "You know name?"

"Flynn. Captain Patrick Flynn. Red hair," he told him, pointing to his own head. "Irishman," he added, but the Indian returned a blank look. It was clear the term "Irishman" was lost on him. "He may be trying to sell a diamond."

At the mention of the word, the Indian's eyes lit up. He suddenly looked very animated. "Diamond, yes. I know sahib with diamond," he cried.

His sudden outburst caused heads to swivel, and Lupton sprang forward and clamped his hand over the Indian's mouth. "Do you want to get me killed?" he growled, before relaxing his hold.

"Surely not, sahib," replied the youth, his head rolling from side to side.

Lupton took a deep breath to steady himself. "Then tell me what you know," he said, producing a silver crown from his pocket.

The Indian eyed the coin as if it were some sort of charm. "I see this man earlier today. I know where he is."

Lupton narrowed his eyes. "You do?" He was not expecting the path that led to Flynn to be so smooth. "He is near?"

"Not far," replied the Indian, his eyes still latched onto the coin.

Lupton suddenly tossed it into the air, caught it on the back of one hand, then slid it across the table with the other. "There'll be another one of those when I find Flynn."

"Very good, sahib," said the Indian. He bit into the crown with his back teeth. They shone very white in the tavern's candle-light. "I take you now."

Lupton drained his glass of rum. He needed the courage. He could not believe his luck. If this Indian did indeed lead him to Flynn, it would be the easiest money he'd made in a while. He only hoped the captain would come quietly. He tapped his pocket. The pistol was still there. He rose and followed the youth, who was already halfway to the door.

By now the moon was obscured by a blanket of cloud and more rain had begun to fall. The Indian dangled a lantern in his hand and lit their way, threading through an alleyway off the main thoroughfare. As they walked at a steady pace, Lupton tried to get his bearings. He sniffed the air. They were heading toward the river; the tang of the Thames began to fill his nostrils. They were making for the Pool of London.

After ten minutes or more, the rain was still pelting down. The narrow dwellings and occasional taverns gave way to warehouses. Avoiding puddles and ruts, they turned into a wider street, lined with a ramshackle collection of buildings. Pulleys and winches protruded from the fascias. The low portals of the city had all but disappeared and given way to doors double the height and width of ordinary ones. These were where the cargoes were stored, full to the brim with hogsheads and crates, bales and barrels. Behind these monstrous doors lay wares from all over the world.

In the shadows, Lupton saw a man ease himself against the wall. Somewhere nearby a man grunted and a woman yelped. A dog chained to the wall, no doubt to ward off intruders, barked ferociously as they passed.

"Not far now, sahib," assured the Indian in a hoarse whisper.

They turned the corner and stopped under the eaves of another warehouse. The Indian lifted the lantern, and Lupton could see a small door set into a larger one. The youth fumbled with the lock, and the door creaked open.

"You come!" He beckoned as he stepped over the high threshold.

Lupton dipped his head and followed through the narrow aperture and closed the door behind him. He was glad to be out of the rain. The pool of light from the lantern did not reveal much at first, but once his eyes had adjusted to the semidarkness, Lupton looked 'round. To his left was a mountain of barrels, piled high on top of one another. To his right there were bales of what appeared to be cotton, perhaps. Next to them were bulging sacks that exuded exotic aromas. But something was not quite right. Lightly he touched his pocket, reassuring himself that he still had the upper hand.

"Why have you brought me here?" he asked. His voice was tinged with suspicion.

In the lamplight, he could see the Indian look slightly indignant.

"Why, sahib? Because you wished to see Captain Flynn, yes?" He tilted his head in the odd way he had before. Lupton could not be sure he was not being mocked.

"Yes."

"Then, please." Once more the Indian held out his arm and beckoned. "Come, sahib. I show you." He turned and ventured farther into the canyon of barrels and sacks. Lupton followed warily. He watched the Indian a few paces ahead, then dipped his hand in his pocket. Suddenly there was a squeak. He saw something in the darkness scurry across his path, and he let out a muted cry. The Indian turned. "A rat, sahib," he said with a shrug. "Just a rat."

Lupton felt his heart pounding in his chest. Now was the time to reach for his pistol; now was the time to show this Indian he was not to be played for a fool. He had just fumbled in his pocket when his guide turned and stood stock-still in front of him so that Lupton almost barged into him.

"What the . . . ?"

The Indian was beaming. "You say you want to see Captain Flynn?" he said. Holding his lantern aloft, he pivoted 'round.

"Well?" queried Lupton, pulling back his head and blinking away the brightness of the lamp.

"Well . . . here he is," announced the youth.

Lupton narrowed his eyes, peering into the gloom. "Where?" he snapped.

"Just there," said the Indian, still smiling and bobbing his head.

Lupton took three cautious steps ahead, where the lantern rays faintly illuminated yet more barrels and crates. He could see very little beyond, but he suddenly became aware of something hanging in his field of vision. He started and his mouth went dry. As he peered into the blackness, he realized what was before him: a pair of feet dangled in the air at eye level. In terror, he cocked back his head to see they were attached to a body.

"My God!" he cried as the shock shot through his chest and down his arms. He plunged his hand in his pocket to grab his pistol, but before he could do so, there was a blow to the back of his head. The gun fell out of his hand and he hit the ground. Through blurry eyes he realized the Indian was standing over him with a curved dagger.

"No!" he screamed as the blade fell. He managed to roll away to the side and, grasping one of the sacks, hauled himself up.

The Indian took another swipe at him, his blade swishing through the air. He missed but slashed through a nearby sack, sending its contents spilling onto the floor in a cascade of ground ginger. Lupton ran on, toward the door. Close behind him he could hear the youth's footsteps and the flailing of the dagger as it sliced through the darkness. His breath was failing him fast, and his legs were turning to lead. Reaching out into the blackness, he grabbed a small cask and, turning, threw it at his attacker. He heard him cry out, then fall with a dull thud against a sack. Only four or five seconds separated Lupton from death. He had to make it to the door. A chink of light slashed through a gap under the doorway, acting as his guide. He headed for it and saw that the handle was within his reach when suddenly he felt the sharp rasp of steel cut his arm. He let out a yelp and staggered, his legs crumpling under him. In the blackness he heard the Indian grunt as he lifted the blade above his head once more and brought it down again. Lupton raised his arm to protect his head, and this time the blade sliced into his shoulder. He could feel warm liquid coursing down his arm as he lunged for the door and careened headlong out of it. Summoning all his strength and clutching his bleeding arm, he staggered down the street, seeking the shelter of the shadows. His strength was deserting him and his vision was blurring.

The Indian stood at the warehouse doorway, his dagger dancing between his fingers. His head switched left, then right; then he looked down onto the cobbles. Blood was mixing with the earlier rainwater that still flowed in rivulets down the gutter. English blood. He returned his dagger to his belt. There was no point in pursuing Lupton any farther. He was already a dead man.

*Chapter 37*

The carriage carrying a dapperly dressed Thomas pulled up outside Sir Theodisius Pettigrew's London town house. Gone was his usual black frock coat, and in its stead one of royal blue with silver buttons that was worn only on the most important of occasions. He had even donned a wig. He was not sure that it suited him, although Lydia had told him it gave him more gravitas. "Lydia," he whispered under his breath, as he tugged at his tightly tied stock. He tapped his pocket. The small box containing the ring was there. Tonight, perhaps? But everything had to be right. No, not merely right. Ordered. Precise. Perfect.

Earlier that day he'd received a message from Sir Percivall Pott. It informed him that, unfortunately, he would be unable to attend Mrs. Hastings's dinner party that evening due to a bad attack of the gout. Naturally the revered surgeon had informed his hostess, and she had been most insistent that Thomas still attend, but bring a guest of his own choosing. The young doctor had jumped at the chance. Lydia had been his obvious choice to accompany him, and now he found himself dressed up like a turkey at Thanksgiving, calling to collect his beloved.

He lifted the knocker on the front door. This was the first time he had escorted her in public for at least two years. Not since just before the Great Fogg had they attended any social function together. The prospect filled him with a new sense of excitement.

There was a second reason for his eagerness, too. The evening would present another opportunity for him to pry a little further into why Mrs. Motte might have an interest in the whereabouts of Captain Flynn. He assumed she would be present, but he knew he would have to tread warily, so as not to arouse any suspicion in her.

The maid ushered Thomas inside Sir Theodisius's London residence just as Lydia was descending the stairs. Dressed in a robe of blue silk, with her chestnut hair piled high and studded with pearls, she appeared to Thomas more beautiful than she had ever looked before. A wave of happiness made him want to rush up to her there and then and ask for her hand in marriage, but he checked himself.

"You look enchanting," he told her, kissing her hand.

Hearing the voices outside, Sir Theodisius appeared in the doorway of his study. At the sight of Lydia, his fat face split into a smile.

"All the diamonds of Golconda could not outshine you tonight, my dear," he told her as Eliza handed her a shawl. "Eh, Silkstone?"

"Indeed no," agreed Thomas, wishing he had been the one to pay his beloved such an eloquent compliment.

"I hear Mrs. Hastings's Indian cooks can conjure up some interesting dishes," Sir Theodisius remarked, suddenly changing the subject. He rubbed his own large belly. "Although I fear they might not agree with my constitution."

"We shall tell you all about it, dear Sir Theo," said Lydia, pressing her gloved hands into his. She saw his eyes glass over, like a proud father who realizes his daughter is fully grown.

"You must not keep the driver waiting," he told her.

She glanced at Thomas, waiting by the open door, and he offered her his arm. "Nor my handsome companion," she replied, taking it with a smile. The night was theirs.

Marian Hastings was greeting her guests in a room she called her salon. Present were Major Scott and the sour-faced gentleman who had accompanied her from India, William Markham. Of Mrs. Motte there was no sign. When Thomas and Lydia arrived at the door, all eyes turned toward them. Mrs. Hastings, her gown embroidered with lizard-green emeralds and her neck adorned with diamonds, moved forward to greet them. Yet the look on her face registered surprise and not a little annoyance.

"Dr. Silkstone," she gushed, fluttering her eyelashes at him and flapping her fan. "Such a shame zat poor Sir Percivall vas indisposed," she told him pointedly. Then, turning to Lydia, she asked: "And zis is?"

"Lady Lydia Farrell," replied Thomas, quickly. Lydia dipped a curtsy, and Mrs. Hastings replied with another. When she rose, however, the look on her face was anything but welcoming. "You did say—"

"Lady Lydia Farrell." She broke off Thomas's explanation and repeated the name as if it meant something to her. "A pleasure to meet you," she said, but her smile was clearly feigned.

Just then Bibby Motte appeared at the doorway, looking resplendent in yellow silk, and Marian Hastings ushered her companion over to make introductions. "Ah, Mrs. Motte," she said with a smile. "Dr. Silkstone you know, and zis is Lady Lydia Farrell."

At the mention of the latter's name, Bibby Motte's eyes darted back to her friend's, but she quickly recovered to curtsy to Lydia, then offered her gloved hand to Thomas.

"A pleasure," she said to Lydia, but Thomas was not sure she meant it.

A moment later dinner was announced and all the guests went through into the dining room straightaway. They sat at a large rectangular table with Mrs. Hastings at its head. As Thomas had anticipated, the governor-general's wife held sway. She was the queen of her court, and those around the table with her were mere players. At first, the conversation was kept light and frivolous. The weather was discussed, as were the ladies' initial impressions of London. The meal was served in a lavish manner, even though those dining numbered only six. Servants wearing brightly colored turbans carried great platters of spiced meats and vegetables. There was chicken cooked with rice, pistachios, and sultanas and a dish of yellow lentils served with flour pancakes.

"This is excellent fare," remarked Thomas. "Your cooks are

most skilled," he added, thinking of Mistress Finesilver's miserable offerings.

"I am glad it is to your taste, Dr. Silkstone," replied Mrs. Hastings. She put down her fork and fixed her guest with an inquiring look, as if to signify that she was done with small talk. "So, Dr. Silkstone," she began, "you are an American." Her manner was almost accusatory, as if hailing from that land was at worst a crime and at best a misdemeanor. "From vereabouts do you come?"

Thomas slid a look at Lydia. Both had half expected such an inquisition. He dabbed his mouth with his napkin. "I was born and raised in Philadelphia, madam," he replied politely.

"Philadelphia, eh?" repeated Scott. "I've heard 'tis quite civilized there." He raised a brow and waited for the mistresses Hastings and Motte to respond with titters, which they did most predictably.

Thomas took such behavior in his stride. He refused to rise to the bait. After almost ten years living in London, he was used to such ribald comments at the expense of either his countrymen or himself. "Its inhabitants enjoy many of the luxuries of their British counterparts," he replied with a measured nod, then added mischievously: "Most of their children even attend schools."

"So what brought you here?" asked Mrs. Motte. She had not joined in the conversation a great deal and appeared very reserved, but her question seemed to show a genuine interest in Thomas.

"My profession, madam," he replied. "My father is a doctor, and he knew of the work of a noted London anatomist. I was accepted as his apprentice before the war, and I have stayed here ever since."

"Zen America's loss is our gain, Dr. Silkstone," commented Mrs. Hastings, a coquettish glint in her eye.

The rest of the meal passed pleasantly enough, and the conversation was kept light until it was time for the women to leave the men to their port and pipes. It was at this point that Thomas hoped to make more headway in his investigations, subtly questioning Scott and Markham in an effort to delve below the surface of this whole murky affair. The servants placed decanters of port and sack on the table, and then one of them produced large pipes that Thomas supposed to be made of bamboo.

"You look perplexed, Silkstone," ventured Markham, seeing Thomas's expression. "Have you never seen an opium pipe before?"

Thomas had to confess he had not. "I use the poppy to ease pain in my profession, sir, but I have not smoked it recreationally."

Scott smirked. "Then it is high time you tried, Silkstone," he told the doctor, taking a pipe and allowing a servant to light it for him.

Thomas felt awkward and intrigued at the same time. He knew that opium could have a most extraordinary effect on a man's behavior and intellect. He believed Professor Carruthers to take it, and now these two. He also knew that whoever murdered Sir Montagu had smoked it, as well. "I shall stick with my usual tobacco, gentlemen, if you please, for this evening."

Markham shrugged. "Of course, you are escorting the lovely Lady Lydia." He smiled as he puffed at the pipe. "I am sure you will need all your faculties about you for later."

Ignoring the insinuation, Thomas lit his pipe. "So you gentlemen knew Captain Farrell?" After witnessing his hostess's reaction to the name, he decided to call the men's bluff. It paid dividends.

Markham, too, lit his pipe, but his face hardened. "They called him 'Ring' Farrell on account of the diamond on his finger," he replied. "Rumor had it that he even murdered for it."

Thomas wondered if they had heard news of the robbery at Boughton. "So he had quite a reputation in India?"

Scott, an unlit pipe in his hand, had remained relatively diffident up until this point. Now, however, he strode toward the mantelpiece and turned his fire on Thomas. "You have some nerve bringing that woman here," he suddenly blurted.

"I beg your pardon?" Thomas was taken aback.

"You must have known that Farrell and his sidekicks used to hire out their services to Philip Francis." The major was vehement in his accusation, pointing the stem of his pipe at the doctor. "And it was Farrell who entrapped Thomas Motte because he was one of Hastings's staunchest allies."

Now Markham joined in. "Farrell, Lavington, and Flynn," he snarled. "They did everything in their power to bring down Hastings. And now it looks like they have succeeded, albeit later than they would have wished."

Thomas recalled Dr. Carruthers's mention of a duel between Hastings and this Francis. The latter had been seriously wounded, but had recovered and returned to England three years ago. Yet he still bore a grudge. Thomas needed to know more. He feigned ignorance and shook his head. "I do not follow," he said.

"Do not play the innocent abroad, Silkstone," flashed Scott. "Hastings is isolated. Thanks to Farrell and his cronies picking off all his allies, he'll not last another year in post. There's even talk of his impeachment. Philip Francis is in league with Charles James Fox to bring him to his knees."

"And you choose to invite Farrell's widow as your guest to this house?" Markham was shaking his head.

Thomas suddenly thought of Lydia. He was used to being treated discourteously by English gentry, but she was not. Fearing she might also be suffering, he rose. "Gentlemen," he said with a bow, "thank you for enlightening me. I now realize why Lady Lydia and I are not welcome and apologize if our presence caused offense. I shall take my leave. Good night to you both."

Not bothering to wait for a servant to show him out, Thomas stalked into the hallway and asked a sepoy to notify Mrs. Hastings of his intention to leave, taking Lydia with him. Keen not to sour the atmosphere, however, he decided to invent an excuse. A moment later both ladies emerged from a nearby room. Marian Hastings looked agitated and Lydia perplexed.

"Dr. Silkstone, I am told you have to leave," said his hostess.

"A patient, I fear," lied Thomas. "I must attend to him urgently."

Lydia frowned, and looked at him quizzically. Suspecting something was gravely amiss, she turned to Mrs. Hastings. "Please forgive us," she said.

"'Tis a matter of life or death," Thomas said assuredly.

His hostess's bejeweled hand reached up to her throat in alarm. "In zat case, you must surely hurry," she replied.

"We surely must," agreed Thomas. "Thank you for a very interesting evening," he said with a shallow bow. And with that he steered Lydia away by the arm and made for their waiting carriage.

*Chapter 38*

"I should never have asked you to come," fumed Thomas, shaking his head. As he sat by Lydia's side on their way back to Sir Theodisius's house, he grasped her hand and held it tightly.

Unsure as to what irked him so, she shook her head. "Will you please tell me what is going on?"

He paused to look at her for a moment. She seemed quite composed. "Mrs. Hastings and Mrs. Motte," he began. "They did not insult you?"

Lydia shrugged. "They were civil enough, if a little distant," she replied. "Besides, I am growing accustomed to being regarded as an outcast," she added.

"An outcast?" He frowned.

Lydia rolled her eyes. "The Farrell name is a blight. I know Michael did some very bad things, and as his widow, it seems I must bear part of the blame."

Thomas clutched both her hands. "You know that is not true, my love. You cannot blame yourself for Michael's misdeeds."

She shook her head. "Clearly other people do."

"They insulted you?" asked Thomas. "About Michael?"

Lydia's eyes slid away from his. "No." She shook her head, but her reply was less than convincing.

"What did they say?" urged Thomas.

Her eyes returned to his. "They did not say anything. It was their manner toward me."

Thomas sat back in the carriage. He was relieved that nothing had been said to hurt Lydia's feelings, but she would not let his behavior rest.

"But 'tis you who owes me an explanation," she told him. "I know there is no sick patient."

Feeling his chastisement justified, Thomas turned to her once more but paused, thinking how to frame his words.

"I am sorry to have whisked you away like that, but I feared that the ladies might turn on you."

"Turn on me?" She looked shocked.

Thomas cleared his throat. "You see I learned tonight something of the governor-general's archenemy."

Lydia lifted a brow. "Philip Francis?"

"You know of him?"

"All of England and indeed India knows of the enmity between the two men. They fought a duel and—" She broke off suddenly when she saw the look on Thomas's face. "You are going to tell me that Michael was in Francis's service?"

Thomas nodded. "And Lavington and—"

"Patrick Flynn." Lydia dived in to finish the list. "You cannot think he would harm Mrs. Hastings, could you?"

The thought had occurred to Thomas the moment he knew of the association. "I fear that perhaps he may," he replied. "But can you think of any connection between Sir Montagu and either Hastings or Francis?"

After a short pause, Lydia shook her head. "You know I was never informed about his business dealings, although—" She broke off.

"Yes?"

"Perhaps Mr. Lupton might know something."

Thomas nodded. "You may well be right. I shall ask him as soon as I am able." He was due to meet with the former Boughton steward the following day to hear him report back on his mission to track down Patrick Flynn. He would also quiz him over how Lydia's card came to be in the possession of Flynn's mysterious caller. "Finding the captain is our only hope of ever discovering who killed Sir Montagu," he told her.

"I know," said Lydia, looking at Thomas. There was both a resignation and an understanding in her tone, and she smiled at him tenderly.

A moment later the carriage had arrived at their destination and Thomas was helping Lydia down the folding steps. "I am so sorry," he said as they stood in the forecourt of Sir Theodisius's town house.

"For what?" Puzzled, she tilted her head.

"For putting you in harm's way tonight," he said. He felt his heart beat faster, and he bent his head to kiss her hand.

"Nonsense," she upbraided him. "And at least you have learned something more to help you in your investigation."

"I have," he conceded, thinking about Farrell's connection to Philip Francis. He paused and looked at her. For a split second he wondered if he should ask her, there and then, to marry him. He heard her catch her breath, as if she was expecting him to say something profound, but he suddenly shrank from the idea. It did not feel right. He took a small step back from her, but it might as well have been a voyage home across the Atlantic. The moment was lost.

"May I call on you tomorrow?" he asked her.

He heard her breath escape in a barely discernible sigh. "I would like that very much," she replied.

*Chapter 39*

That night, as she lay in her feather bed, thousands of miles away from her husband, Bibby Motte cast her mind back over the evening's events. Had she known that Michael Farrell's widow would be at dinner, she would have steered clear, feigned sickness, or tiredness, or both. It was so hard for her to try to make polite conversation when all she wanted to do was tell the world how her beloved husband had been so wronged and betrayed. And then she was reminded so cruelly. Hearing the name Farrell took her back to a night nine years ago that had sealed Thomas Motte's miserable fate.

It had been hot; too hot for an Englishman, as her husband would so often say. The home they shared stood on the other side of the Musi River from Hyderabad. Their residence was on the water's edge, but even the breeze along the river did little to cool the air. During the monsoon season, the Musi was turned into a raging torrent, but back then it was little more than a slow, fordable stream.

From her bedroom window, Bibby Motte had watched her husband pace the veranda. She knew that he had long ago dismissed his punkah wallah, but two sepoys hovered on the threshold, their daggers clearly visible at their belts. They would ensure he was not threatened in any way. At least she could be confident that his personal safety was not at issue.

Once more her husband had wiped away the beads of sweat

that gathered on his forehead. She could tell he was going over the deal again in his mind. Captain Michael Farrell, dashing, debonair officer that he was, had come to the house for their first meeting. There were two others with him, Lavington and Flynn, but Farrell had been the talker—charm personified, she recalled—and Motte had fallen for his wiles. He had given him what he wanted, a length of fabric covered in strange symbols that no Englishman could understand that he had purloined on his travels in Sumbhulpoor. Her husband had confided in her that he considered it a worthless trifle. "Of course there are stories that surround it," he had told her. "But this land seems to thrive on stories." Clearly the Irishman, however, did take heed of the wild tales, believing the embroidered scroll to be some sort of map of the diamond mines. In return for it, the officer had assured her husband of a gem beyond compare. Still uncut, it weighed nearly half an ounce, he was told. In the hands of an expert it could be hewn into one large stone of at least four hundred carats—a cushion brilliant, perhaps, like the famous Pitt diamond—together with several secondary ones. That was what her husband had gambled on. That was why he had handed over twelve thousand pagodas to retain his interest. It was a down payment, Farrell had told him, and a sign of their mutual trust.

Bibby Motte recalled how, that night, her husband had turned toward the river and squinted into the gloom, looking for any lights from a budgerow or other craft. He saw none. But his expression had changed. Lifting her gaze, she wondered what clearly troubled him and found the answer on the horizon. Hyderabad was lit by a bright red light. It seemed there was a fire in the city. Had her husband's plans gone up in smoke, too? Another hour must have passed before he admitted that he had been deceived, or let down, or both. He dismissed the sepoys.

Slipping on her silk robe, Bibby Motte left her bed and joined her husband on the veranda. Draping her arms 'round his neck, she had urged him to come to bed. But it seemed he was not interested in seduction. He was too enraged.

"I've been a fool," he told her, his voice crackling with anger. "I'll wager those three scoundrels will soon be boarding a ship and making their way home to England to spend my money."

"Come, my love." She reached out for his hand, but he refused it, walking ahead of her into the bungalow, shaking his head as he did so. Her advances rebuffed, Bibby lingered a moment longer. She cast an anxious look at the citadel. She'd heard talk among the servants. One of the jagirdar's miners had escaped and was being harbored by a merchant within the city walls. His men were seeking them out, and woe betide anyone who was hiding them.

Shutting out such unpleasant thoughts from her head, she was just about to follow her husband inside when she spotted something odd in the water. The light from the city was reflecting on the river, and she leaned over the balcony for a closer look at what she thought, at first, was a tree trunk bobbing on the surface. It was only when her eyes focused on the object a second or two later that she realized it was not a tree trunk at all that was floating downriver. It was a severed leg. The memory still made her nausated, nine years on. Yet even now, nothing would give her greater pleasure than to see Patrick Flynn's body float down the River Thames, too.

*Chapter 40*

"**D**r. Silkstone! Dr. Silkstone!"

Thomas was rudely awakened from a fitful sleep by cries below his window and a furious rapping on the knocker. It was light, but still early. He lifted his head from the pillow and heard the front door creak open downstairs and Mistress Finesilver's loud reproach.

"What, in the name of heaven . . . ?" she cursed as she saw a rough sort of man, all brawn and no brain, standing on the doorstep. He was a driver, and his cargo was behind him in a wagon. Another ruffian accompanied him, while a third, sheepish-looking dolt sat slumped on the passenger seat.

"Coroner's office," barked the thug, handing her a letter of authorization.

She barely gave it a look, but stepped forward over the threshold and began berating the man.

"What you got in there?" She waved her arms at the cart. She could see from her vantage point on the steps that its cargo lay under a tarpaulin.

The driver sniffed and wiped a stream of mucus from his nose with his sleeve. "Can't you read?" he sneered, pointing at the letter she held in her hand. "'Tis a body. A body for Dr. Silkstone."

Mistress Finesilver's hands flew up to her face. "Not here, you fools!" she cried. "Take it 'round the back!" She seemed more anxious about what the neighbors might think than the fact that a corpse had arrived on her doorstep.

By this time Thomas had slipped on his breeches and shirt and was careering down the stairs. He arrived at the doorway just in time to witness the driver setting off in the direction of the side street that led to the rear gate and the laboratory.

"Well, I never!" Mistress Finesilver was still fuming. "Who do they think they are bringing a body to the front door?"

"A body?"

She turned and, still scowling, handed Thomas the letter. "From the coroner's office," she told him. He scanned it quickly. It was written in Sir Stephen Gandy's own hand.

> *Silkstone,*
> *I have authorized the removal of this corpse*
> *from the mortuary. The man accompanying it is a*
> *shopkeeper, an ironmonger, who found the victim*
> *still alive but mortally wounded. Apparently the*
> *unfortunate gentleman repeated your name sev-*
> *eral times before he died. The ironmonger duly*
> *reported the death, and I took custody of the*
> *body, but thought it best if you inspect it in the*
> *hope that you might identify it—as it seems he*
> *knew you by name. If you think necessary, I*
> *would also ask you to conduct an examination to*
> *ascertain who might be responsible for his death.*
> *Please inform me of your intentions as soon as*
> *you are able.*
> *Yours,*
> *Sir Stephen Gandy*
> *Westminster Coroner*

Thomas hurried back through the hallway and out into the courtyard to see the back gate opening and two men carrying the covered corpse on a stretcher. He called to them to follow him and unlocked the laboratory door to allow them access.

"Here, if you please," he said, directing the porters to lay the body, wrapped in dirty sacking, on his dissecting table.

The two coroner's men took their leave, but a third, the one Thomas assumed was the ironmonger, held back.

"You found the man?"

"That I did, sir." He nodded his head, but regarded Thomas with eyes that were so askew that the doctor could not tell where his gaze was focused.

Thomas approached the table and inhaled through his nose. The corpse was relatively fresh. He was not sure who he would find. All he could be certain of was that the victim knew his name. Bracing himself, he pulled back the sacking, and his stomach suddenly lurched as he saw the face for the first time.

"Lupton," he muttered.

Catching a glimpse of the dead man, the shopkeeper turned away. "You know him, sir?"

Thomas did not reply. The shock of seeing his old enemy lying dead on his dissecting table caused the bile to rise in his throat.

"Where did you find him?" he asked after a short pause.

The ironmonger clutched his tricorn nervously. "In my shop doorway, sir," he bleated in a thin voice. For a moment his tongue was hobbled in his mouth; then he lifted his head toward Thomas again. Sticking out his chin, as if he had suddenly found a little courage, he added: "The coroner said you'd see me right, Doctor. I've had to close my shop to come here. I'll lose a day's takings."

Thomas gave a weary smile and reached into his pocket. Even the most timid of men, it seemed, would seek to make money from someone else's misfortune. But he would make this chancer sing for his supper. He took a shilling from his purse.

"Here," he said, holding the coin up in front of the man's crossed eyes. "Tell me all you know and this will be yours."

The ironmonger seemed to accept that this was a fair exchange for his information. He nodded and began to relate how he had come upon Lupton. "Yesterday morning, I found him, sir. He were lying at the door of my shop. Blood everywhere."

"And where is your shop?"

"Over in Fenchurch Street." The ironmonger waved his arm toward the east.

"And he was still alive?"

"If you could call it that. White as a sheet, he was. Moaning a lot, too. He kept saying, 'Silkstone. Silkstone.'" The ironmonger fixed Thomas with one of his disconcerting looks. "That's you, ain't it, sir?"

Thomas nodded. "What did you do?"

"I called for help. I'm a widower, you see, sir. And we took him 'round the back. Still bleeding like a stuck pig, he was. We got some rags and gave him some gin, but he died a few minutes later." The ironmonger dropped his gaze.

"Did he say nothing else, apart from my name?"

The man shrugged. "Mumbling, he was. He did say something . . ."

"Yes?" Thomas leapt on his words a little too eagerly, and the ironmonger saw it in his manner.

"I might need a sixpence to recall it, sir," he said, touching his forehead.

Thomas dipped into his purse once more. "Here," he told him, depositing a coin in the man's grimy hand.

"I remember now," he responded cheerfully, pocketing the coin. "It were something like 'gin' or 'fin.' He said 'I found gin' or 'fin' or—"

"Flynn! Could it have been Flynn?" Thomas pressed him.

The ironmonger's eyes swiveled in his head. "Flynn," he cried, nodding. "That was it. 'I found Flynn,' he said. Then he went to meet his Maker."

Thomas allowed his own eyes to return to Lupton's corpse. "So, he found Flynn," he muttered to himself.

The ironmonger dipped his head low, as if trying to attract Thomas's attention once more. "Is that all, Doctor?" he asked, then added with a laugh: "I've got a shop to open, you know."

Thomas turned and looked at the man, who bobbed a bow. "Yes, thank you. You have been most helpful," he said.

Left alone with his old adversary, Thomas shook his head and slowly pulled down the sheet a little farther. Although Lupton was still dressed, Thomas could see through the blood-caked coat that there were at least two great gashes on the arm and shoulder. His prognosis was easily reached. He did not need to conduct a postmortem to see that Boughton's former steward had bled to death. The brachial artery had been slashed. The end would have been slow. But whose hand had brandished the murder weapon? Flynn was the most obvious suspect. Lupton might have found him and approached him, and the errant captain might have responded with a blade. But not just any blade. Thomas examined the wounds more closely. He took out his tape measure, then reached for his magnifying glass, and after less than five minutes, he was convinced. The blade responsible for such mortal injuries was curved.

Now Thomas felt the burden of responsibility press down on his shoulders once more. Even though Lupton had volunteered to assist him in his inquiries, he still counted himself partly to blame for his death. He had warned him of the danger, but perhaps he should have accompanied him in his search. Lupton's endeavors had cost him his life. Now, however, Thomas knew it was up to him to locate Flynn and seek him out.

He felt his heart cringe below his breastbone as he pulled back the winding sheet even farther to inspect Lupton's body. "You will have to tell me where you found Flynn," he told the corpse. "The secret lies in you."

Carefully Thomas stripped Lupton of his upper garments, the topcoat and shirt. There were indeed two great gashes that had slashed through the material and the flesh to stop just short of the bone, one by the ulna and the other just shy of the scapula. This latter wound had severed the brachial artery, causing the fatal bleeding. He would examine the wounds later, in more depth, but for now, it was Lupton's hands that snagged his attention.

He lifted up the right one first. It was caked in dried blood, but beneath the crimson, he spied something else. He reached for his magnifying glass and squinted through it. A reddish powder was sticking to the blood. With his scalpel he scooped under the fingernails and sniffed the powder as it sat on the blade. "Ginger," he said to himself.

With renewed energy, he rolled back the rest of the sheet to reveal the lower half of Lupton's body. He scanned the breeches before his eyes latched onto the stockings. Beneath all the dried blood, he could make out another color. Again he grabbed his magnifying glass and peered at Lupton's calves. They were smeared with a dark purplish color. Thomas felt his heart lurch in his chest once more. The legs were streaked with indigo.

*Chapter 41*

"Dear boy, is that you?" Dr. Carruthers's voice carried from the study as Thomas grabbed his hat from the peg in the hall and made his way to the front door. He stopped in his tracks. He did not want his mentor to know of his mission.

"Yes, sir," he replied. He was aware that he would have to engage in conversation if he was to avoid attracting unwanted attention.

Thomas put his head around the door to see the old doctor sitting by the hearth, opposite his brother.

"What was all that kerfuffle this morning?" he asked.

"Mistress Finesilver seemed most perturbed," added the professor with a sympathetic twitch.

Thomas swallowed hard. "I had a delivery, sir."

"A delivery?" repeated his mentor. "By which you must surely mean a corpse." Nothing escaped the old man.

Thomas was forced to concede. "I do indeed, sir."

Dr. Carruthers nodded. "A corpse in August, eh? You'd best work on it quickly in this weather."

For a moment Thomas remained quiet and shifted uneasily, switching his nervous gaze to the professor, who arched a suspicious brow.

"Surely 'tis not someone you know?" asked the old anatomist.

Thomas knew that the professor could read his reaction. He tried to steady his voice before he replied. "'Twas Nicholas Lupton, sir."

"God's wounds!" cried Dr. Carruthers, grasping the arms of his chair. If his joints had allowed it, he would have leapt up at the news.

"The steward at Boughton?" queried the professor.

"The very same," answered Thomas.

"Murdered?" asked the old doctor.

"Yes, sir."

"Flynn?"

Thomas hesitated. "Perhaps."

"So where are you going in such haste now?" His mentor's tone had turned inquisitorial.

Thomas was forced to concede it made no sense to hide his actions. "I believe I know where I might find the captain," he replied.

"Oh? So on what do you base this assertion?" Dr. Carruthers tapped his stick aggressively on the floor.

Thomas suddenly felt like a schoolboy again, being quizzed by his old master. "Apparently, just before he died, Lupton said that he had found Flynn."

"Did he, by Jove?"

Thomas continued. "Lupton was found in Fenchurch Street. Under his fingernails there was ground ginger, and on his stockings were traces of indigo."

The old anatomist harrumphed. "Ah, the all-important fingernails!" he said knowingly. "So you will begin your search in warehouses around Fenchurch Street?"

"I will, sir."

Dr. Carruthers nodded, as if satisfied with Thomas's logic. "I believe that is a sound premise," he agreed, but then he added: "However, I must insist on one thing."

Thomas let a sigh escape from his lips. "What might that be, sir?"

"You must take Oliver here with you," he said, waving his stick in his brother's direction.

The professor's eyebrows lifted simultaneously in surprise.

"Professor Carruthers?" Thomas was taken aback. He had no wish to be accompanied, least of all by a man who constantly challenged his trust.

Dr. Carruthers chuckled but remained firm. "You're a lamb to the slaughter in those parts. You know you should not go alone, dear boy. I insist you go together."

Thomas knew what his mentor said was right. The dock area was the haunt of thieves, cutpurses, and, of course, murderers at any time of the day. He did not wish to put the professor in harm's way, but at the same time he knew there was safety in numbers.

"Very well, sir," he replied, shooting a glance at the professor. "We shall search for Flynn together."

The coach soon left the pleasant environs of west London and journeyed into Cheapside, where the landscape—and the smell—of the city changed. The elegant houses and shops had long given way to meat markets and butchers' shambles, and the summer stink of entrails, so familiar to Thomas, caught on the back of his throat.

He did not find the professor easy company. And, of course, because he was a reluctant passenger, their conversation was naturally stilted. But Thomas decided to make the most of the opportunity to venture a little further into his territory.

As they rattled along the narrow streets of the Square Mile, Thomas decided to find out what Carruthers knew about the mysterious Bibby Motte. "My dinner with Mrs. Hastings and her friends last night proved interesting," he said, gazing out of the window.

The professor, taciturn for most of the journey, now seemed prepared to engage.

"I trust she was in good health."

"Yes, she appears very well," said Thomas. "She enjoys much company."

"And her companion?"

Thomas arched a brow as the professor looked him in the eye. "Mrs. Motte?"

"Yes. How fares she?"

Thomas thought of her enigmatic expression and the faraway look in her eyes that he had noticed at the dinner table. "She seems a little subdued, perhaps," he observed, eager to see how the professor might react.

"Subdued, eh?" The professor's left eye suddenly started to twitch again.

Thomas switched 'round, puzzled. "Do you have a notion why might that be?" he asked.

"You do not know?" asked Carruthers, turning to face Thomas, his brows dipping into a frown.

"Know what, pray?"

"Thomas Motte was a minor official."

"*Was?*" Thomas picked up on the professor's use of the past tense.

"He was declared bankrupt. He is in jail in Calcutta," came the wholly unexpected reply.

"Jail? For debt?"

The professor pursed his lips. "He owes several thousand pounds."

"Does he indeed?"

Thomas's mind suddenly flashed to his chance encounter with Bibby Motte at East India House. "Might Patrick Flynn be one of his own debtors?"

The professor sniffed and twitched again. "It would not surprise me."

Thomas nodded. That might explain Mrs. Motte's anxious efforts to find Flynn and the diamond, he told himself. The proceeds from the sale of the stone would surely be enough to secure her husband's release. Professor Carruthers might just have furnished him with a missing piece of the puzzle.

A moment later the carriage drew into Fenchurch Street and stopped, as directed, outside the ironmonger's. It was a district that was already familiar to Thomas, yet it still filled him with a sense of impending danger. Close to the quayside, yet set back a little from the river, it was an area where every street corner was home to a downtrodden doxy and every alley concealed cutpurses and, worse still, cutthroats. Gentlemen venturing along the lanes lined with warehouses would, no doubt, attract the attention of the wrong sort, but it was a risk that Thomas would have to take. He suddenly found himself glad that he was not alone.

"What is your plan, Silkstone?" asked the professor, his voice raised over the street noise. Both men stepped out of the carriage onto the cobbles.

Thomas pointed ahead of him. "This, I believe, is where Lupton was found yesterday morning." He strode a few paces to his left, keeping his eyes to the ground that was already littered with detritus, namely horse dung and sawdust. There had been no rain for the last few hours, and sure enough, there was blood on the stones. Keeping his eyes firmly on the uneven ground, Thomas was able to follow the intermittent trail of crimson. It stopped outside the entrance to the ironmonger's.

"Lupton was badly injured," he told the professor, pointing to the dark brown stain on the stone porch. "He could not have traveled far." He looked up toward the row of warehouses on the opposite side of the street.

The professor nodded, still looking about him warily. "Ginger and indigo, eh?" he said, recalling that Thomas had found traces of both on Lupton. "An East Indies warehouse, for sure."

The two men set off down the street, looking from side to side. Now and again Thomas returned his gaze to the ground, looking for any sign of blood, but there were several feral dogs in the district and he guessed that by now they would have licked most of it up.

Ahead of them a wagon was partially blocking the street, so passersby had to squeeze through a narrow gap in the road. A winch on the second floor of one of the warehouses was lowering large bales of what appeared to be silk into the waiting trailer. Farther along men were rolling barrels down a plank and onto a waiting dray cart. There were shouts and whistles, punctuated now and again by the loud neighing of a nervous horse. There was, however, one saving grace in this scene of mayhem. The aromas of countless spices hung in the air, and their pungency blocked out the usual stink of piss in the open gutters.

Thomas stopped outside one of the buildings where a piquant perfume was wafting underneath high double doors. Set inside the large doors, designed to take wagons, there was a smaller door. He dropped his gaze to the threshold. There was no blood. His hopes faded. Nevertheless he pulled at the padlock.

"What d'you think you're about?" came a gruff voice from behind.

Thomas turned to see a docker behind him, scowling. Theft from warehouses was rife, and Thomas had to admit he was acting suspiciously. He bowed graciously to the man.

"My mistake. The wrong door," he said meekly and backed away.

Moving on a few more paces, they came to another warehouse with similar doors. Thomas stopped and sniffed. It smelled promising. The professor agreed.

"Ginger and turmeric," he said with a nod. The ability to determine the source of smells was obviously a family trait, thought Thomas as he tried the lock. Making sure he was not seen, he shouldered it and it budged slightly.

"Stand here," he told the professor, keeping his back to the door. "I think I can open it."

Carruthers obliged, shielding Thomas as he took out a lancet he had pocketed should such an eventuality arise. Within a minute he had managed to pick the lock. "We're in," he said in a loud whisper, and he stepped over the threshold, swiftly followed by Carruthers.

Inside, the heady smell of spice was overwhelming, but it took a while for both men's eyes to adjust to the gloom. Fingers of daylight managed to penetrate through the odd broken plank in the large doors, and within a few seconds their partial sight was restored. But what they could now see disturbed them both greatly.

As Thomas stepped forward, he could feel something sticky under his shoes. He looked down to find he had trodden in syrupy blood. The men swapped anxious looks and sidestepped the pool to continue in silence. A few paces away, to the left, they saw a sack had been slashed and its contents spilled out over the floor. Thomas scooped up a little of the reddish powder in his fingers.

"Ginger," he said.

Ahead of them barrels and crates lay piled high, eight to ten feet tall. They walked on through the man-made gorge in the semidarkness.

Suddenly the professor grunted. "Indigo," he whispered.

Thomas turned to see him poised over a bale that had been broken open, exposing its inky blue contents.

"This has to be the place," he said, his eyes darting from left to right. "Flynn has been here. I'm sure of it."

They walked on in the gloom until suddenly Carruthers stumbled on something beneath his feet. It clattered as he kicked it. He looked down.

"A pistol," said Thomas, bending low to pick up the weapon. He smelled the barrel. "It hasn't been discharged recently," he whispered. He inspected it more closely. "But it's cocked."

"Do you think 'tis Flynn's?" asked the professor.

"Or Lupton's," he ventured. He gripped it by its handle and pointed it in front of him. He only hoped he wouldn't have to fire it.

They ventured farther into the ravine of hogsheads and sacks. Thomas glanced up. Overhead, across the ceiling, stretched long beams, and from them hung a variety of hooks. There were ropes and pulleys, too, that festooned the rafters. Through a hole in the roof, a shaft of daylight lanced its way, casting a pool of light into the middle of the warehouse. Thomas stopped suddenly. He could see more clearly now. They were coming to a crossroads. To their left there were more crates; to their right more sacks, and something else. A brazier, half filled with coals, sat in the middle of the aisle. He'd say the heat had long been allowed to dwindle. The embers no longer glowed. Nervously he leaned into a corner crate and peered around it. Everything appeared in order. He could see no further signs of an intrusion. It was only when he turned back to signal to the professor that all was clear that something caught his eye. A strange shadow was being cast onto the bank of sacks. He glanced back, compelled to look up to the rafters to see what might be making it. A large sack at the end of a pulley, perhaps? But no. He edged closer, not daring to breathe, until shock forced the air out of his lungs in a horrified gasp.

"What is it?" asked the professor in a hoarse whisper. He did not need a reply. He lifted his gaze and saw for himself Captain Patrick Flynn, late of the East India Company. He was suspended by his arms ten feet above the ground. His lifeless body was dangling from the end of a rope.

*Chapter 42*

"Dear God!" Sir Theodisius's eyes widened and he turned away. Patrick Flynn's corpse lay on the dissecting table in the Hollen Street laboratory, his red hair plastered 'round his skull. But Thomas was paying particular attention to the lower limbs. The coroner's constitution was as strong as an ox, and his stomach could, and very often did, handle much more than the average man's, but on this occasion even he had been pushed to his limits.

"I should have warned you, sir." Thomas watched Sir Theodisius hitch up his coat tails and place his very large behind on a stool at the far end of the room.

From the safety of his new refuge, the coroner, his brow still puckered, tried to make sense of what he had just seen. "What in God's name happened to him? His . . ." He hesitated and Thomas jumped in for him.

"I fear he was burned, sir." He was studying Flynn's feet and calves. The soles were blistered and blackened. Thomas recalled the brazier he had seen in the warehouse close to where he had made the gruesome discovery. The burning coals had obviously been held to Flynn's feet as he dangled helplessly from the rafter. Death was possibly the result of a heart attack, but he could not be sure until he had examined the corpse more thoroughly.

"You mean he was tortured?" asked Sir Theodisius, his voice an octave higher than usual.

Thomas saw no point in softening the truth. "His feet were

chained together," he said as he cut through the iron links with a tool usually reserved for the trickiest of amputations, "and then hot coals were applied."

Sir Theodisius winced at the thought. "Presumably so that he would divulge information?"

Thomas never liked to presume anything, although on this occasion the coroner, he felt, made a fair assumption. "Yes, that is likely."

"So whoever did this wanted the diamond?"

Thomas nodded as he snapped a link and the fetters fell away from around Flynn's charred feet. "It is a possibility. Professor Carruthers tells me this burning is a common torture in India."

"Ah, the professor." Carruthers's name appeared to stick in the coroner's craw. "He seems to be well versed in such methods, if I'm not much mistaken."

Thomas paused, taken aback by Sir Theodisius's tone. "You suspect him of involvement in all this?"

The coroner pushed out his bottom lip, then said: "I left him singing the praises of the Indian way of doing things. He is taking tea with Lydia and the doctor in your drawing room, dear fellow."

Thomas was fully aware of the professor's admiration for many aspects of Indian culture. "He is what I believe you call an Orientalist, sir," said Thomas. "He has begun translating several ancient texts into English."

Sir Theodisius gave a skeptical grunt. "Do you not think it a coincidence that Sir Montagu's murder, the diamond theft, and now all these ghastly killings have all occurred since his arrival?"

Such an aspersion did not surprise Thomas—the thought had also occurred to him—although he felt the coroner's candor needed to be challenged. He turned to face Sir Theodisius. "Do you base your accusations on anything other than coincidence, sir?"

The coroner pulled a sour face. "There is just something about the fellow that I do not trust," he said bluntly.

Thomas knew what his old friend meant, but he did not let

on. He, too, had seen an unnatural intensity in the professor's eye. At first he put it down to his belief in a different type of religious asceticism or spirituality; what was that he practiced—meditation? There were times, when Oliver Carruthers had been unaware he was being observed, when Thomas had caught him as if in another dimension, one that transcended time and place. It had occurred to him that this devotion might yet mask a deeper truth. The thought had started to lurk in the shadows of his mind long before Sir Theodisius had voiced his own suspicions. They could not be discounted. And then there were the nervous twitches. Thomas knew these often developed after experiencing a psychological problem or an emotional trauma or stress. Despite such suspicions, Thomas would not be rushed to judgment.

"You know full well, sir, we need facts before we make accusations," he admonished, turning back to the corpse. "And the fact is that I need to open up Flynn here to find out exactly what killed him."

Sir Theodisius glanced at the outstretched body on the table and looked slightly bilious at the thought. He cleared his throat. "Then I will let you get to work," he said. "Besides, I do not wish to leave Lydia in the professor's company any longer than I have to."

Thomas looked up from the table. "I fear I will be a while here," he called to the coroner as he lumbered toward the door. Before he began his work, Thomas arched his aching back and as he distanced himself a little from the corpse, his eyes suddenly latched onto something out of place. Flynn's neck. It was an area he had not yet properly examined. And there was something odd about it. The captain's body had many secrets to yield up, he was convinced of it, and this might be one of them. He squinted at the throat and the large bulge at the side. A swollen gland, perhaps? A distended thyroid? He felt the lump. The protrusion was hard. He frowned and picked up his scalpel, directing the blade at the trachea. He made a deep incision at the edge of the protuberance, then folded back the flesh. What he saw caused him to gasp out loud in amazement. There, lodged not in his windpipe, but in Patrick Flynn's esophagus, was a large diamond. The captain had choked to death.

"Sir Theo!" cried Thomas.

The coroner, halfway out of the door, turned. Peering toward the far end of the laboratory, he saw Thomas walking toward him. He narrowed his eyes, then widened them.

"No, sir," said Thomas, fast approaching, brandishing something in his hand. "Your eyes do not deceive you."

Thomas drew level with him and lifted up the forceps that held in their grasp a gemstone the size of a plover's egg.

"The diamond!" exclaimed Sir Theodisius. "Where did you find it?"

"In Flynn's throat," replied Thomas bluntly. "It killed him."

The coroner's forehead crumpled. "You mean . . . ?"

"I mean it was shoved into his mouth and he was made to try and swallow it, sir, knowing that it would cause asphyxiation."

"Good Lord!" Sir Theodisius shook his head in disbelief as his eyes remained fixed on the bloody gemstone. After a moment he asked: "But if Flynn was not tortured for the diamond, then why . . . ?" The coroner had come to the nub of the matter.

"That is the question we must strive to answer, sir, and I suspect the answer lies behind all four murders," said Thomas. Originally he had thought that, once he found the diamond, he would be able to make a clear judgment on the murderer. But this discovery had changed everything. Now the imperative was to find the motive that he was sure linked all the brutal murders. Then, and only then, could he hope to find the crazed killer.

*Chapter 43*

"So Flynn's murder makes four," ventured Dr. Carruthers, tapping his stick on the floor four times, as if he needed to press home the point. "And all killed in a most vile way."

Tea was being taken in the drawing room, as Sir Theodisius had informed Thomas. Once again Sajiv had made an infusion and was serving Lydia, Dr. Carruthers, and his brother with great ceremony, but no one was in the mood for polite chitchat. Earlier in the day, not only had Thomas been obliged to break the news to Lydia of Patrick Flynn's murder, he'd had to inform her that Nicholas Lupton had been killed, too. As a result the occasion was tempered with shock and laced with a certain sense of fear.

The professor clearly disapproved of his elder brother's forthrightness. He shot a look toward Lydia and saw the pained expression on her face. "You must not talk so in front of your guest, brother," he chided him.

Dr. Carruthers shook his head, apologetically. "Forgive me, my dear. I quite forgot my manners." He reached for his tea bowl, and Sajiv, watching intently, stepped forward and guided it to his lips.

"Ah, thank you." The old anatomist smiled. "Your man is most attentive, Oliver."

The professor nodded and looked approvingly at his servant. "Yes. Sajiv has been with me almost nine years now. Loyalty and service are very much part of the Indian culture," he replied before sipping his own tea.

Lydia agreed. "Yes, my late husband, Michael—" She paused and began again with proper formality. "Captain Farrell, that is, always spoke highly of his sepoys." Her eyes slid toward Sajiv, who was at the grate, boiling another kettle of water.

A slightly awkward lull ensued as the professor stirred his tea.

"Yes. India really is a fascinating country." He paused, as if framing a thought. "I have an idea," he said suddenly, looking up from his dish. "Why do we not go and see the elephant in St. James's Park?"

Lydia's face broke into a bemused smile. "An elephant?"

"Yes, by Jove," piped up the old doctor. "Paraded daily, apparently."

"Then I am sure my son would love to see such a sight. As would I," replied Lydia.

"What sight might that be, my dear?" The door opened wide to allow Sir Theodisius to shamble inside and slump into the nearest chair. It groaned in protest under his weight.

Lydia spoke across the room. "Professor Carruthers was saying there is an elephant that is walked often in St. James's Park. I thought Richard might find it amusing. The poor child deserves some diversion," she suggested. "I am such poor company at the moment."

"Tush, tush, my dear. You must not blame yourself for the calamitous events that have occurred," Sir Theodisius assured her. "We are all most perturbed by them." As he spoke, the attentive servant put down a tea bowl by his side, but he waved it away. "No tea," he snapped. "I need a brandy." Then, as an afterthought he added: "And biscuits. Where are the biscuits I was promised?"

"You are out of sorts, dear Theo," ventured Dr. Carruthers with a frown.

"I fear I never find your laboratory very amusing, sir," he countered, sliding a sideways look at Lydia. Had she not been there, he would have added: "Especially with a corpse in it."

"Ah!" said the old doctor. "You have been with Thomas. How is he faring with the latest delivery?"

Sir Theodisius nodded, but wary of offending Lydia's sensibilities, he skirted the question. Instead he replied in vague terms. "There has been an interesting development," he conceded, but added: "Yet I fear we are no nearer to getting to the bottom of this unholy mystery, sir." He reached up for the brandy that the professor's servant handed him. "I regret to say we may never know who killed Sir Montagu, or even why."

It took another hour for Thomas to finish the autopsy on Patrick Flynn's body and to ensure that it was in a satisfactory state to be received back into the custody of the Westminster coroner's office. Two burly ruffians were sent to collect it. By the time the young anatomist had scrubbed away the blood from under his fingernails and donned his topcoat, it was almost time for Sir Theodisius and Lydia to leave. Exhausted, he walked into the drawing room to find them about to make their exits.

Professor Carruthers turned and smiled as he saw Thomas approach. "Ah, Dr. Silkstone," he said, "your guests are about to depart. Sajiv has called their carriage to the front."

Thomas, catching Lydia's eye, tilted his head. "That is a great shame," he said, smiling at her. She returned his smile, but the exchange was short-lived.

"Ah! Thomas," barked Sir Theodisius, "a word, if I might." He beckoned the doctor toward him and looked very earnest. Thomas obeyed and followed the coroner out into the hallway.

"You have news, sir?" he asked. He wondered if Sir Arthur Warbeck had uncovered something in Boughton and sent word during his short absence in the laboratory.

Sir Theodisius shook his head. "Not exactly," he began, "but seeing the diamond today jogged my memory."

"Oh?" Thomas arched a brow.

"Yes. 'Tis about Farrell."

"Farrell?"

The coroner directed his gaze toward the drawing room door to ensure it was shut. "I recall he came to me a few months before the sixth earl's death. Told me he had a business proposition that might interest me." He shifted his weight. "Said that it was widely thought that the diamond mines at Golconda were all but exhausted." Thomas was aware that avaricious eyes were now turned on South America as a new source of diamonds. "But he told me he knew otherwise."

The doctor's eyes widened in surprise. He leaned in. "Did he indeed?"

Sir Theodisius nodded. "Said he had a map, an ancient map that showed where there were more reserves of diamonds. Bigger and even more valuable than any found before."

"And he wanted you to invest in an expedition?" ventured Thomas.

The coroner's jowls flapped as he nodded. "Exactly so."

"What did you tell him?"

"I said that such a venture was too risky for me, but I wished him luck elsewhere."

"And you heard no more of it?"

"No. I thought no more of it, either, until I saw you holding that infernal stone." He lifted his hands up in a show of revulsion.

Thomas nodded. "You are right. It puzzled me why Flynn stole the diamond, then supposedly returned to murder Sir Montagu. We now know that whoever killed him was looking for something other than the stone. Perhaps it was this map."

"'Tis my thinking, too, Silkstone," replied the coroner. "But where to start to look?" Sir Theodisius paused for a moment; then his eyes latched onto the wall clock in the hall. "Sir Montagu's will," he said suddenly.

Thomas frowned. "What of it?"

"I am to accompany Lydia to the attorney's office this afternoon for the reading," he said. "Perhaps it might contain something"—he broke off in search of the word—"interesting?"

Thomas nodded. "Perhaps," he replied, "because at the moment, sir, I am at a complete loss as to where to turn next."

# *Chapter 44*

In the morning room in South Street, Marian Hastings sat working on her embroidery. She was alone and bathed in the warm sunlight that flooded through the full-length casements when the door suddenly flew open and in rushed Bibby Motte. She was looking most distressed.

"My dear, vatever is ze matter?" asked Marian, putting down her sewing frame. "Sit down, please." She patted the chaise longue where she herself sat, but her companion declined. She was close to tears and began pacing the room.

"He's dead," she wailed, clutching her handkerchief and shaking her head.

For a moment, Marian Hastings froze. "Your husband?"

Bibby Motte shot her a horrified glance. "My God, no," she countered. "Although he may as well be now," she added. Her shoulders began to undulate in sobs.

"Zen who is dead, my dear?" Marian rose and walked over to her, putting an arm around her friend.

"Captain Flynn," she bleated.

"Flynn?" repeated Marian. Now she understood. With Flynn's death, any hope of raising the money to pay Thomas Motte's creditors had evaporated. He would remain in jail in India.

"How? How did he die?"

Bibby looked her companion in the eye. "He was murdered."

A gasp escaped Marian's lips. "Not . . . ?" She knew that her friend had engaged a man to track down the errant captain.

The younger woman shook her head. "I do not think so."

"You do not think so?" Marian repeated, a note of frustration in her voice. Her obvious shock prompted another flurry of tears from her friend.

"There has been no word from Mr. Lupton," Bibby told her between snivels.

Marian's chin jutted out. "So you think he vould have told you if he had murdered Flynn?" She was finding it impossible to hide her exasperation. She walked to the mantelpiece, then back to the window. "And vat does ze major say about this?"

Bibby looked up at her with red-rimmed eyes. "He is unhappy."

"Unhappy?" repeated Marian incredulously. "Unhappy? I should say he vill be unhappy ven his name is linked to ze murder of a former East India Company man and one of Philip Francis's henchmen to boot." She knew of the major's part in arranging Flynn's apprehension. "If vord gets out zere will be ze scandal." She dropped back onto the chaise longue at the very thought of all the gossip and recriminations that would surely follow. If word spread that one of Warren Hastings's closest allies was linked to a murder, his political enemies would surely see it as valuable capital. The possibility of the governor-general's impeachment would come a step closer. For a moment Marian sat in silence, listening to the intermittent sobs of her friend; then she rose. "Ve must take action," she said decisively.

"Action?" echoed Bibby, looking up from her handkerchief.

"If Flynn vas found murdered, zere may vell be a post-mortem."

"I do not understand." Bibby narrowed her glassy eyes so that more tears spilled over and ran down her cheeks. She watched as her friend strode purposefully over to the fireplace.

"Ve need to find out who vas responsible for ze captain's death," she said, reaching for the calling card propped up against the mantel clock. "And I think I know ze man who might be able to tell us."

\* \* \*

Hardacre's apothecary shop lay not five minutes away from Hollen Street. Over the past few weeks it had become a regular haunt of Oliver Carruthers. Mr. Hardacre was, by now, used to welcoming the erudite gentleman from India, with his tall frame, slightly stooped gait, and melancholy air. The main thing was he always left happy, even though he might have been a shilling or two lighter.

That morning, as soon as the apothecary clapped eyes on his regular customer, he signaled him into the back of his shop. Dipping low through an archway screened by a thick velvet curtain, the professor was received by Mistress Hardacre, a homely woman with a large bosom and a broad smile. She led him into a darkened room, where the heavy red drapes were always drawn and the banter was always the same.

"Good day, Professor. A fine day, sir." Or: "A cold day, sir." Or: "A wet and most miserable day, sir." But whatever the weather outside, Oliver Carruthers knew that he could always look forward to the warm embrace afforded by the bountiful poppy.

As usual he settled himself onto a sizable daybed to enjoy a pleasurable smoke. Mistress Hardacre handed him a freshly prepared pipe, and he lit it, as he always did, with a relish and anticipation of the ecstasy to come. In such a state he would spend a good two or three hours each day, drifting off into a state of unparalleled pleasure afforded by the opium. Sometimes he was joined by other gentlemen—Mr. Markham from Benares, for one, might occasionally imbibe—sometimes not. It did not trouble him because his mind was elsewhere, flying over the mountains of the Himalayas or swimming in the coral seas of the Bay of Bengal. Swathed in the sweetest of exotic smells, he became oblivious to all his troubles. The past and the future became irrelevant. He was living in the glorious moment. Nothing else mattered. Nothing and no one. For a few hours each day he could be at peace with himself and all was right in his fantastical world. The problem was that reality, when he returned to it, was becoming increasingly difficult to bear.

*Chapter 45*

Thomas's eye sockets felt as though they were full of gravel, and his chest wound was throbbing again. He had spent the rest of the afternoon in the laboratory, writing up his post-mortem report on Flynn. He therefore welcomed the tapping of Dr. Carruthers's stick on the flagstones outside. A moment later the door opened and in his mentor walked.

"I heard what you said to Sir Theo," he told Thomas without ceremony.

Thomas looked puzzled. "Oh?"

"That you are at a complete loss when it comes to getting to the bottom of Sir Montagu's murder, not to mention the other terrible goings-on."

Thomas was glad the old anatomist could not see his expression. He hated to admit defeat, but on this occasion he felt his dogged determination alone was not enough to solve all four murders. He needed a stroke of luck—a coincidence, an unintended consequence—to fire him up once more. He was going 'round in circles, chasing his tail, looking for a motive for murder. And he feared that the longer he did so, the more likely it was that the killer or killers would strike again.

"Do you have chalk, dear boy?" asked his mentor, settling himself down on his customary stool.

A large rectangle of slate covered one wall of the laboratory above a workbench. It was where Thomas sometimes formulated his physic and made various calculations, or left aide-mémoires to himself. He reached for a piece of chalk from a jar. "I am ready, sir," he said, walking over to the slate.

"Then let us get to work," pressed Carruthers. "We have four men dead, and you have conducted four postmortems. Is there anything that links all of them?"

Thomas, his sheaves of notes in front of him, had asked himself the same question many times over. The answer remained unchanged. He began to write on the slate. "In the cases of Sir Montagu, the servant, and Flynn, there were traces of the same coir rope on the bodies. In the cases of Sir Montagu and Lupton, the injuries were inflicted by a curved blade. In the case of the servant and Flynn, Indian torture methods were employed. There was also an Indian word carved on the servant's chest." He chalked up the word "*gaddar*" on the board, then went on: "The bloody footprints in Sir Montagu's study may have been made by an Indian slipper. The smell of opium was also detected at the scene of Sir Montagu's murder and on the servant's body."

"So your thoughts at the moment veer to . . . ?" The old anatomist threw out an open-ended question as Thomas studied his jottings on the slate. When the reply came, it reconfirmed his initial suspicions.

"India," said Thomas. "The motive for these murders lay there."

"India?" repeated Carruthers. He rubbed his chin in thought; then, as if picking up on the thread of Thomas's thought, he began to nod vigorously. "Flynn was with Farrell and Lavington in India, yes?"

"Yes, sir." Thomas nodded.

"And Motte, too?"

Again Thomas nodded. "Yes, he was known to them, as well."

"But Motte is in jail, you say?"

"Yes, sir."

"So who else may be caught up in this tangled web?"

The chalk remained poised over the slate as Thomas considered his mentor's question.

"Did you not mention other East India Company associates?" asked Carruthers.

For a moment Thomas was puzzled; then he grasped the old doctor's meaning. He thought of the awkward dinner party and how he had been rounded upon afterward by two of Hastings's allies: the weasel-faced opium smoker and the bottle-bloated military man, who clearly pulled strings on behalf of Warren Hastings. "Markham and Scott," he murmured. He paused to gather his thoughts. "They were probably trying to track down Flynn, too. You are right, sir, although Markham arrived in England too late to have killed Sir Montagu."

"And Scott?" asked the old anatomist. "Did you not tell me that he was sent on ahead to prepare everything for Mrs. Hastings's visit?"

Thomas's eyes opened wide. "I most certainly did," he said, remembering that he had read out a newspaper report to that effect to his mentor a few weeks back. He hurried to a drawer and rifled through it, pulling out an old newssheet and scanning it quickly. "You are right, sir," he said, slapping the paper.

Carruthers nodded his head. "So it is possible that he commissioned the murder. He must have several men, Indians, under his command."

Putting down his chalk, Thomas marched over to his desk and picked up a note he'd received earlier in the afternoon. It was an invitation to take supper with Marian Hastings at South Street the day after next. "Yes, sir," he replied. "The governor-general's cronies certainly have some questions to answer."

"But you do not sound convinced?" The old anatomist, sensing that Thomas was holding back, handed him the opportunity to raise a very thorny issue.

Thomas took it, even though there was no easy way to put it. He braced himself. "There is one other person within the frame of my suspicion, sir." He could not believe that his words had tumbled out so clumsily.

"Oh?"

Thomas saw his mentor's nose twitch. He sniffed trouble, he could tell. But the die was cast.

"Professor Carruthers."

"Oliver?"

"You are aware, sir, that your brother smokes opium?"

Carruthers frowned and puffed out his chest defensively. "'Tis not a crime to partake of the poppy," he huffed. "Did not the great Dr. Johnson say only recently that 'no happiness in the world can surpass the charms of this agreeable ecstasy'?"

Thomas disagreed. "No, sir, 'tis not illegal to smoke opium. But you know as well as I that such narcotics can sometimes prove addictive, not to mention poisonous. They can also induce the most irrational and pernicious behavior in people."

Both the old anatomist's brows shot up simultaneously, and he nodded slowly. "And these latest killings bear all the hallmarks of a crazed mind acting under the influence of narcotics."

Thomas nodded. "Certainly the deaths of the Indian and of Flynn showed utter depravity which may well have been induced by opium."

Dr. Carruthers's brow dipped. "Surely you cannot be suggesting . . . ?"

Thomas felt his chest tighten. "This is not easy for me, sir. And I know it cannot be easy for you to hear, either . . ." he began.

"But . . ." The old anatomist straightened his back as if tensing himself for an assault.

Thomas reluctantly took the plunge: ". . . but we are conjecturing that whoever murdered Sir Montagu, the Indian servant, Lupton, and of course Flynn had recently arrived from India. Furthermore the person, or persons, was well versed in Indian customs and methods of torture and may have acted under the influence of opium as they carried out these heinous crimes."

Dr. Carruthers remained stony-faced. "You will need more than that for a conviction."

"I fear there is more, sir," replied Thomas. "Apparently the professor's servant was tasked to boil his master's clothes in the copper the night after the murder of the Indian."

Carruthers inhaled deeply. "Who told you that?"

"Mistress Finesilver mentioned it, sir."

"Blah! That woman!" barked the old anatomist, sticking out his tongue to show his disapproval. "I do not believe it." He hit the floor hard with his stick. "I cannot believe it, Thomas! What possible motive could Oliver have for murder?"

Thomas knew he needed to recap. The doctor was not cognizant with all of the facts. "Whoever killed Sir Montagu may have done so thinking he was James Lavington, sir."

"What? The braggart lawyer who did for Farrell?"

"The very same, sir. Captain Flynn only discovered he was dead when he visited Boughton. There was no question that he arranged for the theft of the diamond. But it always puzzled me, if the diamond was in Flynn's possession, why he should return to kill Sir Montagu. It made no sense."

"And what did you conclude?"

"That whoever killed Sir Montagu mistook him for James Lavington, because they believed he had whatever they wanted in his possession. At first I thought it was the diamond. I supposed Flynn's servant had been so cruelly tortured in order to obtain information about the stone. But no. Lupton was set on Flynn's trail and was lured into a trap in the warehouse. He was a hindrance. No more. That's why he was attacked but allowed to escape, only to bleed to death. That leaves us with Flynn himself. Again he was tortured, but I found the diamond stuck in his gullet."

"Good God, no! The diamond? In his gullet?"

Thomas had not had time to inform his mentor of his findings earlier. "I was as shocked as you, sir."

The old anatomist shook his snowy head. "But that means the diamond was not the motive for all these murders."

"Precisely, sir. The killer, or killers, is after something else."

"A bigger prize?"

"Much bigger."

"And you know what?"

"I believe I do." Thomas backed away from the slate. "I believe Michael Farrell had in his possession an ancient Sanskrit map of a region that was virtually unexplored, just north of Golconda, and certainly unexploited. He had heard that the most enormous gemstones, bigger than anything as yet mined, were still to be unearthed."

"You sound most sure of yourself," remarked Carruthers, tapping the flagstones with his stick.

"I have something here," replied Thomas, crossing over to his desk and pulling out a small leather-bound book. "I came across this account of an excursion undertaken by Thomas Motte."

"Motte?" repeated the old anatomist. "The man married to Mrs. Hastings's companion?"

"The same Thomas Motte who now lies in a debtors' prison," said Thomas with a nod. "He was employed by Lord Clive on a mission to Sumbhulpoor to open a trade in diamonds with that country. He wrote a detailed account of his travels, and I happened to find a copy in the library at Boughton."

On his last visit to the hall, Thomas had trawled the well-stocked shelves looking for works pertaining to India. Quite by chance he stumbled across an intriguing document entitled *Narrative of a Journey to the Diamond Mines at Sumbhulpoor in the Province of Orissa.* He went on: "I had hoped to discover something about Indian curved swords in light of the postmortem on Sir Montagu, but events overtook me. I pocketed the work, but the volume remained closed," he explained.

It was only since the ill-fated dinner party with Marian Hastings that he had realized its significance. Earlier in the day, he had managed to grab a few minutes to read the account and had been amazed by what he found. He set the book down by his mentor and opened it. "Motte tells how he journeyed to a far-off land where he found several mines full of priceless stones. It is said he also came back with a map."

"Interesting," commented Carruthers.

"And when Farrell and Lavington returned to England, I do not believe they returned empty-handed."

"No?"

"By fair means or foul, Farrell managed to obtain the map— a map that, unbeknownst to Motte, is the key to the ancient diamond mines."

"And you think this map is here, in England?"

"I firmly do. And I believe the killer does, too."

Carruthers took a deep breath, as if to ready himself for what he was about to say. "By 'killer,' you mean my brother?" The words left his mouth like ashes.

Thomas had been uneasy about Mistress Finesilver's complaint that Sajiv had been boiling clothes for his master, but when the professor had produced a curved dagger at tea, his suspicions were aroused even further.

"There is only one way to find out if that is so, sir."

His mentor nodded slowly. "You want to set a trap?" He always read from the same page. "You want to set a trap for my brother and his naukar?"

Thomas loathed himself for suggesting it, but as much as it pained him, he hoped such a gamble would be worth the risk.

Dr. Carruthers sighed deeply, mulling over the proposition. He closed his watery, unseeing eyes, as if to blur the thought. Finally he replied: "I will, but only to prove you wrong." He jabbed a finger toward his protégé. "A negative proof will suffice on this occasion."

Thomas very much hoped that would be the case. "I know it is hard for you, sir."

Carruthers managed to pull his lips into a smile to reassure the doctor that he understood the need to take such action. "What do you propose?"

Still feeling uneasy about such underhanded methods, Thomas nevertheless outlined his plan. "I suggest you tell the professor that an acquaintance of Flynn's has come forward with some of the captain's effects and that among them was a map. Tell him it is stored here, in the laboratory, and will be taken to the coroner on the morrow. If the map is still here in the morning, then the professor will be exonerated. He will not realize he has been tested and will be none the wiser."

"And if it is gone?"

"Then your brother will not be the honorable man I believe him to be."

The old doctor lifted his head toward Thomas. "I have your word that, if the map remains, he will never know of this?"

Thomas walked forward and shook his mentor's hand. "My word."

"Very well." Carruthers nodded emphatically.

Just as Thomas patted his mentor on the arm, Franklin, who had been shuffling in the corner by the window, let out a squeak and ran for his cage.

"What ails the rat?" asked the old anatomist.

Thomas looked toward Franklin, suddenly eclipsed by a shadow. The loss of light from the window high up in the wall had unsettled the creature. Thomas looked up to see the shadow fall away. "A fly, sir. Only a fly," he replied, even though he had the distinct impression someone had been listening to their conversation.

# Chapter 46

The offices of Hoxton & Fothergill lay within the vast precincts of Lincoln's Inn. Lydia recognized the place from her dealings with the late Charles Byrne, also known as the Irish Giant. As her carriage swept through the New Archway, she saw dozens of lawyers swathed in black gowns scurrying about. The very sight of them filled her with dread after all she had suffered at the hands of at least three of their kind.

Sir Theodisius, seated beside her in the coach, patted her hand reassuringly. "You look nervous, my dear."

"Should I not be?" she asked with an anxious smile.

He shook his head. "This is a mere formality. I am sure of that."

On their arrival a somber-looking clerk led the pair of them into a dark office. Much of the daylight was blocked out by piles of legal ledgers and bills that leaned precariously in front of the small windows.

Behind a commodious desk that made him look even smaller than he actually was sat Gilbert Fothergill. If Sir Montagu had been a raven, then his clerk was a sparrow, all disheveled and fidgety, thought Lydia. He rose to greet his visitors. Although he had spent much of his time in Sir Montagu's employ, it seemed he was also in partnership with another solicitor, and now acted as the deceased's attorney.

"My condolences once again, m'lady," he told Lydia. She nodded graciously, even though she felt nothing but loathing for the little man. He had, after all, colluded to have her committed to Bedlam. He was not to be trusted. "So," he said, busying his hands with the papers in front of him, "shall we begin?"

"The sooner, the better, man." Sir Theodisius felt almost as much contempt for Fothergill as Lydia, although he was prepared to show his feelings.

"Very good, sir," he replied, peering over his spectacles. He cleared his throat. "*I, Montagu Henry Ambrose Malthus, being of sound mind, do hereby revoke all former testamentary dispositions made by me and declare this to be my last will and testament.*" Fothergill's eyes darted from Lydia to Sir Theodisius and back.

"Get on with it," grunted the coroner in a curmudgeonly fashion.

"*Subject to the payment of my debts, funeral expenses, and administration expenses, and having no legal issue, I give all my estate, to include Draycott House, its adjoining lands and farms, both real and personal, to Richard Michael Frederick Crick, the seventh Earl Crick, to be held in trust by his mother, Lady Lydia Sarah Farrell, until he reaches the age of twenty-one,*" pronounced the solicitor.

Lydia had not realized that up until that point she had been holding her breath. She now allowed herself to exhale. Sir Theodisius reached for her hand and patted it once more. She felt there was a certain justice to the legacy, a righteousness in Sir Montagu bequeathing his entire estate to her son by way of an apology for the torment he had caused her.

It was then, however, that Fothergill produced a trump card, or rather the ace that Sir Montagu had held up his sleeve. "There is, I must warn you, a caveat," he told Lydia without daring to look her in the eye.

Sir Theodisius scowled. "A caveat?" he repeated. "What the deuce . . . ?" He leaned forward in an attempt to grab the document from Fothergill's hands. "Caveat? Give me that!"

"Sir, please!" urged Lydia, staying the coroner's hands. "Allow Mr. Fothergill to continue."

The solicitor's feathers were clearly ruffled, but he carried on:

*"The said bequest is made on condition that the said Lady Lydia Sarah Farrell shall not remarry, but remain in her widowed state. Failure to comply will result in the trusteeship of the estate reverting to the Court of Chancery."*

For a moment there was silence in the room. Outside a blackbird chirruped in a tree, and a bell tolled the hour, but inside the solicitor's chambers Lydia was in shock. She had not expected this. "A mere formality," Sir Theodisius had said.

"Oh, my dear, even in death he continues to haunt you," said the coroner, the edges of his mouth sloping sharply in his disappointment.

Lydia, however, straightened her back and stuck out her chin. "Can I not challenge this, Mr. Fothergill?" she asked.

"In court, m'lady?"

She nodded. "Yes, in court."

Sir Theodisius intervened. "That would be most costly, my dear, and—"

"And if I do remarry, Mr. Fothergill, what happens then?" She leaned forward, her voice growing more agitated.

The solicitor lifted the document from the desk, then put it down again nervously. He pushed back his glasses, which had slipped down the bridge of his nose, and focused once more on the will. "There is a clause here that will put the entire estate in the hands of the Treasury," he said. "In that case, m'lady, I fear the earl would lose all his inheritance."

*Chapter 47*

That night Thomas set the trap. Over dinner Dr. Carruthers had informed his brother about the existence of the map and that it lay, until its collection the following morning, in the laboratory. It would then be presented, the professor was told, to Sir Stephen Gandy, the Westminster coroner. Thomas had spent the evening with both siblings; then, as the clock struck ten, he announced he would retire. The brothers followed suit, and Thomas saw both enter their respective rooms. He, on the other hand, after a decent interval had passed, grabbed a candle and returned downstairs to the laboratory.

Deliberately leaving the door unlocked, he entered the darkened room. The street lamp up above shone through the high windows, providing a little extra light. In the corner Franklin could be heard rustling and squeaking intermittently in his cage. Feeling his way through the gloom, Thomas headed for his desk and lit the lamp he kept primed on top of it. As the light pooled, he opened the top drawer and took out a scroll of paper. It was an old map of the Boughton Estate. He had secreted it in his case a few weeks back so that he could show it to Lydia at the height of Sir Montagu's efforts to enclose the common land. Now it was, to all intents and purposes, redundant, but he had a much more valuable use for it. As long as the professor did not inspect the map too closely at first, there was every chance he would be fooled. In the dark, such a document might well pass for a sketch of the diamond fields. At any rate, that was what he was gambling on.

Next Thomas walked over to a large barrel in the corner in which sand was stored. He started to shovel some out, spreading it thinly on the flags below, as was his practice before an autopsy. It soaked up blood and body fluids. Now, however, its purpose was different. It would, he hoped, help trap a murderer. Even if, by some strange twist of fate, he failed to apprehend the professor, or perhaps an accomplice, stealing the map red-handed, the culprit's footprints would be left behind. If they matched the bloody imprint he collected from Sir Montagu's study, then he would have more evidence that might lead to a conviction.

Satisfied that the sand was evenly spread around the desk, Thomas then snuffed out the lamp and groped his way through the blackness toward the large store cupboard. He was relieved when he felt the handle of the door and opened it. The dank space, crammed as it was with bottles and jars and casks of all sizes and descriptions, was large enough to accommodate three men comfortably, but it was not an enticing place to spend the night. Preserved livers and pickled brains did not make good bedfellows. Nevertheless, Thomas did find a moth-eaten blanket that had been used to wrap a femur. He laid the bone in the corner and pulled the blanket around himself. Leaving the cupboard door slightly ajar, he settled himself down to watch and to wait.

He knew it would be an interminably long night, but he also knew that by the end of it, there was a real chance he might have some answers. Not that he relished the prospect of catching Professor Carruthers, or his servant for that matter, in the act of stealing this elusive map. He hoped he would be proved wrong, and if he was, although he would be none the wiser as to the murderer's identity, neither would anyone else. There could be no aspersions cast and no recriminations.

For the first hour or so, Thomas managed to keep awake, listening to the sounds of the street above as they crept through the grille. As the night wore on, however, so the music of the humdrum died away; the carriage wheels stopped turning, the horses' hooves ceased clattering, and sleep came calling, until suddenly . . . The sound of the lifting latch startled Thomas from his half-sleep. His eyelids sprang open, and he shook the fug from his head. Someone was entering the laboratory. His heart beat fast as he listened to footsteps cross the floor. He frowned. They were light, not a man's heavy tread. He held his breath as the intruder came into view and stood in the circle of light cast by the street lamp. So stunned was Thomas by what he saw that he cried out.

"Mistress Finesilver!"

Leaping 'round to face him, the housekeeper crossed her hands over her breasts as if to try and still her own heart.

"Dr. Silkstone!" she cried, steadying herself by the desk.

Thomas jumped to his feet and marched out of the cupboard. "What on earth . . . ?"

Still panting, Mistress Finesilver straightened herself and pulled her wayward shawl around her shoulders. "You gave me such a fright, sir!" she wailed.

Thomas reached for the lamp and lit it quickly. "May I ask what you are doing creeping 'round in my laboratory at this time of night?"

The housekeeper lifted her peevish face to his, but the normal look of resentment was replaced by embarrassment. "I . . . I . . ." she began hesitatingly.

"Well, mistress?" Thomas knew that she sometimes trespassed into his domain for her laudanum in his absence, but this foray was so brazen that it beggared belief.

"I came to see if you had any honey, sir," she said.

"Honey?" repeated Thomas. "Whatever for?"

"For Dr. Carruthers, sir. He asked me most particularly to have acacia honey for breakfast the other day."

"Yes." Thomas recalled the occasion.

"I knew we had three or four jars that an old patient had given to him a few weeks back, but when I went to the pantry, I couldn't find them anywhere."

"So you thought I might have taken them?" he asked in a more measured voice, realizing it was a thoroughly plausible explanation.

"Yes, Doctor. I didn't want to cause a fuss. I thought you might have used the honey for your experimenting, sir, or your pills and potions."

Thomas let out a deep sigh. "I can assure you I did not, Mistress Finesilver," he replied, thinking that she made him sound more like a warlock or a wizard than a medical practitioner. "Perhaps it might be easier to ask me directly in future."

In the lamplight Thomas saw her purse her lips together, as if she were slightly wounded and wished to retort. She did not. Instead she dipped a curtsy. "Yes, sir. Sorry, sir," she replied, even though the apology seemed to stick in her gullet. Nevertheless there was a smattering of humility that Thomas was not used to. "Good night then, sir," she told him, dismissing herself.

"Good night, Mistress Finesilver," he said as he watched her go. "Honey," he said to himself with a shrug, but then the memory of Flynn's hapless servant returned. "Acacia honey," he mumbled. He grimaced as he recalled the man's face smothered in the sweet substance to attract ants. Dr. Carruthers had been certain that it had been acacia honey when he smelled it. Thomas flinched suddenly as the unwelcome thought took root: Could someone in this very household have stolen the honey and used it to torture the Indian? His mind turned again to Professor Carruthers and his servant. Were they, between them, capable of such barbarity? It was difficult to tell what heinous crimes a man might commit under the influence of opium when his reasoning and senses were in altered states. The store cupboard door remained ajar. The professor might yet venture into the laboratory in search of the elusive map, Thomas told himself. He returned to his place. The wall clock opposite remained in his sight. It was not quite eleven. The night was, regrettably, yet young.

*Chapter 48*

"Still no honey?" moaned Dr. Carruthers, munching his buttered toast at breakfast the following morning. He stuck out his tongue to signify his displeasure.

Mistress Finesilver, pouring him a glass of milk, was about to answer when Thomas entered the room. He had slipped upstairs just as the housemaid rose to light the kitchen fire and managed to change his clothes. Nevertheless, he still bore the scars of a virtually sleepless night: dark bags under his eyes and a pale complexion.

At the sound of the opening door, Mistress Finesilver's gaze met Thomas's, but hers slid away almost immediately. She busied herself collecting dirty plates.

"No, sir, still no honey, I fear," she mumbled, conscious that Thomas's eyes were upon her.

The news made the old anatomist more insistent. "But I swear Joseph Crossley gave me some jars from his own hives a few weeks back."

Seeing the situation might escalate, Thomas intervened. "I am sure they've been put safely somewhere," he soothed, seating himself opposite his mentor.

Carruthers wiped his chin with his napkin. "There you are, dear boy!" he greeted through a mouthful. "That will be all, thank you, Mistress Finesilver," he said, waving a dismissive hand. The housekeeper was pleased to oblige and, gathering up her stack of dishes, left the room as quickly as she could.

"Well?" asked the old anatomist as soon as he heard the door click shut. Thomas could not decide whether his tone was conspiratorial or self-righteous.

"The professor is..." Thomas began slowly, wanting to make sure they would not be disturbed.

"My brother is not yet up. We are quite safe."

"Then I am pleased to report that no one attempted to steal the decoy last night."

Carruthers gave a triumphant nod. "By 'no one' you mean my brother and Sajiv?" There was an aggrieved righteousness in his tone.

Thomas could see that the old anatomist wanted him to eat his words. "I am sorry I doubted the professor and his man," he said, humbly. He was happy to make such an apology, although he did not regret laying the trap. Nor did he let on that he had not ruled Oliver Carruthers and his servant entirely innocent.

The old anatomist let the words hover on the air for a moment, allowing himself to savor them before he asked: "So what now?"

Thomas shrugged as he buttered a slice of toast. "What now indeed?" he repeated, letting his knife slice easily through the soft pat before him. "Tomorrow I shall be seeing Major Scott and I shall try and prize some information from him."

"And in the meantime?" Thomas detected a mischievous note in the question. "Might you take a little time off from the laboratory to clear your head?" The old anatomist paused. "And perhaps pay a visit to Lady Lydia later on? I know she is engaged this morning, but..."

"Engaged?"

Carruthers nodded. "My brother, my blameless brother," he added with relish, "is taking her ladyship and young Richard to see the elephant in the park, I believe."

Thomas arched a brow. "Oh?" was all he could say. He did not divulge that there was still something about the professor that made him uneasy. His rapid speech, his intense gaze, and, above all, his nervous tic—so often associated, in his experience, with stress or a singular trauma. He was, Thomas deduced, a troubled man with a hidden past.

His mentor picked up on his reticence, and his features hardened a little. "You still harbor your suspicions about Oliver?"

Thomas's mind knew it was useless being anything less than absolutely honest with his mentor. "I confess there are certain things . . ." he admitted, pouring himself coffee from the pot.

Carruthers shook his head. "O ye of little faith," he muttered. "My brother may be a little eccentric, but he is no murderer. You will be proved wrong."

"I hope I will, sir. I really do," replied Thomas. He downed his coffee quickly, then rose from the table, his chair scraping on the floorboards. "And now if you'll excuse me."

The old anatomist raised a buttery knife in the air. "Just one more thing," he called as Thomas made for the door.

Thomas switched back. "Yes, sir?"

"Lady Lydia left her shawl here yesterday. I think Mistress Finesilver put it over there."

Thomas scanned the room and spotted the wrap folded over the back of one of the dining chairs.

"Perhaps you could take it to her?" There was a wheedling note in the old man's voice.

Thomas caught his meaning. "Perhaps I could," he said with a smile. He lifted the shawl and instantly smelled Lydia's perfume. For a moment it was as if she was standing next to him.

"Promise me this," said Dr. Carruthers suddenly, breaking the spell.

Puzzled, Thomas looked up. "Sir?"

"Do not let Lydia go again, dear boy. Even if you neglect your own happiness, you cannot put right all the wrongs in the world. You know that, don't you?"

Thomas nodded and let a sigh escape from his lips. He acknowledged his mentor to be right. He needed to rekindle the fire between Lydia and himself that had been doused by countless absences and obstacles. In among all this murderous mayhem, he still had to find time for her. "I do, sir," he replied.

## Chapter 49

**P**rofessor Carruthers was in good spirits when, as arranged, he called at Sir Theodisius's mansion at a quarter to eleven o'clock later that morning. Unaware that his integrity had been tested and appeared to be unimpeachable, he arrived to collect Lydia and Richard. Nurse Pring was in attendance, too.

"Richard is most excited," Lydia told the professor as they made the short carriage ride to St. James's Park. "He has never seen an elephant before." She paused to look at her son, who was leaning out of the carriage window, his curly hair blown back from his face. "Nor have I," she added with a slight shake of her head.

"Then I am honored to be the one to introduce you. I am sure you will both be most impressed. Yes, indeed," the professor told her with his usual brusque delivery.

The party decanted at the grand gates of the park—carriages were only allowed inside by express permission of the king—before making its way on foot. Inside was a hive of activity. There seemed to be more deer and cattle than people, and the squawking of the waterfowl only added to the general sense of gaiety. On strict orders, the park sentinels were to bar any rude boys, beggars, or anyone hawking their wares, so Lydia felt quite at ease. There was little else to do but promenade with the other gentlewomen around the park, but still she found the novelty of it all quite enchanting. The trees were in full leaf, and there were displays of flowers in beds dotted alongside the shallow lake.

Beyond the commonplace sights and sounds, there was, however, another novelty that vied for Lydia's attention. An army of carpenters was camped at one end of the park, putting the finishing touches to a long wooden structure.

"What are they doing over there?" asked Lydia as she strolled along with the professor. Up ahead Nurse Pring trotted along behind Richard.

Carruthers crinkled his nose and stared intently ahead. "I believe they are constructing a gallery for the display, m'lady," he replied.

"A display?"

The professor stopped to study the large awning being fixed into place to form a covered gallery. "Fireworks," he told her curtly. "There is to be a firework display in honor of some visiting prince or foreign potentate tomorrow."

The prospect of such a display clearly pleased Lydia. "It is open to the public?" she asked.

"Yes, indeed. There is a poster at the gate. 'Tis possible to pay for seats in the gallery." He jerked his head toward the embryonic structure in front of them.

"Then we must go," she said excitedly. "We shall make up a party."

Meanwhile Richard was tugging at Nurse Pring's hand. "Where is the elephant, Mamma? Where is he?" He was jumping up and down impatiently.

The professor bent low to address the child, who backed away, a little afraid. Undeterred, Carruthers explained: "The creature will come from the direction of the King's Mews." He pointed beyond the trees. "Here should be a good spot from which to see him. Yes, indeed."

They had stopped at the side of the path, along with a few other parties of women and gleeful children. Carruthers looked intently at Richard as he held his nurse's hand. "He is so like you," he remarked to Lydia as they waited in the sunshine.

Lydia caught something sad and doleful in his tone. "Do you have children, Professor?" she asked.

Carruthers's eyes still played on Richard. "No children. No wife. I am married to my work," he replied wanly.

Lydia felt as though she had intruded on his personal life when he suddenly lifted his gaze and gave a tight smile, something she had rarely seen him do. For a split second, she felt the professor had lifted his mask. But it came down again soon enough.

"Mamma, look!" Richard cried excitedly. His hand shot away from hers to point to her right. Just emerging from the tree-lined avenue a few yards ahead was an enormous elephant. Draped in a large blue cloth that was fringed with gold, the beast was being led by a keeper dressed in a jacket of matching blue with a rose-colored silk robe and a cap in the Turkish style. Two liveried Indians followed on behind, carrying long staffs.

By now a number of other onlookers were also lining the path to watch the regular ritual. Several of them cheered as the elephant passed, its trunk swaying placidly from side to side. Richard seemed transfixed by the sight at first, but as the creature advanced to within a few paces of where he stood, he seemed to grow more anxious. He suddenly clung to his mother's skirts and hid his face.

"There is no need to fear," Lydia told him, stroking his head. "Look, my sweet. Look!"

Whether it was because of the cheering of the crowd or the fact that a flock of cackling geese took off from the nearby lake was not clear, but the elephant suddenly raised its trunk and trumpeted loudly. Some of the women screamed, a few men laughed and jeered, but the combined effects of the noise seemed to make the creature even more agitated. It shunted its rear off the path, and in response, its keepers hit its flanks. Their actions only appeared to irritate the elephant further, however. Its slow, measured pace suddenly turned into a trot, and it veered off onto the grass. The little clusters of onlookers started to disperse, and some children broke away from their mothers and nursemaids and began running hither and thither.

"Get back!" called the professor, grabbing Lydia by the hand.

"Richard!" she cried, reaching out to her son. She managed to grasp him and pull him to her. Nurse Pring, picking up her skirts, ran, too. Retreating into the shelter of the trees, they huddled together and watched anxiously. The elephant had stepped up its pace and started to run amok, trampling through the carefully tended flower beds up ahead.

The keepers ran behind it, shouting and waving their sticks to warn any unsuspecting walkers who found themselves in harm's way.

"You are unhurt?" asked the professor, still catching his breath.

Lydia nodded and drew Richard closer to her.

"Look! Soldiers!" yelled the boy.

From the direction of the main gate, half a dozen guards suddenly appeared. With muskets at the ready, they hurtled toward the elephant, which by now had reached the outer perimeter fence. A loud cry went up and a volley of shots rent the air. A deafening trumpeting followed, then silence.

"Oh no!" exclaimed Lydia, shielding Richard's eyes.

"Mamma! What has happened?" he wailed.

Lydia glanced at the professor, who had ventured out from the shelter of the trees. He stood a few feet away, within view of the soldiers. His back was toward her, but she suddenly heard another low trumpet, then an enormous splash. The professor stood motionless, watching the action. Lydia dared not look.

"Is the elephant hurt, Mamma?" Richard was pulling at her arm, straining to see the creature.

A moment later the professor turned and started making his way back toward them. Lydia read his expression. He seemed relieved.

"All is well," he told them.

"But the gunshot . . . ?" pressed Lydia.

"They fired into the air," he replied, shaking his head. "A foolish move, but the creature plunged into the water. He is calmer now. See. Yes, indeed. Calmer now." He pointed to a large dark mound on the edge of the lake. The elephant was half submerged, scooping up trunksful of water and showering itself. It appeared much more contented as its keeper tried to soothe it with pats and soft words.

"We must be thankful that no one was hurt," said Lydia.

"Quite so. Quite so," agreed the professor.

Lydia nodded and took Richard firmly by the hand. "Now let us return to the carriage, shall we?" she said. "We have had quite enough excitement for one day."

Thomas felt his pulse race even though he was standing stock-still. His bedchamber was chilly. The sun had not yet come 'round to heat it, but it was too warm to have a fire laid. And yet the palms of his hands were clammy. After another moment's pause, he reached for the desk drawer. Once more he took out the ring case and opened it. He held it to the light. It was a modest jewel, certainly compared with the magnificent diamond brilliant he had retrieved from Flynn's throat, and certainly by the standards of the English aristocracy. The meagerness of his offering suddenly seemed quite pathetic. He was not Lydia's social equal, not in English eyes, at least, and his income was paltry when measured against the wealth of the Boughton Estate. Most would say he was mad to even contemplate marriage to a titled lady. And yet . . . she had said yes to his proposal before. They were standing in the orangery at Boughton Hall on the morning of his departure after her mother's death. He had asked her to be his wife, and without hesitation she had said yes and nestled her head on his shoulder. There had been no ring, then, just a tacit agreement between them that they would be conjoined in holy matrimony. Events since had marshaled against them, but now that Sir Montagu was dead, there were no more obstacles, no more excuses. Why should she not agree again?

"Lydia," he whispered under his breath as he slipped the case into his pocket and tapped it gently. This time there would be no prevarication, no hesitation. His mentor was right. He could not afford to lose his beloved again. He would propose to her that very afternoon.

# Chapter 50

Lydia took a deep breath. She was relieved they were all safely back at Sir Theodisius's house after the incident with the elephant. Although none of them had ever been in any real danger, the whole episode could have turned out very differently. Professor Carruthers had called it "an adventure," and he and Richard had talked animatedly about the episode until they dropped him off in Mayfair to visit a friend. She had seen a whole new side to him on the excursion, and for that, too, she was gratified.

"Shall I take Master Richard for his nap now, m'lady?" asked Nurse Pring as they congregated in the hallway.

"Yes, please," replied Lydia, stroking her son's curly head. "Go with Nurse," she told him with a smile; then, turning to Eliza, who had just appeared, she said: "I think I will lie down, too."

The maid curtsied. "Very well, m'lady," she replied and began to climb the stairs to turn down the bed for her mistress.

Hearing the general commotion, Sir Theodisius put his head around his study door. "Ah, you are back, my dear," he remarked. "I trust you had an enjoyable excursion?"

Lydia nodded, but before she could answer in full, a scream tore through the house.

"What in God's name?" thundered the coroner.

"Eliza!" Lydia gasped, hurrying toward the foot of the stairs. "Eliza!" she called again as she climbed to the second floor as quickly as she could. Dashing along the upstairs corridor, Lydia saw Nurse Pring leave Richard's bedroom and head toward her chamber. The housemaid, too, appeared from the linen store and hurried in the same direction. They all converged at the open door at more or less the same time to see Eliza, her hands still clamped over her own mouth in shock, as she scanned her mistress's room.

Lydia gulped back a cry. "What the . . . ?"

The others at the door drew aside to allow their mistress to pass. Lydia's mouth first opened wide, then shut again as she walked into the scene of devastation. Every cupboard had been emptied, every drawer pulled out, every pillow and bolster slashed open so that fluff and down were scattered all around. A breeze suddenly blew in from the open window and caught a pile of the feathers, lifting and whirling them like snowflakes.

Lydia dropped onto her bed, as if the shock had made her light-headed. She surveyed the room. Pictures were torn from the walls, a vase had been upturned, and even the heavy drapes had been lacerated.

"God's wounds!" cried Sir Theodisius breathlessly. He had lumbered up the stairs in the wake of the ear-piercing scream to see for himself what calamity had been visited upon his household. His jaw dropped as he contemplated the scene.

By now Eliza's shock had turned to tears. "Who could have done this, m'lady?" she sobbed, standing by the window.

Lydia rose and walked over to her maid. Putting a comforting arm around her, she shook her head. She did not have a reply. There were no words.

"Only Dr. Silkstone can find the answer to that," mumbled the coroner, still trying to catch his breath. "We'd best send for him immediately."

As good fortune would have it, Thomas was already on his way. The weather was pleasant and he had decided to walk the mile or so to Sir Theodisius's house. Banishing all thoughts of the many burdens that weighed heavily on his shoulders, he concentrated instead on how he was going to frame his proposal of marriage to Lydia. He patted his frock coat pocket. The shawl was there. Its return gave him a good pretext for his visit. Not that he should need one, but it could be used to his advantage. After he had placed it in Lydia's hands, he might suggest they take some air. Together they would venture into the garden, and there, in the sunshine, surrounded by flowers and birdsong, he would hold her hand in his and ask her to be his wife. Or should he be more formal? In the absence of Lydia's father, should he first ask Sir Theodisius's consent, even though he held no official role? Should he ask her in the drawing room? Either way, should he go down on one knee, or should he remain standing? Spontaneity was not in his nature, and yet on this occasion and in these circumstances, he really could not make up his mind. As he walked through the wrought iron gates of the mansion, he was forced to concede that he might have to do what seemed most natural when the time came. Feeling slightly more confident, but nevertheless nervous, he climbed the front steps and lifted the knocker.

The sound of the rapping broke into the shared sense of bewilderment and fear of those who had gathered upstairs in Lydia's ransacked room.

"Who . . . ?" barked Sir Theodisius, almost jumping out of his skin.

But Lydia's finger flew up to her lips to call for silence. The butler was heard to answer the door, and a familiar voice inquired if her ladyship was at home.

"Thomas," she cried. "'Tis Thomas." She hurried out of the room and onto the landing to see the young doctor hand the butler his tricorn.

"Dr. Silkstone," she called down, more formally. "Thank God. Come, please."

From the distraught look on her face and the note of panic in Lydia's voice, Thomas could tell that something terrible had happened. He loped up the stairs two at a time and within seconds witnessed for himself the devastation wrought.

"What the . . . ?" He cast his gaze around the room: the slashed curtains, the ruffled bedding, the drawers tossed onto the floor. "Is anyone hurt?" he asked, hurrying over to Lydia.

She shook her head. "No, mercifully not. I was out and came back to find this." She flapped a hand distractedly.

"But I was in my study," exclaimed the coroner indignantly. "Such dashed nerve!"

"Has anything been stolen?" asked Thomas.

Lydia and Eliza exchanged a quick glance, and the maid rushed over to the casket where her mistress kept her jewelry. It lay discarded on the rug by the bed. She picked it up and inspected it. The lock had not been tampered with. She shook her head.

Striding across the room, Thomas headed for the open casement. "I fear this was no random intrusion," he said, sticking his head out of the window. The branches of a large tree reached to within inches of the ledge. Glancing at the pavement below, he could see a few broken twigs and several fallen leaves. It was clear to him that the intruder had climbed the tree to gain access.

Sir Theodisius, running his fat fingers over the shredded drapes, nodded in agreement. "Whoever did this must have known you were out, my dear," he told Lydia.

Thomas turned to her frowning. "And you were with Professor Carruthers," he said.

Lydia looked puzzled. "How . . . ?"

"Dr. Carruthers told me about your planned excursion to the park," he replied. "I thought you would have returned and—" Thomas suddenly stopped mid-sentence, realizing that the real reason for his visit needed to be postponed in the circumstances.

"And . . . ?" Lydia pressed, sensing he was holding something back. Her suspicion forced him to think on his feet.

"I wanted to return this to you." Suddenly remembering the shawl that Lydia had left at Hollen Street, Thomas delved into his pocket and brought it out.

"Thank you," she told him with a smile, taking the wrap from his grasp. She let it fall open, then slipped it around her shoulders, shivering as she did so.

Seeing her body judder, Thomas recognized the telltale signs. "You are in shock, m'lady," he told her. "You should rest."

"The doctor is right, my dear," agreed Sir Theodisius, lumbering forward and hooking an arm around her.

"And you?" she asked, fixing her eyes on Thomas.

He gave her a reassuring smile and cast a look around the room.

"I fear I have work to do here," he replied.

"Come, my dear," said the coroner, guiding Lydia toward the door. "We must leave the good doctor to his own devices."

Lydia nodded, but turned back suddenly. "You think you might be able to discover who did this?" she asked.

Thomas nodded. "There will be clues somewhere among this mess," he told her. "It is my task to find them."

"Come, my dear," repeated Sir Theodisius, growing slightly impatient.

Thomas watched the pair leave the room, followed by Nurse Pring. Eliza stayed behind and, bending low, started to pick up the shards of a broken mirror from the floor.

"No!" Thomas called out.

The maid froze. She switched 'round, her eyes wide.

"Please do not touch anything," he told her. "I need to inspect the damage for myself."

"Yes, Doctor," she said. "Shall I . . . ?" She pointed to the door.

"If you please."

She dipped a curtsy and scurried away, once more on the verge of tears, shutting the door behind her.

The escritoire near the window had suffered most in the burglary. Not only had all the drawers been cast aside, the leather that lined the inside of the drop-down lid had been slashed, too. This was not the work of some opportunist thief. This destruction, he could tell, was targeted and purposeful.

"The map," he muttered to himself. The lining would have been an obvious place to hide the ancient Sanskrit document that appeared to be in the murderer's sights. He would wager that it was the object of this search, conducted with the same frenzied fury as all four killings.

Suddenly a breeze rustled the drapes once more and he strode over to the casement, this time armed with his magnifying glass. Bending low, he inspected the window ledge. The intruder clearly had climbed up the nearby sycamore tree. But it would have been no mean feat. The trunk was relatively smooth. There must have been rope. He squinted at the branches once more. There was no sign, but there were marks on the sill. Muddy smears—the prints of fingers, no doubt, holding onto the ledge. He peered at them through his glass. There were three—no, four—marks of varying size. Something did not ring quite true about them, although he was not sure what. Nevertheless he moved on, inspecting the slashed pillows and the ransacked drawers over the next few minutes. No bolt of lightning struck him. There was no eureka moment. No inspiration. No hard evidence that told him who was responsible. As so often happened with this mystifying case, at the end of his inspection, he had drawn a blank.

*Chapter 51*

"Ah, Thomas!" Sir Theodisius greeted the young anatomist when he entered the drawing room half an hour later. "Found anything of note?" he asked, cocooned in his favorite armchair. Lydia sat opposite him.

Thomas sighed and closed the door behind him. "Nothing conclusive, sir," he replied, walking into the room, "although I do believe that the intruder may well have been searching for the map."

"A map?" asked Lydia. She was seated on a sofa, still wrapped in the shawl.

Sir Theodisius recapped his conversation with Michael Farrell about the existence of a rich source of stones.

"Did he ever mention anything to you about the mines?" Thomas asked her.

"Never." Lydia shook her head.

"And you found no evidence of any documentation when you were going through the captain's papers?" ventured the coroner.

Again Lydia shook her head. But in the ensuing silence, the mention of the affairs of a dead man raised the specter of Sir Montagu in all their minds. It was as if the very thought of him cast a dark shadow across all their faces. Thomas broached the subject.

"And there was nothing telling in Sir Montagu's will?" He

switched his gaze from Lydia to Sir Theodisius and back. "The reading went ahead as planned, I assume?" he asked quickly.

Sir Theodisius and Lydia swapped wary glances, and Thomas caught the anxiety in their expressions.

"Something is amiss?"

All along he had harbored a fear that Sir Montagu would, even in death, have the last laugh. He imagined the tyrant acting like a puppet master, pulling the strings of those left behind to pick up the pieces of his empire from the comfort of his coffin. It was obvious they were holding something back from him. He needed to know. "Tell me, I pray."

Sir Theodisius pointed to the mahogany cabinet that held several decanters. "Pour yourself a brandy, Thomas," he directed.

Thomas protested. "What is it?" He felt the cold steel of a knife twist inside him.

"Please." The coroner lifted up his flattened palm in front of his face to silence him.

Thomas reluctantly obeyed and seconds later, glass in hand, sat down beside Lydia on the sofa. His stomach began to knot once more. He braced himself for bad news.

The coroner took a gulp of his own brandy. " 'Tis a case of both good news and bad," he began.

Thomas straightened his back as if readying himself to bear the blows. "The good first, then, if you please." He needed to remain positive.

Sir Theodisius nodded to Lydia. "My dear," he said, inviting her to take the lead.

She took a deep breath and forced a smile to lift her lips. "Sir Montagu left his entire estate to Richard."

Thomas considered what she had said for a moment. He had feared that neither Lydia nor Richard would benefit at all from the late lawyer's will. Such a bequest would ensure not only the young earl's financial security but that of Boughton, too. "That is indeed good news!" he said, casting around for appreciation. "Is it not?" For a moment he could not understand why neither of the others shared his pleasure.

"It is indeed good news," agreed the coroner, nodding enthusiastically. "Of course until Richard's majority 'twill be held in trust by his mother." He jerked his head toward Lydia.

Thomas nodded. "That seems reasonable."

"Ye-es," drawled Sir Theodisius.

"But there is a caveat?" Thomas had already guessed there was a negative aspect to this arrangement.

"Of course there is a caveat," said Lydia, no longer able to contain her frustration. She rose from the sofa and headed over to the window, as if she could not bear to face Thomas when he heard the news.

Sir Theodisius remained seated, but the anatomist made to rise.

"No, wait," snapped the coroner, his outstretched arm barring his way. Thomas looked at him askance and stayed where he was. Sir Theodisius took a deep breath, put down his glass, and tried to compose himself again. He lifted his troubled face. "All this can come to pass only on condition that Lydia remains unmarried," he said. He clasped his hands behind his back so that his large stomach was thrust forward.

And there was the rub. For a moment Thomas remained rooted to the sofa as the news and its implication sank in. His shoulders sagged and his expression darkened.

"So Richard cannot inherit Draycott if we marry?"

Sir Theodisius sucked in his cheeks. "'Tis not just you, Thomas, 'tis . . ."

Thomas leapt to his feet. This time the coroner did not try to stop him. "Of course the clause was designed specifically for me. That tyrant could not bear to think of me as the master of Boughton," he cried. He could hear his own heart pounding in his ears. "He could not bear it if we were wed." Looking over to Lydia for some shred of comfort, he suddenly remembered the ring. Plunging his hand into his pocket, he brought out the box and opened it. He strode over to where she stood and thrust it in front of her.

"This is the real reason I came here today. I was going to ask you to marry me, again," he said, the words almost choking him. "But I can see I wasted my journey." He snapped shut the box and turned, not wishing her to see that his eyes were welling up with tears.

"No!" cried Lydia. "No!" she called out again, rushing after him as he headed toward the door. Tugging at his sleeve, she pulled him around to face her. Her eyes were glassy, too. "You don't understand, my love," she said, her hands reaching for his jacket.

Thomas nodded his head and swallowed back his anguish. "I do understand, dearest Lydia. I understand that your son's inheritance and the continuation of the Crick line is more important than any love we ever had for each other." His voice remained measured. "And the fault is all mine. I was deluding myself if I ever thought an American anatomist could be considered worthy of an English noblewoman," he said. And taking her right hand in his, he kissed it and bowed low. "Good-bye, m'lady," he said. He turned 'round and bowed to the coroner. "Sir Theodisius," he muttered, then continued toward the door.

"No!" cried Lydia once more. "Thomas." She rushed after him. "I will marry you," she called after him as he grasped the door handle.

At her words he stopped still, then wheeled 'round. His brows remained dipped in a frown.

"What did you say?"

Hurrying forward, she threw herself into his arms.

"I will marry you," she repeated. "I have no care for what others might think."

"But Richard? His inheritance?"

Sir Theodisius intervened. Judging from his startled look, this decision was clearly news to him. "My dear, are you sure?"

Lydia turned and lifted her face toward the coroner, thrusting forward her chin.

"Richard will come to understand that a person's happiness is worth so much more than any land and property," she said.

"That is true," conceded the coroner with a nod.

"Yes. Yes, it is true," replied Lydia, reaching for Thomas's hand and gazing at him. "Richard will not miss something he has never had. And I want to be your wife, my love. More than anything else, I want to be your wife."

Thomas took a breath and looked deep into her eyes for a moment. He knew she was speaking the truth. He smiled and reached into his pocket once more. "Then, you will consent to wearing this?" he said, opening the box. Removing the ring, he took her hand in his and slipped the stone on her finger. She held her hand out for a moment, studying the small sapphire. "'Tis the most beautiful ring I ever set eyes on," she said.

# *Chapter 52*

"**B**ut we must celebrate!" Dr. Carruthers clapped his hands gleefully.

"We must indeed! Yes, indeed!" chimed in his brother. "Hearty congratulations, Doctor," he said, shaking Thomas's hand, then muttering, "'Tis welcome news in among all this murder."

The professor's mumbled words did not, however, go unnoticed. They jabbed sharp as a stiletto, suddenly deflating Thomas's buoyant mood. For several hours he had barely given a single thought to the four unsolved murders that had hung over him for the past few days. He had returned to Hollen Street in the late afternoon. Sir Theodisius had insisted he stay for a celebratory luncheon washed down with liberal amounts of wine and port and had loaned him his carriage for the return journey home.

"A dinner! We shall host a dinner!" exclaimed the old anatomist.

"And fireworks!" added the professor.

"Fireworks?" queried the old anatomist.

"There are fireworks in St. James's Park tomorrow evening. 'Twill be most spectacular, and Lady Lydia was anxious to make up a party," explained his brother, barely pausing for breath.

Thomas regarded this verbal sparring with a mixture of amusement and dismay. His happiness at Lydia's acceptance of his marriage proposal was tempered by the thought that he was really no nearer to unmasking the killer or killers at large. His unease was compounded by the fact that he had also just remembered he had accepted a supper proposal with Marian Hastings and her coterie. He knew the meeting could prove very useful to his investigations. He also planned to find out if any of them knew of the existence of this ancient map. Finally he interrupted the brothers' banter.

"Gentlemen. Gentlemen, your attention," he pleaded. Both men turned in his direction. He went on: "I have accepted an invitation to sup with the governor-general's lady tomorrow."

The old doctor looked crestfallen. The professor's expression registered disappointment. Any plans for a celebratory dinner were thrown into disarray.

Thomas raised a finger. "But the fireworks will not begin until dark, so I propose that we all rendezvous in the park a little later."

His suggestion was considered in silence for a moment until first the professor and then his mentor nodded slowly.

"Yes. Yes," agreed Dr. Carruthers, adding: "As long as you describe the displays to me, dear brother."

"'Twould be an honor. Yes, indeed," came the reply.

"Good, then 'tis settled," said Thomas, clapping his own hands and rubbing them together. Tomorrow evening would be a combination of business and pleasure. He was aware that to mix the two often proved wholly unsatisfactory. He very much hoped that his plans would prove the exception rather than the rule.

Thomas retired to his room a little earlier than usual. Slipping off his clothes, he laid them neatly over his chair, and eased on his nightshirt. Then, after plumping his pillows, he climbed into his bed to contemplate events. It had been a momentous day; a day of surprises, both welcome and unwelcome, but above all a day of celebration. Thanks to Sir Theodisius's hospitality, he still had the headache to prove it. The wine had flowed freely and future plans were discussed. When the late hour forced him to go, he had left Lydia happier than he had seen her in many a long month. She was positively flushed with excitement. They would read the marriage banns as soon as possible, as soon as Lydia felt it safe to return to Boughton. Their wedding would take place before Christmas. At least that was what was hoped. Of course until Sir Montagu's killer had been apprehended there could be no ceremony. Even in death he stood in the way of their happiness.

Thomas turned over to lie on his side. And yet, he told himself, by making Lydia Richard's executrix, the dead lawyer had, in effect, been testing her. It was not beyond the bounds of possibility that he had staked everything on her acceptance of his terms: that, for Richard's sake, she would not turn down the Draycott Estate. Sir Montagu had not, however, bargained on her putting her love for an American before her duty. But then again, neither had he. When faced with such a choice, Thomas had feared Lydia would put Richard's future before their own in order to secure the vast acreage that adjoined Boughton. Instead, she had chosen to follow her heart rather than her head. For that he would be eternally grateful. He only hoped that Richard would not resent his mother's decision. He turned onto his back once more.

Somewhere in the night a dog barked. It set a baby crying, who caused a man to shout. Thomas sat up and walked over to the open window, reaching for the latch. As he did so, he remembered the devastation of Lydia's room and the casement through which the intruder had gained access. He thought, too, of the large thumbprints on the window ledge. They had puzzled him at the time and now he suddenly realized why. Stepping forward, he felt something beneath his feet. He looked down to see a pencil on the floorboards. He stepped back and bent down to pick it up from under his toes, and that was when it struck him. The strange prints had not been made by a thumb at all. They had been made by toes. Big toes. Whoever shinned up the tree and slid in through the window did so in bare feet— a climbing boy, perhaps, although there was no sign of any soot. Few Englishmen would have been capable of such a maneuver. An Indian mayhap? He thought of the coir rope, the curved blade, and the bizarre ant torture. It was suddenly even more important that he attend Marian Hastings's supper. The more he thought about it, the more convinced he was that the murderer was of Indian origin. Somehow he needed to question members of the large entourage that had accompanied her.

Glancing over at his desk, he saw the pile of letters written by Patrick Flynn. In the light of all he now knew, he would go through them one more time. Perhaps he had missed a vital clue. It would be another long night.

*Chapter 53*

It was all arranged. Shortly before dark, at nine o'clock, a carriage was to call at Hollen Street to pick up Dr. Carruthers and his brother, accompanied by his naukar. They would be transported to St. James's Park. There they would make their way to the grand viewing gallery to meet the rest of the party. Sir Theodisius and Lady Pettigrew, Lady Lydia, and the young earl and his nurse would all be there, no doubt in a high state of excitement as they awaited the start of the firework display. Thomas would join them as soon as he could make his excuses from his prior engagement in South Street.

By late afternoon the young doctor had readied himself upstairs. Bewigged and perfumed, he was about to leave the house when he looked in on Dr. Carruthers to make sure he was happy with their plans. However, what he saw as he opened the door disturbed him. He found the old anatomist very out of sorts. Ensconced in his usual chair, he barely acknowledged Thomas's presence when he entered the room.

"Sir, you are unwell?"

"I fear I am most light-headed," came the feeble reply.

Thomas felt the old man's pulse. It was weak. He had seen him in a similar condition before and was forced to acknowledge that his aging body was beginning to falter.

"Some of my tonic, perhaps?" he suggested, walking over to a bottle on a nearby table that was kept for such eventualities.

He poured out the thick, syrupy fortified wine and handed his mentor a glass. He guided the rim to his mouth.

Carruthers slurped the tonic. "I fear I will not be able to come tonight, dear boy," he said, licking his lips.

Thomas squeezed his hand. "I think you are wise, sir," he replied. "No doubt the fireworks will be very loud."

"But there is no reason why my brother cannot go."

Thomas shook his head. "No. If he still chooses to."

The old doctor smiled. "Oh, he seems most excited by the prospect of roaring rockets and thunderous explosions!"

Thomas smiled, too. "Then I shall see him there," said Thomas. "If you are sure . . ."

Carruthers waved a feeble hand. "I am much better off here," he assured his protégé, "although I doubt I'll get much rest with all the bangs."

"I doubt if any of London will, sir," agreed Thomas, letting the old man's hand drop. "But now I must away to see Mrs. Hastings."

"Ah, yes," replied Carruthers. "The enigmatic Marian. She has clearly fallen for your charms, dear boy," he remarked with a chuckle, then added: "But your interest is purely professional."

"I shall be asking some surreptitious questions about her servants, yes," he admitted.

Thomas had remained awake until the early hours, reading and rereading Flynn's letters to Lavington. With the benefit of the knowledge now gleaned, he had paid particular attention to the account that reported in horrific detail the execution, by elephant, of an Indian merchant. It was then that he discovered something he had previously overlooked. Buried in the tiny text, he had picked up the fact that the merchant was reported to be from the Gujarat region, and his name was Bava Lakhani. In the solitude of his room, Thomas had coupled this new intelligence with a throwaway remark made by William Markham after dinner the other night. Referring to Michael Farrell's diamond ring, he'd said there was a rumor that the captain had "murdered for it." He feared there might well have been blood on the precious stone long before he'd removed it from Patrick Flynn's throat.

Acutely aware that he needed to act with caution, Thomas settled into the sedan chair to take him to South Street. He had no desire to arouse suspicion among the select party, and yet he was convinced that there had to be a link between the arrival of the governor-general's wife in England and the four murders, even though Sir Montagu was killed before her coming. The strongest connection surely lay with Mrs. Motte. Her husband languished in a debtors' prison in Calcutta, thanks, at least in part, to Patrick Flynn. There was no doubt she had a motive to murder the captain, but what of the others? He contemplated Scott, a close ally and friend of Motte's. Was his bite equal to his bark? He had arrived in an advance party and had been in England when Sir Montagu was so brutally murdered. Might he have mistaken the lawyer for the late and not-at-all-lamented James Lavington? Could he have commissioned a lascar to inflict such horrendous torture on the Indian servant and Flynn? Or Markham? Quietly efficient William Markham, with his addiction to opium. Warren Hastings had enlisted his organizational skills to ensure that his wife's stay in London passed effortlessly. Perhaps he had also applied these skills to murder. The countless possibilities whirled around Thomas's head as he alighted from the sedan chair. He marched up the steps of the town house.

Shown into the drawing room by a turbaned servant, Thomas was greeted by Mrs. Hastings and Mrs. Motte.

"Ah, Dr. Silkstone. Ve are delighted to see you again," Marian Hastings gushed.

Her companion also seemed more lively than usual, and her smiles appeared more forthcoming than on previous occasions.

"Good evening, ladies," Thomas said with a bow.

An Indian servant immediately appeared with a tray of glass cups containing some sort of punch. Thomas waited until the ladies had taken theirs. He had expected to be joined by Major Scott and Mr. Markham, but after a minute or two of small talk and idle pleasantries it became obvious that neither was going to make an appearance.

"Ve vanted you all to ourselves, Dr. Silkstone," explained Mrs. Hastings. She slid a sideways look at Mrs. Motte. "You see, Dr. Silkstone"—she hooked an arm through Thomas's—"ve heard about ze murders: first Captain Flynn's servant, then Mr. Lupton, and now Captain Flynn himself."

Few things, Thomas knew, could be kept secret in London, so it did not surprise him to discover they knew of the murders of the captain and his man, but it beat him how the ladies could have known about Lupton's death.

"You are well informed," he told them, "but how—"

"I told them," said an unfamiliar voice from the doorway. Thomas's head jerked 'round to see a smallish gentleman, smartly dressed, making his way toward them. Bibby Motte turned as he approached, then linked her arm in his.

"Dr. Silkstone," she said to Thomas, "allow me to introduce you to my husband."

"Mr. Motte?" Thomas could not hide his shock. "Forgive me, sir, but I understood you were—"

"In jail, Dr. Silkstone? In Calcutta?"

Again, Thomas could not hide his shock. "Yes."

"Indeed I was, up until four months ago, when I was mercifully freed," explained Motte, his cheeks hollow and his skin weathered. "A close friend of mine paid my passage, and my ship anchored in the Channel two days ago. I made it to London yesterday to discover my worst fears founded."

Bibby Motte beamed and looked up at her husband. "It was a complete surprise, but a most wonderful one."

"A surprise?" repeated Thomas, thinking aloud.

Motte nodded. "You are wondering why I did not inform my wife of my release, Dr. Silkstone?"

"I . . ." Thomas found himself floundering.

"It was because I came to warn certain people."

"Warn? Warn who?" asked Thomas, growing increasingly agitated.

Motte turned to Mrs. Hastings. "Perhaps I could be permitted a moment alone with Dr. Silkstone," he said.

"Of course," agreed Marian Hastings, fluttering her fan. She glanced at Bibby Motte, who slid her arm out of her husband's. Both left the room.

"Please." Motte gestured Thomas to a chair by the fireplace and the doctor sat. "I understand you have been investigating these terrible murders, Dr. Silkstone," he began, settling himself opposite.

"I have," replied Thomas, eager to allow Motte to explain himself.

The chair in which Motte sat swallowed him up, making him look even more emaciated than before. It was clear to Thomas he had been through a great ordeal.

"My only regret is that I arrived too late to prevent them," he said, shaking his dark head.

Thomas leaned forward, eager to know more. "Pray explain yourself, sir," he urged.

Motte took a deep breath, but his eyes slid away from Thomas's.

"The information I am about to divulge is for your ears and yours alone, Silkstone," he began. "Mrs. Hastings tells me you are a man of integrity and can be trusted." His gaze switched back and latched onto Thomas's face.

"Sir, if you have any intelligence about these murders, I beg you tell me. I fear more lives could be at stake," Thomas told him.

Motte nodded gravely. "You are right, Dr. Silkstone. You are right." Suddenly he rose and leaned his elbow on the mantelshelf. "While I was in prison, I shared a cell with a merchant." His head darted back to Thomas. "Have you ever been in a jail, Dr. Silkstone?"

Thomas nodded. "I have had the misfortune to see its appalling conditions several times," he said.

Motte stuck out his chin. "Then you'll know that it can be the loneliest place in the world and that any companionship is most welcome."

"I can imagine it must provide some comfort."

"This merchant and I passed the days avoiding the scorching

sun and the nights avoiding the rats, but in between we talked."
There was a faraway look in Motte's eyes. "We swapped our life
stories, as you might expect, but little did we know that our
paths had already crossed."

"How?"

Motte returned to his seat and faced Thomas. "This merchant was a bania, a Gujarati, who once had an associate with
a diamond to trade, a huge diamond from Golconda that had
been brought to him by an escaped miner."

"Go on," urged Thomas, feeling his muscles tense.

"So my cell mate's associate made a deal with some East
India Company men."

Thomas's eyes widened as a picture suddenly began to take
shape.

"By the names of Farrell, Lavington, and Flynn?"

Motte nodded, "Farrell, Lavington, and Flynn," he repeated,
spitting out the names as if they were venomous. "The scoundrels had already approached me and told me of this magnificent gem. They wanted to make a trade for it and they knew I
had a map of Sumbhulpoor."

"Showing the location of the untapped mines," interjected
Thomas.

"That was what they believed and I did not discourage them,
but in truth, I thought it worthless. I had brought back many
mementos from my travels to the interior, and Farrell wanted
what he thought was a map."

"What he *thought* was a map?" queried Thomas.

"India is a land of mysticism, Dr. Silkstone, of rich and fanciful things, where legends abound. Rumor had it that I had an
ancient map in my possession. It was a decorative silk scroll,
embroidered with lines and symbols. No Englishman could either read it or translate it. But for some reason, Farrell thought
it valuable."

"Sanskrit," murmured Thomas.

"Meaningless patterns," Motte countered with a flap of his
hand. "Anyway, the scoundrel insisted I give him a down payment to secure my interest in the merchant's stone that he in-

tended to purchase. Twelve thousand pagodas I gave him. That's almost five thousand pounds. He assured me it was worth at least fifty times that amount."

"And that was the last you saw of him?"

"Oh, I waited for him to show up with the stone, of course. But he did not. He was meeting with the merchant and the miner at the appointed time, but he never returned. I was forced to cut my losses."

"You were plunged into debt?"

Motte shook his head. "Hear me out, if you will, Doctor." He sighed deeply. "I was still reeling from the financial blow when, three days later, I was invited by the nizam himself to witness an execution. As an Englishman of some standing, I was to be the honored guest. I never relished the prospect. I had been to a couple before. But this, this was to be a special execution. It was the nizam's birthday and he had selected the method of death. A merchant had been found guilty of murdering one of his escaped miners and stealing a large diamond. His punishment was to be pulled limb from limb by an elephant."

Thomas thought immediately of the newspaper cutting and the same wave of revulsion flooded over him. "But I have seen a report of this, sir."

Motte shrugged. "It was much talked about at the time, but I doubt it mentioned that the merchant's young son fell at the nizam's feet and begged mercy for his father."

Thomas pictured the heart-wrenching scene. "What happened?"

A look of disgust swept over Motte's face. "The nizam ordered the child strapped to a chair by his throne and forced him to watch his father's anguish in front of the cheering crowd." He closed his eyes for a second. "I am not squeamish, Silkstone, but the sight will stay with me for as long as I live. Can you blame the boy for swearing to avenge his father's death by killing everyone who had betrayed him?"

Thomas's mind was racing to catch up with the shocking story Motte was telling. "What happened to the child?" he asked.

Motte's tone lightened slightly. "The boy was shown pity by an Englishman who took him into his service."

"An Englishman?" Thomas was intrigued.

"Yes." Motte fixed Thomas with a stare. "An Englishman who arrived in London but recently, bringing his trusty servant with him."

"And this trusty servant . . . ?"

". . . is the very same." Motte nodded.

"And you fear that this young man is still hell-bent on revenge?"

Motte reached into his waistcoat pocket. "I know he is." He flourished a letter. "Shortly before he left India, he wrote to me in jail. After all these years, he was finally traveling to England. He taunted me with his intentions, knowing I was powerless to act. Before I could warn anyone, his ship had set sail for London." He handed the letter to Thomas, who scanned the poorly formed characters. The English was poor, but the intention very plain.

"Who is the young man's master?"

Motte shook his head. "I fear I have not managed to find out. All I know is that he is a surgeon."

"A surgeon!" repeated Thomas. He leaped to his feet. "A surgeon turned academic?"

Motte's head jerked up. "You have someone in mind?"

"I do," said Thomas, heading for the door. Everything was suddenly falling into place. "And from what you've told me, I fear he could be the next victim."

## Chapter 54

There was a great flurry of excitement as Professor Carruthers's carriage pulled up outside Sir Theodisius's house. Plans had changed due to the elderly anatomist's indisposition. Rather than arrive at the venue alone, the professor had decided to rendezvous with the rest of the party prior to setting off for St. James's Park. He had therefore hired his own carriage.

The Oxford coroner stood on the threshold to greet the professor. Lady Pettigrew was dressed in all her finery and even sported two stuffed finches in her hair. Richard, too, was dressed in a new pale blue silk coat.

"Can I travel with Sir Theo, Mamma, please?" asked Richard as they gathered on the steps.

"You may, my dear, if that is well with Sir Theo," replied Lydia, looking at the coroner as she spoke.

Sir Theodisius chuckled. "Lady Hattie and I always welcome young company. Of course you may, young sir," he said, and with that Richard was ushered into the first carriage, together with Nurse Pring. In Dr. Carruthers's absence, Lydia was left to take the other.

"Then may I have the honor of accompanying you, your ladyship?" asked the professor from the carriage window.

Lydia looked up at him. "The honor is mine, sir," she said with a smile as she settled herself into the carriage, smoothing her skirts. The professor sat opposite, with Sajiv, resplendent in a saffron turban, next to him. A moment later the whip was cracked and off they went, and at a goodly pace behind the coroner's carriage.

"And I believe congratulations are in order?" The professor's droopy face suddenly lifted as he struck up the conversation.

Lydia smiled back. "Yes, indeed," she replied. She touched her hand almost involuntarily, just to reassure herself that the ring remained on her finger.

The professor noted it, and an odd look returned to his face, as if an unwelcome thought or memory had reminded him of a past event. "A little more modest than your late husband's diamond," he said, thinking aloud.

The remark shocked Lydia, and she withdrew her hand like a crab retreats into its shell. "You knew my husband, Professor?" she asked, hiding the ring in the folds of her skirts.

Seeing her displeasure, however, Carruthers tried to rectify his thoughtlessness.

"Forgive me, your ladyship, I . . . I did not . . ." he said, groping for an excuse. "Yes, I did encounter your late husband."

Although she was taken aback by his candor, Lydia had no desire to make the professor squirm with embarrassment any more than he already was.

"My late husband was an interesting character," she told him with an enigmatic smile. "Perhaps we should leave it at that."

The professor, eager to seize the diplomatic lifeline she had thrown him, had just begun to nod his head enthusiastically when their vehicle, which had made painfully slow progress, suddenly came to a halt.

The two carriages had originally set off in convoy, but as they approached the park, the thoroughfares had become unusually busy. Several times, the driver was forced to pull up to allow another conveyance to pass or overtake them. As a consequence the party became separated, Sir Theodisius's carriage making better progress. Such delays put Lydia a little on edge. She began looking out of the window, wishing the buildings to pass faster.

Now that they were stationary, the professor put his head out of the window to see what was amiss.

"Some chickens have escaped from their crate!" he told Lydia. " 'Tis mayhem!"

Lydia looked out to see for herself several men running hither and thither after a dozen squawking fowl. Shouts and cater-wauls filled the air, and it was a full five minutes until the road was once more cleared. By this time it was almost dark and buildings were no longer landmarks but obstacles to be avoided. In the gloom, the streets merged into one long thoroughfare that twisted and turned, with long bends and sharp angles. Indeed such was the general confusion of the journey that both Lydia and the professor assumed when the driver veered down a side street that he was taking a short cut to avoid the traffic.

Shortly after, however, Lydia began to express her doubts.

"Surely we must be nearing the park soon," she said, lifting her gaze to the window once more.

The professor shrugged. "It is madness out there, your lady-ship," was all he could say.

Soon, however, they felt the carriage start to slow. Lydia craned her neck. "But surely this is the King's Mews?" she asked.

The professor also peered out. "The King's Mews?" he re-peated incredulously. "By Jove, so it is."

Although they were only a quarter of a mile from the park gates, Lydia knew they were not in the right place. They drew to a halt in front of a large brick block with grilles high up in the tall walls.

"This is where all the king's carriages are kept," she pro-tested. "We are in the wrong place. We must tell the driver."

A loud roar suddenly tore through the air, followed by sev-eral hollers or grunts.

"What on earth?!" Lydia's hand flew up to her chest, as if to still her heart.

The professor smiled. "It must be one of the king's tigers. Yes, indeed. There is also a small menagerie housed there, I believe, your ladyship."

Lydia remembered the elephant. "Ah, yes," she replied with a nod. "But what are we doing here? Surely we do not have to make our way to the park gates on foot?"

"Most strange," agreed the professor as his left cheek began to twitch. "Most strange. Yes, indeed."

*Chapter 55*

Darkness now cloaked St. James's Park as Thomas frantically elbowed his way through the throng. Somewhere in the near distance the strains of violins could be heard. They mingled with the calls of vendors selling nosegays for the ladies and pies for the men. Ignoring the pain that had flared once more in his chest, the doctor sprinted toward the long gallery. Here the more genteel people who had paid a pretty penny for their tickets could be found. He prayed Lydia's party would be there by now.

As Thomas ran, the first punch of a volley of rockets burst forth, scattering white sparks like diamonds into the dark blue sky. Screams went up from the crowd, which was taken unawares by the thunderous bangs. Next came a cascade of red feathers spilling out from a huge explosion of gold, then shards of silver that exploded and shimmered like stars. Loud alarums and squeals of delight rose into the air. A group of ladies nearby flapped their fans excitedly. Others broke into spontaneous applause.

The night air was heavy with the bitter smell of sulfur. Gray clouds of it rolled along like fog. There were other notes, too. Had he been there, thought Thomas, Dr. Carruthers would have been able to identify them: antimony and possibly a hint of phosphorus. Noxious gases billowed in puffs where the fireworks had been ignited, as if from the mouth of some great unseen dragon. Where amid all this was Professor Carruthers, and where was Lydia?

Soon he reached the gallery and his heart missed a beat when he managed to pick out Sir Theodisius in no time at all. He and his gentlemen friends were laughing loudly, downing cups of punch. Lady Pettigrew was one of a huddle of elderly ladies, whispering and nodding as they watched the crowd like hawks. But of Lydia and the professor, there was no sign.

Richard, licking a lollipop, sat next to Nurse Pring. Spotting Thomas in the crowd straightaway, he leapt up.

"Dr. Silkstone!" he called, waving. The doctor hurried toward the young earl. "Where is my mamma, Dr. Silkstone?" he asked as Thomas drew level.

Thomas looked anxiously to Nurse Pring for an answer. "Her ladyship and the professor were following in the carriage behind, sir," she replied with a shrug. "They must have been delayed."

The news sounded alarm bells in Thomas's head. His heart began to pound even faster in his chest.

"There you are, Silkstone!" The coroner's voice boomed across the gallery. His face was flushed red, and it was immediately clear to Thomas that the punch had gone to his head. "By Jove! What a show, eh?"

"Lydia, sir," replied the doctor, ignoring the coroner's question. "Have you seen Lydia or Professor Carruthers?" His eyes were firmly set on the sea of heads in front of the gallery, scanning their familiar faces. Thomas edged forward. "Are her ladyship and Professor Carruthers not here, sir?" he asked. It was no use trying to suppress his mounting anxiety.

"Dash, no!" declared the coroner. "Must have got lost. Be about somewhere, Thomas. Do not worry yourself." He lifted his tankard. "Here, have some punch. It's got a real kick to it," he added with a wink.

Lady Pettigrew chimed in: "'Tis a pity dear Lydia is missing the display."

Thomas nodded. "Indeed," he acknowledged solemnly. "And you do not know why she might be delayed?"

The elderly lady shook her head so that one of her bird ornaments dislodged itself slightly. "Although I believe the driver was new," she added, not taking her eyes from the crowd before her.

"A new driver?" Thomas frowned.

"Yes, the professor's boy recommended him. An Indian, I believe," she said, fluttering her fan excitedly.

Thomas's eyes widened, and his stomach churned at the news.

Lady Pettigrew noted his fearful expression. "Whatever is it, Dr. Silkstone?" she asked. She did not receive a reply. Thomas melted back into the crowd, his brain awash with nightmarish thoughts. An Indian driver? A stranger, recommended by Sajiv? Loyal, dutiful young Sajiv. He tried to suppress the thought, but like an infected swelling it kept rising and throbbing in his brain. Could he be the dead merchant's son? How easily he could slip out of Hollen Street to commit his heinous crimes. Where had he been the other day when the professor was at the park with Lydia? Ransacking her bedchamber perhaps? Thomas suddenly thought of the other opportunities the servant had been handed: Had he not had access to the opium and the acacia honey? Perhaps it was he who was listening when he had hatched the plan to trap the professor? And now he was missing along with Lydia. Thomas had to get away from these crowds. He had to find her before Sajiv took yet more revenge. If Professor Carruthers was, indeed, the surgeon who showed pity to him, then perhaps he was safe, but Lydia, as Farrell's widow, would surely be the deluded servant's next victim.

# Chapter 56

Apparently marooned outside the King's Mews, Professor Carruthers grew more agitated by the second.

"But we shall miss the display," he complained. Lydia nodded in agreement. The professor turned to his servant, who'd sat in silence throughout the journey. "Sajiv, go and see what the driver thinks he is playing at," he instructed.

Sajiv, however, remained motionless, his palms resting on his thighs, his eyes set straight ahead. The professor frowned. He switched to his naukar's native tongue. "*Manne samaj nathi padtee Sajiv,*" he said, his tone much firmer. "I don't understand. What is wrong?" There was still no response.

"Is there something amiss with him?" asked Lydia, watching the servant, a puzzled look on her face.

Carruthers shook his head in frustration. "*Jaldi!*"

Just as he was about to remonstrate further, the driver suddenly flung open the carriage door. Although he was dressed in a tricorn and frock coat, Lydia noticed he was an Indian. By the look on his face, something, she knew, was wrong. Her alarm seemed to be the signal for Sajiv to act. He lunged across the carriage to land beside her. In one swift move, he drew a familiar dagger from his belt and held it to Lydia's breast.

"My khanjar!" cried the professor. "What the..." Carruthers lurched forward in an effort to save his companion, but the driver produced a dagger, too, and barred his way.

"You right, Professor," said Sajiv, his English broken. "This is royal menagerie, and we make special visit to one of the animals."

"Have you taken leave of your senses, man?" The professor's eyes bulged with fury.

"No, Professor," came the servant's reply. "I am *taking* my revenge. Out. Now!" He jabbed the air with his dagger, motioning his master to alight. Carruthers shuddered but reluctantly obeyed. Lydia, the khanjar now at her back, followed.

They stood at the bottom of a flight of wooden stairs that hugged the side of a high building.

"Up!" growled Sajiv, gesturing with the khanjar.

"What do you think you are doing?" cried Carruthers.

"No talk!" Sajiv screamed back.

"There is no need for this," pleaded the professor, holding out his arms to signify he had no idea what was happening.

But Sajiv was unyielding. "*Jaldi karo!*" he screamed, jostling the professor up the stairs.

In the gloom, they climbed up to stop in front of a door in the wall. The Indian driver unlocked it and pushed the professor and Lydia inside. The first thing that struck them as they crossed the threshold was the stink of ammonia. It stung their eyes and the backs of their throat. Lydia coughed. It took a moment for her eyes to adjust to the darkness, and when they did, she realized they were standing on a raised mezzanine platform in a huge high-ceilinged building. From the stink she gleaned it must be a stable that had never been cleaned. The orange light of the street lamps was glowing through the high grilles, but below all was in deep shadow. Suddenly something stirred.

"What was that?" Lydia gasped.

Sajiv, lighting a lantern, smirked. He motioned her forward to the wooden gallery railing, the rays of his lamp pooling on the floor below. Warily, Lydia peered down, and there, in the gloom, she saw something large lumbering about restlessly. She could hear it slurping and sniffling as it shuffled toward the light. Then, when she saw its eyes, small and wide set, looking out from its enormous head and its long trunk dangling from its head with ivory tusks on either side, she realized. The elephant they had seen in the park, that had shown both the majesty and the menace of its wild nature, was standing a few feet below them.

She wheeled 'round to face her captor. More than fear, it was anger that burned inside her. "Why have you brought us here?" she demanded. She watched as the professor, too, leaned over the railings to see the elephant shuffling in the shadows.

"What the . . . ?" Carruthers looked askance at his servant.

"Does this bring back a memory, Professor?" asked Sajiv, still holding the khanjar threateningly. "Or should I say *Doctor* Carruthers?"

Lydia switched her gaze to the professor. "What does he mean?"

Fear flickered across the professor's face like the candle flame in the lamp hanging on a nearby peg. He grasped the gallery rail as if to steady himself. "I don't know what you are talking about," he snapped, although it was clear from his expression that he did.

"Do not lie!" Sajiv suddenly lurched forward and jabbed him in the ribs, forcing the professor to look again at the elephant.

"No!" cried Lydia, her hands flying up to her mouth. But the naukar motioned to his accomplice. He was guarding the door, but now came forward to keep her in check while Sajiv devoted his attention to the professor.

"Does it remind you of something?" he barked, catching hold of his master's jaw and wrenching his head to the side. "Look," he cried, suddenly switching back to his native tongue. He forced the professor to double up over the railings, his hand tight around the nape of his neck, so he had no choice but to look at the elephant.

"Does it remind you of seeing a man, his hands tied behind his back, a blindfold on his head, kneeling on the dusty ground, surrounded by a crowd baying for his blood?" With each word, the Indian became more inflamed. He brought the dagger up to the professor's neck and pressed the curved blade against his flesh.

Seeing the professor in danger, Lydia lunged forward. "No, please!" she cried, tugging at the Indian's sleeve, but he thrust her back with a single blow from his elbow. She lost her balance, falling to the floor.

Still forcing the blade against the professor's neck, Sajiv continued. He spat out his words so that spittle flecked Carruthers's cheek. "Does it remind you of seeing the elephant slowly advance to within a few paces of the man, then, at the command of its mahout, lashing out with its trunk to knock him to the ground?"

The professor gritted his teeth and closed his eyes for a second as the blade suddenly broke his skin. He dared not breathe, but the Indian went on, his words roiling in his native tongue and his mind caught up in a maelstrom of violent memories.

"Does it remind you of the piteous cry that went up just before the elephant's foot crushed his chest? Or the groan that he made as he was tossed into the air, then speared by one of the tusks?" The Indian's eyes were wild with a mix of rage and terror as he recalled the execution. "Does it?" He pushed back the professor's jaw.

"Yes. Yes!" he replied, in the Indian's own language.

The acknowledgment seemed to break the spell for a moment. Sajiv withdrew the blade, and the professor's chin dropped down.

"I do, too," said the Indian, wiping the spittle from his lips with the back of his hand. He reverted to English. "I was twelve years old and that was the last memory I have of my father."

Lydia had, by this time, hauled herself to her feet. "Your father?" she repeated.

Sajiv switched his gaze to her. "Yes." He nodded before his eyes latched onto the professor once more. "Bava Lakhani. He was a trader. A diamond trader." He pointed to the professor with his khanjar. "And this man has his blood on his hands!"

"You remember how you and your friends killed the miner and stole the diamond?"

In the candlelight Carruthers's eyes were glinting with tears. "No. No. 'Twas not like that, I swear!" he protested.

But his protestations only served to anger the Indian, who once again thrust the khanjar to the professor's throat. "You cut off the miner's leg—to steal the diamond, then left him to die."

The professor's hands flew up to his ears. "No. No. I refused to amputate. I couldn't do it. It was Farrell who did it. Farrell, I swear!"

"What!?" cried Lydia. At the mention of her dead husband's name, she barged forward.

The Indian suddenly turned on her, thrusting the khanjar under her chin. "Farrell. Yes. Your husband." Released from the servant's grasp, the professor fell to his knees, gasping for breath. Lydia stepped backward as Sajiv now turned his fire on her. "They all in it together. They should all have been charged with killing one of the jagirdar's miners. Not my father. He tried to save him. But Farrell, Lavington, and Flynn, they run away, and Bava Lakhani took all the blame."

The professor heaved himself up against the railings. "Please believe me, Sajiv. I wanted no part in it."

The Indian jabbed the dagger against Lydia's bodice. "My father tell me the whole story. As he clung to the bars of his stinking jail, he tell me about the three English officers and he tell me about the map."

"The map?" repeated Lydia. Things were beginning to fall into place. The fear that she had held at bay for so long now began to make its presence felt. Her chest tightened and her palms became clammy.

The Indian nodded. "The ancient map of the lost diamond fields. It was supposed to secure his future and mine and my children's."

"So it was you who ransacked . . . ?" Lydia trailed off, the words cleaving to her mouth made dry by fear. She suddenly realized, too, that this silent, loyal Indian must have murdered four souls. He would surely not care about murdering two more.

Suddenly a sound like a loud thunderclap broke overhead. The noise reverberated around the lofty stable, bouncing off the walls and ceiling. The boom set the door frame juddering. The Indian raised his eyes heavenward.

"The fireworks," he said. Worse still, in the darkness below, the startled elephant let out a mighty trumpet. The Indian's lips split into an unsettling smile. "He does not like them," he said. "They make him restless."

Lydia's heart pounded. She saw her chance. Thinking of Thomas and his reasoned manner, she wondered how he might act in such a situation. She spoke in a measured tone. "Your father's suffering was terrible, but the past cannot be changed. We cannot undo what has been done." She paused for a moment, hoping for some reaction. There was none, so she continued. "I am sorry for what happened. I am truly sorry, but you do no good holding us here. What purpose can be served?"

For a moment she thought her words might have made an impact on the troubled youth before her. Watching his expression, she held her breath. In the candle glow, she saw the whites of his eyes, moist with tears. She saw, too, his humanity and the fragility of his condition. He had been so wronged. Slowly, she held out her hand. She hoped he did not notice she was shaking. "Your dagger," she said softly. He remained still, his breath rasping in his chest. She took a small step toward him and was suddenly so close that she could smell his breath, sweet and exotic, in the gloom. Then, without warning, he raised his arm and, with a roar, coshed the professor with the hilt of his dagger. He watched Carruthers fold like a rag and fall to the ground before he lunged after Lydia. In one bound he had pinned her up against the wooden pillar.

"*Tie her up!*" he ordered the other Indian, and in a second she felt a coarse rope cut into her wrists as she was bound tight against the wood.

"You are Farrell's widow. In my country that means you must die, too. We call it suttee."

"Good God, no!" cried the professor, hauling himself up from the ground. He lunged at the servant. Sajiv lashed out with the khanjar, and the blade sliced through Carruthers's coat sleeve, drawing blood.

"No!" screamed Lydia, pulling at the bindings. But it was no use. She was held fast.

"Down!" ordered Sajiv, pointing to the wooden stairs from the gallery with the dagger. "We go down."

The professor mouthed a protest, but confronted once more with the blade at his chest, he turned and started to stagger down the stairs into the darkened bowels of the enormous room. Sajiv followed, pausing only to unhook the lantern from its peg. "Down," he shouted again.

*Chapter 57*

As Thomas walked out from under the canopy of a tree, another cascade of sparks exploded from a large scaffold a few yards away, pouring down smoke. It was swiftly followed by a burst of maroons. The explosions ricocheted around his head. Each blast was a hammer blow to his brain. The sulfur stung his eyes and nose. He coughed for want of fresh air. His head, too, was fit to burst. He needed to escape the cacophony of the battlefield. He needed to find Lydia. He quickened his pace toward the main gate, and the farther he walked away from the display, the thinner the crowd became. He could see whole people once more, not just disembodied hats and wigs. It was then that he spotted a young woman, her chestnut hair piled on top of her head. She was wearing a peacock blue dress, his favorite color.

"Lydia!" he called, hurrying his step. She did not respond. "Lydia!" he cried again. He was within a few inches of her, and hearing his breathless approach, the lady turned. His heart sank when he realized his mistake. "Forgive me," he told the scowling woman.

Growing more anxious with every step, he walked on, all the while searching, his eyes latching onto every lady he saw. Within a minute he had reached the main gates, where stalls selling gingerbread and hot cross buns were ranged along the park railings. Bootblacks were doing a good trade, too, polishing the muddy shoes of those who were leaving the display. The sounds of exploding fireworks, although still loud, had dissipated with the distance. Thomas could even hear the hawkers barking their wares on the other side of the perimeter rails. But below their raucous cries, he detected something else: unfamiliar sounds, discordant and jarring in the distance. He stopped dead to listen, then hurried on through the gate. Turning to his left, he saw the great edifice of the King's Mews up ahead. Suddenly he could make sense of the resonances; they were neighs and bleats and roars and squawks. The animals and birds in the nearby menagerie were unsettled by the fireworks. Cooped up in their cages and stables, many of the creatures had been thrown into paroxysms of fear by the deafening explosions overhead.

What made him walk on toward the mews, he did not know. That the animals were clearly in distress rattled his nerves, but he knew he was powerless to help. Yet his footsteps took him faster and faster, and as he drew level with the great edifice, he noticed that something was not quite right. There seemed to be a flurry of activity around a side entrance. He sniffed. The familiar tang of sulfur from the fireworks already hung heavy on the air, but now there was something else. He hurried through the gate, narrowly avoiding colliding with a dark-skinned man fitted out in a tricorn and plain dress. The two exchanged wary glances, and the latter seemed agitated. He barged past Thomas, forcing him against the gatepost, and began to run toward the park. Thomas shouted after him, but there was no time to chase him, he knew that. As soon as he sniffed the air again, he understood. As the fireworks continued to pound the night sky, it seemed all hell had broken loose. Men and boys rushed around with pails of water amid volleys of shouts. Animals were braying and barking and kicking against the doors of their pens. And amid the chaos Thomas saw a stable lad tugging two blindfolded horses across the courtyard. Then he heard someone shout the dreaded word: "Fire!"

Within a minute the courtyard began to fill with smoke. From the corner of his eye Thomas saw men hauling a wooden engine over the cobblestones. They positioned it outside one of the large stables, where smoke was arcing up from under the huge closed doors. Suddenly a loud boom buffeted the air. It caused Thomas, standing nearby, to jump. But the sound was not made by a firework. It came from inside the stable.

"Keep clear!" shouted a hostler nearby.

"What's in there?" called Thomas.

"An elephant!"

Through the smoke, Thomas spied the outside staircase. He ran up the steep flight to the side door. As he did so, he could hear cries coming from within and a woman's screams for help. Frantically, he tried it. It did not budge. Cupping his hands around his mouth, he shouted down: "There's someone inside. Open the main doors. For God's sake! Open the doors!" He stumbled halfway back down the stairs and shouted again. "Open the doors."

Most of the men ignored him, but one of them shook his head. "The elephant!" he screamed over the sound of the cracking flames. "It'll run amok!"

Thomas ran back up the stairs and listened at the door once more. There was the cry again. Terror fused with panic as he realized the voice belonged to Lydia. There was no time to lose. He shouldered the door. It remained held fast. He tried again. Harder. This time it yielded. Inside the smoke was thick and choking. He felt his lungs fill with it immediately.

"Lydia!" he called.

Nearby he could hear her coughing. "Thomas!" she croaked through the fumes. "Thomas," she called again, and he followed her voice to the pillar.

Scrambling to untie her hands, he tried to reassure her: "You'll be safe in a moment," he told her.

"Professor Carruthers," she coughed, wringing her bleeding wrists. "He is down there." She pointed to the flames that licked around the hay feeders below them. The elephant could still be heard, stomping and kicking the door and trumpeting loudly.

"Get out of here!" Thomas pushed her toward the open door.

"But . . ."

"Out! Now!" he cried from the top of the staircase. It was iron, and as soon as he touched the banister, it seared his flesh.

He squinted through the smoke but could see nothing. He ventured farther toward the blaze and suddenly felt himself stumble on something halfway down the stairs. He looked down. A leg. His eyes followed it to make out Professor Carruthers sprawled, head down, on the treads. There was no time to check if he was still alive. The fire was taking hold of the wooden pillars that supported the roof, and the elephant was still lashing out, its great bulk smashing against the wooden door as it tried to free itself. Bending low, Thomas hooked his arms under the professor's and hauled him up the half dozen stairs. By now a group of men had stationed themselves at the door by the outside staircase at Lydia's bidding. They knew there were men in the building. Thomas delivered the unconscious professor into their waiting arms. Then, snatching a towel from a hook on the wall, he turned to go back down.

"What are you doing?" cried the head keeper after him. But Thomas did not reply. He was already halfway down the stairs, the rag tied over his nose and mouth. By now the elephant was weakening. It had collapsed on its side just by the main doors, and although it was still bellowing, it was rapidly losing its strength. Its life was ebbing away as the flames advanced, sucking the oxygen from the air.

Thomas looked to the source of the fire and managed to make out a water pump in the corner. Dodging the flames, he took off his coat, and winding it 'round the metal handle, he began pumping water furiously. Seconds later he realized he was not alone. Three stable hands joined him and began to fill leather buckets.

"Quick, men. The h-hay," he stuttered through his coughs.

The stable hands passed the pails in a human chain, dousing the blaze as fast as they were able. The flames began to retreat, hissing like snakes as they did so, enabling more men to move in with beaters. Soon the fire was under control.

Hauling himself up the stairs, his face gray with soot, Thomas made it back to the gallery and staggered out through the door, gulping down lungfuls of air. The keeper was waiting for him.

"Open the main doors," Thomas ordered.

"What?"

"The elephant may yet be saved. Do as I say!"

The keeper sprang into action. He nodded to his men, and together they ran down the steps to the great doors. It took two lads to lift the huge bolts and heave them open. Thomas arrived just in time to see the unleashed smoke billowing out in thick clouds, but the flames were all but extinguished. After a moment, the keeper wrapped a damp cloth 'round his face and entered. He did not have to venture far into the building to find the elephant. Its huge bulk stretched across the doorway. It lay on its side, struggling to breathe. Its massive sides labored up and down, and now and again its trunk twitched. It was in a bad way, but it was alive.

Falling to his knees, the keeper leaned over one of its ears and spoke softly to the creature, patting its sooty hide as he gave it encouragement.

Thomas was heartened by the sight, but he had more pressing matters. He cast around the chaotic scene to see Lydia, who was sitting on a crate, being tended to by one of the stable hands. She was supping small beer.

"My love," he called to her. He ran over to her and knelt beside her, taking her by the hand. She winced, and he saw her bleeding wrists. "They must be dressed," he told her, examining her wounds.

She shook her head. "You must see to the professor," she told him firmly.

"But your wrists!" protested Thomas.

"'Tis nothing. Please." She waved one of her hands. "The professor needs you, Thomas," she urged him.

Oliver Carruthers was lying on a bed of hay on the back of a cart in the courtyard. His heavy lids were closed and his skin gray beneath smutty patches. Thomas ordered an Indian youth—he assumed he was an elephant attendant—to take down the side so that he could examine Carruthers properly. His pulse was weak, and he was breathing out his distress in short, panicky breaths.

"He go die, sahib?" The Indian was peering over his shoulder. The doctor knew that the professor's lungs would be suffering the aftereffects of the choking smoke. Rest and soothing linctus would be the only remedies in the days ahead.

"With good care, he will live, yes," he replied with a nod, adding: "Call for a carriage." He knew the sooner the professor was transported back to Hollen Street, the greater his chances of survival. He would follow on immediately.

Meanwhile, Thomas returned to the stable to find the keeper dousing the elephant with water from a nearby trough. With a large mop, he was lovingly swabbing its sooty flanks. The animal clearly found it rejuvenating and responded by halfheartedly lifting its enormous head. Its trunk slithered before it on the floor, coiling, then straightening like some monstrous snake. Thomas knelt down by its massive shoulder, next to the keeper, and patted the animal.

"Will he live?"

"He's a strong old beast," replied the keeper. Another Indian lad, standing on the other side, sluiced its trunk with another bucketful of water. Just as Thomas allowed himself a smile, the elephant suddenly snorted and lifted its head again, this time higher. It endeavored to right itself by planting a great front foot on the ground. Huffing through its trunk, it tried in vain to heave its great hulk off the cobbled floor, but as it raised its head and shoulder, the lad at its back let out a scream and yelled something in his native tongue.

"God Almighty!" cried the keeper.

"What is it?" exclaimed Thomas. Leaping to his feet, he ran 'round to the other side of the creature to see what had so shocked the boy.

At first he thought it a pile of dirty rags, but then he spied the saffron yellow bursting from beneath the grime and soot, and saw the curved dagger. And there, lying flattened and broken, lay the body of a man, an Indian. Sajiv Lakhani had been crushed under the weight of the elephant.

## Chapter 58

Professor Carruthers lay propped up on fat pillows that made his face seem even longer and thinner. A light sheen of sweat glistened on his skin. The patient did not open his eyes at the sound of the door, and Thomas assumed he was still sleeping as he set down his case. Mistress Finesilver followed behind him with a bowl of bread and milk and a spoon, which she put on the bedside table. She stood away from the bed, and arms crossed over her saggy breasts, she studied the professor, her head tilted to one side. A sudden cough broke the silence. It was dry and rasping, and it lifted the professor's shoulders as he slept, then dropped them down again. He frowned but did not wake.

Mistress Finesilver remained unmoved. "'Course I never did like that Indian. There was something shifty about 'im. 'E only got what was coming to 'im," she whined as Thomas opened his case.

"Thank you, mistress. That will be all," Thomas told her, opening his case. Her mistrust of Sajiv had been evident from the start. Thomas only wished that he had heeded her unease and acted upon it sooner. He should have suspected that it was Dr. Carruthers's stolen honey that had been smeared all over the dead servant's face. Or that the khanjar had indeed been responsible for almost beheading Sir Montagu. Or that his slipper had made the bloody footprint in the study. Or even that Sajiv could easily have traveled from Oxford to Boughton to commit murder. The clues had been there, but he had been blind to them.

The housekeeper shot the professor another narrow-eyed look and tutted her disapproval, as if transferring the blame for all that had occurred onto his shoulders. As she did so, he stirred, and his head began to roll from side to side in a most agitated fashion.

"Perhaps you would care to fetch Dr. Carruthers?" Thomas asked her. In her present mood, it seemed she did not *care* to do anything, but she nodded and left the room.

Now it was Thomas's turn to study his patient. He noted the professor's complexion had improved. For the first time in three days, the color had returned, but Thomas also remarked upon a seeming restlessness and an excessive sweating that were new symptoms. A thin stream of mucus was running from the professor's left nostril, too. It was as he reached for a kerchief to wipe his nose that Thomas realized what ailed his patient, on top of smoke inhalation. True, the cough remained, and would no doubt do so for a few more days, but it was the professor's addiction to opium that was causing his various ills. They were the undoubted signs of withdrawal.

Thomas was bending low to feel the pulse when suddenly the professor grabbed him by the wrist. The quick-fire gesture made the doctor start. There was a strength in his grasp that he would not have believed possible in one so weak. He switched to the professor's face, his eyes now open wide.

"Sir, I thought you were asleep!" he exclaimed, feeling his own pulse racing. "You are a little better?"

The professor pulled a face as he let go of Thomas's wrist. "Better?" He shrugged as if the word were a bitter pill that he was trying to swallow. "I have been trying to feel better about myself these past nine years, Silkstone," he said, his voice cracking. Thomas gave him a cup of linctus from the bedside table, and he downed it, grimacing at the taste. He handed it back without giving the doctor a look. Instead he fixed his watery eyes straight ahead of him. "*No one saves us but ourselves. No one can and no one may. We ourselves must walk the path.*"

Thomas frowned. The lingering melancholy that he had detected in the professor's look when they first met clearly still remained. No doubt the opium had dulled his senses and for brief periods made him insensible to the terrible events of the past.

"Very profound," said the doctor after a moment's pause. "But if I might suggest, sir, contrary to what your sacred texts may say, you are fortunate in that you are not alone. Your brother—"

The professor broke him off. "Opium!" he croaked. "Please. I need some." He raised his hands and held out his palms like a beggar.

Thomas looked at him, full of pity. "Sir, you must wean yourself off the poppy. It can have a most deleterious effect on a man," he told him. As he spoke, he suddenly thought of the Indian servant. "Did Sajiv take it, too?" He recalled the pungent smell at the scenes of at least two of the killings.

"Sajiv," repeated the professor. "Yes," he croaked, grasping at Thomas's wrist once more. "I gave him opium for his own pleasure. Now, please, I would have some for mine."

Thomas struggled to free himself from the professor's insistent mauling. "I cannot give you any, sir. I—"

"Sajiv!" Carruthers exclaimed, wide-eyed, as if his servant had just appeared to him in a vision. "What has happened to him? Where is he?"

Thomas took a deep breath. "He is dead, sir." He recalled the blackened skin, crushed and mangled into an unrecognizable heap under the great weight.

The professor was silent for a moment; then his lips began to tremble. "How?"

"The elephant fell on top of him."

The professor gasped, triggering a cough once more.

"He was crushed by the elephant?"

"Yes, sir," said Thomas. Once she had felt able, Lydia had related to him Sajiv's sorry tale. She told him how he alleged his own father's end was the result of a betrayal by Farrell, Lavington, Flynn, and, to a lesser extent, the professor himself.

Carruthers closed his eyes for a moment. He seemed in pain.

"I know he committed all four murders, sir," said Thomas, extricating his hand from the professor's. The latter made no attempt to hold onto it.

"Then you also know why I was to be his next victim?"

"I understood that you took pity on him when he was a boy after he witnessed his father's execution."

Professor Carruthers blinked rapidly. "If only it had been that simple." He groaned. "I took pity on the boy because I felt guilty. I was burdened by my past deeds, and they still weigh heavy on my conscience to this day."

Thomas nodded. "What happened?" he asked.

The professor lifted his head slightly. "I was ashamed to acknowledge to you that I practiced medicine in India because I abused my position. Farrell approached me, you see." He coughed once more. "He and his associates told me a miner had escaped with a huge diamond that he'd secreted in a wound in his leg. He'd been given protection by a merchant. They wanted to get their hands on the stone, and in return they would fob the trader off with some fanciful map of the lost diamond fields of Sumbhulpoor." He paused for breath.

"And the merchant was Sajiv's father?" asked Thomas.

Carruthers nodded. "Aye. Bava Lakhani." He lingered over the name. "They asked me to cut open the miner's leg to retrieve the diamond. I was to stitch it after. The miner could have escaped and no one would have suspected."

"And in return you were promised a generous share of the sale of the gem?" pressed Thomas.

"Curse me, I was." He groaned and rubbed his chest.

Thomas could not judge the man. The professor's physical welfare was his utmost concern. "Sir, you must rest," he urged him.

Ignoring his advice, however, the professor grew more vexed. "They were coming for the miner."

"Who, sir?"

"The nizam's men. They were armed. There was no time." His wiry gray head rose from the pillow. "Farrell wanted me to amputate the miner's leg there and then."

Thomas suddenly understood the professor's dilemma. "And you refused?"

Carruthers thrust out his bottom lip. "I may have been a greedy fool, but I was not prepared to hack off a man's leg and let him bleed to death." He coughed once more. "Yes, I refused. I refused, and Farrell took a machete to him." He paused to swallow hard.

Now Thomas understood. "So the miner died, but Farrell let the merchant take the blame for his death and the theft of the diamond." Suddenly it was all fitting into place. "And the merchant was executed?"

"Pulled to pieces, then crushed by an elephant," said the professor, the tears now flowing down his cheeks. "And I was responsible."

Thomas reached for the professor's hand and patted it. "You cannot blame yourself, sir," he said, knowing that he was guilty of avarice, not murder.

Carruthers switched his reddening eyes to Thomas. "That was why I offered the boy a home. I have lived with the memory of that execution all these years. I only took Sajiv as my servant to assuage my conscience. He was orphaned because of me. I don't know when he found out that I shared the guilt. I cannot blame him for wanting me and all those who betrayed his father dead. He called Flynn's servant a traitor because he used to be his father's naukar."

"Did you not suspect him when you saw that word carved on Manjeet's chest?" Thomas pressed.

Carruthers blinked. "I should have had my doubts, yes, before he killed Flynn and Lupton. But he was like a son to me. I could not conceive that he could be capable of such . . ." He shrugged and sighed. "I suppose each one of us was a *gaddar* in our own way."

Thomas understood the professor's pain. He had been weighed down by guilt for all these years. That was why he tried not to dwell on the past. That was why he wanted to live in the moment. That was why he found solace in opium. He could not face his own demons.

"So you stopped practicing medicine and instead sought to heal your own wounds through the ancient texts?" suggested Thomas.

The professor looked Thomas in the eye and nodded. "The mind is everything. What you think, you become, Dr. Silkstone. That is what the Buddha said, and he is so right."

Thomas had to agree that what the professor said was true. It did not matter if the words were spoken by the Buddha or by Jesus or by the Prophet Mohammed. It was a universal truth, common to all men. A man's thoughts frame his character and therefore his actions. "I believe it to be so," he replied, fixing Carruthers with a sympathetic smile. "And I believe you to be a good man." He took his hand. "You have paid the price for your misjudgment, and now you must put the past behind you," Thomas told him. "As the Buddha would say, I believe, 'Concentrate the mind on the present moment.' And in this moment, that means you must concentrate on getting better."

With those words Thomas rose just as the sound of Dr. Carruthers's walking stick could be heard tapping its way across the landing.

"How fares the patient this morn?" the old anatomist asked, bumbling into the room.

"I am happy to report he is on the mend, sir," Thomas replied, taking his mentor's arm and leading him to a chair.

"Then an extra visitor will not go amiss?" a familiar voice sang out from the landing.

Thomas's head swung toward the door to see Lydia standing at the threshold. He hurried to greet her and swept both her hands up in his. He noted she was wearing long gloves to cover the ugly scabs left by the rope cuts on her wrists. He frowned.

"Have no fear for me, my love," she whispered. "How is the professor?" She jerked her gaze over to the bed, where Dr. Carruthers was patting his brother's counterpane.

"Physically he is stronger, but mentally . . ."

"Do I hear billing and cooing from the lovebirds?" The old anatomist cupped his hand 'round his ear and laughed. "Over here!" He beckoned Thomas and Lydia to join him. They seated themselves on either side of the foot of the bed.

"So, dear brother, this terrible mystery is over and we can all sleep easy in our beds again, eh?" He tapped his stick on the floorboards. "And to think we had a murderer staying under our very roof!" The old anatomist shook his head in disbelief.

"Are we not forgetting something?" asked Lydia.

"What might that be, my dear?"

Thomas knew exactly what she meant. He intervened. "The reason why four men were not just murdered, sir. They were tortured before they were cruelly put to death."

"Ah!" Dr. Carruthers nodded. "You mean the map, dear boy."

"Indeed I do, sir. The ancient Sanskrit map that holds the key to the untapped diamond fields."

Lydia agreed. "That was the reason my bedchamber was ransacked, and the reason poor Professor Carruthers was subjected to his ordeal."

The professor shook his head. "Not so, I fear, my lady."

"Tosh, Oliver. What are you saying?!" huffed the old anatomist, slapping the counterpane.

His brother was, however, adamant. "There never was a map."

"What?" interjected the old anatomist.

The professor fixed Lydia with an earnest regard. "It was a figment of your husband's imagination, I fear, my lady." Suddenly ashamed, he switched his gaze and bit his lip. "Captain Farrell knew I was good with a pen and brush. He commissioned me to create a map to fool the merchant." A sudden cough ruptured his speech before he concluded. "I forged it myself."

Thomas remained quiet throughout this exchange. He had heard of the map's existence from Thomas Motte himself, even though the latter counted it unintelligible and therefore worthless. He was certain of its existence, but it was best left forgotten, he told himself. It had caused enough blood to be spilled already.

*Chapter 59*

It was the night before the wedding. Guests had been arriving from all over the country for the past few days. Lydia's closest surviving relatives, a maiden aunt and three cousins twice removed, had decamped in Boughton Hall itself. Others stayed with friends or, in the last resort, at the Three Tuns in the village. Thomas's relatives, however, were even fewer in number. His dear father had written to inform him that he was too frail to make the voyage. That left only two distant cousins from Yorkshire, whom the doctor had never met but whom his father insisted should be invited.

Thomas was thankful that he had escaped most of the planning and the inevitable altercations. Aside from being present for the reading of the banns, he had remained in London. Lecturing to eager anatomy students made a welcome change from dissecting the victims of murder and hunting down their killers.

At Boughton, it seemed that Lady Pettigrew had assumed charge of the proceedings, but she and Lydia had not seen eye to eye over a number of details, not least over the color of the bridal gown. When the mantua maker had called and shown the ladies samples of silk, Lady Pettigrew had much preferred the primrose yellow over Lydia's palest cream. Happily Lydia had won the day, but there were other tussles over seating plans and the choice of entrees that led to icy silences and the drumming of agitated fingers. Even Thomas's arrival caused ructions. Lady Pettigrew thought it only proper that the groom lodge at the

Pettigrew residence before the ceremony. Thomas had, however, argued his case for staying at Boughton and had, with a little pressure from Sir Theodisius, finally prevailed.

While Lydia and the other ladies remained in her boudoir, Thomas dined with a few of his gentlemen friends: Sir Theodisius, Dr. Carruthers, Professor Carruthers, Professor Hascher, who was to be groomsman, and Sir Arthur Warbeck. The latter had been invited on the insistence of Sir Theodisius, who said it was politic to do so. The claret and port flowed freely, but Thomas, knowing that such occasions could, if allowed, get very out of hand, guarded himself against temptation by colluding with Howard. A glass jug was filled not with claret but black currant cordial and set at his side for his exclusive consumption. He drank copiously throughout the evening so that his guests believed him to be imbibing liberally, as expected of a groom on the eve of his wedding. The result was that by nine o'clock all the others were in their cups. Thomas pretended that he, too, had drunk far too much and needed to sleep it off before the morrow. He was therefore easily excused, and while the other men continued their merry talk of women and horses over a farcical game of piquet, Thomas was able to retire.

Acknowledging that sleep was unlikely to call on him that night, Thomas made his way, candle in hand, to the silent cocoon of the library. Surrounded by hundreds of volumes, he felt most at ease here. Away from the challenges of the laboratory, the stench of the dissecting room, or the battles of the courtroom, this was where he truly belonged. And yet, even now, on the eve of what should be the happiest day of his life, there was still a many-headed worm of discomfort that was wheedling its way into his psyche.

Despite Professor Carruthers's insistence to the contrary, the possibility, however remote, that a map of the diamond fields existed still gnawed away at him. His business was unfinished. That was why he found himself in the library on the night before his wedding. That was why he was determined to analyze once more, in even more depth, the copy of Thomas Motte's account of his journey to the diamond mines of Orissa.

Glancing around the room that smelled of dust and old leather, Thomas's eyes settled on the portrait of the fifth Earl Crick that hung over the mantelshelf. He had been a man of some erudition and stocked his library well. Next to him hung a portrait of Lydia's late brother, the dissipated sixth earl, Edward, and beside him, another smaller portrait of a young man. Thomas drew nearer to inspect it. The large brown eyes, the small mole by the mouth, and the lustrous curls were so familiar to him. The resemblance to Lydia was overwhelming. So overwhelming in fact that he found it hard to believe that Cousin Francis, whose portrait this was, was not, in reality, related to Lydia at all. If, as Sir Montagu claimed, he was Lydia's real father, then Lydia and Francis shared no blood. The similarity, Thomas concluded, must be purely coincidental. Yet it still troubled him.

Seeing Francis Crick's portrait reminded him of the first time he had set foot in the library. His purpose had been to research the many varieties of poisonous fungi that grew on the estate. He had been convinced that Lydia's brother had died after ingesting a deadly mushroom and he had been proved right.

In the candle's glow, he saw Lydia's tearstained face in the drawing room at Hollen Street when she told him of her pain at discovering she was not of the Crick line, that Crick blood did not run in her veins. It did not matter that no one else knew, and that Sir Montagu had gone to his grave taking his secret with him. "I am a fraud, Thomas," she had cried. "I am living a lie and so is Richard. Boughton should not be ours." Her illegitimacy was a stain that, it seemed, could not be expunged. It was her guilty secret that would, no doubt, weigh heavily on her for the rest of her life.

Thomas lit a lamp from his candle flame and retrieved his case, which he had deposited under the desk on his arrival. Opening it, he took out his notebook and sat himself down to thumb through it. Soon he came to the relevant pages: the postmortem notes on Sir Montagu. Seeing his jottings made at the time, when his nemesis lay cold and bloodied on the table, made him shudder. In his mind's eye he was back in the game larder, replaying the whole procedure. He had first examined the neck wound, taken the relevant measurements; then he had moved on to the hands and wrists, lacerated by the coir rope. At the time he had not deemed it necessary to inspect the heart and lungs. Although he had made a cursory inspection of the entire corpse, he had left it to Professor Hascher to examine the rest of the lower torso.

He turned another page, and as he did so, a loose folio slipped out from between the sheets. He recognized the writing immediately. It was Professor Hascher's intriguing Gothic script. Narrowing his eyes to decipher the oddly formed letters, Thomas saw that the professor had made an especial note of the lawyer's genitals. It read: *A large and ancient scar in the groin indicates severe injury.* With bated breath, Thomas read on, then jabbed the relevant passage with his forefinger: *Could feel no testes.*

"Could feel no testes," he mumbled, this time out loud. It was then that he had a sudden recollection. Just prior to performing surgery on Sir Montagu for his aneurysm last year, Thomas had asked his patient whether he had ever suffered any serious illness or injury. The lawyer had been circumspect, but had told him that he had suffered a serious riding accident shortly after his marriage almost thirty years ago. Could it be that his testes had to be subsequently removed? If he did not have any, surely that could be the only explanation?

"Thomas!" a soft whisper came from behind him.

He jumped in his seat. He had been so lost in his thoughts, he had not heard the creak of the door, nor the footfall of slippers.

"Lydia!" He leapt up.

She moved toward him, her arms outstretched.

"But the other ladies. . . ."

She smiled excitedly. "They sent me to look for a volume of Shakespeare's sonnets. We are in a very romantic mood." Scanning the desk and noting Thomas's wary look, she frowned. "But what are you doing?" she asked.

Thomas lifted his forefinger to his lips. "No one must know I am here," he told her, putting his arms around her and holding her to him.

She looked up into his eyes. "Is something wrong?"

He swallowed hard, then smiled at her, his eyes wildly excited. "I cannot say."

She searched his face for some sort of clue. "Do not talk in riddles," she chided him. "We are to be married in the morning. We must be honest with each other. There must be no secrets."

"No secrets," he repeated. He took a steadying breath. "No secrets."

"What is it, my love? Tell me, please." Lydia grew anxious.

Thomas glanced at the French doors that led out into the garden. "Let us take a walk," he said.

She threw a look back at the door. "But . . ."

"They can wait five minutes. I have waited almost five years."

The evening was cool and Lydia shivered slightly. They stood on the terrace looking out across the parterre as they had done on so many other occasions. The stars blinked in the black sky. The scents of the late roses wafted across the lawns. Up in the nearby woods an owl hooted. Another replied. But Lydia was suddenly in no mood for romance.

"What is it, my love? Do not keep me in suspense any longer," she told him anxiously.

The doctor put his arm around her, but continued looking out across the garden. He had been given little time to frame his words. His theory had only been confirmed a few moments ago, but he knew it had to be right. There could be no sidestepping, no prevarication. He must tell her straight.

"I do not believe that Sir Montagu was your father."

Lydia pulled away from him. "What?" Her eyes suddenly blazed.

"I had my suspicions before, but now I am almost certain he could not father children. It was physiologically impossible."

Lydia had turned to look out onto the lawns. "I . . . I don't know what to say."

Thomas could not fathom her mood. He had gambled that she would be relieved.

She switched back. "You are *almost* certain?"

"Sir Montagu had an accident shortly after his marriage. Professor Hascher spotted an anomaly during the postmortem, and I now believe that surgery after the accident robbed him of his fertility."

The color drained from her cheeks and, again, she looked away in thought, stepping back and placing her arms around her own body, as if to hug herself.

"I know it must be hard for you to hear," he told her. He did not try to follow her, allowing her a moment of solitude to formulate her response.

After a second or two she turned back to face him, and he saw her shoulders heave in a sigh. "I cannot tell you how happy that makes me," she blurted. Her words tumbled from her mouth in a cascade, and she reached out and hugged Thomas to her. He kissed the top of her head, then pushed her back gently to look into her eyes.

"I loved the fifth earl very much," she told him softly. "It pained me to think he was not my real father, but now, knowing that he was, well . . ." The tears brimmed over and trickled down her cheeks.

"Sir Montagu wanted to control you. He wanted you to feel beholden to him."

"So I owed him nothing, except, perhaps, contempt." She shivered at the thought. "Yes."

Thomas pulled her back into the moment. "You are a Crick, my love," he told her.

"And so is Richard," she added. The thought reminded her that her son had no legal entitlement to Sir Montagu's estate. "Draycott was not his to inherit anyway," she said, thinking out loud.

Thomas knew the truth changed everything. Order could return. Integrity could be restored.

"I cannot wait till we are wed," Thomas told her, taking her in her arms.

"Nor I," she said.

# Chapter 60

The bells of Boughton Chapel rang out in celebration for the first time in several years. Recently they had tolled the passing of many a Crick family member, but now they pealed joyously. The whole of the estate and the village of Brandwick and even beyond had turned out to witness the wedding of Lady Lydia Farrell to Dr. Thomas Silkstone.

Lydia walked up the aisle on the arm of a very proud Sir Theodisius. She wore a dress of oyster silk, and her flowing veil gave her an ethereal look. She carried a bouquet of Amos Kidd's roses. As page boy, Richard walked behind his mamma, holding up her long train.

Thomas, nervous as a schoolboy, awaited his bride in front of the altar. He wore a fine blue velvet frock coat made especially for the occasion, an embroidered waistcoat, and cream silk breeches. As groomsman, Professor Hascher stood at Thomas's right hand, while Dr. Carruthers had been given a front-row seat next to an unusually cheerful Mistress Finesilver.

The ceremony, conducted by the Reverend Unsworth, was a fittingly solemn yet joyous affair, and Lydia's choice of hymns meant that spirits were roused even higher. An hour later, the couple walked out into the early autumn sunshine as man and wife to a shower of rose petals from excited well-wishers.

Sir Theodisius, now relieved of his duty to the bride, stood back to watch Thomas and Lydia process toward the lych-gate to the waiting chaise. Freed from Sir Montagu's hold over him,

Dr. Fairweather had indeed confirmed that the lawyer had been rendered infertile by a riding accident three years before Lydia's birth. He could not possibly have been her father.

Will Lovelock, the stable lad, had decked out the chaise with flowers and ribbons, and Jacob had made sure that the bay that drew it looked its best.

"Such a fine young couple," muttered Sir Theodisius, suddenly finding himself a little overcome.

"Yes, indeed," agreed Professor Carruthers, who stood supporting his elder brother by the church path.

Together the three men closed in through the gate to join those who surrounded the chaise. Thomas climbed aboard first, then helped Lydia mount the steps to join him. He was to drive them back to the hall, where Mistress Claddingbowl had prepared the wedding breakfast. Despite the sunshine, there was an autumnal nip in the air, and Eliza, ever mindful of her mistress's comfort, offered Lydia her embroidered wrap.

"Good God!" cried Professor Carruthers from below, his eyes bulging at the sockets.

Sir Theodisius switched 'round. "Damn you, Carruthers. You near made my heart burst!" he scolded. The coroner followed the professor's gaze. He could see his eyes were clamped onto Lydia's shawl.

"What is it, pray?" Dr. Carruthers tugged at his brother's coat sleeve.

"The shawl," replied the professor, pointing at Lydia. Thomas was helping her to drape it 'round her shoulders.

"What of it, man?" barked Sir Theodisius.

The professor was flapping his hands wildly. "'Tis Sanskrit!"

"Sanskrit?" repeated Dr. Carruthers. It was only then that he realized why his brother was so agitated. "You mean 'tis the map?" he blurted. "The ancient map?"

"Yes. Yes!" said the professor, beginning to elbow his way to the front of the crowd that surrounded the chaise. "We must tell them. Here . . ." He lunged forward, trying to catch Lydia's eye, but Sir Theodisius clamped his arm in his grasp and held him fast. In among all the cheering and waving of the villagers, neither Lydia nor Thomas saw him.

"Do you not see? We must have it!" protested the professor, flailing his free arm.

"I do see, brother," piped up the old anatomist, an ironic smile on his face. "But I choose not to. Not now."

Sir Theodisius looked at his friend and nodded. "Nor I. Not when the two young people I hold dearest to me are about to embark on a great adventure together. The Western world has waited several centuries for that map. I think it can wait a little longer, don't you, Professor?" he said.

Suddenly, amid the glee and the commotion, Thomas stood up from the seat of the open carriage.

"Good fortune to one and all," he cried at the top of his voice and, true to an old custom, he threw a large handful of sixpences into the air.

As he did so, a great cheer went up. The waiting children surged forward, their hands outstretched to catch the silver coins that, for a split second, spun and bounced and glinted in the sunshine. For a moment they sparkled like diamonds.

"Good fortune to us all," echoed Dr. Carruthers. He patted his brother's arm, and lifting his face to the bright light, he smiled. "Good fortune to us all."

*Postscript*

Warren Hastings resigned as governor-general of India in December 1784 and returned to England, where he was later impeached for misconduct in a public office. His trial lasted seven years and proved financially ruinous to him. He was, however, cleared of all charges against him. He died in 1818.

Up until the discovery of diamonds in Brazil in 1725, India and Borneo were the only sources of diamonds in the world. Today, the exact location of the so-called "lost mines of Golconda" remains unknown, and only one diamond mine is still open in India.

An estimated five to six hundred women each year died in the practice of suttee, or sati, in British-controlled India. The act was finally outlawed by the British Raj in 1829, although it was not until 1861 that Queen Victoria issued a general ban.

# Glossary

## Chapter 1

*Hyderabad.* The capital of India from 1724 to 1948, which is at present the state capital of Andhra Pradesh in southern India. The nearby Golconda Fort, now in ruins, remains a huge tourist attraction.

*bania:* A merchant from the commercial Indian caste, which also included lawyers and bankers.

*nizam:* The name given to rulers of the Deccan area in this period.

*jagirdar:* The feudal owner/lord of a jagir, or area of land, given as a gift by a superior was called a jagirdar, or jageerdar.

*bulse:* A purse or bag of diamonds.

*old rulers' tombs:* The enormous domes of the tombs of the seven Qutub Shahi rulers are found close to the famous Golconda Fort, just outside Hyderabad.

*vakil:* An attorney.

*Lord Indra:* The most important god in the Vedic religion, he is also a major figure in Hinduism and Buddhism and is often associated with storms and rain.

*naukar:* An Indian male domestic servant.

*second:* A gentleman chosen by the principal participants whose job it was to ensure that the duel was carried out according to the rules.

*duel:* By about 1770, English duelists had adopted the pistol instead of the sword. The first rule of dueling was that a challenge to duel between two gentlemen could not generally be refused without the loss of face and honor. If a gentleman invited a man to duel and he refused, the challenger might place a notice in the paper denouncing the man as a poltroon for refusing to give satisfaction in the dispute.

*cuirass:* A piece of armor that covers the wearer's front.

*commoners:* In this case the term refers to people who share rights over an area of common land in a particular locality.

## Chapter 2

*Woodstock:* A market town eight miles northwest of Oxford.

*tansies:* Plants belonging to the daisy family. They were used for medical purposes.

*laudanum:* In 1753 the Scottish surgeon and physician George Young published his *Treatise on Opium,* which exalted the virtues of laudanum.

*aloe balm:* Although aloe was used to enhance women's skin and in the embalming process in Egyptian times, it was not until the eighteenth century that Europeans discovered the plant's additional healing properties for conditions such as skin irritations, burns, and wounds.

*bury man:* The archaic name for a grave digger.

## Chapter 3

*allotment:* When commoners lost their land as a result of enclosure, many were awarded an allotment of land as compensation.

## Chapter 4

*Bedlam:* Bethlem Royal Hospital, to give it its full name, was originally founded in 1247 but did not begin to treat the insane until the fourteenth century. In 1676, the hospital moved from the site of what is now Liverpool Street station, London, to a magnificent baroque building, designed by Robert Hooke, at Moorfields. The hospital moved to its third site in 1815 and now forms part of the Imperial War Museum.

## Chapter 5

*thieftaker:* Prior to the establishment of a police force, individuals were often hired to capture criminals.

## Chapter 6

*microscope:* Antoni van Leeuwenhoek (1632–1723) became the first man to make and use a real microscope in the late seventeenth century.

## Chapter 7

*Great North Road:* This was a coaching route used by mail coaches between London, York, and Edinburgh. The modern A1 mainly follows the Great North Road. The inns on the road, many of which survive, were staging posts on the coach routes.

*Biggleswade:* A market town and important staging post for traffic on the Great North Road, with many inns providing accommodation, stabling for the horses, and replacement mounts.

*Clerkenwell:* By the eighteenth century the area was home to many small workshops that housed watchmakers and bookbinders.

*Fleet:* Now a subterranean river following Farringdon Street.

*East India Company:* The company ruled India after the Battle of Plassey in 1757 until 1858.

*Blackfriars:* The outfall of the Fleet can still be seen beneath Blackfriars Bridge.

*lascars:* Indian seamen working for British ships. One hundred and thirty-eight lascars were reported arriving in British ports in 1760, rising to 1,403 in 1810.

*Cockpit Tavern:* Although the current pub dates back only to the 1840s, a tavern has stood on this site, the junction of Ireland Yard and St. Andrew's Hill, since the sixteenth century.

*without a nose:* In the Mysore region, an Italian traveler reported that the inhabitants often cut off the noses of Mughal enemy riders. In the eighteenth century, the practice continued as soldiers were rewarded according to the number of noses and upper lips of their enemies they took to their leader. The Sikhs of Punjab also followed this custom.

*The* Atlas *reached St. Helena six weeks ago with the* Besborough: The *Atlas,* carrying Marian Hastings, sailed from Bengal and was accompanied by the East Indiaman ship the *Besborough.*

*Marian Hastings:* Anna Maria, to give her her full name, was first married to Baron Carl von Imhoff, but following a scandalous relationship with Warren Hastings, she married the latter in 1777. She attracted much speculation and gossip and amassed a large personal fortune. One satirical poem at the time ran thus: "Your gaudy charms to public view,/Admiring swains with rapture eye."

*Warren Hastings:* Joining the British East India Company in 1750 as a clerk, he rose to become the first governor-general of Bengal, from 1773 to 1785.

## Chapter 8

*coppicers:* The men who made their living by managing woodland trees.

*sawyers:* In order to cut tree trunks lengthwise, they were placed over pits known as sawpits. Balanced on smaller logs, the trunks were attached to them with iron hooks called dogs. Cutting was done with a two-man saw. The sawyer on top was known as the "top dog," while the "under dog" stood in the pit and would be covered, unfortunately, with all the falling sawdust.

*enclosure:* Between the fifteenth and early twentieth centuries, landowners began fencing off common land previously available for common use.

## Chapter 9

*Aston Abbotts:* A village five miles northeast of Aylesbury in Buckinghamshire.

*ague:* A fever or shivering fit.

*Oxford Castle:* Most of the castle was destroyed in the English Civil War of the 1640s. By the eighteenth century, the remaining buildings had become Oxford's local prison.

*its forbidding prison:* In the 1770s the prison reformer John Howard visited the castle jail several times and criticized its size and quality, including the extent to which vermin infested the prison. Its keeper was the incredibly named Solomon Wisdom. Work began on a new prison on the site in 1785.

## Chapter 10

*gibbet:* During the eighteenth century there were fifty-six public executions at Oxford Castle, for crimes ranging from sheep stealing to arson and spying.

## Chapter 11

*schnapps:* A type of distilled spirit made from fermented fruit, this remains a popular drink in Germany.

*hemp or wool:* Most rope was woven from hemp or wool at the time.

*coir:* Not until 1840 was a factory making coir products established in London.

## Chapter 12

*Great Fogg:* A persistent dry haze hung over Europe during the second half of 1783, thought to be caused by an eruption of the Laki fissure in Iceland. (See *The Devil's Breath*.)

*charcoal burners:* Men who lived in the woods and operated large kilns that burned wood to produce charcoal.

*glean for corn:* A privilege granted to poor parishioners, who could gather the stalks and ears of grain left behind by reapers.

*pannage:* In autumn domestic pigs were allowed to forage on fallen acorns, beech mast, or other nuts. It was a right granted to local people on common land or in royal forests and still exists in some woodlands today.

*coupes:* Areas of woodland that are cut on a rotation. Many other terms are used, such as burrow, hagg, fell, cant, panel, or burrow, depending on the locality.

*sack-'em-up men:* The London anatomist Joshua Brookes refused to pay a retainer to a gang of resurrectionists and found a rotting corpse on his doorstep. His neighbors were so scandalized that they almost beat him to death.

*fulling stocks:* Large wooden hammers used for part of the process of fulling (or thickening) and cleaning woven cloth by matting the surface texture.

## Chapter 13

*Chiltern Hills:* A chalk escarpment that stretches from the River Thames in Oxfordshire to Hitchin in Hertfordshire.

# Chapter 14

*Dick Whittington's day:* The children's rags-to-riches story is based on the life of Richard Whittington (c. 1354–1423), a wealthy merchant and later Lord Mayor of London.

*New Bond Street:* In 1720s London, the original Bond Street was extended to the north, running from Burlington Gardens to Oxford Street. It was then called New Bond Street.

*William Gray:* A 1784 trade directory lists Robert & William Gray, jewellers, 13 New Bond Street.

# Chapter 16

*Great Tom:* Housed in Tom Tower at Christ Church, the bell is the loudest in Oxford.

*runners:* Founded by the magistrate Henry Fielding in 1749, the small band of constables operated from his Bow Street home, hence their full name, the Bow Street Runners.

# Chapter 17

*Oriental scholar:* Several English scholars studied Indian texts during the eighteenth century, but the most famous was Sir William Jones, who arrived in Calcutta in the early 1780s. He founded the Asiatic Society of Bengal with the enthusiastic support of Warren Hastings, who was also a keen Oriental scholar.

*Sanskrit:* The classical language of India. Many ancient Hindu, Buddhist, and Jain texts are also written in it.

# Chapter 19

*in the presence of the nizam:* No English language newspapers existed until 1784 in India. This is a fictitious report, although a firsthand account of one such torture and execution at Baroda in 1814 has been preserved in *The Percy Anecdotes*. It makes for very distressing reading.

## Chapter 20

*pakar tree:* Akin to a fig tree, it is commonly known as the Portia Tree.

## Chapter 21

*banyan:* A gentleman's banyan was a loose, informal robe that was influenced by Oriental fashion. The robes were also called Indian gowns.

*the Great Snake:* In an account of a journey to Orissa in 1766, Thomas Motte wrote that he visited Naik Buns, "the Great Snake worshipped by the mountain rajahs, which they say is coeval with the world, which at his decease will be at an end." Goats and fowl were carried once a week to the cave entrance where the snake lived to satiate it.

*"You have examined the wound?"*: According to legend, a miner escaped from the Golconda mines with a huge diamond hidden in a leg wound.

## Chapter 22

*the commissioner of the dockyard at Portsmouth:* John Woodman, described as a "cautious lawyer," was Warren Hastings's brother-in-law. He gave a detailed account of Marian Hastings's landing on July 27, 1784. He and his wife were waiting to welcome her at Portsmouth.

*William Markham:* Little is known about this person apart from the fact that he was a resident of Benares and a close ally of Warren Hastings.

*Benares:* Now called Varanasi, Benares is regarded as sacred by Hindus, Buddhists, and Jains.

*Sir Percivall Pott:* Perhaps the most esteemed surgeon of the day, Pott found an association between exposure to soot and a high incidence of scrotal cancer in chimney sweeps in 1775. This was the first occupational link ever made to cancer.

## Chapter 23

*Mr. Pitt's India bill:* The forerunner of the India Act of 1784, introduced by Parliament to bring the administration of the East India Company under the control of the British government.

*South Street, close to Hyde Park:* John Woodman wrote to Warren Hastings that the house he had found for Marian was "scarcely to be equalled for situation, as well. . . . It is airy, with an uninterrupted view to Banstead Downs."

## Chapter 24

*the headquarters of the East India Company:* The original East India House was demolished and completely rebuilt in 1726–9. Further remodeling took place after 1796, but that building, too, was demolished in 1861.

*the coat of arms of Warren Hastings:* Coats of arms and crests are awarded not to a family or a name but to an individual.

## Chapter 25

*Indian philosophies:* In the eighteenth century onward, a number of Buddhist texts were brought to Europe by people who had visited the colonies in the East. These texts aroused the interest of some European scholars who then began to study them.

*championing a new movement:* Sir William Jones, with his *Grammar of the Persian Language* (1771), was an authority in the field for a long time. His *Moallakât* (1782), a translation of seven famous pre-Islamic Arabic odes, introduced the poems to the British public. Along with Henry Thomas Colebrooke and Nathaniel Halhed, he founded the Asiatic Society of Bengal.

*Mr. Hastings has a great affection for India:* Unlike many of his successors, Hastings respected and admired Indian culture. He once wrote: "The writers of the Indian philosophies will survive, when the British dominion in India shall long have ceased to exist, and when the sources which it yielded of wealth and power are lost to rememberances."

*like jackdaws:* These birds are notorious for picking up shiny objects such as jewelry to hoard in nests. John Gay, in his 1728 *Beggar's Opera,* wrote: "A covetous fellow, like a jackdaw, steals what he was never made to enjoy, for the sake of hiding it."

*an executioner dropping hot balls:* In Buddhist texts like the *Milinda Panha,* belonging to the second century AD, mention is made of some strange tortures, including the kettle of gruel, where the skull is cut open and an iron ball is thrown onto the brain, which boils and "runs over."

*surrounded by their own amputated noses and ears:* In the Mysore region, the inhabitants attacked their enemies with an instrument that resembled "a sort of half-moon of iron."

## Chapter 26

*agents for none other than Prince George:* George III's son was a notorious debtor and owed money in many quarters.

*Bond Street roll:* In the eighteenth century Bond Street was filled with the "Bond Street Loungers," who cultivated a special walk called the Bond Street roll.

## Chapter 28

*Kew:* By this time the gardens at Kew Palace, just outside London, were already known for their rare and exotic collections.

*sepoy:* A term used in the East India Company for an infantry private or servant.

*Major Scott:* John Scott was a close friend of Warren Hastings and in 1780 was appointed to command a battalion of sepoys, or Indian soldiers. He was political agent to Warren Hastings and arrived in London in 1781.

*Mr. Hales:* Stephen Hales, (1677–1761), was an English clergyman and the first person to measure blood pressure.

*Mr. Fox and his "ghastly" Whigs:* Charles James Fox and his Whig party were fierce opponents of William Pitt the Younger.

*"In my opinion":* In a letter, Percivall Pott promised that Marian Hastings would be in perfect health before the winter and made light of any complaint.

## Chapter 29

*Indians in his homeland:* Native American Indian tribes, including the Apache and Comanche, are known to have tortured and killed victims by securing them over anthills.

*Kooma.* This small caste was apparently performing reconstructive rhinoplasty as long ago as 3000 BC, using a skin graft taken from the forehead.

*skin from the forehead:* In a well-documented case, a Hindu bricklayer performed surgery on a Parsi whose nose had been cut off. The operation was witnessed by Thomas Cruso and James Findlay, senior British surgeons in the Bombay Presidency. Their account was published in the *Madras Gazette* and later reproduced in the October 1794 issue of the *Gentleman's Magazine of London.*

*smeared with honey:* According to George Ryley Scott's *History of Torture,* one method peculiar to India was to tie the victim against a tree, smother him in honey, and allow red ants to eat him. Another insect employed for this gruesome purpose was the carpet beetle.

## Chapter 30

*news from the customhouse:* Major Scott had written earlier that he hoped he had arranged for Mrs. Hastings's baggage to pass without being rifled, "but there are not such a Sett of Vermin in England as our Custom House Officers."

*the customs men have detained*: A list of goods belonging to Marian Hastings that were detained can be found in the British Museum. Everything made of silk was prohibited, as well as a velvet riding habit worked with pearls, and curtains and dresses containing gold or silver thread. It seems she was in danger of forfeiting all her own clothes except those taken ashore with her at Portsmouth and all the items brought as gifts.

*Arab horses*: According to the *Lady's Magazine,* on October 8, 1784, "a few days ago two very fine young Arabs, a horse and a mare, were presented to his majesty from Mr. Hastings." Scott later wrote the king was delighted with them.

## Chapter 33

*Carl Linnaeus's Systema Naturae*: The Swedish botanist and physician published a system of classification in 1753 that divided the natural world into three "kingdoms": animal, plant, and mineral.

*acacia honey*: This honey has a distinctively sweet smell.

## Chapter 34

*White's on St. James's Street*: During the eighteenth century the exclusive gentlemen's club gained a reputation for the shocking behavior of its upper class members.

## Chapter 35

*khanjar*: The widely used name for a dagger that varies from region to region, but usually has a curved blade.

## Chapter 36

*Magpie Ale House*: The current pub on this site, the East India Arms, is located on Fenchurch Street next to the place where the East India Company once had its headquarters. From at least 1645 the Magpie Ale House stood here.

*hot springs at Bath:* These are the only hot springs in Britain. Bath's spa reached its zenith in popularity in the late eighteenth and early nineteenth centuries.

*moon-curser:* A linkboy with a lantern to guide a traveler through the dark streets.

*Pool of London:* An area of the Thames between London Bridge and Rotherhithe. As early as 1586 William Camden declared: "A man would say, that seeth the shipping there, that it is, as it were, a very wood of trees disbranched to make glades and let in light, so shaded it is with masts and sails."

## Chapter 37

*Philip Francis:* Francis was a civil servant in India and is best remembered for his animosity toward Warren Hastings, whom he accused of corruption in India. The two men fought a duel on August 17, 1780. Francis was severely wounded but recovered shortly afterward and left India a few weeks later. He continued to oppose Hastings in England.

## Chapter 39

*Musi River:* A tributary of the Krishna River in the Deccan Plateau, upon which Hyderabad stands.

*famous Pitt diamond:* Thomas Pitt was the grandfather of William Pitt the Elder, and his exploits caused the latter much embarrassment. Later known as "Diamond" Pitt, he is best known for buying a huge diamond that was purportedly smuggled out of a mine in the wound of a worker's leg. In 1791 the stone, which was sold to the regent of France, was valued at £480,000. It was placed in the French crown, and is now in the Louvre.

*twelve thousand pagodas:* The pagoda was a unit of currency, a coin made of gold or half gold minted by Indian dynasties, as well as the British, the French, and the Dutch.

*budgerow:* A large Indian boat with a long cabin that ran the length of the craft.

## Chapter 40

*indigo:* A blue dye derived from the leaves of a leguminous plant, it was a popular crop in India and was supplied to Europe since the Greco-Roman era.

## Chapter 41

*Cheapside:* The area takes its name from "*chepe,*" a Saxon word for a market. It was long associated with the nearby Smithfield meat market, although in 1775 a visitor observed that with its "many thousands of candles . . . the street looks as if it were illuminated for some festivity."

*Square Mile:* The boundaries of the City of London have remained almost constant since the Middle Ages, and it is often called the Square Mile as it is almost exactly one square mile (2.6 square kilometers) in area.

*jail in Calcutta:* Among the Impey manuscripts in the British Museum is a petition from Thomas Motte written from Calcutta Jail in 1783 in which he begs his creditors to assent to his release.

## Chapter 42

*a common torture:* Buddhist texts like the *Milinda Panha,* from the second century AD, catalog some strange and inhuman methods, such as flaying and boiling a victim alive. Torture was abolished in England and Wales in 1641, and in Scotland in 1707, but remained common practice in India until the start of the nineteenth century.

## Chapter 43

*the elephant in St. James's Park:* King George III was presented with an elephant in 1763 that is thought to have been exercised in the park. The British Museum has a print of this elephant, *His Majesty's Elephant, from Bengall,* and the curator mentions the animal being exercised in St. James's Park, but gives no reference. According to historian and London guide Peter Berthoud, the *Gentleman's Magazine* says the animal was presented "at the Queen's House," later to become Buckingham Palace, adjoining St. James's Park. If it was kept in the vicinity, it is possible that it was exercised in nearby St. James's Park, and is most likely to have been stabled in the King's Mews, close by.

*mines at Golconda were all but exhausted*: The last large diamonds were mined around two hundred fifty years ago.

## Chapter 44

*the governor-general's impeachment:* Talk of Warren Hastings's impeachment first surfaced when he was personally attacked by Charles James Fox during the presentation of the India bill in 1783.

*opium:* Smoking opium was not illegal. The British began trading in it after they took Bengal in 1757. By 1764 the British exercised a monopoly over opium production.

## Chapter 45

*Dr. Johnson:* The literary genius took opium as a painkiller, but cautioned that it should only be taken as a last resort.

*Lord Clive:* Major-General Robert Clive, also known as Clive of India, was a British officer who established the military and political supremacy of the East India Company in Bengal.

*Narrative of a Journey to the Diamond Mines at Sumbhulpoor in the Province of Orissa:* Thomas Motte's account was not published until 1799.

## Chapter 46

*Charles Byrne:* An Irishman measuring almost eight feet, Byrne came to London to exhibit himself. His tragic story is explored more fully in *The Dead Shall Not Rest,* the second novel in the Dr. Thomas Silkstone series.

*the New Archway:* Built in 1697, it is one of three principal entrances to Lincoln's Inn and leads to New Square.

## Chapter 49

*by express permission of the king:* In 1775, King George III ordered that only those whose names were on a list were permitted to pass through St. James's Park and Green Park. Access to both was only gained via approved ivory passes.

*fireworks:* In 1746 nearby Green Park was used for a national party, celebrating the end of the War of Hanoverian Succession, that included a great firework display set off to music by Handel. Another huge celebration was held in 1763 to mark the signing of the Treaty of Paris.

*a keeper dressed:* In *Splendour at Court,* authors Nigel Arch and Joanna Marschner describe how George III commissioned special liveries for his elephant keepers in 1763. An embroiderer named Richard Harrison made a large blue cloth and lined it with red baize and fringed it with gold, while renowned tailors made suits for the two Indians who had been sent with the elephants.

*King's Mews:* These were located in a building that is now the site of the National Gallery in Trafalgar Square.

*half a dozen guards:* The fate of Chunee, the Indian elephant who was brought to Regency London, was a cause célèbre. In 1826 he became agitated, killed his keeper in the Strand, and was finally fired upon with muskets by soldiers at nearby Somerset House. Still he refused to die and was finally put out of his misery with a sword or harpoon.

## Chapter 52

*a climbing boy:* Also known as a pipe boy or a chimney sweep's boy.

## Chapter 53

*the execution, by elephant, of an Indian merchant:* The warrior Santaji Ghorpade (1764–1794) delighted in this form of execution and, for the slightest misdemeanor, would order an offender to be crushed under the feet of an elephant. The punishment was also adopted by Tipu to suppress a revolt at Seringapatam. Many English prisoners were dragged to death by means of elephants or hanged after having their ears and noses cut off.

## Chapter 54

*loud roar:* Several exotic animals were kept in the mews, but most of the dangerous ones were housed in the Tower of London.

## Chapter 56

*mahout:* The man or boy who rides on the back of an elephant and commands it.

## Chapter 57

*a wooden engine:* The 1708 Parish Pump Act ordered every parish in London to keep a water pump and designate men to help extinguish fires. Several people began to design fire pumps, but it was Richard Newsham's creation that proved most effective. His famous No. 5 engine could throw 160 gallons of water per minute to a height of 165 feet.

## Chapter 58

*"No one saves us but ourselves":* This quote is said to have come from Buddha.

# Chapter 60

*a dress of oyster silk:* Red was a popular color for a wedding dress at the time that Jane Austen's parents were married in the eighteenth century.

*wedding breakfast:* Weddings were normally held in the morning, traditionally after a Catholic mass, so the celebratory meal was a breakfast.